If you want world history, ancient archaeolo[...] theology all intertwined in a drama of hu[...] thinking person's novel. By masterfully weavir[...] time and geography, Harris reminds us that [...] work in the midst of heartbreak and loss, invisibly ordering the visible messiness of our lives to further his mysterious purposes. And he does it with gracious glimpses of his presence with us through our pain and lament.

—**David Guretzki, PhD**
Executive VP and Resident Theologian
Evangelical Fellowship of Canada

An exquisite tale of love, longing, and loss, set against the coastlines of Nova Scotia and the Aegean. Harris deftly intermingles Greek myth with the concreteness of love and the horrors of war. A stunning first novel.

—**J. Richard Middleton**
Author of *A New Heaven and a New Earth*
Professor of Biblical Worldview and Exegesis,
Northeastern Seminary at Roberts Wesleyan College

THOUGH I

Walk

— A NOVEL —

Dale Harris

THOUGH I WALK
Copyright © 2021 by Dale Harris

Scripture quotations taken from the Holy Bible, King James Version, which is in the public domain.

ISBN: 978-1-4866-2059-3
eBook ISBN: 978-1-4866-2060-9

Word Alive Press
119 De Baets Street Winnipeg, MB R2J 3R9
www.wordalivepress.ca

WORD ALIVE
—P R E S S—

Cataloguing in Publication information can be obtained from Library and Archives Canada.

Dedicated to Dani,
who has walked with me every step of this journey.

ACKNOWLEDGEMENTS

ABOVE ALL ELSE, I AM THANKFUL TO THE LORD JESUS CHRIST, WHO STEPPED into this story years after I had given up on it, redeeming it for his glory and transforming me in the process. I pray it will touch many with a deep sense his love for us, even in—perhaps especially in—those times of doubt or darkness.

I owe an immeasurable debt to my wife Dani, my greatest encourager and most discerning reader. Without your help, insight, support, and inspiration, this book could never have been written.

I am profoundly thankful to all the family and friends who read early drafts of this manuscript, and whose honest feedback made it a far better book than it otherwise would have been: to Natalie Harris for working your way through one of the earliest versions of this story long before it was readable, to Michelle Middleton for your thoughtful feedback as one of the most avid readers I know, to Joshua Chalmers for your theological insights, to Matthew McEwen for a good friend's honest opinion, to Kim Kacaba for helping me believe this story really might impact others the way I hoped it would, and to Pam Verhagen for being the kind of determined prayer warrior every aspiring writer needs in their corner. I also need to say a special word of thanks to Mary-Elsie Wolfe, who responded so warmly to my writing and kept her eyes peeled for publishing opportunities. If you had not brought the Braun Book Awards to my attention, this novel may not have seen the light of day.

Besides all these, I am grateful to all my brothers and sisters in Christ at the Corner Church, who so graciously supported me in taking a three-month sabbatical to finish this project in the spring of 2020, a gift of time and a vote of confidence that was truly invaluable to me.

I would like to thank the wonderful staff at Word Alive Press, for their enthusiastic reception of this book and their gracious encouragement and support. I am humbled that *Though I Walk* was selected as the winner of the 2020 Braun Book Award for fiction, and honoured to be given this opportunity to share it with others. To everyone at Word Alive, you have helped to make a lifelong dream of mine come true.

In researching this novel, I relied on a wide variety of historical sources, some of them consciously and others no doubt by osmosis. I would be remiss, however, if I didn't acknowledge my special debt to the following works: *Crete, Past and Present*, Michael Nicholas Elliadi's fascinating description of life in 1930s Crete; *Crete: The Battle and the Resistance*, Anthony Beevor's gripping account of the battle for Crete and the heroic resistance effort that followed; *Halifax: Warden of the North*, Thomas Raddell's classic history of the city of Halifax; and *Wordstruck*, Robert MacNeil's wonderful memoir of growing up in wartime Halifax. There were others, of course, many of them looted from the classics department of the Rutherford Library at the University of Alberta, but these books in particular helped to give my story some of its rich texture and historical detail.

Finally, I have it in mind to thank that Australian tourist I chatted with on the waterfront of the Heraklion harbor, whoever you were, at four o'clock in the morning back in 1996, while we were both waiting for the ferry to arrive. Your offhand comment about the freedom fighters who lived up in the mountains of Crete for years after the war—can you imagine?—inadvertently planted the seed that would eventually grow up into this novel.

Having lived with this story for so many years, I hope now that it will be as inspiring to those who read it, as it was for me to write it.

Soli Deo Gloria, 2020.

*L'anima amante si slancia fuori del creato, e si crea nell' infinito
un Mondo tutto per essa, diverso assai da questo
oscuro e pauroso baratro.*

The soul that loves projects itself beyond the created world and
creates in the infinite a world all its own, very different from
this obscure and fearful abyss.
—Percy Bysshe Shelley, *Epipsychidion*

Nihil humanum ab archaeologia alienum est.

Nothing that concerns humanity is alien to archaeology.
—Ralph Van Deman Magoffin, *The Romance of Archaeology*

PART I

Artefacts

CHAPTER ONE
Mementos, 1961

A BITTER BUT BEAUTIFUL TRUTH ABOUT HEALING IS THAT SOMETIMES THE only way to become whole is to embrace our wounds. Grace probably never would have put it in quite those words, but that's how it seemed to her the day she came across that tattered shoebox, lying forgotten at the back of their closet, stuffed with the letters her husband Stephen had sent her when they were young and he had been in Greece. It had already been three months since his death, and she supposed she was far enough into her grief that she could bear to go through them, that it might even help.

Even so, she sat on the floor of the closet for a long time, staring intently at the box full of letters and wondering if she really had the strength.

She had known it was there, of course. She was the one who had put it there, in fact, filled almost to overflowing with paper and tightly secured with twine, when they had moved into this old beach house years ago.

She hadn't thought of it for ages, though. She might not even have thought of it now, except that she had taken a long walk by the seashore that morning. Though it was late in the spring, still it was very cool, so she had gone to the closet for one of Stephen's old jackets. Since his passing, she hadn't yet found the resolve to go through any of his personal effects, but they had often used to walk the beach in front of their house—to stroll the rim of the wine-dark sea, is how he had sometimes put it, quoting some Greek poem or other she didn't understand—and once, when it had been unexpectedly cold, he'd draped her with his coat to keep her warm. He hadn't said much when he did this, but the memory was so tender, and her longing for it so profound, that she had finally dared to rummage through his side of their closet for a jacket. She had felt so uneasy among his things that she hadn't lingered when she pulled it from its hanger, but when she'd returned from her walk, scrubbed fresh and rosy by the salt breeze, she'd needed to push aside his overcoat to hang it up properly again.

That's when she had seen the shoebox.

She took a deep breath and drew it towards her, placing it gently in her lap. She was surprised to see that her hands were trembling, and it occurred to her that her grief was more raw than she had imagined, but she clenched her fingers into fists until they were steady again, then pulled the twine and lifted the lid.

The box was quite full—Stephen had been a prolific letter-writer—and the lid was pressing down far more paper than the box could properly hold, so that as she lifted it, the top dozen or so letters seemed to burst out from underneath, two or three of them spilling to the floor. She picked up the first of these, turning it in her hand and looking at the date.

As soon as she saw it, she felt a great surge of sadness sweep through her. It was the last letter he had ever sent her, the one she cherished most and knew best. The Royal Canadian Navy officer who had delivered it had appeared on her doorstep a long time ago, placing it into her hand with a clumsy expression of condolence.

Closing her eyes, she was almost startled by how vividly the memory came back to her.

———————

It was early September 1941. The day was wet with the grey of autumn, rain pouring down on the dirty streets of Halifax and shining in the gutters. She was just about to step out, a pale raincoat draping her shoulders and a black umbrella hooked over her arm, when she met the officer coming up the steps to her door.

A half-stifled "Oh!" escaped her lips at the sight of him. Her father, Captain Edward Stewart, was at that very moment fighting Germans somewhere out in the Atlantic, and she knew the kind of news that typically lay behind a visit of this sort.

The officer hesitated, recognizing the fear that accompanied him. "Miss Grace Stewart?" he asked. Rain sighed in the street behind him.

"Yes?" She steeled herself for some grim announcement about her father.

The officer held out an envelope in his gloved hand. "I do beg your pardon, Miss Stewart, but this letter came into the hands of the British Navy in Alexandria. It was a New Zealander, a soldier escaping from Crete to Egypt after the battle for the island. He gave it to them."

Confusion passed over her features, and the officer began speaking more quickly, racing towards his point and in his haste saying more than he ought to have.

"This New Zealander, like I say, he and two other men found an abandoned raft and took their chances across the Mediterranean. One was also a New Zealander, the other a British officer. They say the New Zealander killed himself before the raft landed at Sidi Barrani. Delirium and despair, I suppose. The British officer, one Lieutenant James Percy, died of dehydration during the trip. Before he died, however, Lieutenant Percy gave the other New Zealander this letter, and urged him to see it delivered. The man was all but dead himself, but he promised. It's a miracle, really, that he survived the journey, but he did. When the Brits in Egypt heard the story, they passed the letter on to us. And, well, here you are, Miss Stewart: your letter."

She took it unsteadily, muttering some formality about his kindness, and sank to the steps of her porch. The envelope had already been opened, of course, and resealed after the Department of National Defence had determined it contained nothing that might compromise the war effort.

Grace opened it again and extracted a single, folded page. Sitting there in the streaming rain, before an awkward junior officer, she unfolded it carefully and drank deeply with her hope-parched heart. It had been many, many months since she had heard anything from Stephen at all, and she had almost given him up for lost.

Sitting on the floor of their closet, years later and alone again, she read it one more time.

June 15, 1941

Dear, dear Grace,

If this letter, by some miracle of fate, does actually reach you, please do not cling to some false, empty hope. Know that I am alive, and that I love you desperately, but it seems so unlikely I will ever be home again. It would hurt me deeply to know that you held on for nothing.

We are surrounded by death here. It falls from the sky. It wells up from the earth.

This morning we crossed Mount Ida, pursued by Germans, hoping to escape by boat in Sfakia. It was like a march across hell. On the south slope of Ida we crossed a vineyard, scorched out and blasted. The Cretan boys and girls who were defending it lay dead with kitchen knives and scythes still in their hands, cut down by German machine guns.

In other places, corpses litter the landscape. Greek dead, British, New Zealanders. They lie about in heaps, festering and swarmed with flies. I watched a Cretan girl cut down and—but no, I will not recall that. The island has fallen, but the death continues.

I will give this letter to Percy, who is escaping for Egypt tonight. If he makes it, this last note may reach you. I don't know. I am only writing to tell you this: do not wait for me. I have decided to stay on Crete, to fight against these horrors. I don't expect to see home again, but I know that I must stay here and fight.

I am sorry if I have failed you, if my staying to fight alongside these people causes you pain. Please do not double that pain by hoping vainly for my return. Know that I love you, and live your life, but do not wait for me.

Yours always, Stephen.

Grace's eyes misted over the page. She recalled the waves of emotion that had washed over her the day she'd first read it, rocking herself on the rain-streaked porch and clutching it to her chest. Fear, anger, confusion, and joy had each taken its turn in her, till at last she had settled on hope—despite the letter's clear warning against it. The simple truth that he was alive and still loved her had been enough that day.

It was the memory of that hope that finally sealed her resolve to bring the shoebox out of the closet, to go through all the letters it contained and find in them, if not healing—that might be too much to ask—then at least the strength to move towards healing. After all, she had dared to hope back then, and back then her hope had been realized.

Stephen had seldom talked about what he had seen and done in Greece, of course, but miracle of all miracles, after writing that final letter he had made it through the unspoken traumas of the war and back to her.

And this morning, still warm with the comfort of a long walk along the seashore wearing his old jacket, she found she was more open to the possibility of hope than she had been in a long time. So she gathered up the rest of the letters that had spilled out, pressing them back into the shoebox as best she could, and brought it out of the bedroom closet.

The kitchen table was probably too small to lay them all out, and anyway, somehow it didn't feel right to her. Neither did the living room. There was really only one place in the house, she knew, that would suit.

It had to be Stephen's study.

But she hesitated, even longer than she had when she'd first glimpsed the shoebox. After all, his study was the room where she had found him, the day he'd died and left her alone. If it had taken great resolve to open the shoebox, it would take real courage to open the door to his study. At least, she hadn't done so once since that awful day three months ago.

As she stood wrestling with indecision, the memory of it all came back to her more sharply and vividly than even the memory of his last letter.

———————

It had been a morning something like this one, bright with sunshine, though colder, since it was still winter. Nevertheless, they had planned to take a walk along the beach before the day got underway. He had left a heavy woollen sweater in his study, and when they'd seen how cold it was he'd gone to fetch it. Grace had been waiting for him by the door, bundled in her hat and scarf, when she'd him cry out in a stifled voice.

The study was at the far end of the house, so it was hard for her to make out what he had said.

"Everything all right, dear?" she called back.

No answer came, but that didn't register with Grace as especially alarming. He usually got distracted by work when he entered his study, even if it was only supposed to be for a minute, and when he did it was often hard to get his attention again.

She waited another minute or two, and when he still didn't appear, long after she thought he should have, she called out again. "What are you doing in there? Knitting the sweater from scratch?"

It was the kind of thing Stephen might have responded to with some sort of ironic rejoinder, so when still no answer came Grace wondered for the first time if something really was the matter.

"Stephen?" she called out a third time, and as she did so she became aware of an unnatural silence that seemed suddenly to have filled the house. She moved down the hall towards the door, the silence giving her voice a surreal timbre. "Are you okay?"

The door to the study was closed, and even though she was quite sure now that something was wrong, the habit of not interrupting him in his study was so ingrained in her that she paused and rapped on it with her knuckles.

"Stephen?"

She didn't wait for an answer but pushed the door open. With a sickening thud, it stopped against something soft and heavy. She felt a kind of horror surge through her and she leaned on the door handle, shoving past the weight and forcing it open.

He had collapsed in a heap, and she fell to her knees, gathering his sprawled body into her lap, holding him against the beat of her heart and cradling his inert face in her palm. She felt for a pulse, and though she was not trained to do that kind of thing, the lifelessness of his hand was enough to tell her there wasn't any. Blind with horror, a fervent prayer welled up instinctively from within.

Though it had been an agony to do so, she'd left him lying there and rushed for the phone, to place a call for an ambulance that even now, months later, she couldn't quite remember making.

When the ambulance attendants arrived, they had found her clinging to him and praying, as if her prayers alone might keep his lingering warmth from fading altogether.

———————

Of course they hadn't kept it from fading. Even though he had been barely fifty-one—far too young, everyone agreed—still the hospital had blamed his death on the heart. While he'd stood there, rummaging among the clutter of his study—looking, presumably, for a misplaced sweater—his heart had quivered somewhere deep in his chest and left him to die.

And now all the shoeboxes in the world, filled with every scrap of writing he'd ever written, would not be enough to bring him back. The thought almost cowed her, but she breathed deeply again and stepped to the door of the study. Instinctively she reached to rap with her knuckles, but she caught herself, remembering how unnecessary it was to do that anymore, and instead simply turned the handle and crossed the threshold.

Almost immediately she felt like she was intruding. Even when he had been alive, she'd always felt like she did not belong in this study. She knew he had never meant for her to feel that way; it was just that his work as a professor of classical archaeology had always seemed so inaccessible to her. She might ask a random question about a box of broken pottery he'd brought home with him from Greece, and something in his answer—a wistful tone, maybe, or a tinge of regret—would discourage further inquiries. One time he had found her flipping curiously through a handful of old black-and-white photos from his fieldwork in Athens, and something in his manner had told her he would much rather she not.

So it didn't surprise her that she felt like an intruder in this room, though the feeling was far more intense than she had expected.

She passed a hand over the books lining the shelf closest to the door, and their worn spines seemed almost to glare back at her. She knew some of them: a world atlas stuffed with newspaper clippings from the war, a copy of *The Odyssey* scratched with his notes in pencil. Others she had heard him refer to in his lectures, Pausanias' *Description of Greece*, or Herodotus' *History*. One or two he'd even quoted to her, mostly poetry, in their courtship before the war. But still they were his books, and not theirs.

One shelf was lined with potsherds. Most of these were on loan from the university, she knew, and very precious. Many of them still bore the ancient markings of the sea they'd been painted with—a dolphin's dorsal fin here, the vine-laden prow of a ship there—and she had always admired the delicate artwork. She noticed a faint film of dust covering everything, and it bore down upon her, all over again, how long it had been since she had been in this room, and why.

The room was shrouded by a Venetian blind drawn low over the window. She stepped slowly though its striped shadows to the massive oaken desk at the far end—the only piece of furniture in the house that he ever really seemed to care about—and sat in his worn leather chair. It was still cluttered with his papers, research he had been working on the night before he died, perhaps, or maybe even work he had laid out for himself that morning. She lingered over it, as if discovering for the first time some final testimony to his life.

A huge book sat open in the middle of the desk. She turned back the cover to read the title—*Art of the Ancient World*—and then lay it down as it had been.

The page was open to an image she had seen before: a photograph of a mural that had once adorned the wall of some ancient Greek palace, a broad-chested bull, caught mid-lunge while three beautiful youth danced about it. The smallest and most lovely of the three had just vaulted the sweeping horns and hung, poised and graceful, above the animal's dappled flanks, her lithe body arched in a thrilling curve. The caption read "The Toreador Fresco, ca. 1500 BC. Heraklion, Crete."

It struck her strangely in that moment how well she knew this picture. Even to her untrained eye, it was quite stunning, and she knew it had been a favourite of his. A reproduction of the same bull-dance hung in a frame above his desk, though whenever she had asked him about it, his answers had been unclear, almost evasive. "It's the Bull of Minos," he would say, as though no other response was needed, and in his more talkative moods he might add something especially obscure, like: "Though Evans invented more than discovered the style."

She wondered vaguely why he would have set out this book, to this particular page, on the morning he had died. Not that it was an especially unusual thing to have done, but it touched on something deeper, his strange obsession with the image she had never understood. She gazed another moment at the bull and its three dancers, as if they might reveal to her the secret of the Bull of Minos that he had never explained. Like the other objects in this place, however, they had nothing to say, except to assure her that he really was gone, with no one to help her make sense of these strange, silent artefacts.

She closed the book and started to straighten up the papers, to make room for her shoebox of letters. As she did, her eyes fell on one more treasure lying among the clutter, perhaps the only thing in the room she knew for certain they had shared together. It was a seashell, dark and polished by years of sand and waves, the commonest of seashells one might come across on any beach around Halifax. She took it up and turned it in her palm, smiling in spite of herself.

And as she did, a healing flood of memory finally overcame her and she embraced, at last, the wound.

CHAPTER TWO

Seashell. 1927

GRACE PICKED HER WAY CAREFULLY AMONG THE ROCKS THAT LITTERED the beach. Out over the ocean, the sky was rolling in the last throes of summer, grey with a tinge of early autumn. The wind was cool but refreshing, and it tousled her, kicking the skirt of her summer dress about her knees, coaxing strands of her light blonde hair loose from the braid that held them in place.

She made her way slowly, stopping occasionally to overturn an abandoned sea star, or to poke the washed-up sack of a jellyfish with the squeamish toe of her canvas shoe. Though she would be twelve this fall, and in other settings would have tried hard to act mature beyond her years, a rocky beach at low tide and nothing to do but explore still aroused the childlike curiosity that was very much alive in her.

These were, after all, the last few days of their summer vacation on Prince Edward Island, and she wanted to make the most of them. Early in the season, Dad had ferried the family across Northumberland Strait to the island, and the four of them—Mom, Dad, Grace, and little William—had spent a golden summer together in a cottage just outside the drowsy little town of Annandale. Dad had rented it from a distant relative of his, a modest, white-washed arrangement standing on the seaward edge of a potato field, as close to the water as the beach would allow.

And it had been a glorious vacation. When it returned to her in memory, it always came in flashes of vibrant colour: picnicking on bright red strawberries with Mom and Willie, exploring the endless ochre stretches of the shoreline, together with Willie gathering spiral-coloured pebbles in handfuls, red sand, silver seafoam, bright blue sky.

In the late days of August, however, the colours had begun to dim. The changes were subtle, of course, but even at eleven she noticed them. The wind was cooler, the sky moodier, the sea more brooding. Even the beech trees around the cottage, it seemed, had begun to droop. Not that any of this dampened her spirits, but it left her determined to soak up as much of the summer as remained. With no clearer objective in mind than this, she had set out that morning to explore the shoreline, following whatever route her curiosity or her fancy suggested to her.

She came to a place where a tumble of large rocks blocked her way across the beach right down to the shore. She had wandered further than ever before but wasn't yet ready to turn back, so she clambered up, grazing her knee on the rough lip of the rock but reaching the top otherwise unscathed. She could see the beach, trimmed with silver foam, stretching off again into the distance.

She jumped down on the other side, a bit undignified in her billowing summer dress, and landed with a muffled thump.

"Oh!" The startled gasp came involuntarily from her lips as she spotted a boy. She hadn't noticed him, crouched there in the lea of the rock.

He sat on his haunches, hunched over his thighs with his chin resting heavily on his knees. He wore a knitted pullover and knee-length trousers from which protruded his slightly bruised shins. His bare toes curled around clumps of sand, helping him to balance in his awkward crouch. Soft brown hair hung straight over his forehead, his cheeks freckled from a summer spent playing at the seashore.

He was staring at something in the shelter of the rocks, his freckled brow furrowed in concentration.

When he looked up at her, Grace found herself suddenly self-conscious. She smoothed the skirt of her dress with a distracted sweep of her arm and brushed away the clumps of sand that clung to her knees. Her fidgeting hand secured the loose hair behind her ear.

"What are you doing?" she asked.

"Look," he said gently, almost whispering. He nodded in the direction he had been staring.

She sank beside him, arranging the skirt of her dress neatly over her knees. "What is it?" She found herself whispering, too, and looked to where he had nodded.

A haggard-looking bird, a gull, was wedged tightly into a cleft of the rock. It stared back at them, its head cocked, its bright black eye flitting nervously. She looked closer. An ugly-looking length of fishing net, crusted with sand and sea salt, fraying but still tight and fast, was bound at least twice around its bedraggled body. The story told itself: this bird had become entangled somewhere out in the surf, had barely escaped drowning, and dragged itself desperately to the lea of this rock to wait for death. The gull opened its orange bill and screamed at her, but weakly, unconvincingly.

The boy said nothing for a moment, then, still whispering, "I tried to loose the net, but it wouldn't let me near." As proof, he held out his hand to her. "Look." His wrist was torn where the gull's bill had fended him off, not deeply, but it bled.

Grace looked shyly from the boy's wrist, to his face, and then at the gull again. She felt herself suddenly in the presence of weighty matters: pending death, profound compassion, a faint admiration.

The boy reached for the gull again, but the screaming bill warned him off.

After another moment of silence she said, "It's going to die." The note of finality in her own voice caught her off-guard. "I mean, unless we could... could we save it?" He was sucking his wrist thoughtfully, so she continued. "If we could hold back that bill somehow. Without hurting it, I mean." She shuddered at the thought of touching this wild living thing but found herself determined to hide her squeamishness. "Maybe if one of us held it down, the other could pull the net away?"

The boy said nothing for a long moment.

"My name's Grace," she said at last, more to break the silence than by way of introduction. "What's yours?"

He looked at her again. "Stephen."

Suddenly he leaned forward off his haunches and onto his knees in the sand. Without explanation, he began pulling the knitted jumper up over his shoulders, dragging it off. When his head finally pulled clear, he flashed her a freckled grin, his hair upended by the static of the wool. He tossed the jumper to her.

"Here," he said. "Use this."

She understood, but hesitated. "It's sure to ruin it. Won't your mom..."

He grinned again. The weighty presence she'd felt before pressed on her more strongly, and she found herself strangely drawn to him.

"Go ahead," he said. "It's okay. You can put it over the head. Watch that bill. When you've got it held tight, I'll try to loose the net."

She followed his directions. The bird screamed murder at them, more convincingly than before, but after a couple of false starts she managed to pinion the head and bill together with the jumper. The gull struggled for a moment and then went still. But for the nervous trembling she still felt in the bundle of wool beneath her hands, she would have thought she'd killed it. It was difficult to wrap the jumper around the bird firmly enough to be sure it wouldn't struggle free.

"Okay, I think I've got it," she finally said.

At the sound of her voice, as if it could sense what was coming next, the gull set to thrashing wildly.

"Hold it!" Stephen said, firmly but not angrily. He placed his hands on hers to help. The knitted jumper held. Her heart, she found, was racing. When the bird's struggles had subsided again, he said, "Okay, gently now, pull it away from the rock."

She did, slowly, until he could get at the strands of fishing net from all sides. He grinned at her again. Very gently—far more gently than she'd ever seen her cousins or the boys at school move—he reached for the net and began to explore the knotted mass with his fingers.

"When I pull this back from the shoulders," he said, "I bet it'll start thrashing like nothing with its wings. Can you hold them down?"

Grace adjusted the jumper, pulling it further down the bird's body. "I'll try."

He was right. The struggle was so desperate that the gull almost broke free, but she was able to hold it back.

As more of the net came loose, she saw that the tangle around its leg was the worst, both because it had wound more tightly there and because the gull kicked viciously whenever it became aware of Stephen's hands. She watched him closely as he unwrapped the last of the netting, gently and carefully.

She became aware something awaking in her—and if she was older, she would have recognized it immediately.

"There," he said. "I think we've got it. Only, when you let that bird go, watch it doesn't lash out at you. It's gonna want to."

She nodded. Together they moved to their knees, still holding down the gull but ready to leap back if it came to that.

"Count of three?" she suggested.

On three, they pulled the jumper away and moved back. The bird lay perfectly still, its head turned to the side, its black eye fixed on them. It squawked once, tentatively, and then screamed outright. Rising on shaky legs, it tested its wings, awkwardly sweeping the air with them, but it could not fly away—at least, it did not. It swept the air again and screamed. Then, tucking in its wings, it scuttled clumsily a few yards down the beach, watching them with its beady black eye the whole while.

Grace suddenly became aware that she had taken the boy's hand in hers, perhaps in that thrilling instant when the gull had risen up screaming, perhaps out of that eleven-year-old habit she still had of reaching for her father's hand in startling or uncertain moments. She released it quickly; if he had noticed, he didn't say anything.

"I'm Grace," she said, because she didn't know what else to say.

He grinned again. "You told me that already. I'm Stephen."

She felt shy, but also that unfamiliar admiration. "Do you live here?" she asked.

"I'm from Halifax."

"Us too. We're on vacation."

They both still watched the gull. It had waddled to the edge of the seafoam but hadn't yet flown away.

"Do you think it will live?" she asked. "Can it even fly anymore?"

He shook his head. "Don't know. That net was wrapped pretty tight." He sat on one of the larger rocks. He began brushing the sand from his feet and reached for his shoes where he'd left them in the sand. As he put them on, Grace sat down across from him.

"I haven't seen you before," she said. "Where's your house?"

"We're staying at the farm just across that field there." He gestured. "With my Uncle Adam."

He explained how he, along with his mother and two sisters, had been visiting for the summer. Speaking into the sole of his shoe as he shook the sand from it, he told her how his father was a doctor in Halifax, and how they'd all come to stay with Uncle Adam for the summer while he stayed in the city and took care of his practice.

"How old are you?" he asked finally, pulling the laces of his shoe tight.

"Eleven."

"Older than my sisters. Jane's ten, Sarah's eight." Both shoes finally tied, he stood up and began shaking sand from his jumper. "Not quite ruined," he commented. "I'm twelve and… Oh, look!"

He pointed. The gull had finally worked up the resolve to try its wings. It beat them once or twice about its body, and then, still hobbling a bit, raced along the edge of the tide, stirring the air with them. Together they watched as it rose, floated for a few feet, landed briefly, and then tried again. At last it caught the air, sailed a distance out over the rolling water, and landed finally in the waves. They saw it bobbing among the whitecaps.

Her unfamiliar shyness momentarily forgotten, Grace clapped her hands once with satisfaction. "So we did save him after all!"

She felt the impulse to take his hand again, though this time she caught herself.

They started walking. He had picked up a twisted piece of driftwood and was furrowing a line behind them. She walked as close to the reach of the waves as she dared in her canvas shoes. They talked more, comparing schools in Halifax and swapping stories about their time on the island. She wondered how they could have lived so close together for so many weeks and not met sooner. He explained that Uncle Adam had kept him busy with farm chores much of the time.

They came to a tidal pool. For a moment, her childlike curiosity won out over the growing shyness in her and she knelt to explore. He crouched down, too, and probed the water with the length of driftwood. This raised up a swirl of silt, and as it settled Grace thought she saw the blurry flash of a seashell, half submerged in the sand. She reached in and lifted it free, silt and sand splashing from its hollow cup as she pulled it out. She shook it in the water, stirring the remaining muck from its cavity, and finally held it in her palm, black and smooth.

Stephen watched. "It's just a mussel shell. It's a big one, and you don't usually find them whole like that. But still, they're as common as dirt around here."

She looked at the shell closely. She had a full menagerie of them sitting on the windowsill of their cottage, treasures she'd gathered over the holidays, but none of them, she thought, quite like this one. It was still closed, or mostly so, the two sides only slightly parted, like a mouth caught by surprise in the middle of saying something very important. Their outer edges had been polished smooth by the persistent caress of the tide.

She pressed her thumb into the dark depth and gently pried it apart. The hinge creaked until the halves spread from the centre, a pair of black angel wings. The inner surface gleamed brilliantly in contrast to the black exterior, pearly and soft with all the colours of oil on water when the light struck it just so.

Stephen leaned in and examined it again. Her shyness crescendoed in her, but she smiled at him and, with a snap, pulled apart the two halves.

"Here," she said. "You can have this half, and I'll keep the other."

Stephen looked at the gift as she placed it in his hands.

"To remember the day we saved that gull," she added, feeling suddenly childish.

There was that freckled grin of his again, but it was hard for her to read it. "Sure. And I'll always have mine, and you yours?"

She laughed. It seemed suddenly very absurd to her and she stood up. Looking back down the stretch of beach, she said, "I should go."

"Wait."

She stopped, turned back.

"Will you come back tomorrow?" he asked. "I'll be here."

She laughed again, and her shyness seemed lesser now. "Yes."

Grace did return the next day and, scrambling over the line of rock that separated them, found Stephen sitting barefoot in its lea. She sat in the rough sand beside him.

"Hi," she said shyly.

"Hi."

He sat with his back against the rock, listening intently to the sound of the tide, his freckled brow furrowed. She looked at his hand in his lap. His thumb idly stroked the delicate, pearly concave of his half of her seashell.

"What are you doing?" she asked.

"Do you ever wonder what's out there?" he said, not looking at her for a moment.

She looked out over the water, confused. "Just water, I guess." She tried to remember her geography from school. "Cape Breton's out that way, I think. Then what? Europe?"

"That's not exactly what I mean. I mean out *there*." He gestured widely. "Other places, strange places, other people..."

She watched his hand stroke the seashell. She felt glad he had it. In her gladness, she said nothing.

"Just think," he continued. "All those deep, secret ocean places out there. Like that gull yesterday. I mean, who knows where it could be right now? The sea might have carried it anywhere. And the treasures, too. Think of all the lost things the water hides."

Still confused, Grace felt obliged to say something. "Like the seashell?"

"Sure. Like the seashell."

Feeling strangely absurd again, like she had the previous day, she laughed. The sea seemed to be laughing, too. It danced with rolling mirth along the beach.

The children sat for a while, listening to it laugh at them, at their youth, at their clumsiness with each other, at the summer that spread its final golden days before them. And lost in its laughter, Stephen traced his finger along the outer edge of their seashell.

CHAPTER THREE

Atlas, 1927

STEPHEN WAS WAITING FOR HER IN THE SHELTER OF THE ROCK—THEIR rock, as he had begun to think of it—with his atlas in his lap. He had been playing his usual game, though at twelve it hardly felt like a game anymore, more an imaginative exercise, a thought experiment.

He stared intently at a map of Egypt, which he had chosen more or less at random. He fixed his eyes on the intricate web of lines that marked the delta of the Nile, and then followed the great river from Alexandria at its mouth, through Cairo, and down into the heart of the continent.

He squinted, looking through his eyelashes, and tried to imagine people moving through the dust-choked streets of Cairo, a busy market maybe, a crowded square, and then palm trees and papyrus waving sleepily from the riverbank, crocodiles smiling hypnotically from the water as he drifted south. After many years of practice, these images came to him sharply and vividly.

He traced the line of the river with his finger, following it deep into Africa, till it reached the shores of Lake Victoria, bright and sapphire-blue in his mind's eye. He traced his way back, downstream to the river's delta, and out into the vast expanse of the Mediterranean Sea.

"There's more to reading a map than knowing names and places, Stevie," his grandfather used to say. It had been his atlas.

As a little boy, Stephen had often sat on his grandfather's knee as they flipped through the atlas together. Having travelled a fair bit during the Great War, Grandfather had personally visited many of the places they discovered in the pages of this book. When they came to a place he knew especially well, rich stories full of vibrant detail came tumbling out of him, Stephen's young heart soaking it up eagerly like a sponge. It was Grandfather who had taught him how to look at maps, to really see them, and to imagine the faraway worlds they represented.

"We're all of us spots on the map, Stevie," Grandfather had said, his lungs gurgling strangely the way they did when he got excited. Stephen, then a boy of seven, would squeeze the old man's hand and strain to understand. "That inch of dirt under your feet is a spot on a map, somewhere. Look around you. It's all on a map somewhere, isn't it? I mean really look, and what do you see? Labels? Borders? Longitude and latitude?" Sensing it was important, Stephen struggled to keep pace with his logic. "No!" A fit of mucus gurgled through the lungs. "What you see is life! Hills and water and forests—and not even forests, but trees, and trees and trees, gathered together. The trees don't know anything about borders. That's what the map records. It's our world, our existence. Any fool can read labels and borders and whatnot, but a man of vision, he sees—he sees the world in all its beauty and texture."

Often the coughing would interrupt them at this point, or his mother would, warning Grandfather that he was going to overwhelm the boy, and shooing Stephen out to play.

Once Mother had told him vaguely that Grandfather had been hurt in the war, and that's why he talked the way he did sometimes.

He died not long after this, and they told Stephen that he had "passed on." Though he hadn't really understood, it had been enough to know that Grandfather had left him the atlas.

"Because he loved so much to study it with you," his mother had explained.

At seven, he had received it with a deep sense of responsibility. The first time he'd opened it, he had tried to see the things Grandfather had seen in those maps, but all he saw were spots of ink, labels, and borders, and little else.

The more time he spent with it, however, the more he learned to see.

Stephen wasn't sure when, but at some point it had become a game to him. He would open the atlas at random and imagine himself hovering high above the world, the land stretching out so far below that it seemed to be, in fact, nothing more than a map. From such a height, he could only make out the dark outline of a country or a shadowy shoreline, but in his imagination he would begin to descend, and soon the blurred colours would take on life. Pastel green ink, maybe, would wave with the thousand shades of a forest. Pale blue would scintillate like steel and silver, etched with the living patterns of real water. In this game, the images became more and more distinct as he plunged towards the earth. Spidery lines swirled with the rushing water of real rivers. Elevation markings stood out sharply like the rocky peaks of real mountains. Labelled dots became crowded with the buildings and streets of real cities. And he would continue to watch, and fall, until he touched down and felt like he'd seen it—the world in all its beauty and texture.

In the lea of the rock, Stephen turned the page and, still waiting for Grace to arrive, hovered over the next map that spread open beneath him, a bird's eye view of Greece. Even as he did so, his right hand held the seashell Grace had given him, thumbing its edge distractedly. Tomorrow he and his mother, and Sarah and Jane, would take the ferry back across Northumberland Strait and home to Halifax. The vacation was ending and they were returning to the city, leaving the island to ripen into autumn.

This meant, of course, he would be leaving Grace. The fact weighed heavily on him. It was just over a week ago now since they'd met, and they'd spent every day together, exploring long stretches of beach, inventing games, swapping stories. Grace had told him about her father's work on the sea, about her school and the other girls in her class, about the big stone church they attended, where she was going to be confirmed this fall.

In turn, Stephen had told her stories he had read and remembered from his *Children's Book of Mythology*—of Jason and his quest for golden fleece, of Odysseus and his quest for Ithaca. Stephen loved these stories and had found in Grace a patient audience.

Once, while they were writing messages in the sand with driftwood, Stephen had asked her if she knew any poetry. At first she'd laughed dismissively at the strange request, and then, upon realizing he was serious, she refused. But Stephen prodded until she gave in.

"Well, I do know one poem," she admitted. Cautiously, her voice lilting childishly, she said, "*Monday's child is fair of face; Tuesday's child is full of grace…*"

Stephen laughed, but not unkindly. "That's not poetry! It's just a nursery rhyme."

"It is so poetry. It has rhyming and everything, and I read it in a book." She drew another breath. "*Wednesday's child is full of woe…*"

She trailed off, thinking.

Stephen waited. "What about Thursday's child?"

"I don't remember that one, but it's something that rhymes with woe. But I know the rest: *Friday's child is loving and giving; Saturday's child works hard for a living. But the child that is born on Sabbath Day is bonny and blithe and good and gay.*"

There was a very short silence after she finished.

"Do you know what day you were born on?" he asked.

She was shy again for a moment. "I asked my mom, and she said Wednesday." A childish, ominous silence followed.

"Well, it's just a poem."

"What about you?"

"I think I was born on a Thursday."

She laughed. "No. I mean, do you know any poems?"

Stephen drew an aimless line in the sand with his driftwood. "We did poetry recital in English class this year, and I learned a poem called *Ozymandius.*"

"What's an Ozymandius?"

"It's the name of an ancient Egyptian king," he explained. "It's about a traveller who comes across a monument to this king, King Ozymandius, somewhere in the desert. Even though it was a fearful sight at one time, it's all ruined and buried in the sand now. It's about how even the greatest achievements of man get buried, in the end."

"How does it go?"

Stephen cleared his voice, paused for the briefest moment, and then, with an earnestness that seemed somehow older than he was, he began: "*I met a traveller from an antique land, who said: two vast and trunkless legs of stone stand in the desert. Near them, on the sand, half sunk, a shattered visage lies.*"

"What's a shattered visage?"

"It means the statue's broken face." He wasn't annoyed at the interruption—rather, pleased that she was working to follow. He continued, with a conviction in his voice, as though he could see it standing before him even now: the statue's frown and wrinkled lip, its sneer of cold command. "*…and on the pedestal, these words appear: 'My name is Ozymandius, king of kings: Look on my works, ye mighty and despair!'*"

He paused, long enough that Grace shuffled to move, as though he were done, but when she did, he continued.

"*Nothing beside remains. Round the decay of that colossal wreck, boundless and bare, the lone and level sands stretch far away…*"

His voice trailed off, lost in the rush of the sea and sighing wind.

Grace said nothing, until, "I like that: the lone and level sands stretch far away." She gestured grandly with her arm, playing with the drama of the lines.

Stephen grinned at her. He couldn't tell if she felt the weight of the words, but she had enjoyed them, and he was glad of that.

He then scratched the word *Ozymandius* with his driftwood in the sand. Grace, for her part, had written *Wednesday's Child.*

In the sunshine that now blushed across the beach where he sat, remembering and waiting for her, he flipped his atlas to the map that read "Eastern Canada." Whimsically, he traced out the lines of Prince Edward Island, imagining himself suddenly miles above their spot on the beach, looking down on the tiny speck of a boy, studying an atlas in his lap and waiting for a girl, his friend, to arrive.

He remembered, two evenings before last, how his mother, who loved to entertain, had gushed hospitably when he'd told her about the family from Halifax that was renting the small cottage on the other side of the big potato field. Why hadn't he told her sooner? Of course, she said, they would have to have them over for dinner.

Watching the shoreline of eastern Canada rise and fall on the page, he thought about their visit, just last night, when Grace and her family, Mr. and Mrs. Stewart and five-year-old Willie, had come at last to dinner.

Stephen had watched her across the table, stealing playful glances through the soft glow of the candles that his mother had insisted they light. Mother had pressed him into a collared shirt and tight black tie, fussing with his straight brown hair till she was satisfied it wouldn't lay any neater. He'd felt somewhat self-conscious, aware that it was a more carefully groomed and presentable young man sitting across from Grace at the table than she had yet seen. He still grinned at her boyishly, like he had that first day on the beach, but this new setting seemed subtly to change the way they were with one another.

She sat straight with practiced etiquette, wearing, he assumed, the nearest thing to a Sunday dress she had with her on the island. Her blonde hair had been done up neatly in a French braid, and she wore a pendant he'd never seen before. She seemed somehow older, but also more distant.

"You can't imagine our surprise," Mother was saying as she set down the roast and potatoes and took her place at the table, "when Stephen told us about a family from Halifax, vacationing in the cottage just down the beach!" Polite smiles were shared around the table. "I am so glad we were able to meet like this before the summer ended."

The dining room was small for such a large dinner party, but somehow they had all found a place. Willie sat with Mrs. Stewart, and Mr. Stewart next to Grace. Stephen was across from her, with his two sisters, Sarah and Jane, on either side of him. Uncle Adam sat at the head of the table and Mother, talking engagingly, opposite him.

"To think," Mother said, "all these weeks living right next door and never having met!"

"We were just as surprised," Mrs. Stewart agreed. She touched her husband's hand as if an appeal for him to confirm it. "Why, we've passed this house on the road to Annandale any number of times, haven't we, Edward? And never known who was living in it."

Mr. Stewart nodded. He spooned some potatoes onto his plate and passed the dish. "I understand your husband practices medicine in Halifax. I believe I know him. At least, I've heard of him. Dr. Garret Walker? A highly respected physician, from what I hear."

Her face beaming as it usually did when she spoke about Father, Mother began to describe Garret's practice: the office he kept among the mansions of the Northwest Arm, the furniture inside the waiting room she had helped to select, the girl they employed, who admitted patients, filed charts, and so on for Dr. Walker. She mentioned one or two of his wealthier or more celebrated patients by name, about the Christmas cards and thank-you notes they received, one even from the mayor.

"And Stephen tells me, Mr. Stewart, that you're a member with the RCMP?" she said politely.

"Well, technically I work for the Department of National Revenue, Mrs. Walker," he explained. "The Preventative Service. We work closely with the RCMP, but they don't have a marine section of their own as of yet."

He was, in fact, the captain of a cruiser that patrolled the coast for smugglers and bootleggers, bringing their trade of illegal Caribbean rum into Nova Scotia.

"That's right," Mr. Stewart said with a good-natured laugh. "A life of derring-do on the high seas, for me. Chasing pirates from here to Newfoundland!" He thrust a playful jab of his fork at Sarah, sitting directly across from him.

"Daddy fights pirates!" Little Willie bubbled up, wide-eyed with admiration. "Just like Peter Pan. Right, Daddy?"

Mother laughed. "You must have no end of stories to tell, Mr. Stewart."

When dinner was done and cleared, they found their way to the parlour. The evenings were growing cooler this late in the summer and the room was damp. Uncle Adam fussed at the hearth with the makings of a fire, while Mr. Stewart, apparently intent on proving Mother's claim at dinner, and encouraged by his wife and his son both, launched into a story.

"A tale of adventure at sea," he called it, winking again at Sarah as Willie nestled in against him.

The story was, in fact, gripping, and well told, about a midnight chase with some rumrunners from Miquelon.

Sitting in the dimly lit parlour next to Grace, in her best dress and braided hair, Stephen found himself drawn into the story and liking Mr. Stewart very much.

When the evening was over and the Stewarts had left into the soft blue night, once more up the road to their cottage, and after Mother and Jane had done up the dishes, Stephen crept from the house silently. In the distance he heard the water breathing heavily as it rolled along the shore in the moonlight. Over that, closer to hand, a cricket chirped.

Stephen stole along the edge of the potato field that separated their homes, following the fence line as well as he could in the dark. The going was slow, and the night had become very cool and damp by the time he found himself standing, at last, on her edge of the field.

He crouched down among the potato plants and watched silhouettes passing their yellow-lit window. He could make out hers, sometimes, and then the taller shape of her mother, the bulkier shadow of her father. He only watched for a minute, with a strange thing happening in his heart he'd never felt before—like hope, only surer. He searched for a name to call it by and, finding none, slipped back into the darkness. Smiling, he passed silently through the field towards his house.

Sitting now in the glare of the sunlight with the atlas in his lap, Stephen turned the seashell over one more time with his thumb. It had become very important to him. He looked at its pearly concave and thought of the earnest girl who had helped him rescue an entangled sea gull from certain death, the shy girl who had recited lines of poetry with him, the quiet girl sitting across from him in Uncle Andrew's parlour. He tried to name the strange feeling again. The simplest word he could find for it was friendship, but it was not like any friendship he'd known before.

He wanted to give her something in return. He felt this necessity overwhelmingly, something she could remember him by, and see him in, the way he saw her in this half of a seashell they shared.

He looked again at the atlas. He had been thinking about it since finding his way home through the dark last night, and he had finally made a decision: if anything could give Grace the glimpse of himself he so wanted her to see, it was this book. He would give her his grandfather's atlas.

A shadow cast itself over him as he looked up and saw her. Unexpectedly, nervousness grew from the centre of his body.

She sat in the sand beside him. "What's with the book?"

"It's an atlas," he ventured, watching her face cautiously.

"Oh."

He wondered if it was mockery he heard in the tone of her voice, or was it only confusion?

"You're reading an atlas?" she said.

"I like to look at the maps. You can see things in them, you know. If you look hard enough, it's like the places come alive."

Whether confusion or mockery, he could not tell which, it rose from her as a hardly audible though well-meant laugh. "Stephen, that's very strange."

He was quiet as he closed the book. She had started burying one hand in the sand with the other.

"Why do have an atlas out here, of all places, anyway?"

Stephen finally said, "It's… it's nothing."

She laughed, the atlas forgotten. Would he like to explore low tide? He rose and followed her, the atlas tucked tightly, sadly under his arm.

Grace gave him her Halifax address before they parted that day. He pressed the paper into his pocket and promised to write. The next day, he boarded the ferry and returned to the city and his home.

He did not write.

————————

In the dim light of the study, Grace turned the seashell over in her hand, sadly. A full forty years later, he still had it. Memories tumbling, one after the other, she glanced up hopefully at the bookshelf by his desk. It took a minute for her to pick it out among the titles, but eventually she found it, tucked in among his more scholarly tomes: *The World Atlas.*

Tears blurring her vision, she pulled it down. It left a gap on the shelf like the space of a missing tooth in a child's smile. She opened the book on the desk, flipping through the pages and remembering the thoughtful, dreamy boy who had once owned it. It was stuffed with old newspaper clippings she had long ago forgotten, and scrawled with notes.

She flipped through the book randomly until her eye caught on the map of Egypt, and she stopped to read. He had scribbled a few lines in the bottom corner of the map, across the pastel blue of the Red Sea, his young handwriting awkward and clumsy:

Round the decay
Of that colossal wreck, boundless and bare
The lone and level sands stretch far away.

CHAPTER FOUR
Ice Skates, 1932

"TODAY'S LESSON COMES FROM THE PROPHET HOSEA, CHAPTER TWO."

Reverend Elliot had given Grace's father, Captain Edward Stewart, the honour of reading the Scripture in church that morning. Normally one of the deacons would have performed this duty, but the reverend had wanted especially to recognize Captain Stewart today. Only three months ago, the Department of National Revenue's Preventative Service had been absorbed by the RCMP, and he had been transferred to the newly minted Marine Section. His new command was one of the more active vessels in the fleet, and this was the first Sunday he had been ashore in many days.

He wasn't used to reading in church. Though on the bridge of his cruiser he'd have barked orders with all the confidence of a seasoned seaman, in this setting his voice sounded tentative as he mounted the steps of the lectern and read: "'And in that day will I make a covenant for them with the beasts of the field and with the fowls of heaven, and with the creeping things of the ground: and I will break the bow and the sword and the battle out of the earth, and will make them to lie down safely.'"

For her part, Grace sat at the back of the musty-smelling sanctuary, the rose-tinted light from the stained-glass windows shining with red fire in her bobbed hair. She was sixteen now, after all, and surely too old to sit with Mom and Dad in church. She watched her father admiringly from her place at the back, but also distractedly, because of the steady hiss of gossip that her friends, Beth and Margaret, whispered between them.

Her father continued to work his way through the lesson: "'And I will betroth thee unto me for ever; yea, I will betroth thee unto me in righteousness, and in judgment, and in lovingkindness, and in mercies.'"

"Are you going tonight?" Beth asking in hushed tones. The girls were organizing a skating social on Chocolate Lake, and Grace had yet to commit.

"Richard's coming," Margaret said on the other side of her. "And he asked me specifically if you'd be there."

Beth nudged her gently, meaningfully. "I daresay, he's absolutely smitten with you, Grace."

Grace's voice almost rose above a whisper. "Beth! I hardly think so."

"No, it's true!" Margaret pressed the point. "Beth overheard him talking to John, and he was saying he thinks you're the best-looking girl at St. Chris. He's *smitten*, I tell you."

They giggled girlishly.

The pew directly ahead of them creaked. None of the people sitting in it looked back, but the girls could tell a few of them were wondering if a stern look would be necessary to hush their whispering. The friends sat still, affecting an exaggerated solemnity. Beth and Margaret smothered their smiles by staring intently into their prayer books.

Captain Stewart soldiered on through the lesson: "'I will even betroth thee unto me in faithfulness: and thou shalt know the Lord.'"

After a moment's silence, Grace whispered, "Well, let him be smitten. I think he's a pompous—"

"Pompous?" Margaret was near giggling again. "Who cares? The boy's gorgeous. And that *accent* of his?"

"And he's the captain of the Halifax Juniors rowing team," Beth added with a suggestive, sidelong glance at Grace, who still staring determinedly at her prayer book. "I mean, have you *seen* him row?"

At the front of the church, her father finished the lesson: "'And I will have mercy upon her that had not obtained mercy; and I will say to them which were not my people, Thou art my people.'" His voice grew strong as he neared the end. "This is the word of the Lord."

"Thanks be to God." Grace muttered the words with the rest of the congregation, and then, still muttering, added, "Anyway, I'm sure he's not my type."

"But you'll come tonight?"

Grace said nothing. Reverend Elliot had found his way to the pulpit and started his homily, something about how Hosea's faithfulness reveals God's faithfulness. She caught it only in fragments. Richard was sitting just four pews ahead, and her eyes and her mind kept wandering over to him.

It's not that she disagreed with Beth and Margaret's assessment. He was certainly good-looking, and by far the most popular boy at St. Christopher's. And yet there was something about him—his attentions a bit too forward, maybe, his conversation somehow hollow—that made it impossible to be entirely herself around him. Pompous was probably too strong a word, but at the very least she was far less interested in him than he seemed to be in himself.

That day at the beach, for instance. Had she noticed the distance he swam out into the surf? (She hadn't.) Had he told her about winning his last rowing regatta? (He had.) Did she know that his father had served on one of the largest ships in the British navy? (She did, but only because this was the third time he'd mentioned it.) It may be that he was smitten, but even so, it was hard not to feel like a rowing trophy when she was around him.

The reverend was finishing, something about God's faithfulness inspiring our faithfulness. Heads bowed in prayer. The organ burst into song. They stood.

Margaret leaned in during the hymn. "Will you invite me to the wedding?" she whispered mischievously.

Grace tried to ignore her as Reverend Elliot spread his arms and spoke the benediction.

Church was over.

Grace chose to wait on the steps of St. Christopher's for her parents to offer their Sunday morning niceties to the reverend. With Captain Edward's new role in the Marine Service, there was a lot to talk about, and she knew the wait would be long. Her brother Willie had insisted it was too cold and was waiting in the foyer, but it was a mild afternoon for February, and anyway, she didn't mind the cold. She pulled a knitted cap over her ears and buried her hands in her fur muff.

"Hi Grace." Richard appeared beside her; they stood side by side, facing the street. He had turned up his collar and was tucking the ends of a wool scarf down the front of his coat. "Cold today."

"I like it," she said, distantly.

"Me too. Clears the head. And it's good for the circulation, they say. My dad said he knew a man in the navy who bathed in cold water every morning. Even in the winter. Was convinced it would keep his heart strong."

She was quiet. Her cheeks had started to redden. Her nose, too, from the cold.

"The ice will be hard," Richard said. "Good skating, I mean." He adjusted the scarf around his neck and plunged his hands into his pockets. "You're coming tonight?"

From the tone of his voice, Grace couldn't tell if it was an observation, a request, or a directive. She settled on request. "Well, I haven't decided, but I suppose it'll be fun."

"I guess everyone'll be there. Beth and Meg and the rest. John, too. John said his cousin may come. I haven't met him. Goes to Halifax Academy. We rowed against HCA last summer. They have a good rowing team." He had begun to ramble, but she could tell he had a point in sight. "You do skate?"

She laughed softly. "Of course I do."

"I was wondering if…" He shuffled his feet, shifting his weight back and forth against the cold. "If you were going, I could go with you? You are going?"

Her features softened. "Yes," she admitted at last. "I'm going."

Her family was approaching the door of the church. Through the frosted glass next to the door, she could see their cloudy shapes bundling themselves up before stepping into the cold.

Richard had noticed them too, and tried one more time, his voice determined. "Would you like to accompany me then, tonight? I mean, could we go together?"

Grace inhaled and held it for only the slightest moment. When she spoke, she could see the mist of her breath, as if her words were hanging in the air between them. "Sure, Richard. I'd be happy to."

The door opened and they came out: Will first, followed by Mr. and Mrs. Stewart. Richard smiled broadly. Triumphantly, she thought.

"Right, then. I'll pick you up at half past six." He turned to her parents. "Mrs. Stewart, Captain Stewart, good to see you. Will." He punched her brother's shoulder lightly. "Well, so long, and I'll see you tonight, Grace."

And he was down the steps, walking briskly because of the cold.

"A nice boy," Mrs. Stewart said, watching him go.

Mr. Stewart added, "What's at half past six?"

"I know—" Will began, but Grace silenced him with a look.

She linked her arm with her father's and stuffed her hand back into the fur muff. "Can we go now?" she asked. "I'll tell you on the way."

By the time the Stewarts had finished dinner that afternoon, the grey of the morning had deepened. Wet weather crept over the city from the Atlantic, and at some point snow began to fall—not thickly, but consistently.

Grace sat at their parlour window, watching it drift through the air while she waited for Richard. Having learned the details of the evening outing, her mother had curled and arranged her hair about the nape of her neck and had helped choose her outfit, fussing about how nice a boy Richard Turner was. She had even offered Grace her best shawl to wear, which Grace declined.

"It's a skating party, Mother. Not an audience with King George!"

She had opted for her much more practical knitted scarf and cap, though she did accept the string of faux pearls her mother had suggested. No one would see them anyway.

She caught herself wondering all over again why in the world she had agreed to this. Margaret and Beth wouldn't have spoken to her for weeks if she'd refused, and there were girls, she knew, who'd have fallen over themselves for an evening out with Richard Turner. But even so, she felt a strange dread in her. Or was it simply nervousness? He was, after all, a fine young man, captain of the rowing team and all that.

Grace tangled her fingers in the pearls. Of course, there was that time she'd mentioned her father's transfer to the RCMP. And what was it he'd said, laughing, about the Marine Section? Hack sailors playing with toy boats? When she'd spoken up, he'd said again how his father had served on the largest ship in the British navy. Not scornfully, but not modestly, either. Beth would gloss over memories like those; Margaret would say something embarrassing about how only the most passionate couples quarrel.

The snow continued to fall. From her perch at the parlour window, Grace saw his shape, indistinct in the snow and twilight, coming up the path to the house.

He rapped on the door. She checked herself and decided at last that it wasn't dread but simply nervousness. She rose and wished she'd accepted Mother's shawl.

Will was first to the door. "Grace!" he hollered playfully. "Your beau's here!"

She cringed, but Mr. Stewart intercepted her brother as Will opened the door, welcoming Richard in himself. She could hear them talking in the hall.

"Good evening, Richard! Not too cold for skating this evening, is it?"

"Not so bad, sir. I think the snow warms the air a bit."

"Does it indeed? Well, Grace's been waiting for you. She'll be here shortly."

Hearing her name, she stepped into the foyer. "Hi Richard," she said.

His face lit up when he saw her. "Grace, you look…" He became awkwardly aware of Mr. Stewart standing there. "…ready to go. Shall we?"

He helped her wrap herself in her wool overcoat; she hung her skates across her shoulders, and they set out.

The walk to Chocolate Lake lasted a good quarter of an hour, but what Richard had said was true: the snow had softened the edge of the cold. And it kept falling. They talked about superficial things, and joked a fair bit. Grace felt she was beginning to feel at ease with him, though she also wondered if he wasn't walking a bit closer to her than he might have. At one point, he walked with one hand hanging at his side, and she was glad she'd brought her fur muff, as she felt sure he'd have otherwise wanted to take her hand in his.

When they arrived at the lake, it only took a few minutes to locate the St. Christopher's crowd. A few dozen yards down the beach, someone had cleared a large patch of ice and a good number of young people were already gliding around playfully. Some of the boys had even brought sticks with them, and a half-hearted scrimmage was underway. A small fire had been lit on the beach and the girls had arranged to have some haybales dragged down, which they used as seating. Margaret was there now, lacing up her skates.

"Richard! Grace!" Margaret called. Something in the tone of her voice greatly annoyed Grace. "You made it! And how do you like our little winter bivouac?" She gestured to the fire and straw seating.

"Hi Meg," Richard said. "This is," he paused only very slightly, looking for the best expression, "a first rate affair."

Margaret laughed. "Sure it is. First rate, I like that. You've got your skates? Beth's out already, and the rest. Even John made it. And his cousin. Though his cousin says he doesn't skate, if you can believe it. Said he never learned."

Richard laughed. "How do you grow up in Halifax and not learn to skate?"

Grace said, "I've never met John's cousin. Where is he?"

"Oh," Margaret said, "he's around here somewhere. He tried coming out on the ice anyway, but it's pretty tough without skates. I'm not sure where he's at just now."

Richard had already taken a seat on a haybale and was lacing his skates. Grace sat, too, and pulled on her skates. But before she could lace them herself, Richard knelt in the snow and took her foot in his hands.

"Can I help you tighten the laces?" he asked.

She was taken aback but said nothing and let him. He could, after all, get them much tighter than she could.

Out on the ice, he cut a wide orbit around her as she glided at a more leisurely pace. It required some work to avoid the jostle of the hockey scrimmage that kept threatening to break out into a full-on game. Once, Richard seemed to misjudge his trajectory, and slid directly into her. He didn't crash against her, and he was laughing all the while, but still he tumbled to the ice and the weight of the collision dragged her down on top of him. He helped her up, gallantly, playfully.

"Not bruised, I hope?"

She was good-humoured about it, of course, and brushed the ice from the skirt of her overcoat. "I'm fine."

They skated closer together now, and when Grace wobbled on an uneven patch of ice, he reached out and took her hand to steady her. He didn't let it go for a long while, not until Grace herself relaxed her fingers and made to drift away from him.

They had been skating for quite a while, and found themselves at the far end of the cleared ice, a good distance from the rest. The snow fell thicker and the sky had grown almost fully dark. She could see the fire, yards away on the beach, and behind that a few lighted windows from the city. The laughter and play of the others seemed suddenly miles away.

He glided up close to her. "I like this," he said.

She deliberately missed the point. "Skating is good fun."

"That's not what I mean, Grace. I mean, I like *this*. Being here with you."

He reached for her hand again. An uncertain thrill passed through her as he took it and she wished she'd brought her fur muff out onto the ice.

She grasped for new topics, lamely. "It's not too cold for you?"

He laughed. "Not as long as I'm with you."

With a sudden sweep, he glided around to face her, taking both her hands in his, and skated backwards in front of her. The same vague thrill passed through her, but more clearly this time.

"Richard," she said with a note of reprove in her voice. "The others will be wondering."

"Let them wonder." He stopped suddenly. She heard the slice of his skates braking on the ice, and in her momentum she glided helplessly into him. His arms closed around her, not aggressively but confidently. His breath was warm, from the work of skating, and the mist of it hung heavily in the space between their faces. They stood there, silent on the ice for what seemed an eternity.

A third time the thrill went through her, and she recognized it at last. "Richard, I don't want you to—"

The noise of hockey and playful shouting reached them, growing louder as the party approached their end of the ice. Grace raised her arms and pushed him away gently.

"Richard, I think you've maybe misunderstood something." Her voice was unsteady.

He started into another wide circle around her, his composure unruffled. "What's there to misunderstand?" he laughed, innocently.

Before she could answer, Beth had found them. "Grace! Richard! There you are. Charlie and George want a go at 'crack the whip.' Are you in?"

She found her limbs were trembling. "I think I need to rest my ankles," she said, and then added, "The laces are a bit tight." She drifted off towards the glow of the fire, grateful that Beth had recruited Richard for the game before he could follow her.

She found a seat on one of the straw bales and loosened the skates, warming her shins by the fire. Her shivering began to subside. She could hear laughter out on the ice, but also the muffled pelting of snow as it grew heavier and wetter. She knew they would be coming in soon.

A voice spoke from the outer edge of the firelight. She had thought she was alone.

"Not one for skating, either?" It was a young man's voice. She turned to it, but could make out very little in the shifting light.

"Just taking a breather," she said guardedly.

"I never really learned, myself. My cousin John invited me out tonight, but now I'm thinking maybe I shouldn't have come."

The young man moved closer to the fire. She could make out the indistinct shape of his face, his cap pushing the hair low on his forehead, the flaps pulled down over his ears. A boyish grin lingered at the edges of his mouth.

Something very faint and distant appeared on the far edge of her memory. "You're John's cousin?" she said. "My name's Grace."

"Hi, I'm Stephen." He stepped nearer and sat on a bale near her. He cocked his head, thinking. "Stephen Walker," he added, offering her his hand.

She looked more intently at him, that distant something in her memory taking more distinct shape.

"Stephen Walker?" she repeated, taking his hand tentatively. "Do I... do I know you?" Even as she asked it, she heard in her voice the echo of a rising Prince Edward Island tide, and beneath that the thin strain of an eleven-year-old girl sitting at its shores. "My name's Grace Stewart."

In the dancing yellow light she saw a smile of recognition break across his face. "Grace *Stewart*? Were you... are you...?"

She nodded, her eyes smiling as the memory took hold for him, too.

"I can't believe it!" he said. "What's it been? Five years? More? What are you doing here?"

"What am I doing here? What are you doing here?"

"Like I say, John dragged me out. I had no idea you'd be here."

"*You're* John's cousin."

"You go to *his* church? This is—"

"It's incredible! How have you been?"

"I'm fine. Fine. You look… well."

The intensity of her feeling caught Grace off-guard. "And you do, too." She looked at him closer still, through the firelight.

Just then, a holler of delight reached them from the darkness, over the ice. The whip cracked and young bodies went tumbling over one another.

"Crack the whip," she said, vaguely.

"Like I said, I don't really skate." His tone was apologetic, misunderstanding her.

"Well, I'm glad you came anyway."

The noise of the party sounded closer. They were coming in at last. She thought of Richard, as though she could feel his arms even now, confident but unwanted, around her waist. A flush rose to her cheeks.

With it came an inarticulate fear that Stephen and Richard might meet, filling her with a strong sense that this should not, must not, happen. She squinted out over the ice in the direction of the laughing voices. They were close enough now that she could make out their silhouettes against the dim grey shadow of the frozen pond.

"Stephen?" Her fear welled up in her as a resolve, and she focused it on him. "Can we get out of here?"

She started pulling off her skates determinedly.

"Go?" he said.

The resolve intensified in her. She wasn't sure where it came from, but she knew she couldn't face Richard again. "Can we go somewhere? Would John miss you terribly if you left?"

"No, I guess not. But shouldn't we at least tell them we're going?"

She had pulled on and laced up her boots. "Oh, they'll figure it out, I'm sure. It's just, I don't want to see Richard again."

"Richard?"

"I can't be seen. Not by him."

She was on her feet now, feeling urgent. Stephen followed.

The way up from the lake to the road was unsteady and there was almost no light at all now, the snow wet and slushy. When they finally reached the lamplight of a street, they were flushed and breathing deeply, clouds of mist hanging about their faces.

They began to make their way along the road, snowfall clinging to them as they went.

"I'm sorry," she said. "You must think I'm completely insane, but I had to leave there. Margaret and Beth and the rest are fun, but sometimes they can be a bit much."

"It's okay. I don't mind. Anyway, I don't skate."

She laughed. "So you say."

They said nothing for a moment, as though they'd reached an unspoken agreement not to talk about it anymore.

"I must say, Stephen, I don't think I ever expected to run into you again. I wondered about you now and then, that funny boy I met on Prince Edward Island. I was going to write—at least, I wanted to write—but, you know... sometimes..."

"Way leads on to way?" he suggested.

She smiled, remembering. "I thought about you more often, I guess, than now and then," she admitted. "But we were just kids."

"I thought about you too." He was silent a moment and then added, shyly, "I still have my half of the seashell."

Grace laughed. "The seashell!"

They had arrived at an intersection. The headlights of a lone automobile were approaching and they stood in the sodden snow to wait for it to pass.

She turned to him. Wet snow clung to her hair and eyelashes; it was piled around his collar. She reached out and brushed it clear for him.

"What school do you go to?" she said.

"Halifax Academy. I'll finish next year. Probably college after that. Maybe." He spoke for a while about his plans, and she listened. In the streetlight she thought she could see a look in his eye she had seen before but could not place.

"Would you walk me home?" she asked. The cold was penetrating now, and she found herself walking close to his body to avoid it. "Remember when you made me recite that silly poem?"

"*Wednesday's child is full of woe.* Did you ever find out Thursday's child?"

"Far to go," she answered. "Thursday's child has far to go."

After a long moment of quiet, Stephen asked, "Who is Richard?"

"Richard?"

"Back at the ice, you said—"

"Richard Turner. He's just the darling of the gang at St. Chris. Captain of the rowing team. His father was in the British navy. Margaret and Beth have been trying to match us up for weeks now. I don't think I realized until tonight how wrong we are together. I think that's why I had to leave."

"I'm glad you did."

Suddenly she felt anxious. "You don't think I'm cruel, do you, that walking off like that was the worst thing I could have possibly done?"

"I'm glad you did."

Something stirred in her. "Do you ever feel pressure to be something you're not? Like some mould other people are trying to pour you into?" She didn't really want an answer, and Stephen offered none. "I do. I did. At least, that's how it was with Richard."

They walked for a while more, and Stephen asked Grace about herself.

She pulled her fingers from her fur muff, the damp lingering obstinately. The cold seemed to draw them closer to each other, their mutual warmth an almost magnetic force.

A chill trembled through her; she wasn't sure if she had taken his hand, or he hers, but their fingers had interlocked. The cold seemed less now, and they continued like this, hand in hand, until the street brought them to her house.

She turned to face him. "Thanks again. You really saved me tonight."

"It's really good to see you again, Grace."

"I guess some friendships were meant to be." It sounded lame as she said it, but she didn't know how else to put into words what she was feeling.

"I guess." He turned to go, but then, looking back, "May I see you again? Soon?"

She smiled at him. "Yes. Please do."

He shrugged his collar up around his cheeks, smiling, and turned down into the night.

CHAPTER FIVE

Silver Sands, 1932

BY SUMMER, GRACE AND STEPHEN HAD CLEARLY BECOME, AS BETH AND Margaret liked to put it, "a going concern," and though her friends continued to remind her playfully about her lost opportunity with Richard, still they welcomed Stephen warmly into their circle. Not that they had much choice, of course, if they wanted to see anything of Grace herself anymore. She was with him as often as possible—and more often, it seemed, than not.

For his part, Stephen made every effort to fit in with her friends. He laughed at their jokes and nodded at their gossip, joined in their skating parties—though he did not skate—and when the weather warmed, went along on their afternoons playing ball or visits to the waterfront to watch the ships in the harbour.

Often he caught them off-guard, though, quoting lines of poetry when the conversation seemed least to call for it, or making vague allusions to some Greek myth or other that none of them recognized. Such moments left Grace feeling anxious for him, as she watched her friends exchange quizzical glances, but she also felt, deeper down, admiration. He was so wistful, so thoughtful, and especially so unlike anyone she knew; and anyway, her friends humoured him, even seeming to genuinely enjoy his unexpected "Stephenisms," as Margaret took to calling them.

The shortest path between Halifax Academy, where Stephen went to school, and his home in the Northwest Arm didn't necessarily pass by Grace's school, but Stephen had begun taking a more circuitous route so as to meet her just as her classes were letting out. Then he'd walk her home in a meandering way while they exchanged the details of their day.

As the months progressed and their relationship grew, they began to exchange closer things: their passions (his for travel, hers for a family), their dreams (his to study and write, hers to train for nursing, perhaps, or teaching, until she was married), and their hearts (his for faraway and undiscovered things, hers for things close and familiar). These differences didn't give Grace any pause in her affection, though. If anything they deepened it, drawing her out of her world and into his, which seemed so broad and distant and full of possibility.

Then, early in July, only a few weeks after school had let out for the holidays, they made an outing to Silver Sands Beach, a popular surf-bathing destination east of the city. There was to be a dance in the Silver Sands Dancehall that evening, and they planned to make a day of it. Grace had prepared a picnic basket, and Stephen had arranged to borrow his father's Frontenac. This was doubly exciting, as the automobile was new—purchased just last fall—and Stephen had only recently acquired his driver's permit.

At the last minute, Will convinced Grace to let him and a schoolmate of his join them for the day. She didn't really want to—this was to have been hers and Stephen's first real outing alone together—but after saying as much to Will, he teased her so mercilessly that she finally gave in. Stephen and Will were, after all, good friends, despite the difference in their ages, and anyway, there would still be plenty of opportunity to be alone with Stephen.

By the time they arrived and changed into their swimwear, the sun was nearing midday and the beach becoming crowded. The day was bright and warm, though not yet smouldering with the heat of late summer. The surf was high and playful, the long beach strewn with visitors from the city soaking in the sun. Though the sea was very cold, and the waves rolling, still many bathers had braved the water and were playing out in the foam.

The four of them picked their way along the beach until they found a sheltered spot in the lee of some piled dunes. Grace spread the blanket she had brought, and she and Stephen sat together.

"We're going to try the waves," Will told her. "I bet they're freezing!"

He skipped with anticipation once or twice on the sand, then slapped his chest as if bracing himself for the cold.

His friend, an enthusiastic boy named Alex, laughed at him. "I'll beat you the water!" He started running, kicking up sand behind him. Will took up the chase.

"Will! Alex!" Grace shouted after them; they stopped and turned. "Take care with the waves. And watch for the tow."

"I promised your mother I'd bring you home in one piece," Stephen added.

Will waved away their warnings. "Yes, Mom. Yes, Dad!" He then grinned at Stephen. "Or should I say, brother-in-law?"

Laughing, he raced Alex to the water.

Grace watched them a minute and then turned suddenly to Stephen. "And can you imagine, we were his age when we first met?"

Stephen was unpacking items from the daypack he'd brought. "That seems ages ago, doesn't it? And worlds away. I still can't believe we ran into one another like that, again, after so many years. Although, it's funny, you know. I never forgot you. Even though we didn't keep in touch, still, I always remembered that pretty girl from the island. My first…" He seemed to have said more than he meant to. He went back to busying himself with the daypack.

The wind flung her hair gently across her cheek and into her eyes. She brushed it away and tilted her head at him. "Your first…?"

But he would not finish the sentence. Far away, the sighing waves rolled along the beach like laughter.

"I never forgot you, either," she said at last. "Even though I didn't write like I'd meant to. You were just so different from any boy I'd ever met. So sweet and gentle, but also so serious about things, poetry and books and whatnot. I like that about you still."

"And who could have known we'd meet again? What was it? Five years later…?"

"And you, just as sweet and just as serious as ever."

He grinned. "And you just as pretty."

Grace suddenly felt shy. She was wearing a brand-new swimming costume, a short, skirted design with a bright floral pattern that her mother had ordered from the Sears catalogue that spring. Trying it on in the cool light of her bedroom before her dresser mirror, it had seemed perfectly fashionable and modest, but here, under this bright sun and sitting so close to him, she became sharply aware of her bare shoulders and knees. She shifted herself so she was sitting on her calves, her bare ankles tucked under herself discretely; nervously she smoothed the skirt down over her thighs.

She fumbled with her words. "It's the kind of thing that convinces one of the hand of providence."

"Or destiny."

The daypack was empty now. A canteen of water, a towel, his watch, and a couple of books lay in a heap on the blanket.

Feeling foolish, he said it again: "Do you believe in destiny, Grace?"

The question hung in the air between them.

Grace faltered. "Well. I believe… I believe in God, if that's what you mean. Like I said, the hand of providence, watching over us and looking after us and whatnot. *Is* that what you mean?"

Stephen squinted into the sun. "I'm not sure. Maybe not so orchestrated as all that. But destiny, right? Fate. An intention or meaning behind things, moving them on towards an inevitable outcome. Something that transcends the things themselves, and you can't escape it. In fact, trying to escape it only makes the outcome all the more sure. They say that Oedipus was fated to murder his father, and when they abandoned him on the mountainside to *avoid* that fate, it actually, really, only sealed it."

"I feel like we're talking about something a bit deeper than just a boy and a girl meeting a long time ago on Prince Edward Island and then bumping into each other out of the blue years later."

"Maybe, maybe not. Maybe this thing—fate, destiny, or whatever it is— actually *works* in these superficial ways. You know, two friends meeting for the first time, old friends meeting again after a long time. Chance encounters. Fated. Oedipus had no clue that the man he met on the road that day, years later, was really his father."

"Is that one of the stories in there?" She pointed to the pile of books on the blanket in front of him. The direction of their conversation was starting to make her feel unsettled, and she hoped to change the topic.

"No," he said. "That's *The Odyssey*, there."

She began flipping through the pages. "*The Odyssey*," she repeated.

"You know, Homer. The original epic adventure? It's the story of Odysseus and his journey home to Ithaca after the Trojan War. He literally has to sail to hell and back. His men all die. His boat is shipwrecked. And eventually he's trapped on the island of the sea nymph Calypso, who keeps him as her…" Colour rose to his cheeks as he groped for the word. "…prisoner. Meanwhile, his wife Penelope is waiting for him at home on Ithaca. Twenty years she waits, watching the sea for his return."

Still thumbing the pages, she began to read out loud. "'The beautiful goddess led the way quickly and he followed in her footsteps. And they came to the hollow of the cave, the goddess and the man, and he sat down upon the chair… and the nymph set before him all manner of food to eat and drink… But she herself sat over against divine Odysseus, and before her the handmaids set ambrosia and nectar… The sun set and darkness came on, and the two went into the innermost recess of the hollow cave…'"

Her eyebrows arched, and she glanced at him quickly. He reached for the book, his cheeks quite red now, but she held it away, still reading.

"'...and took their joy of love, abiding each by the other's side...'" She was blushing, too, but she continued with a nervous giggle. "'As soon as early Dawn appeared, straightway Odysseus put on a cloak and a tunic, and the nymph clothed herself in a long white robe, finely woven and beautiful, and about her waist she cast a fair girdle of gold...' Well, Stephen, it doesn't sound as though he had it as bad as all that."

Stephen laughed in spite of himself. "No. But however beautiful Calypso may have been, Odysseus always longed to be home again with his Penelope, his one true love and faithful companion."

She flipped ahead again, thumbing through the pages and coming randomly to a stop. She read silently for a while, and then aloud: "'...to me the Olympian has given sorrow above all the women who were bred and born with me. For long since I lost my noble husband of the lion heart, pre-eminent in all manner of worth among the Danaans, my noble husband...'"

"And that's Penelope," he explained, "mourning her lost husband. Every day she tells her suitors that she'll choose a new husband when she's finished weaving her tapestry, and every night, secretly, she unstitches the work she's done that day, so she'll never finish."

Grace saw the familiar, faraway look coming into his eyes. To forestall it, she pushed at him and teased. "It hardly seems like seaside reading, Stephen. You didn't have anything lighter to bring? No *Treasure Island... King Solomon's Mines*? Nothing like that?"

"Well," he said. "It's one of the texts that will be on the exam for the Edward Blake Scholarship next year. I know it's still a year away, but I want to be ready. It is full tuition, after all."

She absorbed herself with thumbing through the book. She knew his plans to study classics at the University of Toronto after his last year at Halifax Academy. Even though they'd talked them over at great length, it remained a tender nerve for her and she was profoundly ambivalent about the whole thing. Of course he should pursue his passion—literature and myth and ancient things—and she knew that, try as he might, he would never be really satisfied with the limited academic scope that the social circle at St. Christopher's had to offer. At the same time, full tuition to study classics in Toronto would mean being apart from one another for months at a time. The thought was a heavy one.

"Yes, I do," she said at last.

"You do?"

"Believe in destiny, I mean. Like you said, some things are meant to be—and no matter what you do, you can't really escape them." Then she added, "I saw you that night, you know."

"Saw me?"

"I mean, way back, on the island when we were kids. That night we came for dinner. Did you come out after we'd left? Come to the yard? I saw you from the window, at the edge of the field."

Again he groped for words. "I wanted to… I don't know… I wanted to see you, to tell you…"

"To tell me what?"

"That I've never met anyone like you before, and I don't think I ever will. And if you'd have me, with my head full of books and dreams and all, if you'd have me, I'd be yours."

"You wanted to tell me that?"

"Maybe not those words, but they're the words I'd use now."

She set down *The Odyssey* and reached for his hand. "I will, Stephen. Have you, I mean. Head full of books and dreams and all. I will have you."

In the shelter of the dune, she felt her self-consciousness giving way. She leaned against him, her eyes closed, and felt his fingers tighten around hers. She wanted so much to kiss him in that moment, or to be kissed by him, even though the thought made her breath shallow. He touched her cheek gently and his fingers lingered at the hair on her temple. She wondered if he would be as clumsy in kissing for the first time, as she herself would be to be kissed.

For a long moment, he did not move, and she waited longer still, the sun and sea sounds and salt air washing in waves against them. The kiss did not come.

She opened her eyes suddenly and sat upright. She had heard it, over the wave-rush, before Stephen had, but the next time it came he heard and sat up, too. Alex was calling them. Even over the noise of the sea, they could hear the note of unmingled horror in his voice. She looked anxiously into Stephen's face.

"Stephen! Grace! Help!"

Stephen was on his feet and moving towards the sea, where she could see Alex pelting across the sand towards them, waving frantically. When he saw Stephen, he began running back where he had come from.

"Come quick!" he called.

Stephen broke into a run, behind him.

Grace was on her feet then, too, running after them, a sickness in her chest. Stephen had reached Alex now, at the very edge of the surf, and Alex was pointing desperately out into the water. She ran up to join them.

"Where's Willie?" She could barely get the words out through the knowing sickness that strangled her breath.

Alex was panting, nearly sobbing. "Wanted to see how far…" he gasped between breaths. "Water so cold… waves and… I turned back… but Willie didn't… we were out so far!"

Stephen scanned the water blindly. Others had joined them, drawn by Willie's cries for help and by the sight of the three of them standing in distress at the water's edge.

"There's a devil of an undertow out there," one was saying.

"I saw the two of them well past the marker," said another. "It can sweep you out pretty suddenly if you don't know what you're doing."

"Where's Willie?" Grace asked again, and the effort of pushing the question past that burning sickness in her chest forced it out as a scream. "Alex! Where's my brother!"

Alex's choked panting broke into full sobs now and he fell to his knees. "I don't know, Grace!" he groaned. "When I got back to shore, he wasn't with me. I thought he was. We were out so far and the tow so strong. I said we should turn back, and I just swam for the shore. I thought he was with me. I thought he was!"

Stephen was already barefoot as he tugged his shirt over his head. He called Willie's name into the wind and waves, a desperate note in his voice.

"Willie!" He splashed into the surf.

Grace's screams rose in pitch. "Stephen!"

She raced after him, the water sweeping around her knees, up to her waist. Stephen was up to his chest now, waves pounding his frame back and then sucking it out further.

"Willie!" he called one last time then plunged in with a flailing breaststroke.

Some of the crowd had already run off to get help. Others splashed up to where Grace stood in the water, putting gentle but restraining arms around her. She yielded to them, screaming both their names now, wildly, blindly, deafly. Stephen had swum out as far as he dared. She could see his head and shoulders bobbing with the surf. Faint on the wind, she heard him calling her brother's name over and over again. Someone had found a boat and rowed it out to where Stephen was treading water. She saw him scramble up over the gunwale, saw men standing with him in the boat, scanning the empty waves.

Time collapsed into a delirium for her at that point. Someone assured her that the coast guard had been notified, another that the police had been contacted. Others suggested that she come up to the Silver Sands Hall, out of the sun. Somehow a tumbler of water found its way into her hand, though she didn't drink it. Strangers made vague offers of hopefulness and optimism that she did not really hear.

At some point, a soft-spoken police officer arrived and she answered his questions numbly. What was he wearing? How long had he been out? How strong a swimmer was he?

It was many hours before Stephen finally found her, sitting alone in the shadows of the hall. He told the whole story of their futile search: they had scoured up and down the beach many times, but Willie was gone. She collapsed wordless and trembling into his arms and sobbed uncontrollably.

———————

The funeral at St. Christopher's was almost unbearable for Grace. Mother would say later that the singing was lovely—"Be Still My Soul" was one of her favourite hymns—and for the scripture reading, the Ninety-Third Psalm was especially fitting, even if it was less traditional than the Twenty-Third.

The Stewart family had endured two full days of numb despair before William's drowned body finally washed up, miles from the Silver Sands Beach. Captain Edward himself had joined the search, though mercifully he wasn't the one who found him. The story had made headlines—*Halifax Boy Drowns at Silver Sands Beach*—and the churchyard of St. Christopher's on the day of the funeral was crowded with mourners and well-wishers alike. The marker was a modest carved stone: *William Edward Stewart, 1921–1932, Beloved Son and Brother.*

After the reverend had pronounced the benediction and everyone else dispersed, Grace's mother and father lingered with her a long time at the graveside. When at last they took her hand and moved to leave, Grace shrugged herself free of them, silently.

"You go," she said at last. "I'll be along later."

Her mother's eyes were bleary with grief, and Grace knew she ached to hold her daughter close, but she seemed to understand, and she and her husband wandered listlessly out of the churchyard.

When they were gone, Grace went back into the church and sat alone in the dim shadows of the sanctuary. Reverend Elliot checked in on her once or twice, but he recognized the inaccessible loneliness of grief. With a simple "Take as much time as you need, my dear," he left her undisturbed.

The window just above her pew depicted a vivid image of Jesus standing in the bow of a boat, sunlit indigo and midnight blue whorls of glass raging all around him. The hand he held out looked at once commanding and inviting. The inscription read: *Jesus Calms the Storm.*

She stared at it for a long time, bitterly, until at last she allowed the question to surface in her.

Why?

It came up like an inflated ball held too long under water. She sobbed. Why would the Jesus who calms storms, whose throne is mightier than the noise of many waters—why? and how?—why could he have let him go like that?

"Inasmuch as Almighty God, in his wise providence, has received from this world our deceased loved one," the reverend had said when they returned ashes to ashes and dust to dust at the graveside, "we therefore commit his mortal body to the ground."

She had fought back then the sobs that shook her now. Was this the wise providence of Almighty God? That a boy so young and full of promise should be swallowed up so suddenly, so randomly, so violently? With her questions came her guilt and the sobs reached a nearly uncontrollable crescendo. Why had she not gone with him to the water? Why had she lounged about with Stephen like a lovesick puppy while he swam out so far alone? And he, only eleven! Self-recrimination surged in her.

"Grace?" someone spoke.

The voice was tentative. She looked up and noticed first how the blue light of the window coloured Stephen's face.

"Reverend Elliot told me you were here," he offered by way of apology for having intruded. "Can I sit?"

She said nothing but shifted on the pew to make him room. He sat stiffly next to her, and they were very quiet for a long time.

"Why?" she said at last.

"I–I can't say," he said bleakly. "But, Grace, I am sorry."

She leaned against him, clinging to him as to flotsam in a tempest. "Oh Stephen," she sobbed. "It's my fault. Mine. I drowned him, or may as well have!"

Stephen put his arm awkwardly around her and pulled her against him. "Hush, Grace," he said softly. "Don't say such things." Words failed him, so he said it again, weakly. "Don't ever say such things."

"But it's true! What can I ever do to make it up to them? To make up for a lost brother, a lost son?"

Stephen was at a loss in the presence of this grief, darker than anything he had ever known before. "Grace, please, don't torture yourself. Please."

And then, in the way that random thoughts sometimes come, swirling disconnected from the depths of grief, she said suddenly, "Please, Stephen, don't ever leave me!" And she whispered it a second time: "Don't ever leave me."

Stephen held her closely and rocked her, like a small child in his arms, and kissed the top of her head clumsily while the light of Jesus, calming the storm, played blue and softly over his down-bent head.

CHAPTER SIX

Love Letters, 1933–1937

IN THE DIM LIGHT OF HIS STUDY, GRACE PULLED MORE LETTERS FROM the battered shoebox. They were strewn randomly over the desk like layers of sediment, artefacts of ink on time-faded paper. She sifted through them, trying to arrange their delicate shards into a tentative whole, like a vessel that might contain her grief. As she did, pictures of the past flooded over her, painful but for all that still rich and good.

September 18, 1933. This was the first letter he had written her from Toronto, the fall he'd left to study classics. He had taken first place in the Edward Blake Scholarship exam, winning full tuition and an invitation into the honours program.

The news had been bittersweet. Through the winter of their final year in high school, their friendship had flowered into something richer and fuller, and he had become a permanent presence in his life. Especially after the loss of Willie, as she'd struggled to keep her chin above the flood of sadness and shame that was always threatening to rise, Stephen had kept her from sinking utterly. Even Mom and Dad had noticed how fully she'd welcomed him into her world, and they'd taken to dropping awkward questions about their intentions.

So when he'd come to visit that day, clutching his offer from the University of Toronto, near-trembling with delight, she'd celebrated with him, swept up in the overflow of his own joy. To see him so eager and excited was, after all, very sweet—but bitter, too, because it would mean months apart.

In the study, she imagined she could feel their embrace again, on the platform of the train station the day he had left. Their kiss that morning had been far less clumsy than it had once been. He had promised to write every week.

Smoothing its creased pages in front of her on the desk, she reread the first of those promised letters.

September 18, 1933

Dear Grace,

Missing you already. I arrived in Toronto yesterday evening, completely exhausted after what seemed an interminable journey. I've never travelled so far by train before. I wish I could have shared the trip with you.

As you travel west of Nova Scotia, the countryside is lovely, with rolling farms and distant forests. And for a kid from Halifax, the city of Toronto is almost overwhelming— big and busy and bustling like nothing I've ever seen.

And the campus is simply stunning. I'm writing this on the lawn directly across from the University College building, this solemn-looking structure all stone spires and arched windows. Neo-Romanesque, I think they call the style. You could almost imagine you're at one of the great universities in England, or Europe.

I've found my dorm room and settled in comfortably. Tomorrow class registration begins. This semester I'll be taking both Greek and Latin. I'm also enrolled in a course on the History of Greece and Rome, with Professor Cochrane. He's a world-renowned expert in the field, and I've heard his lectures are fascinating. Looking at my timetable, I feel almost like a kid in a candy shop, with so many treats to choose from. I can hardly wait to get started.

If only you were here to share it all with me, Grace. Perhaps—one can hope—perhaps one day we'll make the trip together, travel the world. Meanwhile, only four months till the fall term's done and I'll be home for the break. I'll be thinking of you every day from now till then, and loving you dearly.

Always yours, Stephen.

Grace smiled weakly, in spite of her grief. Like a kid in a candy shop! Only Stephen could welcome a semester of Greek and Latin with a watering mouth, but then, how like him to savour it all with such sweet delight.

She had smiled when she'd first read it, too, and then wiped her brimming eyes. She had been sitting on a bench in the sun of the Halifax Public Gardens then, his letter spread across the floral print of her dress in her lap. She had come to the Gardens after a day volunteering at the Barrington Street Mission downtown. She'd wanted to tear into the envelope upon its first arrival that morning, but on some strange impulse for delayed gratification she had shoved it into her handbag instead, unopened, and waited until after her work at the mission was finished. Then she'd walked up Citadel Hill, along Spring Garden Road, and found a quiet corner of the Gardens to sit at last and read. There was something soothing in the gentle sounds of the Gardens—the burbling of a pigeon along the path, the faint murmur of Victoria's fountain, and fainter still the clatter of traffic along Sackville Street—that somehow lessened the ache for him that his letter had opened in her. At any rate, she was less likely to cry openly in public.

This became something of a ritual for her. Whenever a letter arrived—and true to his word, Stephen wrote weekly—Grace would keep it unopened until she was at her spot on the bench in the Halifax Public Gardens. And there, among the turning leaves of early autumn, the gilded and scattering leaves of late fall, even among the naked tree limbs of early winter, until the snow came and it was too wet and cold to sit and read, she would follow him, letter by letter, as he wound his way into the world of classical antiquity.

October 7, 1933

Dear Grace,

The window of my dorm room looks down on the main court of the college. The Quad, they call it. From my writing desk I can see the lawn and the great old trees. They're turning now. I can watch students bundled up against the chill of autumn, shuffling back and forth on their way to class.

I've started a tutorial in Homer's Odyssey. It's for second year students, mostly, but they've let me sit in. I still have my old copy of The Odyssey. Now that I'm reading it in the original, in Homer's Greek, it's like meeting an old friend for the very first time, or finding, after searching so long, a treasure buried just beneath the surface of thought.

His style and tone seemed to get more ponderous and distant as the months went by. Sometimes she grasped very little of it.

This afternoon a professor from the British School of Archaeology at Athens, a Dr. James Percy, was on campus, speaking at a symposium on the Archaeology of Antiquity that the Classics Department is hosting. What a remarkable lecture, Grace! He spoke about the discovery of ancient Greece—the "Homeric World," he called it—with such passion, about the "Golden Age of Greece," the Grecian "Heroic Awakening." And his manner, so fluid and literate, so animated, brought these things to life like no one I've ever heard. What I wouldn't give to be there, Grace, to see them for myself.

But if his style grew obscure at times, it also grew, at other times, warmer and more intimate the longer they were apart. Some passages brought colour to her cheeks to read them, out in the open of the Public Gardens.

Could barely sleep last night thinking of you, Grace. How I long to hold you again. It's like my arms actually ache for you. Or my chest. I remember your soft hair against my face the last time we were together, the warm smell of it all around me.

In the study, Grace smoothed this letter next to the others, passages racing with youthful desire sitting alongside plodding descriptions of his studies and their impact on him. Two desires, side by side.

On the park bench in the Public Gardens, however, at eighteen and in love, she folded these sections quickly closed and pressed them into her lap when she came to them, with a happy but also furtive glance around her. Only when she was sure she was completely alone would she continue, the blood warm in her face and rising at her throat.

These weekly letters from Stephen had brought happy relief to her otherwise grim days, which were for the most part consumed with her volunteer work at the Barrington Street Mission. By the time Stephen had left for university, the city of Halifax had begun seeing with alarming regularity the dreary scenes of economic depression that had become commonplace in the larger cities across the country. The men appeared on their own at first, poor, hungry, and looking for work, piled desperately on the backs of train cars pulling into Halifax. Soon whole families were arriving, some from Toronto and Montreal, some as far west as Winnipeg, others from the ferries out of Newfoundland or Portland, all plying the countryside hopelessly. Finding little welcome and less relief, they congregated along the docks or meandered the streets, chasing rumours of work. Once or twice, the papers printed stories of tussles between the police and drifters. Long editorials wondered out loud what Halifax was to do about the "problem with the unemployed."

Grace's work at the mission, a soup kitchen for the jobless, began one afternoon when her walk home from an errand brought her along Barrington Street just as the soup line was opening. The sidewalk was packed with bodies, mostly men with haggard faces and battered hats, though there were a few ragged-looking women, too, and even once or twice a forlorn child, holding feebly to someone's hand. The crowd was so close that she had been forced to step into the street to get by.

"Can you spare anything, miss?" a voice called, bringing her up short.

She looked and saw a young man sitting on the curb, apart from the others, holding a cardboard placard that said something about working for food. He was young, perhaps her age, or just barely older. A wild thought flashed through her mind that the eyes, or maybe his grin, reminded her of Willie.

"I'm sorry," Grace had stammered, feeling as though something like a well was opening in her. "I don't have much."

"A dime, maybe? Even a nickel? A cigarette? I don't suppose you smoke."

"No, I don't smoke." She reached into her handbag trembling, but not with fear and sadness; rather, with profound compassion bubbling up in her. "I'm sorry. But what I have, you can have."

She pulled out her change purse: two nickels and a dime. He took it with thanks and that slight but honest grin.

Then he said something that opened the well in her deeper, and wider. "Do you pray much, miss?"

"Well, I do—sometimes. At least, I go to St. Christopher's Methodist Church." She trailed off uncertainly; the question was so unexpected.

"I'm not much for praying, myself. But like the preacher says at the mission there, at least prayer don't cost anything. And you've got nothing to lose by it. Which is good, because me, I really got nothing to lose." He grinned again, thinly.

"No, I don't suppose you do… have anything to lose by prayer…"

"I'm asking, miss, because I was wondering if it would be too much trouble for you to pray for me? You see, I've got the worst toothache you can imagine. I suppose it's infected, but what with me having nothing to lose, I sure don't have anything to give the dentist neither. And so I was wondering, if you're much for praying at all, maybe you wouldn't mind praying for me? That the Lord would heal it?"

He pulled his hat off his head as he asked this. His hair was unwashed and thick, plastered to his forehead. Without knowing how she knew what to do, she reached out her hands, trembling with the new compassion welling up in her, and placed them gently on his head as he bowed it towards her. She whispered something uncertainly about this young stranger and his toothache, about pain and healing and relief. And she wasn't sure, but her palms felt warm, almost hot, while she prayed, though this may have been the shyness in her.

"Amen, miss," he said when she was done. She was finding it difficult to look into his face. "God bless you."

"God bless you, too," she said, her hands still trembling. She turned and looked at the crowd milling about the door of the soup kitchen waiting for it to open, and the well finally overflowed in her. "Is it like this every day?"

He laughed. "Oh no. Some days it gets really crowded. But this is a Wednesday, right? And most anyone who's getting work this week will have had it by now."

She turned to go, but instead of continuing on her way down Barrington Street she pushed past the crowd to the front of the line, where a man in a Salvation Army uniform stood at the door, watching until the kitchen opened and they could be let in. She asked about volunteering, was referred to the director of the mission, and left an hour later with her name added to the roster of volunteers.

In this way, while Stephen explored the mysterious world of ancient Greek epics and their mythic adventures, miles away and worlds apart from her, Grace threw herself into the charity work of the mission, serving soup to the unemployed every afternoon, and coffee and doughnuts most mornings.

In the study, as she pieced together the past with his letters, she remembered back to those days fondly. There had been bleak moments, to be sure, encounters with poverty that had left her reeling, but she'd also found something purging, or purifying, in the work. However dismal things had been, it only made his letters all the more welcome when they came. Their earnest talk of translating Ovid's *Artis Amatoriae* or writing a paper on Homer's *Hymn to Aphrodite* seemed to echo mysteriously from above, or beyond the grey world of soup kitchens and relief work.

May 2, 1933

Dear Grace,

And so the semester is finally over! I will keep this letter short because in just a week I will be home and seeing you, holding you again at last. They've posted the grades and I've made honours in all my courses.

Professor Norwood has recommended me as a candidate for the honours scholarship, which will mean full tuition again next year. There's a new course they will be offering in the archaeology of ancient Greece that he's encouraging me to take. He said my work with Ovid's Artis Amatoriae was first rate.

How madly I miss you. I can't wait to see you. There is so much to catch up on. Give my love to your mom and dad.

Always yours, Stephen.

This letter found its spot alongside the others on the desk. With it came a vivid memory of a beautiful spring afternoon at the mission. He had been due by train that evening, home for the summer after his first year of studies. They had been together at the Christmas break, of course, but the time had been preciously short, so short as only to sharpen the pang of their separation rather than relieve it.

But now he would be home for a full four months. And though he would be working for much of that time, still he would be home, and they would be together, and life could return to some small semblance of normalcy.

She had spent the lunch hour ladling out soup to the never-ending line of the needy, and now worked in the stuffy back room, organizing care packages. Canned food, used clothing, old toys, and other assorted donations had been collected from around the city, and they were packed into boxes bound for other parts of Canada, places where the need was even greater than in Halifax.

As she filled each box, she scratched down their contents on a pad of paper: canned peas, canned beans, pears and peaches. Beside her, a volunteer named Katie stacked tins in piles at her elbow: coffee, flour, canned pork. When the box was full, she pulled the flaps closed and addressed it with a thick black pen: *Portage Street Mission, Winnipeg Manitoba.* She pushed it towards Vivien, who sat next to her, to seal it with tape.

She hummed as she worked.

"Well," said Vivien absently. "You're certainly chipper this afternoon."

Katie agreed. "What ray of sunshine is shining in your life today?" she asked, not looking up from her inventory of canned food.

Grace's cheeks coloured only slightly. "Oh, it's nothing."

"Don't keep secrets, Grace," Vivien said. "This place can always do with a ray of sunshine or two. What is it?"

"Well, Stephen's coming home tonight."

She was still humming when her work was done and she left the mission late in the afternoon. After dinner, the Walkers were to call for her and they would go down to the train station to welcome Stephen together.

Being so late in the day, the mission was almost empty when she left, but a young man sat idly on the steps as she came out the front door.

"Afternoon, miss," he said.

Something familiar in his voice gave her pause. It was that same young man who had asked her for change so many months ago.

"Well!" she said. "I haven't seen you in ages."

"No. I got work at a warehouse on the quay for a few months. Then I was working at the logging camps in New Brunswick, but that dried up a couple weeks back. And so here I am again."

"It's good to see you. Though I'm sorry, I haven't any change." She had stopped bringing her change purse with her to the mission. The need was just too great and it pained her to say no so often to requests.

"Oh," he said. "No. That's not why I'm here. I wanted to see you especially, to tell you: it got better."

"Better?"

"The tooth. You do remember praying for me? Well, three or four days later—not more than five, I'm sure—the pain left. Overnight. Went to bed groaning and woke the next day good as new."

"Well, I am glad," she said, hesitantly. "Only… I'm not sure my prayers made any big difference."

She felt that warmness in her hands again, all up her arms, though this time she was sure it was only the shyness in her.

"No, miss," he said. "Don't take it away from me. I'm sure the Lord did a healing in me. And I'm sure it was your prayers that did it. And I just wanted to say thank you."

He grinned at her—a big, broad, painless smile—and if there was something about him that had reminded him of Willie before, it shone bright and sharp in him now.

She wanted to say something to encourage him, but somehow her words stuck in her throat. "You're very welcome" was all she could manage.

Trembling, she turned down the steps.

———————

More and more letters fell into place as Grace worked her way through those four long years. They would reunite in the summers, only to separate again each fall, the long grey winters lit just briefly by the bittersweet break at Christmas. But for all that, the time away made their times together warmer and closer. Rather than pulling them apart, the separations pushed them together. Anyway, Grace's work at the mission had grown from a simple weekly volunteer role to a full-time position as assistant to the director, and as much as she threw herself into it, she had yet to find an end to the need.

Phrase by phrase the memories rushed at her now.

Professor Norwood has asked me to be his research assistant for his class on the Archaeology of Greece and Rome... my paper on Homer's Hymn to Aphrodite won first place in an essay competition on the literature of ancient Greece... have started tutoring first years in Latin... took top honours in my fourth year archaeology seminar.

The desk was utterly strewn with faded paper, four years' worth of love letters arranged like a kind of monument. For one fleeting instant, the memory of him, a picture complete and solid and poignant, rushed into Grace's mind and filled her to the very edges of her grief.

And then, the page of one letter, hanging unbalanced over the edge of the desk, spilled to the floor, bringing more letters down with it. The picture of the past she had so painstakingly pieced together began to slip back into formlessness.

She brought her elbows down on the desk, laying her arms over the scattered pages and resting her forehead on them. The movement caused more letters to slide to the floor, and with them the now empty cardboard box. An involuntary surge of grief passed through her and she clenched the letters beneath her palms into crumpled handfuls, blindly.

––––––––––

A cool morning breeze, exuberant from the harbour, danced at Grace's shoulders as she walked up Carmichael Street towards the green slope of Citadel Hill. It was late summer, the last day before Stephen would return to Toronto for his fourth and final year of university. He was leaving the following afternoon, and they had planned to spend this last day together before the train took him away from her one final time.

The Old Town Clock was just ahead of her, the early sun brilliant on its white pillars, its green dome looking down over the harbour. They'd arranged to meet here, and she could see him sitting on the steps already. He was reading while he waited, and the shape of him, shoulders sloped and head bent intently over a book, reminded her of another time, of a small boy waiting for her, pouring over the pages of an atlas.

She sat beside him, and together they looked out over the city, down towards the waterfront. At a quay near Prince Street, a crisp-clad crew of seamen were scurrying about to moor a British navy sloop. At the harbour's edge, out beyond

George's Island, the black shape of a ship, barely tangible against the glimmer of the morning sun, crept slowly out to sea.

"Stephen Walker," she said teasingly, "head in the clouds and nose in a book." She tilted her head to look at the cover, which he turned up for her to read. "What's on the menu this morning?"

"A book of poetry by Percy Bysshe Shelley. I'm reading a poem called 'Epipsychidion.'"

"Doesn't exactly roll off the tongue. What's it mean?"

"It's Greek. It means something like 'This soul out of my soul.'"

"What's it about?"

"A man in love."

Grace laughed. "What poems aren't?"

But Stephen explained. "In Plato's *Symposium*, there's a story about how, in the beginning, every soul existed as a union of two halves. Two halves of a soul joined together into one." He laced his fingers together. "But something happened that caused the soul of every person to be split. To divide." He pulled his fingers apart. "Ever since, every soul has always felt a longing for the half of the soul that has been separated from it. And we're all on this quest, you know, to find the other half of our souls. And to find it, the soul that completes you, to unite with it, that's what love is: to reunite with the soul out of your soul."

"Well, that is lovely. But I'm not so sure it's right."

"Neither was Plato. His Socrates, the main character in *Symposium*, rejects this theory."

"So this poem, the Epi—" She stumbled over the word.

"Episychidion."

"It's about his soul's search for its other half?"

Now he laughed. "What poems aren't?"

He took her hand and they watched the waterfront bustle with its morning work. The British seamen had nearly secured their sloop.

She closed her fingers tightly around his hand, feeling warm and close and content.

"I'm going to miss you when you leave," she said, breaking the spell of contentment at last. "It gets so hard to be strong here, when strength is so needed, it seems. It's hard without you to help me."

The city was noisy all around her—gulls calling to one another, cars clattering along Brunswick Street, the distant noise of the men on the waterfront shouting as they made fast their ship. Even so, an ominous silence seemed to fall between her pauses.

"Of course, the thought of you there, doing what you love, it strengthens me, in a way. I'm proud of what you're doing there, and glad you're able to. Especially," she added vaguely, "when so many men don't have the chance. It's just—"

"I know it's hard, Grace. And not just for you. I know how difficult things have become in the city for everyone. It makes every moment I have to study seem like a precious gift to me. And I don't take it for granted. I don't take you for granted."

Though they were meant kindly, the words pained her. "I know," she said. "It's not that I feel taken for granted."

He pressed on. "And I see the work you do. Your work at the mission, with the jobless and the poor. The difference you're making. And I love it. You're beautiful for it. And I love you for it. And your waiting for me like this. Grace, I don't take that for granted either."

"I know." And then very softly, almost beneath her breath she said, "After Willie, I have no choice."

Stephen looked at her closely. "What did you say? Grace, please don't do this to yourself again. It wasn't your fault."

She spoke quickly now, the view of the harbour blurring in her eyes. "It's not that, Stephen. I don't mean that. It's just that, I mean, without Willie, and with Mom and Dad so sad for him all the time, I mean—" and she looked at him tentatively "—after him, who do I have but you? How could I… how could I not wait?"

She squeezed his hand courageously and offered him a thin but sincere smile.

"Just one more year, Grace," he said. She nodded silently as he spoke. "Give it—give me—one more year."

She said nothing but leaned against him warmly, and when he bent down to kiss her forehead she lifted her mouth to him and received him tenderly.

CHAPTER SEVEN

Lighthouse, 1937

"STEPHEN, COME BACK!"

The wind swallowed her voice, flapping about her like a sheet on the line, snapping damp and white in the sun. She sat up to look over the edge of the rocks that had been sheltering her, along the tousled tufts of grass that spotted the slope, towards the cliff's edge where he stood looking out over the ocean. The wind caught strands of hair and flung them across her face. She brushed them away and called again.

"Stephen! What are you doing?" The shadow of his back was turned to her, one hand held to his brow against the light on the water. "Lunch is almost ready," she said loudly as she sat down again in the shelter of the rocks.

Behind her stood the lighthouse, a brightly painted sentinel staring east across the water. Its noonday shadow lent no shade, but the day was mild and the air cool despite the brilliant sun and cloudless sky. All around its base, the ground was strewn with dark grey rocks, rusted with white lichens and orange mosses, yellow, and green grasses bristling up between them. Far below, she heard the ocean foam, bursting into a cascade of curling diamonds and mixing with the wind in a roar.

She smoothed her palms over the red-checked cloth she had spread on the rough grass, pushing its corners flat. From the wicker basket in front of her she brought out the makings of a picnic lunch: cheese and ham wrapped in waxed paper, a pair of apples, a loaf of bread. Each found its place in the arrangement before her. She withdrew a thermos of hot tea and set it out beside two tin cups. Last of all came a bit of cake, a special treat for a special occasion.

This was Stephen's first weekend home. After four long years, his degree was finally finished. He had taken top honours in classics, with generous accolades and high praise from his instructors. He'd even won an award of distinction for research in the literature of Greek antiquity.

Grace was happy for him, of course, but happier still simply to have him home at last. To celebrate, both his successes and his homecoming, they had borrowed Mr. Walker's Frontenac and planned a daytrip along the coast north of the city, exploring the sights. It was Grace who had spotted the abandoned lighthouse, lonely and isolated on the cliffs, and suggested they stop for lunch.

When lunch had been laid out, she rearranged the shawl she had draped over her shoulders and turned again, calling once more to Stephen. He stood as close to the edge as he dared, watching the bright backs of gulls below, poised on updrafts from the sea. From his vantage, they seemed like wraiths drifting idly and peacefully against the whipping lash of the wind, the cacophony of their cries reaching his ears over the haunting noise of the ocean. Below, the water swept up violent and grey between the black feet of rock, drawing off again with a suck of bubbles and spray.

He looked pensively up and down the coastline as it heaved and plunged in both directions. He'd heard her call but had lingered, watching intently the drifting gulls, the surging sea, his head full of thoughts. With a deep breath, he filled his lungs and moved his hands distractedly over the front of his tweed vest. As he did, he thought again of the folded paper he'd placed in the front breast pocket. The thought turned him sharply, at last, towards the lighthouse, where she was sitting in its lee, waving a beckoning arm in an exaggerated gesture. She looked lovely to him, her hair in the wind, the cloth of her dress pushed in sharp wrinkles against her shoulders. He stepped away from the edge of the cliff and came towards her.

"What was keeping you?" she asked when at last he took his place on the blanket.

"I was just thinking. It's so peaceful here."

"A lovely spot for lunch. And what a feast we have." She filled both cups with tea, handing him one. "Well, it's hardly champagne, but it'll have to do." She lifted her cup. "A toast?"

Stephen stared at the white and red pattern of the blanket a moment. "To what?"

"Isn't it obvious, silly?" She studied his face, though he kept his gaze lowered. "To us, together—again—at last." She extended her cup in invitation.

So he brought his to hers, and then took a sip. From over the rim of her own cup she watched him drink, her eyes radiant, until his finally fell into their embrace.

She began slicing the bread, talking quickly as she worked. "What a marvellous idea this was, Stephen! It's simply wonderful being alone together at last." She passed him some bread. "Really, you know, I wonder if anyone even knows this little lighthouse exists, stuck way out here on this peninsula and all. We were lucky to have found it. It's so quaint. And the air up here, so exhilarating!"

The wind seemed to sweep Grace's words unheard across the slope, combing them through the grass.

Stephen said nothing, chewing thoughtfully, so she continued.

"And wasn't it generous of your father to loan us the car? I daresay he's happy to have you back." She paused. "We all are, Stephen."

She felt the cool touch of his palm on her hand.

"Grace. There's something important I need to tell you. Something I want you to know…"

She leaned forward, resting her palms on her knees in front of her. "What is it?"

But he said nothing and looked away again, shyly. The ensuing silence was filled with the murmur of gull cries, faint and far away.

"Stephen, I know. It's okay. I know how you feel about your studies, your poetry, your Greek and whatnot. And Stephen…" She ran gentle fingers through his hair, bringing her forehead to rest against his. "I know how hard the last four years were for both of us. Not just me, but you, too. Of course it was hard, but I'm so proud of you and all you've accomplished. And anyway, being together now, like this, makes all those months apart worth the sacrifice."

The wind and surf and distant gull cries filled the silence to bursting.

"I love you, Stephen."

"And I love you too, Grace." He raised his hand to her cheek. "And I want…" Again his words floundered; he looked down. "I want… you. But…"

She shifted her weight and moved closer. As she did so, the breath of the sea caught a loose strand of her hair, dragging it across her cheek. She smoothed it back along her temple and inclined her head, lowering her eyes into his downcast gaze, like grey doves settling into their nest. The collar of her dress caught the wind and danced briefly at her throat, her breath drawn and tentative. Then her lips moved, opened, and pressed against his.

He lingered in the kiss briefly, and then pulled away. But she held his eyes in hers, searching. She could feel him tremble, fingers of crimson spreading from his neck and creeping along his jaw. Her palms came up gently on his chest, and beneath their touch he felt more than heard the paper he had stuffed into his breast pocket.

His voice, nervous from flushed cheeks, broke dry over his lips. "I do love you, Grace." His hand smoothed down her hair. "I do…want this. But we can't. Not yet. Not here. I want to ask you…"

And to quiet him, she pressed her lips against his mouth again, drawing away his voice.

Then she was lowering her weight onto the red-checked cloth, and her arms drew him down onto her body. Under the flowing tide of yellow-flowered cotton, he felt her warmth as he sank down, the fragrance of her all around him, the blood roaring in his ears. Alone beneath the blind and forgotten watch of an isolated lighthouse, white and blue in the crest of the sun, their warmth pushed together, one warmth, the flesh of their palms folding into each other. A soft and gentle rocking started, like the undulation of the tide, and far below the sighing of the ocean drowned out all other noise. The tide rushed up and out, caressing with its foam the dark concaves of the base of the cliff, the soft but urgent hands of the surf pushed fondly against the shore, finding and filling its secret warmth. The wind quivered. The dark waters of the deep convulsed.

Even after the roar of blood in their veins had stilled, Stephen lingered in her arms. Her fingertips drifted along the curve of his spine, dragging furrows in the loosened folds of his shirt. And then he pulled away from her, shivering in the wind as he sat up on the blanket, adjusting the disarray of his clothing, watching her.

Grace sat up then, too, and with delicate movements of her wrists began smoothing down the cloth of her dress, the disorder of her hair.

As he felt the buttons and rough tweed of his vest work through his fingers, he became aware again of the paper in the breast pocket. He inhaled deeply.

"Grace," he said, a new rush of blood roaring anxiously in his ears. "I still have to ask you—tell you—" Far away, the gulls cried mournfully. "—ask you something."

"What is it, darling?"

"This is hard, Grace, but I need—I want to ask you if—if you could—" His hand rose involuntarily to his heart, his palm pressed against the paper in the pocket. "If you would…"

"If I would?"

And, swallowing his heart, he asked her. "Will you marry me?"

The words hung, wraith-like, poised and paralyzed in the air between them. As if they hovered still, he stared at them, surprised.

Light spread across Grace's face. "Yes," she said.

She moved towards him and they folded together in a new embrace. With her breast against his, he felt again the paper he carried in his pocket.

Grace spoke now, enraptured, as he held her close. "Oh, Stephen! Really! You and I, married? Like the winter is finally over," she murmured into his shoulder, softly to herself, with words she didn't quite understand.

When they pulled away and had settled on the blanket around the scattered remains of their lunch, Grace gathered together their tin cups, the thermos of tea. She refilled the cups and placed one in his palm.

"Another toast?" she ventured. "To our love?"

"To our love," he said quietly and raised his cup. "Forever."

"Forever." She met it with her own.

They drank, and then Grace, overflowing with joy, began discussing their wedding, how to tell their families, the future that awaited them. Stephen listened quietly, thoughtfully.

"But Grace—" Finally he interrupted her meandering joy.

Something in his voice stopped her short.

After an interminable pause, he spoke. "Grace, I have to leave first."

Confusion clouded her eyes. "Leave? What do you mean?"

Stephen drew the paper at last from his breast pocket. A letter, folded away into an envelope, addressed to him, appeared in his hand. He reached slowly, measuring the look in her eyes and placed it in her lap. She did not touch it.

"Stephen, I don't understand. What do you mean, leave?" Her voice was heavy with fear, or anger, or both.

"I got this letter last week. I didn't tell you about it, because I didn't know how to react to it myself. The director of the Classics Department in Toronto mentioned something about it just before I left. But honestly, Grace, I didn't expect anything to come of it when I applied."

The letter lay untouched in her lap. "What is it?" she asked.

"I told him I couldn't afford it, that I couldn't leave Halifax, but he said I should apply anyway. He even applied for funding for me."

"What is it, Stephen?" Her voice rose in pitch.

"It's an acceptance letter. For archaeological fieldwork."

Grace looked at the paper in her lap.

"In Athens," he added into the pallor of silence that had fallen over them.

"And you've accepted?"

"They're providing me a one-year research grant. I'll be working at the best school in Athens."

"Athens? But Stephen—us? What about us?"

Though she turned her face away from the touch, Stephen placed his hand on her shoulder. "Grace, listen to me. There is still 'us.' There will always be 'us.' I do love you. I do want to spend the rest of my life with you. I—"

"And marriage? Was that just some big ploy?"

Stephen held her against his heart. "We will get married, Grace. I promise. The thought of spending the rest of my life without you in it... it... kills me."

Grace pushed away from the embrace, fear and grief, shame and rage washing over her in successive waves.

"Don't you see?" he said. "I have to do this. This is who I am, what I was made for. If I don't, I'll always have the what-ifs and should-have-dones hanging over me. Oh Grace, we will get married. I'll do this trip to Greece and I'll get back and we'll be—"

"But why do you have to leave at all? When you get back—when you get back! I don't know if I can wait any longer! I love you so much, and it breaks my heart to see you leave..." Her voice faltered, lost somewhere between anger and sadness. "I want to be with you. We are supposed to be together."

"We will be together, Grace. Fieldwork doesn't start until the fall. We'll have this summer together. And then in the fall, I'll leave for Greece. But only for one—"

"One year? One year! Why not just say eternity? Stephen, why can't you follow your heart here, find your dream here? In Halifax? In Nova Scotia? Why does it have to take you across the world?" Her sadness settled simply into anger, and it welled up in her hotly.

"Don't you see?" His voice was urgent, with a deep need for her to understand. "What is there for me if I stay here? There's no work, even for men with more useful education than a classics degree. The world here is in shambles. What kind of life could I offer you if we were to get married today, or tomorrow? A life of poverty? Deprivation?"

"Being without you is deprivation, for me."

"But Grace, there is nothing here! I'd never find work in Halifax, and the rest of the country is no better. Think about what an opportunity this is for me. Suddenly, from out of nowhere, comes the chance for me to work. And not only work, but work in my field. It is the chance I've been waiting for. How can I pass this up? I can work over there, gain experience… and maybe by then conditions will have improved here. And when I come back I'll be able to give you the life you deserve. I need to do this, Grace, not only for me, but for us."

"What kind of life together can we have," Grace asked, anger still trembling through her, "with you in Greece and me here?"

She gestured around her at the windswept peninsula, accentuating its isolation.

"And what life could we have together, poor, dependant, starving for work?" he asked. "What could I provide for you?"

"I don't care about that, Stephen. What I care about is you. And being with you. Those other things will work themselves out. I love you for you."

"For me to be me, Grace, I have to do this."

Grace stared for a long time into his eyes. The silence grew unbearable. Finally, the levee of her heart broke and a great surge of feeling flooded from her.

"I know. I know, Stephen." She moved to him, clinging to him bitterly. "I know," she murmured into his shoulder. "I know."

"One year. I promise you. One year." And then, hesitantly, "Please let me follow this dream." And then, feebly, "Please, love me for it."

"I do."

"Will you marry me?" And this time, the words fell warm and earnest from his lips.

"I will."

CHAPTER EIGHT
Journal and Field Notes, 1967

GRACE PLACED THE LAST LETTER ON THE DESK BEFORE HER. *PLEASE, DO NOT double that pain by hoping vainly for my return.* A final piece of his memory, it stared up at her from the hard, wooden surface: *It would hurt me deeply to know that you held on for nothing.*

A tear still burned on her cheek. Because she had held on. For twelve prayerful years, she had waited for him.

She lifted herself through the darkness of the study, hovering over the desk and its scattered memories, her palms pressed on the surface. With a gentle push, she moved to the window and stood in the striped shadows of the Venetian blind. She looked out from the shroud of darkness in which she stood and remembered those hard years.

In the fall of 1937, he had left the warm fold of her arms, a final embrace, and disappeared into the echoing hull of the ship that had borne him away. After what had been one of the richest summers she could remember, all the more rich for the time they spent together, he had sailed off. And with him on that ship went a small, vital piece of her soul.

As it happened, Stephen and his father had had a dreadful row right before he left. Mr. Walker had insisted that he ought to stay in Halifax, that it was a "fool's errand" to chase off to Athens with no clear prospects for the future. He'd wanted Stephen to stay, to marry Grace, to settle down. Stephen had insisted, however, and Mr. Walker told him that if he did go, he could expect no help from him whatsoever. His mother had remained painfully torn between the two. She'd wanted Stephen to follow his dreams, but the thought of losing him broke her heart.

And so he had left, estranged from his father and barely saying goodbye to either of his parents. They did not come to see him off. From what Grace learned from his sisters Jane and Sarah, he seldom wrote his parents from Greece, and when he did the letters had a perfunctory tone. He wrote to his sisters more warmly, but even those letters were rare.

He wrote Grace almost weekly, however, letter after affectionate letter from across the Atlantic. These, too, were spread chaotically across the desk. Each one, when she received it, had given her the strength and hope she needed as she waited for that piece of her soul to return.

The letters revealed the story of those empty times, how a one-year research scholarship had been extended—only by a few months, his letter had assured her—by his decision to tour the islands in the spring of 1938. A year away turned into two, when he landed the opportunity to do research at the Heraklion museum on Crete that fall, after which he would come home. And then they would be married.

She, the dutiful bride, had waited earnestly and faithfully for the return of the man who would be her husband.

Of course, the letters also explained how the brooding political climate in Europe had extended his absence month after uncertain month. Rumours of war had swirled around him everywhere he'd gone and travel from Greece had become impossible.

Even as she stood there, watching the garden from the window of his study, the paralyzing anxiety of those times washed over her again. Fearing the outbreak of war in every ominous radio announcement and apprehensive newspaper report, Grace had teetered at times on the edge of despair, certain she'd never see him again.

And then came that shadowed day in September 1939 when she'd heard, muffled and distorted from the depths of radio static, Britain's declaration of war on Germany. A short while after this, Stephen's correspondences had stopped abruptly. From that distant island somewhere in the Aegean on which he was now trapped came only silence.

War took hold of Halifax, too. The citadel bristled with militant life. The harbour filled with fighting ships from around the world. She watched as men boarded these vessels and disappeared across the horizon of the sea. She watched, too, as her father, in command of a Royal Canadian Navy corvette, hunted German U-boats in the North Atlantic. She remembered those days, sitting prayerfully by the radio, absorbing the minutest details of the operations on the Eastern Front, listening with meticulous care for any promise of Stephen's safety. She had followed the Italian invasion of Greece tremulously and breathed a sigh of guarded joy when it had been repelled. She'd wept later with open grief when Germany finally conquered Greece, succeeding where Italy had failed. With the fall of Greece, she lost all hope of his return and almost gave up praying.

And yet, by some miracle, a final letter from him had fallen into her trembling hands, from the starved hands of a dying New Zealander, through the confused hands of a Canadian Naval officer. *Please do not double my pain by hoping vainly for my return.* Such a strange way to say it, and yet, despite his admonishment, she had hoped… she'd clung desperately to it.

No more letters came, but she'd continued to pray, fervently, earnestly, defiantly.

And then, nearly ten years after his leaving, her prayers were answered. Stephen emerged from the terror of war, from the far ends of the earth, back into her arms, back into the life she had kept nurtured in his absence. They were married, and though she never ventured to break the frail silence that seemed at times in their new life together to bring itself ominously between them, she always wondered what dark secrets he had witnessed in the war. His silence shrouded them from her, burying within him the horrors he had been part of, horrors he would never share with her.

Grace turned back from the window to face the study. Letters were scattered over the floor and strewn across the desk, the remembrance of him finally, fully complete.

Almost as if she were seeing them for the first time, she realized what a mess she'd made. She knelt on the floor and with gentle movements began to gather the letters together again, returning them to their carboard urn. She had found at last what she'd come for, and these reminders of him, although they pained her, were cathartic and healing, too. She even dared to smile, thinly.

When the box was full again, she sealed it with the lid and twine. She didn't want it to lie hidden anymore in some forgotten corner of their closet, so she sat at the desk and pulled open its lowest drawer, hoping to lay it to rest among the other mementos of his life.

But as she did, she noticed something thick and flat in the darkness of the drawer, something she didn't recognize. Reaching, she felt the smooth leather cover of a book.

She pulled it out—tattered, age-stained pages bound by a worn cover. Opening it to the first page, she read, in his thin hand *Journal and Field Notes*, written in black ink across the top of the page. And lower down, *Stephen David Walker (1937)*.

She had never seen this before. Nor had Stephen ever mentioned it. She dragged a thumb through the pages. Each had been packed thickly with black ink. Her eyes, touching momentarily on phrases or words that passed before them, began to piece together its contents. This was his journal from those dark times—a chronicle of his work in Greece, a personal record of his life during those years of absence and exile.

She closed the book. Before her lay the veiled secrets of war and trauma he had never shared with her, the memories lurking just below the surface of his mind that she had never asked of him. A thrill of fear and a tremble of anticipation convulsed in her.

Outside in the garden, the sun shone brightly. Caught in a solitary shaft of light that pierced the room like a wound, Grace leaned over his journal. She opened the book again to the cover page, then turned it. And as she did so, she thought she felt the frail surface of a dark shadow shatter before her.

PART II
Fieldwork

CHAPTER NINE

Athens, October 1937

Started excavations on the Eponymoi today, with a promising first day back in the field. Discovered two remarkable marbles north of what we have tentatively identified as the Altar of Zeus. While still unidentified, they may be two of the Eponymous Heroes, as named by Pausanias; though they may also belong to the remains of the Temple of Ares, which we are just beginning to uncover some 60' N of this find.

While the first theory is more likely, if they do belong to the Ares temple, it would make these sculptures important in my search for the Aphrodites. Despite the beautiful marbles we have already unearthed this season, these two images have yet to be discovered. Pausanias mentions them in connection with the Ares temple...

Near the figure of Demothenes is the sanctuary of Ares where are two images of Aphrodite... though so far, nothing in our work on the Ares has uncovered anything that matches the description. If the marbles we found today do belong to the Ares temple, they could potentially point me in the direction of Pausanias' Aphrodites.

STEPHEN SET HIS PEN DOWN AND LEANED OVER THE TABLE, SCATTERED with the various sketches, diagrams, and field notes he had made during the day's excavations. Near his elbow, marked heavily with pencil and scrawled with notes, sat his well-worn copy of Pausanias' *Description of Greece*, a tattered volume he had purchased for a few drachmas in the Greek bookshop near his residence early on in his work at the excavation. He reached for a pencil and underlined a passage carefully: *"the sanctuary of Ares, where are two images of Aphrodite."* Beside it, he indicated its importance with two asterisks: the Temple of Ares, the two Aphrodites.

He cradled his face in his palms, closing his weary eyes to the evening-coppered light that spread over the street and pressing the heel of his hand firmly against them. Thinking back over the day's excavations, he could see again, in his mind's eye, the marble statue he had discovered that morning emerging from the dust of the past.

———————

The sun had been hot all morning, filling the basin of the Agora where they were working with hard light and pressing heat. Their excavations had stirred up the dust and it hung over them, heavy and still.

His neck bent beneath the glare of the sun, burnished and bright from long days beneath its watchful eye, Stephen sat supervising the two hired men in their slow and meticulous work, removing the last of the hard-packed earth that encased the marble. Perched on the makeshift bench of an unearthed block of stone, the unidentified foundation of some forgotten monument, Stephen scrawled down the details as the figure emerged: *Matrix: packed silt, slightly sandy.* One of the Greeks called out numbers, using the ruled stick he had erected near the find to measure the depth, and Stephen scratched them down in his journal: *Horizontal provenience: 5' 9" to 7'2".*

He watched the two men, their browned hands moving gently over the emerging torso, chipping away the crumbling silt with the gentle chisel strokes of their tools—a garden spade, an artist's brush. Like sculptors themselves, he thought whimsically, they carved the ancient statue out of the earth and into new existence. He scribbled down more notes: *Association: Torso facing east, 12' west of previous marbles. Smaller fragments nearby.*

In this way, the marble materialized slowly from the matrix that contained it: the broad chest, the poised torso, the balanced hip. *Description: Marble, male image. Size: Standing intact, possibly 5'9". Head, left hand at wrist, right arm at shoulder, all missing. Torso pose: classic contra-posto; nude, with shoulders draped.*

The stone was heavy. It took four men to finally unearth it and carry it up the slope to the edge of the excavations, where they laid it in the shade of an olive tree. Stephen prepared a tag with the artefact number scratched on it, attaching it to the statue's broken forearm with a length of string.

He lingered for a moment to examine the statue closely. He pressed his fingers into the deep crevices of the stone, around the drapery of the shoulders, along the inside of the arms, brushing away any clumps of earth that still lingered. He tried to imagine the ancient hands that had moved so long ago over a mute block of marble and with the careful strokes of hammer and chisel breathed this figure to life; he thought, too, of the Grecian youth who had once stood and posed, whose young, vibrant image now was stamped forever in this ancient, cold stone. Who had he been? Who had this image been meant to represent? The stone offered no answers, so at last he turned away, back to the slowly emerging mysteries of the Agora.

From where he stood at the edge of the site, at the border between old Athens and new, he could survey the whole of the excavation. The rubble of the ancient city spread out before him in all its broken glory—the sprawling foundations of once ethereal temples tracing crumbling lines in the earth, the sunken remains of once graceful pillars tumbled randomly over the ground. Strewn about the site lay huge mounds of earth and rubble, smouldering fine dust into the heat of the day. They would be sifted one last time for artefacts before being loaded onto the horse-drawn carts that waited to haul them away. Groups of local Athenians milled about these carts, watching the work and commenting amiably on its progress. As the carts gradually filled with sifted rubble, their owners led the horses off, and the crowds dispersed and regathered around a new carter awaiting a load. In this way, the tide of locals supervising the discovery of their own glorious past continually ebbed and flowed, swirling about the shores of the excavation.

Stretching wearily, Stephen pulled a handkerchief from his pocket, removed his hat, and sponged his brow. He looked up along the edge of the Agora at the squat villas and close-backed buildings of modern Athens, peering over the ruins of its golden past. If these buildings recognized the glorious city that was their mother, the cradle of their birth, nothing hinted at it. Stoic and gaping, their earthen-red roofs shimmered in the heat, the streets of new Athens crowding out the remains of the old.

———————

A waiter appeared at Stephen's table, where he sat with his hands still pressed against his eyes. He looked up and smiled at the man, who nodded pleasantly in return and set a tumbler of ouzo among the clutter of Stephen's books and papers.

Stephen tried to thank him in Greek, feeling all over again the irony of his learning. While he had devoted so much of his life to studying the ancient mother of this man's language—could recite whole sections of Homer or Hesiod—still he fumbled the simple task of addressing a waiter in modern Greek.

The waiter waved off his efforts. Like many of the Greeks Stephen had met in Athens, the man was clearly proud of his simple command of the English language and was determined to give it a try.

"You have ouzo," he said in English. "Good. You want... you will order dinner now?"

Stephen struggled through the task of placing his order in Greek.

Once the waiter had left, he returned to his work. It was getting late, and the last light of the day spread itself through the dusty streets. He closed his eyes against it for a moment, remembering, and then reached for his pen.

It is my hope that our further excavations on the Ares, and with it, our further discovery of frieze work (hopefully) will lead us, finally, to the two Aphrodites. From the time Hephastios caught her with Ares, as the old story goes, she's always been close to the god of war. Surely her images will be uncovered, now as then, in Ares' arms.

When the excavations had finished that evening, rather than accompany the rest of the team back to the residences, Stephen had wandered off alone. His mind full and pensive, he had meandered along the path of the Theorias and up the slope of the Areopagus. The sun had just begun to lower itself behind the hills surrounding the city and the heat had grown soft.

He'd followed the curve of the road between the Areopagus and the Acropolis, until it met the Avenue of the Dionysus. On his left he had passed the ruins of the Theatre of Dionysus, looking forlorn in the twilight, the rock of the Acropolis towering over it.

Eventually the path had brought him out of the ruins of the ancient world and into the bustle and chaos of the new.

As the evening cooled, the city had awakened to new life. Crowds came out, restaurants placed out their placards, children emerged to play on porches and curbs. Still preoccupied with the mystery of the missing Aphrodites and the identity of the marble he'd discovered that day, Stephen had walked along, blind to it all, climbing a steep, narrow street east of the Acropolis. The houses here were packed and close, with chipped plaster faces and weather-worn window shutters.

The dusty maze of narrow streets had led him slowly north and east, into the Plaka district where the crowds were denser. On a curb, a restaurateur had offered him a table with a sweep of his arms. A merchant leaned against a wall, gesturing towards his wares.

The crowds had made it impossible to wander, so Stephen had pulled himself at last from his thoughts, turned down a narrow side street, and found a quiet taverna, hoping to work out the problem of the missing Aphrodites over a drink and some dinner. Ordering an ouzo, he had pulled his notes from his satchel and laid them out on the table.

That was almost an hour ago now, and he was still no closer to making sense of it all. He reached for the tumbler of ouzo, grimacing as he took an acrid sip. The daylight was almost gone, but looking up through the narrow streets he could still see, hazy in the settling dust of the evening, the dark silhouette of the Acropolis watching over the city. The dark skeleton of the Parthenon stood stark against the sky, like a regal circlet crowning the brow of the sacred rock.

He had visited the Acropolis during his first week in Athens. Climbing the ancient path, cool in the early morning light, he had journeyed like a wide-eyed pilgrim to that mythic hill. The morning light had thrown his shadow long over the path before him as he'd followed it up to the Propylaea.

Standing among the shattered ruins of that once resplendent gatehouse, in the shadows of the Doric colonnades that had once formed the gate, he had turned and looked down along the route he'd just traversed. Through the rays of the dawning light, Stephen had tried whimsically to imagine the ancient procession he knew had once followed this path: the parade of horsemen, banners, and trappings ablaze in the sun, the musicians marching in celebration along the processional avenue, the dancing maidens glistening and chanting, the solemn, white robed priests. In his imagination he strained his ears for the lowing of the spotless calf, or the bleating lamb, festooned with garlands and led among the clamour to the place of sacrifice. Sunlight warmed his cheeks and a bird lifted its song somewhere to the dawn, but otherwise everything was silent.

He had then turned down the avenue of the Panathenaic procession, following those long-silent footsteps through the bleached and broken fingers of the half-toppled columns.

Later he tried to capture the moment in his journal:

I remember my first visit to the Acropolis. Arrival in Greece by steamer—a gruelling passage from Brindisi to Patras, second only to the gruelling trip by rail to Athens awaiting me in Patras! Arrived in Athens travel-worn and starving. But somehow this exotic city, so rich with legend and full of life, rid me of my travel fatigue. My first view of the Acropolis, a looming shadow in the evening sky, is burned in my mind. It's like meeting an old friend, a hero stepping alive from the pages of Homer or something. It is like a dream come true, being here. It's as if I'm walking in the footsteps of the very architects of civilization.

In the study, Grace cradled the journal in her palms. Her face intent over the words, her heart hungry for them, she took in every detail voraciously—the concise descriptions of matrices and proveniences, rough sketches of artefacts, hand-drawn diagrams of excavation sites. She lingered especially on the comments and reflections that coloured these dry data, places where his elation and yearning had bled through the restrained details of archaeological discovery.

In these records of the past she was discovering a history she'd known vaguely but never really understood. She spread it before her eagerly, piecing the story together, flipping forward in the journal.

Today a discovery of great importance during excavations of the Post-Herulian Wall, near the Library of Pantainos. In association with what we have identified with great certainty as fragments of the Ares temple frieze work, I have discovered pieces of a female image. Imperious, well over life-sized, a goddess surely, she appears to be wearing a tightly fitted chiton with an elaborate mantle swept over the left shoulder, reaching around the right thigh. Her left hand is spread over the hip, and her right arm appears to have been raised in the pose typically reserved for a divine image. The head, right arm, and right foot are all missing, though we have already uncovered scores of what are probably her smaller fragments.

It was with uncontainable excitement that I worked on her excavation. Although without further evidence—it is still a tentative identification—I am hopeful that we have at last discovered one of the Aphrodites noted by Pausanias.

Stephen's fingers pressed gently into the earth. It was dry and pliable here in the shelter of the Post-Herulian Wall, and it crumbled easily beneath his touch. He hovered over his work, sitting on his haunches with his chin resting heavily on his knees. A rounded bit of marble protruded from the ground, and something about the shape of it piqued his interest. He touched it, brushing aside the earth that hid it until, unexpectedly, it became a knee, delicately posed and graceful.

A thrill of anticipation raced through him and he cleared away more of the debris, revealing the rounded length of a thigh, sharp ridges of sculpted drapery, the curve of a hip. He measured and recorded the provenience, his fingers charged with excitement: *Marble statue: Female. Depth, 3'2". 4'5" east of wall. 8' north of marker 3.*

He leaned in and gently blew away some loose dirt, revealing an elegantly poised hand resting lightly against the hip. Another bit of scraping and brushing and soon the elaborate lines of a mantle appeared, sweeping dramatically over one of the rounded shoulders. It was an hour or more of this painstaking work, but eventually the whole statue, a finely sculpted marble of a female figure lay in full view.

I am cautious to identify this find as one of the Aphrodites without further investigation. It was, after all, uncovered well away from the Ares site, where I would have expected to find it. The pieces of the temple frieze work are promising evidence, but ultimately not enough to make an absolute identification.

Of course, Pausanias does mention two images of Aphrodite to be found in the sanctuary of Ares. The discovery of a second image, in association with this one, and like it in form, would be the kind of decisive evidence I need to make an accurate identification. If this is the Aphrodite, ought not there be a second to discover near it?

At the taverna in the Plaka, Stephen closed his journal and gathered together his field notes. This place had become something of a regular haunt for him. In the distance, the evening mumbled with the noise of the marketplace.

Pausanias lay open on the table, the key to his excavations in Athens. He read the ancient descriptions: *"Above the spring are temples, one to Demeter and Kore, the other to Triptolemos in which there is a bronze bull as if it were led to sacrifice."* Unsure of his purpose, he took his pencil and traced a thin line beneath the words, highlighting the passage about the bronze bull. In the margin he pencilled a note: *to whom the sacrifice?* Then he closed the book and stuffed it into his satchel with the rest of his notes.

Seeing him preparing to leave, the waiter arrived at his table and Stephen paid him.

"You… American? English?" the man asked in broken English as he placed the drachmas Stephen had given him into his pocket.

"No. Canadian."

"Canadian?" The waiter seemed to turn the unfamiliar word over in his mouth a couple of times. "You… work… here in Athens?"

"I'm working on the excavations. I'm an archaeologist."

"Archaeologist?" Another word, unfamiliar over his tongue.

"I discover the past. I dig up clues to the past."

"Ah… Greece… a very big past, no?"

"Indeed. A huge past." Stephen smiled. "It's the mother of western civilization, after all. Right now our team is excavating the Agora."

"The Agora. Is very old. You find very old things there?"

Stephen looked at his satchel. "I've discovered Aphrodite," he said.

"Aphrodite? The goddess of love? A very good thing to find!"

"Well," he began, and this was a confession more to himself than the waiter, "I'm not certain it is the Aphrodite. I believe it is, but I need more evidence. There should be two statues. If I could find the other, I'd know for sure."

"Two Aphrodites? Two?" Something seemed to strike the waiter peculiarly. He laughed. "You sure you not Greek?"

Stephen smiled, too. "I'm sure."

"Well, Canadian. You have good luck. Good luck with goddess of love."

Stephen shouldered his satchel and thanked him. He walked through the crowded Plaka, making his way back to the residences.

Grace read Stephen's record of this question, asked of him so many years ago and scratched down later in the journal: *Two Aphrodites? You sure you're not Greek?* She smiled softly, sadly.

She turned the page and saw next his sketch of the goddess, her broken form done in pencil and then traced out in black ink. She lingered over it—the dark lines of the drapery, the curve of the torso, the fractured limbs. So tenderly, so painstakingly he'd sketched it out, and beneath it, in his wandering hand, he had written, *Aphrodite (?) Pentelic Marble. Possible 4th Century B.C. Discovered October 12, 1937.*

CHAPTER TEN

Sounion, May 1938

THAT SPRING, AFTER A LONG AND REWARDING YEAR OF FIELDWORK, Stephen made an eagerly anticipated tour of the Greek mainland. Most of his colleagues spent their off time relaxing by the seashore of one or another of the many sun-soaked Greek islands, but Stephen knew his days in Greece were now numbered, and he wished to visit as many of the significant archaeological sites as possible before his time was up.

This spring tour took him in a wide loop around the Peloponnesus—the sanctuary of Asklepieion in Corinth, the Lion's Gate of ancient Mycenae, the ruins of Sparta, the temple of Apollo in Delphi, and finally, before returning to the dusty streets of Athens, a trip to the Temple of Poseidon on the tip of Cape Sounion.

Though it was much more modest than the sprawling shrine to Apollo at Delphi, and much less significant, archaeologically speaking, than the noble Lion Gate of Mycenae, it was this temple, the shrine to the sea god Poseidon, that most captured Stephen's imagination. There was something haunting, he thought, about its lonely perch on the edge of the cape, looking forlornly out over the Aegean Sea. He picked his way among the tumbled ruins and scattered stones, scrambling carefully down the slope of the cliff to the very edge of the water, where three or four of the ancient marble slabs, having once formed one of the pillars of the Sounion Temple, had fallen and come to rest. He crouched to examine them—Doric, he knew from the sea-worn fluting that marked their sides—and then shaded his eyes against the glitter of sunlight on the water. Above him, the temple ruins rose noble and broken at the very edge of the cliff, forever watching the rippling rise and fall of the sea.

Off in the distance, at the edge of that hazy line where sea and sky became one, he could just make out the first islands of the Aegean archipelago, rugged shadows rising faintly against the pastels of sea and sky. Water and air and earth, he thought, allowing the lyricism of the scene to work on him; joined in a single mythic landscape, the elements mingled in a tender embrace, stretching off towards the horizon until they became one beneath the watchful warmth of the sun. What secret histories, he wondered, indulging in the poetry of the moment, what ancient mythologies were hidden out there, surging with the movement of the tide?

The moment passed and he began cautiously to pick his way again up and along the sea-calloused boulders. A steep path wound its way up the cliff, fringed here and there with yellow grass and purple wildflowers.

When at last he clambered over the final knoll and stood again on the ledge of Cape Sounion, he began to examine the temple itself. From the crumbling stone pedestal that was its foundation rose the tattered remains of fifteen Doric columns, elegant-looking and forlorn. Perched on three or four of their vaulted capitals rested the few architraves that had not yet come crashing to the ground, dragged down by the incessant pull of time. Far below, the rush of the sea—the voice of this temple's ancient deity, Stephen thought vaguely—could still be heard.

Stephen's guide waited for him, sitting in the shadow of one of the ruined columns. Stephen mounted the crumbling steps and crossed the time-polished stones to take a seat beside him.

"You like Sounion? Yes? Like I say you will?" The guide's English was broken, but he would not let Stephen speak Greek.

"I like it very much. It is beautiful." Near where he sat, two blocks of marble joined in a worn seam, the scented stalk of wild thyme growing up in the fissure between them. Stephen tugged absently at it as he searched for his words. "Haunting."

The guide smiled. "You interested in history of Greece? This place is very important to Greece. Very important to people." His voice trailed off. "You know this place? Why it is so important?"

Stephen tugged the thyme free from the seam of the marble. "This temple? Well, it's a temple to Poseidon, erected sometime around the fourth century. It was built in the traditional hexastyle, with a porch and a sanctuary. The columns are in the Doric style. It was—"

"No, not when it is built, but *why*. This is what makes it important. This is where Theseus is made king of Athens."

Far below, Stephen could still hear the sea, whispering as its waves washed up against the stone.

"You know story of Theseus?" the guide asked. "How Theseus is come to be king of Athens?"

"Do you mean the myth of Theseus and the Minotaur?"

The guide nodded. "It starts here. Story ends here, too. A very important place."

Beneath his words, the sea suddenly surged, like distant siren song, seductive.

"This is long ago, when Crete was ruled by King Minos, and Aegeus was king in Athens," the guide continued. "You see, son of Minos was killed at big games in Athens, and king Minos is angry, makes war. Aegeus is losing war, so he makes promise with Minos, which says Minos will come each year and take seven men and seven girls of Athens as payment. These he will take back to Crete and feed to awful monster he has there, being kept in a labyrinthos... a... a..."

"A labyrinth. A maze." Stephen's imagination sparked and his eyes kindled with the memory of the legend. "And in the heart of the labyrinth lives the Minotaur, the Bull of Minos, the terror of Athens, and seven Athenian youth and seven maidens the tribute."

"Yes... tribute... But one year, when Minos comes to take his... tribute... he sees Theseus, son of Aegeus. And Minos knows he is powerful and mighty, so he picks Theseus to go to Crete and be food for the Minotaur. So Theseus leaves Athens with the others. He goes to face this Minotaur."

In Stephen's imagination, the siren song, it seemed, had grown heady in the air now. He looked out over the misty horizon where sea and air and earth were one, to the ancient place where, somewhere far beyond the edge of his vision, lay the island of Crete. In vague thoughts and indistinct images, he pictured the ominous vessels of King Minos, plying the waves to Athens, exacting their dreadful tribute. Year after year, seven beautiful Athenian boys and seven doe-eyed maids were stolen off to Crete, the lustre of Athens taken to feed the Bull of Minos, lost in the blackness of its labyrinth.

Stephen knew the story.

"You know, on the voyage to Crete, Theseus faces Minos," the guide said. "Theseus, he claims he is son of the sea god and Minos wants proof. He must give proof he is son of Poseidon. So Minos throws a ring into the sea and makes Theseus to get it. Theseus jumps into water and Minos sails away."

Over the horizon of the Aegean, Stephen imagined Theseus among the fourteen Athenians, challenging Minos, a gleam of a ring through the water, and

Theseus diving after it to prove his birthright. He remembered his Bacchylides: "*The Athenian youths trembled as the hero leaped into the sea, and tears poured from their lily-like eyes as they awaited the sorrow of what had to be. Yet the dolphins… dwellers in the sea swiftly brought Theseus to the palace of his father, the ruler of horses.*"

The lines of ancient verse formed on Stephen's tongue: "In the lovely palace he saw his father's own wife, the beauteous Amphitrite, in all her majesty. Round him she cast a purple robe and upon his thick hair the unwithered wreath, dark with roses, which subtle Aphrodite had given her at her own marriage."

"Ah. You know the old poems."

"Some of them. Bacchylides tells this tale in the Dythrambs."

"You know how the old stories say Theseus was born?"

"Aegeus was childless, and travelled to Delphi with Pitteus, the king of Troezen, to get advice from the oracle."

"Yes," said the guide. "And the oracle says to Aegeus, 'Do not open wineskin's mouth until you get home.' Aegeus is confused with this oracle. He asks Pittheus. Pittheus, who understands, makes him drunk with wine and gives him his daughter Aethre, to sleep with. She gets pregnant and when Aegeus leaves Troezen, he tells her not to tell the baby who is his father. He puts a sword and sandals under a big rock and says that their boy should come to Athens when he is older, when he can lift this rock and take the sword and sandals."

"But was Theseus not the son of Poseidon then?"

The guide shrugged. "Some say Thesus was son of Aegeus. Others say son of Poseidon. But could be Aegeus was son of Poseidon. Or could be Aegeus was Poseidon himself. No one really knows, but the stories agree: whether son of Poseidon or son of Aegeus, when Theseus arrives at Athens he lifts the rock and takes the tokens left for him."

Across the vision of his mind, Stephen watched Aegeus standing in the torrid air at the temple of Delphi, the dim light drifting with smoke. Aegeus would be asking his question of Apollo, the chanting priestess transfixed over the ceremonial tripod, the temple fire entrancing her with its pallid light. He imagined then the prophetic ecstasy sweeping over her, what the ancients called the voice of the god, as she begins to utter her riddles, garbling words, guttural. And Aegeus is answered in these frenzied ravings, transcribed from incoherent gibberish into verse by the priest at the oracle's side: "*Loose not the wineskin's foot thou chief of men, until to Athens thou art come again.*"

Stephen's tour of the mainland had, in fact, included a visit to Delphi. He'd rented a room in a meagre stone house built precariously on a rocky escarpment near the site. It was owned by a peasant family who kept goats in the hills, and in the five or six days he spent there he developed a friendship with the young daughter of the family. Though half his age, Themis was bright and curious, and eager to please. As a young goatherd, she knew the hills surrounding Delphi intimately. She had been hired by French archaeologists to fetch their water and carry their meals during their recent excavations of Delphi.

Anxious to share her knowledge with him, Themis had accompanied Stephen on his excursion to the site, guiding him through the mysteries of Delphi.

He could see her still in his mind's eye, waiting for him on the steps of the Theatre of Delphi as he'd made his way thoughtfully among the worn foundations and broken columns of the ruined sanctuary of Apollo. Her scarf had been wrapped about her dark hair, rustling with the wind, as she'd smiled at him.

He had come up next to her and together they'd followed the path along the Sacred Way. She had pointed out to him everything she knew, speaking in the limited, garbled French she had learned from the archaeologists she had served during the excavations.

"Ici, la voie sacrée," she had explained as she led him into the temple. He'd strained to understand, translating the clumsy words as best he could—*This is the sacred way.*

She took a seat on the steps among the broken Doric columns, and with a sweeping gesture indicated the view, the mist-kissed slopes of Mount Parnasus spreading out beneath them. Though Stephen knew these places intimately through his learning, he found himself poised over every name she pronounced, encouraging her answers to his questions.

On the tip of Cape Sounion, the guide continued his story. "And when Theseus is arrived on Crete, she sees him there. She falls in love with him. Ariadne."

Stephen knew this part of the story, too: Ariadne, the Cretan maid of myth and legend, the daughter of King Minos. When Theseus had arrived on Crete, she'd seen him, bold and shining with youth and nobility, and loved him. And for love, she unlocked for him the mystery of her father's labyrinth. She gave Theseus a scarlet thread, to lead him back from the maze, and a radiant wreath, to illuminate its darkness.

Again the ancient whispers of his learning rose up in him: *"She Theseus loved, from Crete with Theseus fled."*

"Ariadne." The word formed softly on his lips. The wind rose up and carried her name out across the water.

"Yes, Ariadne. Own daughter of Minos. She is in love with Theseus. Gives him the magic string so he can find his way in the labyrinth to where the Minotaur lives. She gives him a wreath that will light up the darkness. With these things he goes in the labyrinth and kills the Minotaur."

Stephen remembered his Plutarch, the ancient words running through his head: *"having a clue of thread given him by Ariadne, and being instructed how to us it so as to conduct him through the windings of the Labyrinth, he escaped out of it and slew the Minotaur."* Over the horizon, he imagined Ariadne and Theseus together, scattering the darkness and slaying the beast, the Bull of Minos fallen.

Stephen watched the mingling of sea and air and land more intently, remembering. Theseus had killed the Minotaur with the help of Ariadne, who had betrayed her father for love of him, and together the lovers had fled Crete.

Stephen took his turn with the telling. "Full of their victory, they returned to Athens. And they forgot the arrangement that Theseus had made with Aegeus: that if they were victorious against the Minotaur, they would change the black sails of their ship and return with white sails flying. If they failed and Theseus was dead, they would sail home in black. Theseus forgets to change his sails, and when Aegeus sees the black ships approaching, he despairs for his son and flings himself from a cliff into the sea."

"Yes." The guide took up the story again. "Yes. And here is the cliff where Aegeus died. Here is where Theseus is made king after his father. This place, I say, very important to Greek past. We call this sea 'Aegean,' always after, in memory. And here," the guide gestured to the ruins all around them, "here is built an old temple to always remember the stories."

Stephen rose and walked to the edge of the cliff. From here, Aegeus in despair had flung himself into the bosom of Poseidon. He turned and looked again at the ruins of the temple.

An old temple, he thought, *to always remember the stories.*

The pillars rose up, grey and naked against the sky. The reddish rock of Cape Sounion rolled north into the hills that surrounded the temple. The wind moved quietly among the wildflowers.

The guide stood. "It gets late. We go now." He turned from the temple and began walking.

Stephen nodded but did not immediately turn. His thoughts went towards the woman waiting for him at home, far across the ocean that separated them. His year in Athens finished, his work on both the Ares temple and the newly discovered temple to Aphrodite Ourania completed, it was nearly time for him to return.

And yet he knew what he had written in the last letter he had sent her. If he closed his eyes, he could still see it burning on the page before him:

Though my work here in Athens is done, I feel I am not ready, yet, to leave this place. I have planned a small tour of the islands before I come home. It will be no more than four months, and I assure you I'll be home before Christmas.

Oh, Grace, I long to be with you again, to be in your arms and tell you about the wonderful things I've discovered here, but it seems we must wait still a little longer.

Stephen cast a final glance out over the horizon. His work on the Agora had gone far too quickly. Submerged in the wonder of its forgotten past, he had barely noticed it slip by. And now, with his research grant used up and his work in Athens finished, he had planned one final exploration of this beautiful country before returning home.

He knew the life Grace was preparing for him, for them together, and though it filled him with gratitude, he felt he needed to embark on this last voyage before taking his place in it. He had written to her, trying to explain this need, knowing she would wait, even if she could not understand it.

He remembered sitting on the crumbling steps of the peasants' home at Delphi, on the threshold of the door as the sun had sunk crimson behind the hills. He'd watched the farmer lead a laden donkey along the road and listened to the idle song of the old grandmother sitting near him on the porch, humming vaguely over her needlework. He had been scheduled to leave Delphi in the morning.

Themis had came and sat next to him. They'd quietly watched the sunset with him.

"Vous avez… aimé les ruines du Delphi?" she'd asked. *Did you like the ruins of Delphi?*

Stephen smiled at her, and his French came slowly. "Oui. Elles sont magnifique." *Magnificent.*

"Oui." She had thought through the language again, and added: "Et les hommes… français… qui travaillé ici, ils me dit que… une fois… tout la monde venais a Delpi?"

Stephen watched the evening lengthen through the hills and understood her meaning. "Oui."

Yes. Once the whole world had come to Delphi. At one time, the whole world had come and found here the answers to its questions.

"J'ai… un…" Her the words came more slowly still, but not because of her French now, but for shyness. "Un don… pour vous." *A gift for you.* She watched him cautiously. "C'est un don… du Delphi. Pour vous. Pour souvenez toujours une fois tout la monde venais a Delphi."

She'd moved her hand quickly, and with it opened his palm. She had placed into it a small metal object, warm from her clutching it, and then closed his fingers around it.

When Stephen had opened his hand he found a small silver disk, a tarnished coin stamped with an image he recognized as Apollo. He knew the image well. The god sat on a diphros, his right hand pouring out a libation from a phiale, three stylized pigeons circling his wreathed brow. Perhaps it had been a gift to Themis from one of the French archaeologists who had excavated Delphi, or more likely a small treasure lifted from the dirt by a young girl drawn to the gleam of the silver. And now she had given it to him: a gift from Delphi, that he might always remember a time when the whole world had come here seeking answers.

Themis and her tiny gift had remained prominent in his thoughts since she'd given it to him. He had struggled with it, its significance, its portent. He thought of that young girl, uttering a language that was not her own: "Pour souvenez toujours une fois tout la monde venais a Delphi." *To remember a time when all the world came to Delphi.* The enigma of the words, the mystery of the thing, lingered in his heart. It was this mystery, he thought to himself, this strange prophecy of sorts, that had finally persuaded him to explore more of Greece before returning home. The mystery of a time when Delphi had been the centre of the world is what, after all, had drawn him away from home in the first place. And that mystery, it seemed, still beckoned to him, inviting him to continue seeking it.

The wind moved softly through the Doric columns of the Poseidon temple at Sounion as Stephen turned his back on the Aegean at last and followed his guide down the path that had brought them to this very important place of Greece's past.

CHAPTER ELEVEN
Halifax, August 1938

GRACE HAD RECEIVED STEPHEN'S LETTER ON A THURSDAY. SHE KNEW THIS quite certainly, because she'd started going to St. Christopher's on Thursday mornings to review with Reverend Elliot the hymns for Sunday's service.

Since Stephen had left for Greece, she'd sought to fill her extra time with as much busyness as possible, and in an effort to fill gaps that even her work at the mission couldn't fill, she had volunteered as St. Christopher's primary organist. Typically, Reverend Elliot had Sunday's hymns selected by Thursday, and Grace would spend the morning rehearsing alone in the empty sanctuary, losing herself, sometimes for hours, in the reverberating tones that filled the great, gaping space.

On this particular morning, she had been running late and the mail had arrived just as she was leaving. As she usually did, she hunted through the bundle of envelopes, searching eagerly for anything from Stephen. She found his letter and poured over it, her eagerness turning to shock, then to despair, as she read his news: another four months in Greece, then home by Christmas. He longed, of course, to be with her again, but still they must wait a little longer.

She crumpled the letter in desperate fists, flung it onto the tabletop, and nearly fled the house, walking with an unsteady step the long road to St. Christopher's. Her eyes were almost blind with bitterness, though she did not weep openly. With each step, the words seemed to echo hollowly in her heart: *"I feel I am not ready, yet, to leave this place… a small tour of the islands before I come home… no more than four months…"*

As though four months were not, for her, four lifetimes!

Reverend Elliot could tell something was troubling Grace deeply when she arrived. She maintained her composure as they talked through the music he had selected, but still there was something furtive in her manner, her unwillingness to meet his eyes perhaps, or a slight curtness in her words that told him something was not right. He didn't pry, however, and simply gave her the lists of hymns.

"I've chosen 'Jesus Saviour Pilot Me' as the offertory hymn," he said. "I know you've played it often enough in the past, so I don't suppose it will be a problem for you."

"No, that's certainly fine," she answered distantly.

"And after the homily, I thought, perhaps, 'O Love That Will Not Let Me Go.' The Matheson text. Do you know it?"

"No." Grace still could not meet the reverend's eyes. "No, I'm not familiar with that one."

"The tune is quite lovely, and I think you'll not find it difficult at all." He held out the hymnal to her, opened to the correct page.

She took the book from him without looking. "Thank you. I'll play it through this morning and I'm sure it will be no trouble for Sunday. I know all the rest well enough."

"Yes." Reverend Elliot looked at her closely for a moment, as though he were measuring the distance that seemed to separate her from him and wondering if he might venture across. "Well, I will leave you to it. If you need me, I'll be in my study."

When he had gone, Grace sat down at the organ. The emptiness of the sanctuary seemed almost to taunt her. Though at other times she found its vast open space inspiring, today it only intensified her loneliness.

She pressed the hymnal flat and set it on the organ's music stand, looking over the text of the unfamiliar hymn: *O Love that will not let me go, I rest my weary soul in Thee.* It was hard to focus her eyes, and the music was nearly illegible to her, the words vague and indistinct. *"I give Thee back the life I owe that in Thine ocean depths its flow might richer, fuller be."* She lifted her hands to the keyboard tentatively and pressed down the opening chord.

Sound erupted from the organ so suddenly and harshly that it startled her. Like a child caught at something shameful, she pulled her hands away and set them still again in her lap. The sanctuary echoed with the noise, and then the great silence of the place fell over her again.

She blinked, and swallowed, and tried a second time. *"O Joy that seekest me through pain, I cannot close my heart to Thee."* It was the words now, and not the emptiness, that seemed to taunt her, but she played on, more hesitantly than she might have. The sound seemed so strangely garish to her, or the stillness of the place so implacable.

When she finally reached the end, she brought her hands to her lap again and stared blankly at the page long after the final chord had faded.

————————

"I've finished at the organ now, Reverend Elliot." Grace stood in the doorway of the reverend's study, clutching the hymnal close to her chest.

He looked up from his desk, strewn with paper and books, an open Bible, pen and ink. He removed his reading glasses and offered her a smile.

"Ah. Thank you, Grace. No trouble with the new hymn, I hope?"

She stammered, feeling a weight of tears pushing at the edge of her throat. "No. It was easy enough." To steady herself, she fixed her eyes on the papers littering his desk.

He followed her gaze and, misunderstanding, explained, "Still deep in the throes of study for Sunday's sermon, I'm afraid." He gestured to the Bible. "The text is Mark 10: Jesus heals the blind man. The story's simple enough, but what to do with it is not so straightforward. 'What do you want me to do for you?' That's the question Jesus asked the blind man that day, before he healed him. And I suppose, in a way, it's the hardest question of all to answer, isn't it? What do any of us really want the Lord to do for us?"

"What, indeed." With only the greatest of effort, she held her tears in check. "I'm sorry to disturb you. I… I only wanted to return your hymnal."

She held out the book, and Reverend Elliot wondered if she wasn't trembling slightly as she did so.

"Grace," he ventured at last, "are you quite well today?"

It was the kindness in his tone that finally undid her. The tears pushed past her best efforts to hold them back, and when they came they exploded with overwhelming force. She found herself sobbing uncontrollably, bitterness, anger, grief, and disappointment washing over her by turns. She lifted the book involuntarily to her face and buried her sobs against it.

For his part, the reverend watched her with a gentle but concerned look. If anything in this sudden surge of grief troubled him, not the slightest hint of it appeared on his face. He said nothing for a long time.

"I am so sorry, Reverend Elliot." Her own voice, when it came, sounded to her as though it were coming from miles away. "I don't mean to trouble you. I didn't. It's just, I received a letter from Stephen this morning."

"Ah." There was nothing condescending nor dismissive in his voice, and before she knew it Grace heard herself pouring out the entire story to him.

"He says that he'll be staying in Greece another four months. He's making a tour of the islands, he says, and he'll be home by Christmas. And I'm happy for him, I guess. Only... four months? Home by Christmas?"

"It's a long time till Christmas," he acknowledged. It was simply an observation, but his tone drew something out of her that she hadn't known was there.

"I have waited," she said, trembling again. "As well as I can, I've waited. And I understand what he means when he says that there's nothing for him... no work... here. And certainly, the chance to do what he's doing, where he's doing it, of course I see that such an opportunity doesn't come along more than once in an eternity. I see all that. But it's already been a year. And I've waited. And..."

She looked for something on which to fix her eyes, for fear that the anger seeping now into her grief might overtake her and she'd start sobbing again. Reverend Elliot said nothing but watched her patiently.

When she finally met his gaze, her eyes were red and raw but without tears. "It is a long time," she said. "And if I must, I must. But I don't know if I can, and..."

"And you're wondering if you must?"

Though nothing changed in the kindness of his tone, a great shame flooded over her as she heard the words spoken aloud. She looked down, and her nod was almost imperceptible.

"Grace, you love Stephen deeply. Anyone can see that. And you have been through much together, to be sure. But you and he are not bound together in holy matrimony. No vows were exchanged. I don't believe the good Lord would hold you to him if he is not holding to you. St. Paul says as much in his letter to the Corinthians: 'If the unbeliever depart, let him depart.'"

"I'm not familiar with that one." She smiled weakly, grimly, and the reverend fell silent again. "It's just that he was so good to me, after... he was there for me when I was at my worst, and I don't think I would have made it through without him. How could I leave him now, when he refused to leave me after I... lost... Willie?"

Something in her voice as she said it struck Reverend Elliot, and he repeated it back to her. "*You* lost Willie?"

She averted her eyes. "We all lost him, Reverend. Even Stephen. They were good friends, you know, though Willie was much younger than he, of course. Like a kid brother." Her voice faltered again.

"Grace, do you blame yourself for Willie's death?"

She said nothing.

"And is this—waiting for Stephen—is it a kind of penance for you?"

She looked up quickly. "No. No, of course not. It's only, if I am with Stephen, if I wait for him and I'm here when he returns, however hard it might be, if I am, and I do, maybe then Willie won't have died for nothing. Not if it keeps us together, he won't have."

A sad look, something Grace had not seen before, passed across the reverend's face.

"Or at least," she said faintly, "at least if I still have him, then I won't have lost everything."

They were silent then for what seemed a very long time.

"Reverend Elliot... why does it hurt so much?"

"He was your brother, Grace. Of course it would hurt, very much."

She shook her head. "Not that. I mean, this. All of this—life, and love, and... everything. It's Willie, sure. But it's also Stephen. And it's the ragged men down at the mission. And it's me alone, and my mother's broken heart, and my father. Why does it all hurt so much?"

"Grace, there are many things in this world that are not at all the way the Lord intends, but—"

Grace lifted a hand to cut him off. "Please, don't tell me that God's on his throne, or that he works these things together for His good. I've heard those platitudes any number of times and they don't help." Whether it was grief or anger, she could not tell, but her voice trembled again.

The reverend shook his head gently. "That's not what I was going to say. He does work things together for the good. I believe that. But how he might, or when, is not my place to say. What I can say, what I know, is that the Lord is near to the brokenhearted. And our hurt is his hurt."

Grace kept her eyes averted, and her voice became very quiet. "Before he left, we were together. Stephen and I, we were... alone together. Privately." She felt fingers of red rising at her throat, realizing she was saying far more to her pastor than she had expected to.

"Ah. I see."

She looked into his eyes, cautiously. There was no note of judgment in his voice, only a quiet kind of understanding.

"'I charge you, O daughters of Jerusalem, that ye stir not up nor awaken love, until it so please,'" he quoted, so softly that she could hardly tell if he was speaking to her at all. The words seemed so strange, but they were spoken with such gentleness.

"Does…" She hesitated. "Does that matter?"

"Does it to you?"

"Yes," she said, and she was weeping again. Not uncontrollably this time, but deeply and tremulously, as though something long buried was finally emerging.

The reverend waited until the wave had passed. "Grace, of course I can't tell you what to do. You are certainly not beholden to Stephen. But I do know that no act of faithfulness is ever wasted on God. Of all the virtues, it is faithfulness, I think, that brings us closest to the heart of his Son."

Grace did not fully grasp his meaning, but she found a quietness in what he said. She wiped her eyes furtively and smiled weakly but sincerely.

"Those words you said just now," she asked, "about not awakening love?"

"It's the Song." He gestured to the Bible lying open on his desk. "Song of Solomon, chapter eight, verse four… though I took some liberties with the text. It's notoriously difficult to translate."

"It's very good advice." She had composed herself now, and though her eyes were still very raw, they were dry. She turned to go, but stopped in the doorway and looked back. "Reverend Elliot, does the Lord heal?"

He misunderstood her again. "It won't always hurt like this, Grace."

She shook her head. "No. I mean others. Does the Lord heal other people, when we pray for him to do so? A while back, at the mission, I had a young man ask me to pray for him, for healing. I didn't expect much, but I did pray. And months later I met him, and he was saying God had done so, that he was healed."

She expected a more quizzical look on the reverend's face, but he gestured again at the Bible on his desk.

"There's no doubt the Lord healed many in his time on earth," he said. "And nothing I've read here gives me to believe that he's changed. Not every minister I've known would agree with me on this, certainly, but I see no reason why the Lord couldn't have done for your friend what he says he did."

Grace nodded.

But before she finally left the reverend added, "But I should tell you, Grace, that when the Lord does heal others through us, oftentimes it is our deepest brokenness that he uses to do so."

———————

Grace spent the afternoon at the mission, but that evening she found the crumpled letter and smoothed it out on the kitchen table. She read it through a number of times, and then sat very still for a long time. Finally she rose and found her way into the parlour, where the great family Bible sat in a special place by the chesterfield. She brought it into the kitchen and laid it open, near Stephen's letter. She flipped through the pages slowly, until she found the spot that Reverend Elliot had mentioned that morning.

Song of Solomon, chapter eight. She read it through carefully, and then again, not just verse four, with its sober warning against awakening love before it so desires, but the whole chapter. Some of the imagery caught her off-guard, but something touching and lovely worked in her heart as she read: "Set me as a seal upon thine heart, as a seal upon thine arm," it said, "for love is strong as death; jealousy is cruel as the grave: the coals thereof are coals of fire, which hath a most vehement flame."

She wore a silver locket around her neck, a gift from Stephen shortly after their engagement and not long before he had left for Athens. She had planned to place a photograph of him inside but hadn't been able to find anything small enough, or suitable, and had been wearing it these last ten months empty. She fingered it as she read, and when she reached the end of the chapter, she unclasped it.

She found paper and ink, and in the smallest hand she could manage, wrote out an abbreviated rendition of the verse: *Set me as a seal upon thine heart, for love is strong as death; jealousy is cruel as the grave.* With a scissors, she cut the verse out into a tiny slip of paper and folded it carefully. Closing it in the locket, she clasped it again around her neck and set the words carefully in place, just below her throat.

She closed the Bible gently. There were no tears left in her, and in the emptiness that remained she discovered a quiet resolve. Four months would pass and Stephen would return, and when he did, she knew, he would find her waiting.

CHAPTER TWELVE

Heraklion, September 1938

"*To be abroad, to be an orphan, to be sad, to be in love*
   Put them in the scales and the heaviest is to be abroad
   The man who is exiled abroad should put on black
   For his clothes to match the black fire of his heart..."
   These are the lyrics of a song the men at the digs in Athens
used to sing, translated as best I can from the original Greek.
One of the many they would sing over ouzo in the café after
the work was done. My rough translation misses the ache of
it, though. They would sing it as if it was seeping from some
deep crack in the heart. A "xeniteia," they called it, a song
of exile.

   "*A song for you, Walker!*" *one of them would shout*
sometimes, and then they'd all toast me with a generous gulp
of ouzo. "*A song for the exile from Canada!*"

STEPHEN LOOKED UP FROM HIS JOURNAL AS HIS STEAMER PULLED AWAY
from the harbour at Rhodos Town. While Grace was placing a handwritten token
of her faithfulness in a locket, somewhere on the far side of the world, he stood
on the deck of a boat bound for Crete, watching the sunset bleed its last glorious
rays of red across the sky.

Against the darkening silhouette of the island, he saw the scattered lights of the town glimmering slowly to life. He leaned heavily on the railing of the steamer, his journal propped up against it. He looked down for a long minute into the foaming water along the side of the ship, and then took up his pencil to finish scratching out his lonely thoughts.

Somehow those words are haunting me tonight with a heavy sense of relevance. "Put them in the scales and the heaviest is to be abroad..."

Indeed. I have nothing black to wear, of course, but I feel tonight for the first time since leaving Halifax, maybe, that I am alight with that black fire that burns in the heart of the exile.

Stephen had spent the last week at Rhodos, exploring the sights of Rhodos Town. *Though it was once the site of one of the seven wonders of the ancient world,* he had written on his first night, *this bustling capital of the island bears little vestiges of its ancient glory.*

Later in the week he would make an excursion to the excavations of the acropolis at Lindos, scratching down his impressions in his journal.

The remains of the Temple of Athena provide a wonderful example of late 3rd Century Doric colonnade, but the Italian reconstruction-work going on there is a hatchet job, really, with little appreciation for the true historical value of the place.

From Rhodos, he planned to spend two weeks in Crete, to see the excavations of Knossos especially—and, if time allowed, perhaps a daytrip to Gortyne. From there, a five-day stop to see the black cliffs of Santorini, then on to the Island of Milos, to explore the acropolis of Kilma, after which he would return to Athens. In total, his itinerary had him back by the end of October, after seven stops and some two months of travel.

He had travelled as cheaply as he could, paying for a berth on a cargo ship bound from Athens to Naxos, and then making his way from Naxos to Rhodos by hiring passage on fishing vessels and private boats crossing between islands. Tonight he had paid for deck-seating on a steamer crossing overnight from Rhodos to Crete, and though the idea of sleeping under a Mediterranean sky on the deck of a ship bound for Crete was exactly the kind of adventure he had set out in search of, tonight he felt far too travel-weary to appreciate it the way he once might have.

The steamer lurched slightly, and Stephen closed his pencil in the journal. He straightened himself up from where he had been leaning against the railing and squinted one last time at the setting sun. Tonight it really did seem as though he were burning with the black, lightless fire of exile, and for the first time, almost, since his personal odyssey began last year, he felt a real ache of homesickness.

He thought of Grace, as he often did in these long quiet times of waiting between destinations, but tonight a deep yearning came along with the usual feelings of fondness and whimsy. He had seen so much—the stuff of myth and legend, really—and yet had shared none of it with her. He had sent postcards home, of course, when he could, scrawled with his best efforts to express the wonders he encountered, and his journal was crammed with notes written more as an extended love letter to her than as a mere record of his trip. Often, indeed, he simply wrote down what he might have said to her, if she had been with him when he encountered these things, as though they were somehow recollecting them together.

But she was not with him, and they were not recollecting them together, and tonight, as a humid evening fell heavily over the still face of the Mediterranean and the steamer churned up its luminous wake of iridescent foam, he wanted more than anything to have her there.

He flipped through his journal, letting phrases, dates, sketches, and notes remind him of particular moments in this last year of travel. How empty and meaningless they suddenly seemed to him, standing on the deck of a ship bound for Crete, with the sun like a dying ember on the horizon and he so painfully alone.

He turned to the next fresh page and, holding the book in his palm, took his pen and scrawled out two or three more lines:

What a fool I've been, ever to have left: a wandering restless fool. What have I been looking for here, alone, that I could not have found more richly and more beautifully there, with her? What could I possibly find that could make it worth the months I've been without her?

He looked hard at the words on the page, and then laughed slightly at his own melodrama. He closed the journal again and turned to find a place out of the wind, to see if he mightn't smother that black fire of his heart with sleep.

The morning found him poorly rested, after a fitful night on the deck of the steamer with his baggage as a pillow and his overcoat as a blanket. It had been so damp, and the deck so noisy, that towards four in the morning he had given up on even the pretence of sleep. Wrapping himself in his coat, he tried to shake the stiffness from his limbs by wandering aimlessly up and down the deck. It would be nearly three more hours until the sun rose, fresh and bright on the eastern edge of the dawn. He meandered up towards the bow of the ship, hoping that the slap of salt wind in his face might stir him from his grogginess. He leaned with folded arms on the ship's railing and stared blankly into the blue-grey haze of the western horizon.

Between the growing light behind him and the fading mist ahead, between his dullness from a sleepless night and his impatience for the trip to be done, it was not clear to him when exactly he first became aware of the island on the horizon before him. At some point, however, it had appeared, and despite his weariness he knew it at first glimpse: the mythical birthplace of Zeus, the centre of the Minoan world, the chief among the islands of the Aegean.

Crete.

A stray line from Homer passed quickly across his memory. How had he put it? *"There is a land called Crete in the midst of the wine-dark sea, a fair land and rich, begirt all around with water."* And something, too, about *"many men and many cities."*

Years later, long after his ordeal was ended and he had returned to Halifax, he would never forget this first glimpse of Crete, emerging slowly and somehow beckoning him from the fading mist of an Aegean dawn. Worn though he was, his heart stirred with an indistinct tremor of longing. Dark ridges rose gracefully against the hazy edge of the sea, like the arched back of a dancing youth, he thought, or the sloped shoulders, perhaps, of some ancient god. They became sharper and more distinct as they approached, the colours growing from a dark shadow to a mottled olive to a chalky brown dappled with hard green brush. Soon he could distinguish bright lines of grey and white, sharp with corners and standing out against all the earth tones of the hills. This, he assumed, must be the city of Heraklion.

Somewhere far ahead a gull screamed, wheeling out over the bay.

He made out the dark line of the Koules first, the Venetian fortress that guards the entrance to Heraklion harbour. From the reaching arms of the seawall to the heavy bulk of the kastello, with its bright white tower and jagged battlements, each stood out sharply as they approached. They rounded the mouth of the harbour and a cluster of tall dark lines came into view, along with the naked masts of schooners moored along the pier and a flash of white sails here and there as smaller vessels set out into the morning.

The sun had lifted itself well into the sky by now, and with the fresh morning light warming his back Stephen leaned out over the railing and watched as the boat came at last to dock and the crew worked to secure it. It was a long time before they were ready to disembark, and he was still impatient with weariness, but this first vision of the island, rugged and rising wild into the distance behind the town, was enough to absorb his imagination while he waited.

When at last he stepped from the steamer, the morning had grown hot. He was sweating by the time he had carried his luggage up from the docks and into the town. The streets were crowded now, too. Aproned merchants had opened their shops and were finding their places by their wares. The local kafenion had unfurled their awnings and set out their tables. A few groups of older men had already gathered in the shade, sipping at small beakers of Turkish coffee. One or two of them fingered a set of traditional komboloi, the amber and olive-wood worry beads that older Greek men used to count out the hours, flashing them, bead by bead, over their palm and across their wrist as they watched the world pass by. Crowds of younger men went past, too, laughing and jostling on their way to whatever business the day had in store for them. Some were dressed in the Turkish style, with loose-fitting breeches hanging over knee-length boots, though the younger men were dressed in European jackets and trousers.

The scene was, in fact, very picturesque. White-washed buildings capped with red roofing tiles lined the streets, and brightly coloured awnings shaded crowded walkways. Occasionally a wrought-iron balcony looked out from a second floor, bedecked with flowers or strewn with airing laundry. Here and there a mule waddled by, laden with baggage, and occasionally the crowds pressed back to allow an automobile to rattle through, often with a throng of laughing children chasing behind it.

The city's charm was largely lost on Stephen, his thoughts still clouded with homesickness from the night before and preoccupied with the vague directions the man on the pier had given him when he'd asked where to find lodging. The man had muttered something about finding a hotel near the Plateia Leonton— the Lion's Square—and then gestured broadly up towards the city.

Shouldering his bag, Stephen did his best to follow the route the man had indicated, but by the time he had reached the market district just south of the harbour, he was woefully lost. He stopped at a kafenio and interrupted a game of backgammon to ask the men playing if they could direct him to the Plateia Leonton.

"Ta Liontaria?" said one of them in Greek.

The other recognized Stephen's English accent. "You are looking for the Fountain of Lions?" he offered in thick English. "The Morosini? Yes, we can show." He motioned down the street and then gestured to the left.

The other offered directions in Greek. "Aristera," he said. "Dexia, kai eutheian." Left, then right, then straight ahead.

Stephen nodded and set out again. He turned left where he believed the men had indicated, though the road was really only a narrow walkway between houses. Eventually he came to another left turn, not a right, but he continued along until he was completely lost again.

The path opened up at last into a wide street, but he had no idea if he was closer to the Plateia Leonton than he had been before. He stopped a passerby and asked again.

The man smiled and pointed behind him. "Dexia," he said. "Stripste dexia." Turn right there.

Stephen followed again, and this time the route looked more promising. His right turn brought him out into an open square, crowded with the tables and chairs of the many kafenion lining the street. These were still filling with patrons as the morning waxed. The square was shaded by several stately, broad-spreading trees. There was a soft murmur of talk in the air, and beneath that the faintest sound of clear water trickling over cool stone.

He made his way to the centre of the square and found at last what he could only assume were the lions for which the Plateia Leonton took its name.

It was a stone fountain, intricately carved of white marble. Four stone lions sat on a low pedestal at the centre of a broad, eight-sided pool. Each lion faced out to a different corner of the square and together they supported a stone basin, running gently with water that spilled over and rippled down into the pool. The light danced with the water, jumping up along the marble pedestal and shining like shards of diamond at the lions' feet.

He walked up to the edge of the fountain and stared for a long time into the water. There was something serene, he thought, moving just at the edge of sight in this dance between water and light. From the directions he'd received at the pier, he knew his hotel would be at the far end of the square, but he was overwhelmed now by the heat of the morning, the weight of his baggage, the weariness of the journey, his sleeplessness, and his longing for home. He set his bag down on the fountain's steps and sat beside it, heavily, with his back against the cool marble.

He closed his eyes, fixed his attention on the gurgle of water all around him, and thought of Grace again. The ache he had begun to feel last night had widened now into a gaping wound. As best he could, he imagined her face. It struck him sharply how long the picture took to come, and how dim it was when it did. He inhaled and tried to remember her scent. He tilted his head up towards the sun and felt its light against his closed eyes.

How much he missed her.

"You like the Morosini fountain?"

The voice jarred him from his reverie and he looked up. Not far from where he sat stood a merchant, motioning him over.

"You like the Lion Fountain?" said the merchant. "Very nice. Very famous for Heraklion. The Morosini." He motioned again, so earnestly this time that Stephen felt compelled. He rose and wandered over. The man gestured to a table. "You like? A photographia of Heraklion. For... sending home?"

The table was laid out with a handful of black and white postcards, grainy photographs of various sites on Crete. One he recognized as an image from the excavations at Knossos, which he intended to visit tomorrow. Another was a picture of the Venetian fortress down in the harbour. One or two were portraits of Cretan men and women in traditional dress.

"And here is a photographia of... ta Liontaria..." The man held up a photograph of the Lion Fountain, even as it burbled away in the centre of the square behind him. The image was not sharp, but still it captured the fountain's poise quite well. "A good enthumio, no? A souvenir of Crete, to send home to someone special?"

Stephen smiled ironically: to send something home indeed. He nodded at the merchant. "How much?" he asked.

In Stephen's study, Grace read for the first time the journal entry he had written that night on the deck of the steamer bound for Crete. The words touched her deeply. *"What could I possibly find that would make it worth the months I've been without her?"* Even thirty later, it sounded so typically Stephen, so restless and conflicted.

She turned the page again, and something fell out that had been wedged into the spine between the pages. It was a postcard, a black and white photo of a stone fountain, standing among some trees in a city square. She turned it over. It had never been sent, but it was crammed with Stephen's handwriting.

September 30, 1938

Dearest Grace,

With any luck I will be home to you before this postcard even arrives. I think I will race it back to Canada. I am only sending it now because when it does arrive, I want it to bear witness to my heart today, and my resolve. I spent all of last night on the deck of a steamer, wide awake and thinking, really, of nothing but you. How stupid I've been, chasing God knows what by myself out here when all I've ever really wanted is waiting—how sorry I am to have made you wait, Grace—waiting for me at home. All this to say I've decided to cut short my trip. Today. I will only take the morning tomorrow to visit the digs at Knossos (it would be a shame to have come this far and not see them), and then I will find passage back to Athens tomorrow afternoon. How I miss you, Grace. But barring any disaster I will be back in your arms before the end of the month.

Till then, yours always, Stephen

Grace stared at the postcard for a long time. She turned it over and looked intently at the image of the Lion Fountain.

It bore no stamp. It was not addressed. It had never been sent.

The knowledge welled up in her tremulously. Why had it never been sent? This resolve to come running back to her arms—dated well before the fateful letter she had received from him explaining how he had been invited to do research at the Heraklion Museum on Crete, dated well before the war that would keep them apart for so many subsequent years. She had never seen it before.

For the first time since opening his journal, something very dark passed across her mind, though she brushed it aside almost before she was aware of it. With a trembling hand, she set the postcard down on the desk, beside the journal, and continued to read.

CHAPTER THIRTEEN

Knossos, October 1938

PERCY WAS CLOSE TO THE POINT OF HAVING DRUNK TOO MUCH. STEPHEN had only met him a few days ago, so he didn't know him well enough to say how close, but he knew it was close. The man's grey head seemed to stagger at times with the weight of his words, and sometimes his eyes drifted off randomly before fixing suddenly, if a bit too steadily, on the space between them.

Though Stephen took measured sips at the tumbler of ouzo before him, Percy would drain his glass in three or four generous pulls, and then fill it again from the bottle between them. The liquor weighted his words, of course, but they didn't hobble their eloquence, and Stephen found himself mesmerized by the colourful tapestry of myth and legend they wove.

He had met Percy three days previously, while visiting the Palace of Knossos, just south of Heraklion. After scratching out his heartsick letter to Grace on the back of the postcard he'd purchased at the Morosini fountain, he'd resolved to visit the infamous Labyrinth of Minos just once before finding passage back to Athens and home. It was almost entirely by chance, it seemed, when he met Percy, who worked at the museum in Heraklion and was there overseeing some of the restoration work at the site that day. When Percy learned that Stephen had worked on the digs at the Agora in Athens, he'd offered to take him for a drink.

They had gotten along so famously that Percy had invited him out the following day to view the special collection of artefacts from Knossos, and the day after that, again, to hear the story of the discovery of Knossos, this enigmatic jewel in the crown of the ancient world.

"Schliemann wanted it first, you know," Percy was saying now, between draws at his tumbler of ouzo. He held it poised before him, hovering just beneath his chin while he spoke. "Though Schliemann didn't really discover it." He laughed to himself. "Of course he claimed it was his discovery. He probably even believed it was. But no, he didn't discover it. A Greek—Minos Kalokarinos was his fateful name—was the first to suspect that a ruin of some sort was buried under the mound at Kefala. He dug twelve trenches, trial trenches, and found enough to convince him that he'd found something massive."

While Percy paused to drain the glass, Stephen ventured a question: "Only those twelve trenches, though? He didn't excavate?"

"Oh, he had enough to go on. Great storage jars. Pottery unlike anything seen before. And more importantly…" He set the tumbler on the table as if it were an exclamation point. "The double axes."

Stephen nodded and smiled. "Right. The sign of the labyrs, the double axe."

Percy's head staggered in a tipsy nod. "The sign of the double axe. The labyrs. Right from the start, they knew it was a bloody house of kings."

"But Minos wasn't the one to excavate?"

"The Cretan Parliament cut off old Kalokarinos. Blue-balled him!" Percy began filling his tumbler again, focusing as well as he could on the bottle to steady his hand. "You see, the Turks were still an ominous presence in Crete at that time, and the Cretans were afraid that whatever came out of an excavation would be shipped off to Istanbul—and more likely than not, they were right—so they stopped his dig. But enough of Knossos had come to light to make every antiquities dealer from here to Egypt drool."

"And Schliemann?"

"Schliemann was an opportunistic treasure hunter! He was in his sixties when he first visited Knossos. That was 1866, mind you. It was to be his last great achievement in archaeology. Schliemann was a powerfully driven man, I'll grant you, but he was a butcher of an archaeologist. It was the same hunger for fame and fortune as what had driven his hunt for Homer's Troy. He was there to be the man to discover the mythological Knossos—the Labyrinth of Minos—in all its glory."

"But he didn't excavate, either?"

"It was his own greed—or bull-headedness—that kept him off Knossos. Or maybe a bit of both. He'd made a deal with the Turks who owned the land and was set to begin excavations. But at the last minute, he called it off."

Percy stared for a long moment into the shining liquid in his glass, so long that Stephen wondered if he was expected to say something. Then the man's shoulders began to shake gently with laughter.

"And you know why?" Percy continued. "Because he was told there were two thousand olive trees on the land, and when he counted them there were only eight hundred. Only eight hundred! So he called off the deal." More laughter shook him. "Walked away from the find of a lifetime for the sake of twelve hundred olive trees. He didn't even want the damn things! He was going to dig them up anyway. Bloody fool. He died some years after that, the greatest and the worst archaeologist of all time."

Percy considered his tumbler silently for a moment more, and then pushed it away decisively, as if concluding that he was as close to the point of over-drinking as he wished to come. He looked up at Stephen and grinned.

"And how was it that Evans got to be the one to actually do the dig?" Stephen asked.

Percy leaned back in his chair with a luxurious sigh. "Well, the site just sat there for five or six years. It was his search for the origins of European writing that brought Evans to Crete. He wasn't interested in glory or fame. He was looking for seal stones, of all things!"

"Wasn't there something about finding a Minoan seal in an antique shop in Athens?"

"Well, Evans was trying to understand the similarity between Egyptian hieroglyphs, on the one hand, and the strange script they found on the stones that Schliemann had dug up at Mycenae. He finds some seal stones with a similar script on them in an antiquities shop in Athens. The shopkeeper tells him they're from Crete, so he comes to Crete looking for more. The rest is history."

Stephen toyed with his own tumbler of ouzo, still largely undrunk, and thought back to his first visit to Knossos, some three days ago.

———————

It hadn't taken long for him to find himself hopelessly lost amidst the ruins. As far as he could tell, he was standing at the eastern edge of the central court of Knossos when he finally admitted it. He'd purchased a map at the gate, but the ruins were so sprawling and the rubble so indistinct that he couldn't seem to orient himself. The sun was at its highest, cutting like a razor through the sky and falling hot over Stephen's neck, unstirred by any breeze. The broken pillars and tumbled debris of Knossos marked short, sharp shadows in the dust.

Stephen stepped along the stones, wandering enraptured through this maze of ruins, up the broken cobbles and along the plateau of what he assumed had been the main court. He turned the poorly drawn map again, and then again, but still couldn't make out where he was.

He came to a line of crumbled foundations—the remains of ancient storerooms, he supposed—crossing and intersecting each other symmetrically. To his right rose a short length of reconstructed wall, plastered and frescoed. Though the rest of this section of the palace had crumbled and fallen, Stephen thought he recognized this wall as part of the so-called domestic quarters, labelled on his map. He followed it, passed corridors and dead-ends, and arrived at another reconstructed fragment of the palace. Then came a series of portals, brightly painted in yellow, and a line of tapering pillars crowned with spreading capitals.

Stephen squinted and scratched his head. According to his best take on the map, these pillars ought to have been at the far end of the platform on which he stood, not here. He turned the map again and looked back to try to make sense of how he'd gotten here. At last he gave up the effort. He folded the map, wedged it into his pocket, and started out again, following the ruins more or less at random.

He came to the edge of a ridge marked off and held in place by a crumbling stone wall. A scraping sound reached him as he approached, the cough of a spade through the earth. He stepped up to the lip of the retaining wall and looked over.

The sun glared down against the foundation here, its heat pooling palpably in the air. A young man about Stephen's own age stood close to the wall, labouring over a spade. He wore the traditional garb of a Cretan. Most of the men Stephen had met yesterday in Heraklion had been dressed the same: loose fitting trousers, baggy to the knee, sealed with high black boots. Around his waist the labourer had wrapped a knotted belt of cloth which had been dyed bright red and shone like a single star of colour against the otherwise pitch blackness of his clothes.

Stephen said nothing at first, watching him work. As far as he could tell, the man was clearing away some newly fallen debris from the foundation. His forehead was damp from the digging, his thick black hair clinging to his brow. Because of the heat he had removed his shirt—Stephen could see the black bundle of it draped over a pile of stones behind him—and his torso seemed to shine with sweat.

After a moment, the man stopped and straightened his back. He turned to see Stephen watching him. He plunged the spade upright in the earth and leaned heavily on the handle. He didn't say anything, but he nodded and offered an inquisitive grin while he caught his breath.

Stephen felt suddenly self-conscious and stumbled with his Greek. He asked about the palace's throne room. "Hey aithousa tou thronou?" Where is the throne room?

The man reached for his shirt and pulled it on. "Ho thronos?"

With a slight motion of his hand, he beckoned Stephen down from the ledge of the retaining wall. He began gesturing off to his left, but Stephen shook his head and held out the map.

"Can you show me?" he asked in Greek.

The man took the map. He seemed to realize that Greek wasn't Stephen's first language and tried his best English in return. "Here is north," he said.

He turned his shoulders to indicate the direction and Stephen followed his lead. Then he turned the map to align it with the direction they now faced. He indicated a spot on the map.

"We are here." He moved his finger across the page. "The throne—hey aithousa tou thronou—is here."

The man pointed again at their location, and then across the page to the throne room. He grinned again.

"Wait," he said, fishing a stump of red pencil from his pocket. He marked the spot with an X. "We are here... the throne is here." Another X. He began to trace a red line between the two, thin and winding through the maze of corridors like a thread. "The best way to go... like this."

He traced it a second time, and then folded the map and returned it to Stephen with a grin.

"There you are," he said.

"Thank you." Stephen paused a moment and then said, "I'm Stephen."

The man reached again for his spade. "Stephen?" he repeated, and then gestured to himself. "Ianos. I am Ianos."

That had been three days ago now, and since then Stephen had come to know Ianos as one of the men working with Percy on the restoration work at Knossos. He was a villager from the foothills to the south and had been hired on just last year. It was mostly maintenance work they were doing, the bulk of the excavation having been finished four or five years ago, but Ianos seemed to have a profound curiosity about the ancient past of his homeland.

"Evans began digging in the spring of 1900." In the taverna, Percy was continuing with the story of Knossos. "His first dig lasted about nine weeks— about two hundred men clearing away some two acres of the site. But well before those first nine weeks were up, they knew they'd discovered something *unparalleled*. Every spadeful of earth seemed to reveal some further treasure. He found his writing, too, Evans did. Only a week in, he found a clay tablet with the script on it—what we would come to call the Linear B. But by that point, he knew he had something more monumental on his hands than simply an early form of European writing."

Percy pulled his glass back toward him and gazed into it for another moment, remembering.

"I was just a young officer then, mind you. I was here as part of the British occupation, just as the excavations started in earnest. I was consumed with them, too. Every spare hour I had, I'd walk out here from Heraklion. Sweating like a beast in the bloody heat. And every time I came, something new and fabulous had just been unearthed."

He swirled the drink in his glass but did not raise it to his lips. He stared very intently, as if fixing his gaze on an image long lost to his memory.

"And then, three weeks into the dig, they found it, hidden in the earth like some lost gemstone. The throne room."

Percy paused, long enough that Stephen eventually said it, too, by way of prompting him. "The throne room…"

"I was there, in fact, the day they found the first remains of the walls. Evans was giddy as a schoolboy over a winning game of cricket. It was in severe ruin, of course, the room was. Only some few feet of the walls were left standing, and most of the frescoes lay in fragments on the floor. No one even knew, at first, what it was they'd found. We supposed it might be some ornately decorated chamber, perhaps the royal quarters."

His tone shifted, as though he were reading aloud from old field notes of the dig.

"On the north wall they found the gypsum throne, between the stone benches—no one expected anything so monumental as it was—high-carved back, shaped seat, florid pilasters for the legs. The floor was strewn with alabaster vessels, too. Ritual vessels, they seemed. Could it be, we wondered, the very throne room of Minos himself? How did Homer say it? *A great city called Knossos… there King Minos ruled and enjoyed the friendship of almighty Zeus…*' It seemed to whisper to us. *'Minos… the Father of my father… Minos my father.'* He looked up from his glass, still full, and grinned haphazardly at Stephen. "Well. It is easy to let one's imagination run away, in times and places such as those."

Stephen nodded. "What did Evans make of it?"

Percy laughed. "Oh, Evans was near to wetting himself with wonder. I won't say dancing, but as close as I ever saw him come to it. Giddy as a bloody schoolboy. 'What ceremony?' he kept muttering it to himself, over and over.

'What ceremony? What ceremony?' He believed, you understand, that the last king of Knossos had been performing some desperate ritual or other trying to save the place from destruction—that we had caught him in the act of trying to deliver his people from whatever catastrophe it was that finally froze Knossos in time and left it there, for us to discover, some thousands of years later."

Stephen did his best to picture it all, drinking in the images as Percy poured them out so liberally from his memory.

———

Stephen had found his own way, eventually, to the throne room on that first visit to Knossos, following the red thread Ianos had traced out on his map. Although the room hadn't whispered nearly so hauntingly to him as it must have done the day Evans and the rest had first found it, he could well imagine what they might have heard as they stood there then, in the presence of these ancient and mysterious things, wondering about the hands that had first shaped them.

Hoping to capture something of that mystery, he pulled his journal from his satchel to spend some time sketching the place: the gypsum throne, the lustral basin, the glorious griffins that adorned the walls. He sat in the dust, propping the journal against his knee. Moving his pencil with light, tentative strokes, he traced out the ancient form of that first of kingly thrones, etching out the polished omen of its high back. Under the drawing he wrote, *The seat of Minos' glory.*

Turning to a fresh page, he sketched the griffons from the frescoes. He traced out the lean strength of their leonine bodies, crouched and poised, the upturned shape of their eagle heads, the plumes, the open beaks guarding the throne. His pencil moved lightly and quickly, the image taking shape while his heart, he felt, echoed with beckoning voices, the mysteries of Knossos. It was indeed easy to let one's imagination run away at such times, in such places.

When he finished his sketches, he rose and found his way out of the throne room, through a series of low, narrow stairwells. They brought him out into the west wing of the sprawling ruin, and he followed them up from the shadows of the inner chamber, back and out into the razor-edged light of the sun.

———

"The first man to connect Knossos with the Labyrinth from mythology was actually an American journalist named Stillman," Percy was saying. His voice brought Stephen back from his meandering memories and into the present. "This was long before Evans had even thought of excavating, back when Kalokairinos was still just dipping his toe into the mound at Kefala. He saw how complex it was, what Kalokairinos was uncovering, and the idea that this maze-like building might be the legendary Labyrinth struck him soundly."

"And then there were the double axes."

"Yes, yes. The double axes. They found images of the double axe—which, as you know, the Greeks call the labyrs—carved everywhere. People had made many guesses about King Minos's labyrinth before. The earliest I am aware of goes back to the fifteenth century or so. A fellow named Buondelmonti found the remains of some mines near Gortyne and took them to be the Labyrinth. Stories like that were told and retold, everyone with a different take on the real place behind the myth. But nothing conclusive…"

Percy's glass had sat untouched for so long that Stephen assumed he'd given up on it. But suddenly he raised it—so suddenly that some of it spilled out on the table.

"Then old Kalokairinos digs twelve trenches in a mound outside Heraklion, and they start turning up these labyrs everywhere," Percy continued. "And the ruins… well, you've seen them. They have no bloody end. Corridor after corridor, chambers and antechambers, stairwells and storerooms, all of it marked everywhere with the double axe. It didn't take much to put one and one together."

He tilted the glass slightly towards Stephen, as though toasting the find, or his memory of it; then he put it to his lips and drained half of it with a toss of his head.

"The thought that they'd at last discovered the Labyrinth of King Minos set the archaeological world on fire. Suddenly this dig was more than just some magnificent palace. It was a wellspring of mythology itself, and everyone's eyes began watching to see what else Evans would find. After all, if this was indeed the source of the story, perhaps they would find a King Minos, too, and an Ariadne, a Theseus…"

"And a minotaur?" Stephen interjected, caught up in the enthusiasm of Percy's remembering.

"Oh, they found their minotaur all right. The Bull of Minos, I mean, in all its sinister splendour. At the very heart of the labyrinth they found it."

Stephen understood exactly what Percy meant on this point, for he had found it, too, the day of his visit to Knossos.

———————

He had traced his way through the maze of ruins, stepping among the scattered rubble and crossing the sun-baked central court. He stepped down into the ragged remains of a corridor that brought him suddenly and unexpectedly into the shaded place where the bull fresco was housed. The reconstruction here was complete, the image filling almost the entire length of one wall. A series of brightly painted pillars stood guard, the air laden with a faint scent of cypress from somewhere far away.

Stephen spent a long time at the fresco. He knew it was based as much on the imaginative speculations of the archaeologists who had reconstructed it as it was on the actual fragments of the mural they had unearthed from the site; even so, something about this image of the Bull of Minos enthralled him. It was at once graciously serene and intensely playful, with the fluid slope of its back dancing upwards, the supple flanks taut and lunging, the arching curve of the shoulders balancing the weight. Three slender Cretan youth danced about it, leaping weightlessly and vaulting the tilting horns—doe-eyed maidens, as he imagined Homer might put it—with long limbs glistening, their youthful vitality poised against the lunging energy of the bull.

Bracing his journal against his knee, he raised his pencil again and did his best to sketch out the curving form of the bull and the three bull dancers. His brow furrowed as he drew, working to capture in these thin pencil lines something of the dolphin-like playfulness he glimpsed in the youthful shapes, the floating weightlessness of the bull, like seafoam, perhaps, the arc of its back like a white-capped wave.

He was more than an hour sketching, and once finished he held his sketch up against the fresco itself. It fell short, he knew, of capturing the enigma of the image, but even so, he was satisfied. He closed his book into his satchel again and, after one last whimsical look at the Bull of Minos, turned back toward the squinting brilliance of the day.

———————————

"Because," Percy was saying, finishing off his tumbler and setting it down on the table with a force that stirred Stephen from his memory. "Because, Walker, every myth *happened*, you know? Now, I don't mean that Theseus really slayed some *literal* monster in that maze—what, five thousand years ago?—that there was some real half-bull, half-man beast roaming the corridors of Knossos in Homer's day. Of course not. But that doesn't mean the story isn't *true*."

He did not reach to refill his tumbler. Apparently he had drunk his fill at last, but it was enough. Stephen found it very difficult to follow what he was trying to say.

"Every myth comes to us brimming with something true. A truth about something in here—" Percy leaned forward and placed an unsteady finger on Stephen's forehead. "And in here—" The finger stumbled down to Stephen's chest, landing roughly in the area of his heart. "And if you can unearth that, you will know the meaning of the minotaur. Minos, Daedalus, Theseus, Ariadne— these are all just vessels, really, a way of shaping that truth and breathing it into life, so that it might live beyond the short lives of the ones who first discovered it. We are, after all, no different from them, you know. Five thousand years is a second when measured as the space between human hearts. And it's the myth… the myth is what connects us, with them."

Stephen was trying hard to follow the train of Percy's thought. "And so, the myth of the Minotaur is really about the ancient bull-dancing rituals that happened once long ago in this labyrinthine palace on Crete?"

Percy laughed abruptly. "If you will. But even that's not the *truth* that the myth conveys—that's just the seed it sprang out of. Because even the ancient bull dances were about a truth, something that reached down deeper, and went back further even than Knossos itself."

The man trailed off again. Stephen didn't know him well enough to know what to make of his words, whether they were a sign that his successive tumblers of ouzo had finally caught up with him, or whether they were in fact as profound as they seemed to him in that moment.

Stephen had himself drunk more ouzo that night than he was used to drinking, so he stared at Percy with a somewhat bemused look on his face and said nothing.

———

Stephen had been sitting in the scented shade of a cypress tree when he'd met Percy, late in the afternoon after a long day exploring the ruins. His journal was cradled in his lap and he was working on a last sketch of Knossos before he left for home. He was so intent on his work that he didn't notice the man who appeared by his side and stood for a moment watching him draw.

"You draw with a sharp eye for detail," the man said at last.

Stephen looked up, startled, and with an odd air of guilt he closed the journal shyly.

The man laughed, then crouched down to where Stephen was sitting. "That was a compliment."

As he lowered himself into the shade, Stephen saw him more clearly. His grey head and lined eyes hinted at old age, but his face was brown, coloured by what must have been long days spent under the Cretan sun. It gave him the air of someone younger than his years. He was impeccably dressed, with pristine trousers and a crisply pressed shirt.

Removing his hat and passing the back of his left hand across his forehead, the man offered Stephen a friendly smile.

"Only someone with a particularly keen interest in Cretan antiquities would take such pains to sketch a few heaps of broken rubble." He spoke with a meticulous English accent. "Most people come out to the site, wander around a for bit with the odd ooh or ahh here and there, and then rush back to the tavernas in Heraklion."

"I'm a student," Stephen explained. "Of archaeology. I worked last year on the digs in Athens."

The man smiled. "Well, that explains it then, doesn't it? Don't worry, there are no rules against sketching." He gestured with a sweep of his arms. "By all means!" He was quiet for a moment, thinking, and then: "Have you been on Crete long? As a student of archaeology, there are plenty of sites on this island that I'm sure would suit your fancy."

Stephen found the man compellingly familiar. He started to share far more than he otherwise might have to a stranger, about his work in Athens, his tour of Greece, his home in Halifax. He explained how Knossos was to be the last stop of his journey.

"It's a pity you're leaving so soon," said the man. "There's much more to see on Crete than just the famous Labyrinth of Minos, as fascinating as it is. You could fill that notebook of yours with sketches, if you wished to."

Stephen smiled. "I only wish I could stay longer. But I have people waiting for me at home." He looked at the man closely, the sense of familiarity growing stronger, and reached out his hand. "My name's Stephen Walker."

"And I'm James Percy." He took the hand warmly. "It's a pleasure."

The name stirred Stephen's memory and his vague sense of recognition landed concretely. "James Percy? Professor James Percy, of the British School in Athens?"

Percy smiled broadly. "Sometimes. Though I haven't been in Athens for some years now. I'm currently at the Heraklion Museum, here on the island. Do you know me?"

"When I was in Toronto, you gave a lecture at the university there. In the fall of '33, it must have been. You spoke about the Golden Age of Greece, the Grecian Heroic Awakening, I think you called it. It made a great impression on me."

The man laughed. "Well, Mr. Walker, someone who has had to carry with them for so long the burden of something I said has my deepest sympathy. Perhaps I could make it up to you with the offer of a drink? It's not much, but since this site has become so notorious with the holiday crowd, a taverna opened up just down the road. Unless those sketches can't wait, of course. It would be my pleasure to offer a colleague a drink."

Stephen rose and brushed off his clothes. "Of course. It would be an honour, Dr. Percy."

It was not a long way to the taverna, but the road was hot and their walk dusty, so by the time they arrived their thirst was sharp. Percy ordered them both an ouzo, and they sat in the waning heat of the afternoon, watching it slip gradually into the shadows of evening.

They covered much ground over that first glass of ouzo. They discussed the latest finds at Athens, and also at Delphi. Percy spoke broadly and with intricate knowledge about the various sites worth visiting on the islands. Stephen was especially interested in Knossos and the man's work in the museum at Heraklion, a topic they returned to repeatedly. With a second drink, the professor insisted that Stephen call him simply Percy. After a third, there seemed to be no end to the stories he had to tell, or to his rambling theories about what they all meant.

"Well, the palace itself is really little more than a looted hull," Percy told him that first night. "Stripped of anything worth anything, to tell you the truth. The real treasures of Knossos are the artefacts they pulled from the place. Remarkable stuff, really. Right from the beginning, the finds were so unique, so unlike anything from anywhere else—Egyptian, Greek, Roman—nothing compared to it. They were convinced they'd discovered a culture that predated even the Myceneans. I could show you some of them, Walker, if you weren't leaving tomorrow. They're all in the special collection at Heraklion. You'd find something worth sketching there, I don't doubt it."

Stephen felt a tinge of regret rising at the back of his throat as they continued to talk, and by the time the evening had settled in fully that tinge had become a sharp pang. All the while, Percy's words wove images in his mind of antique splendours and ancient heroics.

When they finally parted that evening, Stephen found his way through the cooling darkness to his room in Heraklion, his mind electric with everything Percy had told him. Even while sitting at last on the edge of his bed, ready for sleep, still his head swam with it all.

The postcard he'd bought at the Lion Fountain the day before lay near his bed, ready to be mailed. He reached for it and read what he had written. He reread it. Then, because he had in fact accepted Percy's offer to meet him in the morning for a tour of the Heraklion Museum, he folded it in half and hid it deep in the pocket of his trousers.

He went to the front desk and booked his room for another four nights.

Just as they had that first night, they now spent another long evening "over a friendly glass or three of ouzo," as Percy put it. In these last three days, the professor had been a gracious guide, showing Stephen all there was to see of the mysteries of Knossos. Stephen had already extended his stay another week, and Percy spoke of hiring him on for intern work, if the money could be found.

Their glasses were empty now, however, and the night growing dark. Percy rose at last, more steadily than Stephen would have expected from the way his words had staggered from memory to memory that night.

"Why don't you come up to the villa tomorrow, Walker?" he said. "I can show you the tablets we've been working on. Do you suppose you might like to have a look at what we've done with the Linear B?"

Stephen rose, too, and though he had not drunk half the ouzo Percy had, he felt his head humming. "Really? Percy, I'd kill to have a look at those tablets."

Percy laughed. "Well, murder won't be necessary; just arrive by nine."

Stephen nodded enthusiastically. "I'll see you tomorrow, then."

Percy clapped him on the shoulder. "Till tomorrow."

The walk back to the hotel in Heraklion took a good hour, and though he was quite sober before it was done, his steps remained light long after the drink had worn off. A thrill coursed through him, more hotly than anything he had drunk that night, to have met in Percy someone who not only shared his passion, but somehow held the key to it. He buried his hands in his pockets, and because they were numb with drunkenness he did not feel the postcard he had buried there as it brushed up against his palm.

CHAPTER FOURTEEN

Villa Ariadne, January 1939

GRACE LEANED INTENTLY OVER THE JOURNAL, LAID OPEN AND BARE before her on the desk. Much of what she'd read was familiar, details she had pieced together both from the many letters Stephen had sent and later from the vague comments about his life on the island he had offered in passing once he'd returned. These, of course, were far fewer than Grace would have liked, but she'd gathered up each one carefully and been able to piece together very much the same story as the one she discovered now in the journal: his first encounter with Professor Percy, the internship at Knossos which Percy had established especially for Stephen, and the six-month stint at the museum in Heraklion, helping to parse out the meaning of the Linear B script.

Though more or less familiar with the story, she had never read it in quite these words before. As she did, details she had never understood began to materialize for her. She had always thought of Percy simply as Stephen's supervisor, but she hadn't grasped how keen a role the older man had played in Stephen's life, taking him into his confidence and mentoring him so closely. Every journal entry that mentioned him did so fondly.

There were parts of the story, too, she had never heard before. The hired man, Ianos, whom Stephen had met on the digs at Knossos, figured prominently in the journal entries from this time, and yet Stephen had never mentioned him. He emerged from these pages a complete and enigmatic stranger to her, and yet, to judge from the journal itself, he and Stephen had become fast friends during his work at the museum. This struck Grace very strangely.

She flipped back a few pages until she found again the sketch of the bull dancers Stephen had made, his drawing of the fresco at Knossos. She smoothed the journal flat before her and stared hard at the picture. A lunging bull tossed about with great, curving horns while three slender youth danced around it, their dark hair waving, their almond-shaped eyes glinting, even in this thumbnail sketch. Two were clearly female, though one seemed male to her. One of the three, the most elegant of all, to Grace's eye, was poised in a sweeping arc, vaulting over the great beast's back. Stephen had always possessed a fine hand for drawing, and the sketch seemed to breathe with life.

She knew the picture, of course. The book he'd left on his desk that last morning before he died had been open to a photograph of the same, and a print of it hung on the wall. *The Toreador Fresco, ca. 1500 BC. Heraklion, Crete.* She looked long at the image, comparing it to the framed picture. It seemed to her in that moment of uncertainty to be the one great cipher that could open to her the meaning of everything she was reading. She squinted at it and turned the journal to view it from another angle. The feeling that this sketch somehow held the answer to finding Stephen again welled up irrationally in her, so strongly that finally she had to turn the page for fear of being overwhelmed by it. Whatever its secrets, the Bull of Minos kept them well hidden.

She flipped ahead to the next entry, dated January 1, 1939.

The work at the museum closed down on Sundays, and of course this was also New Year's Day, so rather than idling over notes and research in his room, as he normally would have done on a Sunday afternoon, Stephen met Percy on the veranda of the Villa Ariadne, where they were both staying, for a game of backgammon. Stephen had never played before, but Percy had insisted that if he were going to spend any serious time on Crete he would eventually have to learn.

They sat down together so he could teach Stephen the basics of the game. The afternoon was cool and the veranda airy, so Percy had brought out a bottle of wine and two glasses.

"There really is nothing like a good glass of Malvasia," Percy said, pulling out the stopper. "The nearest thing to ambrosia that Crete ever produced! A good draught of Malvasia will take the edge off even the worst of a winter's afternoon on Crete."

He poured the glass while Stephen scowled at the board.

"I'm not really sure the best way to start," Stephen said at last.

"It's a game of luck, mostly. But as with most things in life, the better your strategy, the better your luck."

Stephen rattled the dice in the wooden shaker, rolled, and then after another long scowl moved his stones. While Percy took his turn, he leaned back and lifted the glass to his lips. The drink was sweet, and its strength showed on Stephen's face. Percy laughed as he moved his stones and handed the dice back.

"Takes some getting used to, I suppose," Percy said, then watched Stephen take his move. "Remember, Walker, you've got to keep as many points covered as you can, to prevent my moving. But at the same time, leave as few blots as possible."

He took the shaker from Stephen and rattled the dice himself.

"Threes! Remember that doubles count for twice the roll." Percy spread his stones along the board, placing each one down with an enthusiastic clap that jarred the table. "I learned enthusiasm for the game in Turkey," he said after a long sip of wine. "While I was posted there during the war. To watch two Turks play the game, you'd wonder it didn't more often come to bloodshed. An enthusiasm for backgammon is certainly not the least thing the army taught me."

Stephen made his move. "It gave you your first taste of archaeology, did it not?"

Percy examined Stephen's move thoughtfully. "My stationing in Crete, you mean?" He shook his head. "That certainly encouraged me in it, but it wasn't my first taste of archaeology... careful not to spread your stones too thin, Walker."

"What was your first taste, then?"

Percy squinted at Stephen for the slightest moment, and then lifted his glass, pausing for a moment as if in toast. "In some ways, Walker, I wonder if this life—a life in antiquities, I mean, the world of archaeology—if it hasn't been stalking me all my life. It does for some, you understand." He looked hard at Stephen with an indistinct grin. "Stalk us, I mean."

Grace read the journal entry a second time. It was short, simply noting that Stephen and Percy had spent the afternoon drinking Malvasia and playing backgammon on the porch of the villa. It also included a discussion of the Linear B—whenever she came across these in the journal, they seemed unnecessarily opaque—and a line or two about how fine a mentor Percy was to him.

There wasn't much of substance there, but she read it a third time, because it prompted so vividly and unexpectedly the memory of her own New Year's Day, 1939.

She had spent the better part of New Year's Eve at Margaret's house. She and Beth had organized a small get-together, mostly of old friends from the circle at St. Chris's. More than a year earlier, Beth had married a young man named Wallace whom she'd met at Normal School in Truro where she had done her teacher's training. She never did go on to teach, however, as she and Wallace had their first child that summer. They had left little Wallace Jr. with her parents for the evening. Beth had been in especially high spirits, because this was their first evening out alone since becoming parents.

Richard was there too. Grace hadn't seen him since the spring, when his first tour with the Royal Navy had started. He had followed his father's footsteps into the navy, and, though he was stationed in Halifax she hardly saw him anymore. He was posting in the morning, heading off into the Atlantic for another six months.

There were a few others, some of whom Grace did not know. Katie was there, from the mission, and Stephen's sister Jane arrived later in the evening. The parlour of their house was crowded and stuffy. The front windows, looking out onto the snow-sodden streets of Halifax, fogged over with the heat of happy bodies pressed into a space too small for them.

Margaret's father had given her mother a new portable gramophone for Christmas. They didn't have many phonographs—*Shortnin' Bread* by the Andrews Sisters, and a couple of Artie Shaw records—but no one minded the repetition, and the music swayed and swung over them as they all chatted warmly.

Towards the middle of the evening, someone produced a flask and they passed it around with no small amount of bravado. It came to Grace, too, and she did take a reluctant sip, but mercifully it burned so that she would not take another, and it set her to coughing so badly that no one would pressure her to.

"I'll take that from you, Grace," said Richard with a robust laugh. "If you're not having any, I guess I'm drinking for two now!" He took a pull at the flask and made a face, followed by a very faint gasp.

"And you'd better drink for two, Dickie!" called out Beth. Grace had never heard her call him Dickie before, but she herself had taken one or two more sips at the flask than she was probably used to. "You head out to sea tomorrow and it'll be a lonely six months till you're home again! Maybe the drink will keep you warm at night, 'cause there won't be much else to!"

The room laughed, and Richard too, though Grace wondered if a very faint sadness didn't first pass across his brow. He caught her watching him and, with a childish grin half-cocked on his face, lifted the flask as if to toast her, taking another sharp swig.

"And what a pity Stephen couldn't be here!" This was Beth again, talking far more loudly than she might have. "What is old Stevie up to these days, Grace?"

She feigned a smile and looked down. "Well, he's still only two months into his internship, on Crete." She said it quietly, but then looked up and affected a pleasant tone. "He is doing wonderful stuff at the museum there, from all I can gather from his letters. He does write me every week, you know. He tells me he's working on deciphering some ancient form of writing—something they call 'Linear B,' whatever that is—and that they are very close to a breakthrough."

"And any word on when he'll be home? Oh, you must simply pine for him!"

She knew Beth didn't mean to be cruel, only that her head was beginning to hum now, so Grace feigned another smile and nodded.

"Daily!" she said, far more affably even than she had meant to sound. "He won't be home till after summer. But as they say, absence makes the heart grow fonder."

Percy rattled the dice again, and then paused thoughtfully before rolling them out. "Did you know that I once met Heinrich Schliemann?" he said all of a sudden. "I was only a child at the time—I'm not as old as all that—but I did meet him. My father was travelling in west Turkey. He was in the army in those days, just like his son after him, and he visited Schliemann's work at Troy. I remember next to nothing: the intense heat, the dust of the Troad, mostly. My father held me by the hand and I remember him explaining that this was a very old city they were digging up."

He looked at his roll.

"Four and one," Percy said, moving a stone to an empty point and closing it with another.

"And Schliemann?"

"Like I say, I remember very little, but I do remember a man in a clean white suit, whom my father seemed to regard as very important. I was shy of him because of his voice—the German accent, I suppose—and he showed us around the site. Schliemann would do this with visitors, you understand, boasting about his discovery of 'Homer's Troy.' And I followed as best I could, clambering over the stones and thinking it all very dusty and hot. But Schliemann did something that will be forever engrained in my memory. He crouched into the dust, so as to bring his eyes level with mine and placed his hands on my shoulders. I remember being very afraid, this strange man bringing his face so close, and speaking with that voice. And then he said something that simply rang in my head... Are you going to roll, Walker?"

Stephen had lost himself in the story. "Sorry," he offered, rattling the dice and making his next move. "But what did he say to you?"

Percy took a sip of wine and set down the glass quietly. "Get the hell off those stones, little boy!" he suddenly, affecting a German accent as closely as he could. "Those are thousands of years old and not a playground!" He started to laugh. "Oh, the man really was mad! I cried and rushed back to my father, and after that I was too terrified to leave his side."

"And that was your first taste of archaeology? A crazed German screaming at you on the Troad?" Stephen was laughing, too.

"Not the typical story, I admit, but like I say, this world sort of stalks you. Schliemann used to say that when he was seven his father gave him a book of Greek mythology, and a picture of the destruction of Troy so captured his imagination that he asked about it. His father explains to him that it's Troy, and it was destroyed thousands of years ago, and then and there, according to Schliemann's own telling of the tale, he decides that he will be the one to discover the lost city of Troy."

Here Percy lifted his arm and deepened his voice in a pretence towards the dramatic.

"And thus was born the world's greatest archaeologist. Well… that was the kind of romantic rot that Schliemann loved to tell about himself. Rubbish, if you ask me. And it was that kind of romantic rubbish that characterized his work through and through. When Dorpfeld went on with the work at Troy, after Schliemann's death, he found that Schliemann had actually destroyed most of Troy looking for treasure, and that what he had called 'Homer's Troy' was really a much later city built on the same site. The butcher. He'd actually dug away most of the real Troy looking for it."

Percy paused to take his turn.

"So instead of archaeology you went into the military?" Stephen asked.

"Like my father, and his before him. The army is a Percy family tradition. I went in when I was eighteen. 1899. They stationed me in Crete just as the dig at Knossos was getting underway. Everyone was talking about it, and the first time I went up to see the work, I was hooked. No one yelled at me this time, mind you, but I came up to Knossos every chance I had, to watch and help where I could. I was here until the fall of 1906. Most of the work was done by then, and the occupation of Crete was lifted. After Crete, I put my military career on hiatus, much to my father's dismay, and went to study at the newly formed British School in Athens. Do you know, I went back to Troy, too, years later as part of a team working with Dorpfeld, to patch up Schliemann's butchery?" Percy moved his stones with another slap on the board. "So I was in Turkey when the war broke out, and the army reclaimed me. That was where I learned to appreciate a good game of backgammon."

"And after the war?"

"As I say, the world of archaeology stalks you, when it wants you. I couldn't get away. I worked with the French at Delphi for a while, and later returned to Athens. But Crete kept calling me: the island, the Minoans, Knossos. I came back to Crete in 1930, I think it was, to work on the translations of the Linear B tablets. Well, that was—what, nearly ten years ago? And we're still no closer to cracking that nut."

"With all the work going on these days in this part of the world, it's a bit of a wonder to me you're holed up in a museum working on the Linear B—"

Percy laughed somewhat incredulously. "I'm hardly 'holed up,' Walker. The Linear B tablets may very well be man's—at least European man's—first attempt to set down his cares, his thoughts, his passions, in words. Think of it: the origins of human writing itself! Find that and you'll have your hands on something that puts all the potsherds from here to Rome to shame. Walker, this is where archaeology is at its best. Any two-bit grave robber can dig up a few antique bobbles and sell them to the highest bidder. But the meaning behind those bobbles, the hearts that fashioned them and have long since faded from memory—what they longed for, what they feared—Walker, no one can get at that but by getting at the words they left behind. That, there, is the ultimate human connection with the past."

Stephen recognized this effusive burst of eloquence. He had heard Percy talk like this before, and he wondered if the Malvasia wasn't starting to catch up to him.

"But you understand this," Percy said. "I've heard it in your voice, when you wonder out loud over what in hell that Phiastos Disk was for, or who the Snake Goddess really is. I saw it in your eyes the day you looked at the Linear B tablets for the first time. You're after that human connection, too. You keep doing the work you're doing, and you'll find it. I've no doubt."

Grace walked Richard home that New Year's Eve; he was quite drunk by the time midnight arrived and the crowd in Margaret's parlour held hands to stumble their way through a clumsy rendition of Auld Lang Syne.

Beth and Wallace left directly after the song, with some good-natured joke about how they would have liked to have stayed and helped with poor Richard, but they already had a baby to take care of at home.

Grace laughed amiably and gave her friend a warm hug. "Go home," she said, "and give that little angel a kiss for me. I'll make sure this one gets to bed all right."

She waited until the last guest was gone and then helped Margaret with some perfunctory straightening up of the place before finally helping Richard into his coat and boots, bundling him in his woollen scarf and pulling a knit cap over his head. He stood there somewhat dazedly, still warm with what he had drunk that night, and quite pliant to Grace's directions.

"Come along, Richard," she said at last when they were both ready to go. "Say good night to Margaret and let's get you home."

"Peg—" he started with an indistinct wave.

"Don't you 'Peg' me, Richard," Margaret interrupted. "You've never called me 'Peg' in your life and you're not going to start now! Now be a good boy and let Grace get you to bed."

The night was very clear and cold when they finally found themselves in the street. The moon was waxing, and its crisp light somehow sharpened the touch of the cold against their cheeks and noses. It seemed to sober Richard slightly. He still walked with uncertain steps, leaning against Grace's body to steady himself as they went, but his words at least were more lucid than they had been.

"Grace," he said after a moment. "This is so kind of you—I must say, you've always been far more kind to me than I deserve."

He rested his head wearily on her shoulder, his arm clinging to hers for support. And because she knew what Richard had drunk that night—and because she knew that by week's end he would be heading out again into the loneliness and danger of life at sea—she did not shrug away the gesture.

"After what you've had to drink," she said, "I don't suppose it would be that hard to treat you more kindly than you deserve." She was not at all reproving, only gentle and perhaps a bit playful.

"No!" Richard's head lolled a bit unsteadily from side to side. "No, Grace, I mean it. I've always thought that, you know, that you are too kind. Too kind. Stephen is lucky to have you."

She fell quiet for a moment and put her far hand up against his chest, to steady him over an icy patch on the street. "I suppose we are both lucky."

"Do you know, Grace, that I have always thought Stephen was the luckiest man in the world to have you?" He leaned in close to her ear, as if to whisper this like a conspiracy between them.

She shrugged him off this time, but only because he was in fact speaking far louder than he realized.

"No, it's true," he insisted, laughing. "It's true! And I'm not shy to say it, but do you know that I've always sort of envied him?"

She felt something shut tightly inside her, close off abruptly, as she heard him say these words, but still she held him up, compassionately.

"Have you indeed, Richard?"

"Don't get me wrong. I know you're mad about him and he about you. I understand. But even so—" He trailed off unsteadily, as if staggering about for the words. "Even so, I have always carried a flame for you, Grace."

He leaned his head on her shoulder again, but very innocently now, like a baby brother leaning against a far older sister, perhaps, and she let him do so.

"Oh, don't be ridiculous, Richard," she said at last, but not dismissively or cruelly. She stared at the ground for a long time, watching over his unsteady steps as each one found its way in front of the other. "And anyway, you'll be leaving for your next tour in a few days. Who knows what lovely belle or other you'll meet at your next port of call? Save your flame for her..."

"But this is why I'm saying it, Grace! There's a lot of talk these days, about Germany and the troubles over in Europe. Hitler has already taken Austria, and they're saying Poland is next. My father says that the signs are all pointing to war—that it's just a matter of time."

He sounded far more sober suddenly than he had any right to be, but still he had to stop here to steady himself, teetering slightly as he did. Grace lifted her hand instinctively to the bangs of his hair, brushing them back from where his hat had plastered them down over his brow. Another instinct in her prompted her to hush him.

"Shhh, Richard. Shhh... please don't." She added this last part almost inaudibly, and started him moving again.

"Father predicts something will happen by spring, but even if not, it's coming for us eventually, Grace. And it's dark out there. And I wouldn't want to head out into it without at least telling you, that I am carrying a flame for you as I go..."

He fell quiet after this, mercifully.

Grace said nothing for a long time, but she kept his feet shuffling forward through the cold. At last she spoke, and as best she could she affected an air of levity. "You must have had more to drink tonight than even I suspected, Richard."

They didn't say much the rest of the way, but when they finally arrived at Richard's home he didn't let go her arm immediately.

He turned towards her. "Grace, you really are too kind. And I meant what I said… No!" he added quickly as she opened her mouth to interrupt. He lifted his hand between them, to stop her from stopping him. "No, I meant it. I understand, and I won't pry, and all that, but I need you to know that I am carrying a flame for you."

It was dark, and Richard was still drunk, so he didn't see the sad struggle that shadowed her face in that moment.

"Oh Richard, please don't."

He leaned forward and stumbled into her arms for an embrace; it was very warm but also very innocent.

"Stephen is too lucky to have you, and you are too kind," he whispered.

Grace hesitated a fraction of a second, and then lifted her arms around him. She hugged him warmly in return, and then, after a short pause, squeezed him very tightly in her arms, as if for the briefest of moments she clung to him desperately. Then she placed her palms against his chest and pushed away.

"And you are too sweet," she said, keeping her eyes down for fear he would see how they glistened. "And too drunk. Go to bed, Richard." Just before he turned to go, she added quickly, "But do know that I will be praying for you, whatever may come."

Whether or not he heard this, he turned without saying anything more. She watched him pick his way up the porch and through the door, and then turned to find her own way home.

By the time the afternoon began to cool, Stephen and Percy had finished their game of backgammon and were working on their last sip of Malvasia. Percy had won again, quite handily. He had continued to coach Stephen along the way, however, and Stephen was playing as much to learn as he was to win, so he didn't mind the drubbing he received. How to take a drubbing in a good game of backgammon was only one of many things Percy had been coaching him in, and he had come very much to appreciate the comradery of his mentor.

"It really is a shame you can't stay past the spring, Walker." Percy peered thoughtfully into his empty wineglass. "At the rate you're going, it'll be time for you to leave before you become any sort of a challenge in backgammon. Give it a few more months of training, though." He whistled softly and looked up with a grin. "And there's the work, too, let's not forget. There's still a lot to do at the museum, as you well know, and you do have a knack for it, though I won't say there's not a lot you could learn there, too. If you wanted to stay on permanently, you know I could find the money for it."

Stephen looked out over the tops of the pine trees that encircled the grounds of the villa. "Percy, you know we've been over this. I really can't. I've already been away far longer than I intended."

"I'm simply saying that you've a real talent for this work—a calling, if you prefer to spiritualize it—a vocation, let's say. I've seen it. Your help really has been invaluable, and it would continue to be so."

"No, I understand. It's just, I do have people waiting for me at home."

"Your family, you mean?"

Stephen looked down pensively. "Well, we don't speak much anymore, though I do have someone, and I have kept her waiting for a very long time."

"Grace?"

Stephen had told Percy just enough about Grace that he could see quite clearly what he meant. He nodded, still watching the pines. A breeze sighed through them, setting them to swaying.

"Does Grace know?" Percy asked.

"Know what?"

"The heart you have for this kind of work? The passion and the pleasure that's in it?"

Stephen smiled, remembering. "Oh, she knows. She understands."

"But you love her, don't you?"

The sighing of the breeze reached a crescendo and then stilled suddenly. Stephen nodded softly. "I do," he said at last, and he felt a heavy weight sink in his chest.

Percy looked at him not unkindly for a long time. "Then you're a man torn, aren't you, Walker? You can't go home, but of course you can't stay either."

Stephen shook his head resignedly. "No," he acquiesced. "No, I can't stay."

He drained the last lingering drop of Malvasia and began closing up the backgammon board.

In the study, Grace read the entry Stephen had written that night:

Percy offered me a permanent post at Heraklion today. Said that he could find the money for it if I wanted to stay on after the internship ends this summer. How I longed to say 'yes.' How indeed. But I can't, of course. It would not be right. And I couldn't do that to Grace. I promised I wouldn't.

She looked up from the journal and closed her eyes, remembering the promise he'd had in mind when he had scribbled down those words.

The night before Stephen had left for Athens, on their last night with each other, they had lain together, in her bed, in her parents' house. Mr. and Mrs. Stewart had attended a formal dinner that night and would be out late, and Grace had suggested that he might come by for a final goodbye. Her mother and father had hesitated noticeably when she mentioned the idea, but she was a grown woman now, of course, and anyway, he would be away for almost two years. Mom had even made tea and prepared a tray of treats for them to share, setting them out in the parlour and reminding Grace discretely but quite clearly that the two of them ought to remain in the parlour for the evening.

They had meant to. But they had still been quite young and very much in love, and before either of them had finished a second cup of tea they found themselves—almost before they realized it—holding one another tightly behind the closed door and pulled drapes of Grace's room. The light was dim, but not quite fully dark, and when it was over they lay for a long time on the bed, nestled against each other and staring silently into the twilight of the room. Stephen ran his hand thoughtfully through her hair; hers rested lightly on his chest. His shirt was still open, and his skin felt quite warm to her.

"Promise me you won't forget me there," she said at last, very quietly, a whisper offered more to the darkness than spoken to him directly.

He didn't say anything right away, though she could sense his weight stir beside her.

She pressed her hand down on his bare chest and said it again, earnestly but softly: "Please promise me, Stephen."

"Grace…" He was whispering, too. "Grace, of course I will never forget you. What a thing to say. You are my heart… my life…"

She slid her hand into the fold of his open shirt, down along his side, and pulled her body as close in against him as she could. He seemed slight to her, as she came against his weight, slender and warm but somehow fading.

"No. Stephen, please promise me. I know you love me. That's not what I mean. It's just that you'll be in Greece, there, and you'll have all sorts of strange adventures. You'll see all sorts of exotic things, and it may be that when you finally come home, you'll forget this. Being warm and in love and together like this, or if you don't forget it, it will seem just so ho-hum and ordinary to you. I—" she hesitated here, because it was difficult. "I may seem ho-hum and ordinary."

Stephen shifted his weight so that he was leaning over her in the bed and looking down into her eyes. He was about to speak, but she lifted her finger to his mouth to prevent it, and continued.

"And so, I want—I need you to promise—that whatever you find on the far side of the globe, you won't forget this—me—us—here in each other's arms like this, and how good and true it is."

She trailed off, feeling suddenly very silly, but there was only a look of compassion in Stephen's face, no hint of reproach.

"Grace—" He leaned down against her as if he were gathering her into himself. "Grace, you are the soul out of my soul."

"Your epi—psy—" She had forgotten the word, but Stephen laughed and supplied it. "My Episychidion. This soul—"

His hand found hers and held it tightly as he said it. "*This* soul out of *my* soul. And I will never forget that."

Grace smiled faintly, still feeling somewhat silly but also very tender towards him. "Do you promise?"

He reached forward and kissed her forehead gently. "I promise."

In the study, Grace opened her eyes and looked about her. The memory was still so vivid that it took a moment to regain her bearings. The journal lay open before her, the words almost staring back at her with an air of accusation: *I couldn't do that to Grace. I promised.*

And but for the outbreak of the war, she knew, he would have kept that promise.

A feeling of unexpected guilt welled up in her and she almost closed the journal. But the unmailed postcard still lay in one corner of the desk, and the framed photograph of the Toreador Fresco still looked down from its spot on the wall, identical to the sketch she had seen in the journal, and a longing to know overcame her.

She turned the page and came to something that she had never heard him speak of before.

PART III

Labyrinth

CHAPTER FIFTEEN

Ianos

THE THUNDERING RAIN HAD BEGUN TO WANE, LEAVING EVERYTHING DAMP and cool. It still drummed softly about the house, but the noise was only a faint echo of the outburst of storm that had roared to a climax only moments ago.

Stephen sat on the porch of the Villa Ariadne with his journal propped up against his knee, waiting for Percy to emerge. He watched the silty runnels of rainwater as they seeped and foamed their way down the path through the gardens, then took a deep breath of the humid morning air and resumed his writing.

A sudden spring shower, waiting for Percy at the Villa Ariadne, in which I find a moment to sit and reflect. It is hard to believe that only two months now remain of my internship—a short summer to go and then I will have to return. This year at the museum has been more than all my greatest aspirations could have imagined.

Today Percy has arranged for us to visit Gortyne and Phaestos, Minoan ruins similar to Knossos, though far less well-known. We plan to spend the night at Phaestos, and perhaps visit Ayia Tiadha in the morning. Ianos is coming, too, as our driver. Hopefully this rain will pass soon. I expect it will: rain seldom lasts long on Crete.

At last Percy appeared at the door. He stood beside Stephen and watched the rain as it sputtered out.

"Ianos will be here soon. He is surprisingly punctual for a Cretan." He cast a grin at Stephen. "I just hope this rain lets up some. It will be a mess out at Gortyne if it doesn't."

Stephen closed his journal and placed it in the bag on the floor by his chair. "How long should it take us to reach Gortyne?"

"It's not more than thirty miles to the southwest, though the mountains lie between us, and the road is winding. Depending on how much this rain slows us up, it could be anywhere from two to three hours till we get to Gortyne, and Phaestos, the real beauty, is still a good half-hour beyond that."

The clouds had indeed stopped raining and were even beginning to part somewhat when the reckless rattle of an engine finally announced Ianos's arrival from the drive. They took their baggage and walked out to meet him, finding him perched and grinning behind the wheel of a particularly decrepit-looking lorry, the museum's 1927 Albion. It was well-worn from its long and varied years of service, rusted in parts, and splattered now with mud from the recent rain. Stephen cast Percy a look.

"Well, I admit it's no Rolls Royce," Percy acquiesced. "But it's the only vehicle the museum owns. I was barely able to get my hands on it as it is. Don't worry though, Walker, it'll get us there and back again."

The back of the lorry was covered with a canvas, and Ianos stepped down from his perch to help them load their luggage under it. He was dressed very much the way he had been the first day Stephen had met him. Black breeches hung loose about his lean frame, pinched below the knee by high black boots. His close-fitting shirt was held in place by a bright red belt of woven cloth. His thick dark hair fell in curls over his forehead, jutting out playfully from beneath a tasseled cap. The corners of his dark eyes crinkled into a smile.

"All is ready to go, Mr. Percy?" he asked in heavily accented English.

"All's ready, Ianos. How are the roads looking?"

"They are very wet, but our lorry will make it fine." Here he brought his hand against the side of the truck with a kind of determined affection. Clearly Ianos enjoyed driving this vehicle very much. He turned to Stephen. "And you? You are ready to see the beautiful places of our island?"

Stephen hefted his bag into the back of the lorry. "Very much so. I've been here five months already, and I feel like I've spent all of them in hiding at the museum."

"If you wish to see the real beauty of this island," Ianos said, speaking quickly and fluidly in Greek, "I could show you some real beauty. Crete has many beautiful things to see besides ancient ruined stones. If you wish, I could show you—"

Percy clapped Ianos on the shoulder. "Not today, Ianos. Today Gortyne." He said this in Greek, and then, turning to Stephen he said in English, "Ianos comes from a village called Apodoulou. It's a lovely place. Quaint, like most villages in Crete are. Quainter than most, maybe. But like all Cretans, he's convinced that the most beautiful place on the planet is the town of his birth." He cast a teasing look at Ianos. "Though in his case, he may not be far off."

All three of them fit into the cab of the lorry, but only barely, and they had to wedge themselves in, shoulder to shoulder as best they could. Ianos took the wheel while Percy navigated, and Stephen found himself pressed uncomfortably between them.

The road meandered south through the cultivated folds of Crete's lower hills. Quite clearly Ianos relished this opportunity to drive the old truck, speeding along with great gusto. Soon the road rose very steeply and began to ascend the first ridge of the mountains.

"Look north!" Percy shouted to be heard over the roar of the engine and the jostle of the ruts in the road. "Look north behind us as we crest this ridge. The view from here is unforgettable!"

The road wound out from beneath the lee of the first rounded peak. Slowly the sea came into view, slate-grey from the passing of the storm but beginning to sparkle here and there as the sun broke through the tattered clouds. The slopes of Crete, rough with dark patches of cypress and myrtle, tumbled down from this height to meet it.

"The view that conceived a civilization!" Percy's voice rose loud over the noise of the engine. New hills were rolling up and the brooding panorama slipped from sight behind them. "And if I were King Minos, I'd have set up shop here, too!"

Ianos grinned and shoved the lorry into a lower gear; it groaned with protest as it surged over this first crest and into the mountains beyond.

They were approaching a cluster of stone buildings, whitewashed and brilliant in the sun, perched in ascending steps up the side of the mountains.

"Here is the village of Patsides," Ianos called out as they rumbled through. "Very lovely. Very typical of Crete."

The road wound on, passing other such sights as they continued to climb. They clattered past an old woman riding a battered donkey down the hill, then a young boy driving a bedraggled herd of goats. Yet higher they went. Brilliant flashes of colour often dotted the slopes: wild thyme's bright purple, the deep yellow of cerinthe, the fiery violet of echium. Percy named these all as they went.

They approached the very summit of the range, where the road wound precariously along the sharp edge of the mountain, clinging to its terraced slopes. Stephen leaned over Percy to look out the window and felt as if his breath had gone tumbling down the hillside, which dropped off far more steeply than he had expected. In the valley below, a lingering mist drifted through the patches of thick scrub that pocked the landscape.

"We're near the top!" Ianos said, flashing a bright smile. "Very high!" The engine roared pathetically as he found the lowest gear and urged it to the summit. He reached out with his left hand and gestured at the sweeping landscape. "Mr. Percy speaks about the beauty of Crete? Here she is in all her glory."

The road wound west now, and Ianos began pointing out more and more of the sights as they came into a broad flatland, what he called the Messara Plain. The air was scented heavily here. Even over the oily smell of the lorry's interior, Stephen caught the fragrance of wildflowers and pine resin.

"Here is the heart of Crete. Ahead lies Liviko Pelagos—the Lybian Sea—behind us the Oroseira Dikti—the Dikte Mountains." There came a light in Ianos's eye that Stephen had not seen before, and the man began telling him about his own village, with a note of ardour in his voice that even the roar of the engine could not drown out. He traded glances between Stephen to his left and the road ahead, grinning broadly all the while. "We have the finest orchards in all of Crete. And our vineyards produce the most excellent wine. Soon the martolouloudia—the yellow bloom of the vineyard—will be in full flower, and that is when my village is most beautiful. You wish to see the beauty of this island, Stephen? I tell you, my village is the jewel in her crown!"

Percy laughed over the noise of the lorry. "Careful, Walker! You don't know the dangers of starting a Cretan on about his hometown. This could take us hours. And it won't end until the outsider—in this case, you—agrees to test the claim by visiting the place itself. The hospitality of Crete is as unavoidable, you understand, as it is famous!"

Ianos ignored this remark—or perhaps he was emboldened by it, for he flashed an even wider grin towards Stephen. "Should you visit me in my village, Stephen, there we would share a good bottle of raki at my father's table, and you would agree that there is no more beautiful place in the world than Apodoulou."

Something in the tone of his voice made it easy for Stephen to take him at his word.

———————

Within a few hours, the road wound down and among another cluster of brightly painted buildings, swatches of perfect primary colours flashing past them as the lorry rumbled along.

"Here is the Ayia Dheka," Ianos explained, gesturing out his window with a slight nod of his head.

Stephen translated it. "The Holy Ten? It's a peculiar name."

"It is named for the ten... the ten..." He looked to Percy, at a loss for words. "Martyres?"

"The Ten Martyrs," Percy said. "The word's the same in English."

"Yes. Ten Martyrs. Ten villagers refused to worship the Roman gods, long ago, and they were killed for it. There is a church here where we keep the stone where their heads were cut off. And tombs, also."

Stephen did not linger long on the story. "And this is where the ruins of Gortyne are?"

"They call this place a living museum," Percy explained. "The village has somewhat absorbed the ruins of the ancient Greek settlement into its own buildings. You'll find here and there ancient columns, or what have you, built into the modern structures. It's a scandal, really, the mess they've made of the site. But the most significant ruins are yet outside the village."

They followed the road north and west, along a shaded avenue lined with lolling olive trees, until they came to the far edge of the village. Here they stopped their lorry and set off on foot through fields ragged with long grass and scrub. The sun had grown hot by now, and any water that might have been left by the morning's rain had long since burned away. The air was sharp with the scent of cypress, and in the distance they could hear a muttering herd of sheep.

As the first tumbled stones of the Gortyne ruins came into view, Percy began to point out and explain every notable site and structure.

"This is the Nympheon." He pointed to a ridge of sun-bleached stone scattered among the trees. "There's the ancient theatre," he said, gesturing towards a crumbling basin ringed with fractured teeth of white marble. Every random block of stone, it seemed, had some enigmatic name or mysterious import. "Here's the temple of Pythian Apollo. There's the sanctuary of Isis—that's the Egyptian influence there. Here is the Praetorium, though much of that is a later work, from the second or third century."

They came to a semicircle of stone, a curving wall that marked the ruins of the Odeon. The wall was low and worn, but its face had been etched with the characters of an unfamiliar script. As Stephen ran his fingers lightly over the mysterious letters, their angular lines seemed somehow impervious to the passage of time and weather, as if they always had and always would be there.

"This is the so-called 'ox-plough' script," Percy said. "The code dates back to the fifth century B.C., we think. It was the Italians who found these stones and reassembled them the way you see it now. As far as we know, this is one of the earliest law codes in the western world. This is the prize possession of Gortyne, Walker. A most remarkable find."

Ianos grinned mysteriously and shook his head. "There is, you know, a more wonderful thing to see in Gortyne than these old stones."

Stephen looked up at him from where he had crouched to examine the wall. "How do you mean?"

"There is the Labyrinth."

Stephen looked uncertainly at Percy. "The Labyrinth? I thought Knossos was the site of the Labyrinth. You know, the house of the labyrs and all?"

Ianos laughed. "But Crete has many labyrinths, Stephen. A labyrinth for every man. Knossos is Mr. Percy's labyrinth. But this, too, is one of them. Would you like to see?"

"Do you know what he's talking about?" Stephen asked Percy.

Percy was elusive. "Go with him and see."

"Will you come?"

Percy tilted the shade of his hat down over his brow. "No," he said, leaning back to rest against a low stone. "Ianos's labyrinth is too far a walk for an old man like me. You go on ahead. I'll make my way back to that taverna we passed in Ayia Dhkea. You can find me there when you're done."

Ianos had already begun following a trail that led up from the ruins, making his way north and west. He turned and gestured, and Stephen set out to join him.

The walk was longer than Stephen had expected, through gnarled bush and up hazy slopes. Before long he was red with the work of it and beads of sweat glistened against his forehead. Ianos said very little as they went, but led them on through the scrub-mottled ridges of northwest Gortyne. They walked together when the path permitted it and fell into a single file whenever the way became too narrow. Stephen's shirt was clinging to his back and his hair to his brow now, but still Ianos led them on, deeper and deeper into the hills, until Stephen had somewhat lost track of where they were.

Half an hour or more later, they came at last to the stony face of a high cliff, split by a narrow fissure, a cave that opened like a wound in the side of the mountain. They stood before it for a moment, Ianos very silent and Stephen breathing deeply from the effort of their climb to this place. The gaping space in the cliff seem to stare at them blindly.

Finally Ianos spoke in a hushed whisper; whether it was out of reverence or some contrived attempt at melodrama, Stephen could not decide which.

"Here is the labyrinth," Ianos said. "It is a secret place. Always a secret place for Crete. A place of hiding and losing the way." He turned and grinned again at Stephen. "But also a place of finding."

His words were so enigmatic that Stephen gave him a quizzical look.

Stephen wiped his furrowed brow with a folded handkerchief and took a moment more to catch his breath. "The maze of Minos?"

Ianos gave him one more grin. "The maze of Minos," he said in Greek. "Perhaps. Perhaps not. Who knows? But it is a labyrinth: a place of lost ways and hidden secrets."

Stephen's brow remained furrowed.

Ianos laughed at his friend and reached into the satchel he carried, producing an electric torch. "Come," he said, speaking English again. "We will enter."

The man pushed past the reaching limbs of cypress and scrub pine that partially guarded the entrance and stepped into the cave. Stephen followed him.

The air grew suddenly cool, all the more cool in contrast to the dazzling heat from which they had just stepped. It smelled strongly of wet stone and earth, a musty scent that clung to one's lips. A few yards into the passage, the darkness had enveloped them completely, although it was very soft and inviting.

The torch in Ianos's hand flashed open and he spread its light across the shadows. Stephen could sense more than see the black expanse above him; it suggested a cavernous roof many feet overhead, and as they walked forward he perceived side passages branching off in many directions, tunnels and crevices that broke away from the cave's main artery. Every now and then a draughty gust of air rose up from one of these, whispering, it seemed to him, of winding ways that led deep into the heart of Crete, and of the earthy secrets couched there.

Despite these many meandering side passages, Ianos seemed sure of the route, and though he moved forward slowly, because of the dark, it was with no hint of uncertainty. Stephen could see very little in the narrow path of light cast by his guide's torch, and he pressed close to Ianos for fear of losing his way.

The cavern floor descended gradually, and along each side, as the light happened to touch them, Stephen caught sudden glimpses of piled rock, heaps of fallen stone that were clearly the work of someone's ancient hands.

"They are here to mark the way for us," Ianos explained when Stephen pointed them out.

They continued on and, but for Ianos's intimate knowledge of the place, Stephen might have lost his way irretrievably. The air grew damper and the darkness thicker, and in the back of his mind the pressing shadows seemed to him like some great horned beast bearing down upon him.

Finally, the passage seemed to widen—at least the light of the torch no longer fell on the cavern walls when Ianos cast it from side to side—and Stephen felt as though they had stepped into some great chamber. Ianos scanned the area with his torch, and Stephen saw more heaps of stone piled here and there, and every now and then an alcove or recess of blackness that hinted at more tunnels leading deeper into the heart of the hills.

Ianos stepped to the very centre of the space.

"And this is the standing stone," Ianos said in Greek. In the darkness, his voice seemed almost like a sigh. "This stone marks the very heart of the cave. Some call it Ariadne's stone, in memory of the old stories."

For Stephen's sake, Ianos outlined it with the beam of his torch. In the indistinct light Stephen could make out a great, stoic horn of earth, a pillar of stone standing straight and erect, as though it alone held up the darkness looming all around it.

"It was put here long ago," Ianos said after a moment. "Back when these caves were first used. And it has marked this spot ever since."

Stephen could not say why, really, but he found himself sinking into a strange stillness, almost awe. It was like, he thought later, an ancient finger held up to hush the darkness all around them—though whether it did so to hold in some dark secret, or to soothe some dark distress, Stephen could not decide.

After what seemed a long time, Ianos spoke. "Mr. Percy will be waiting. We should go."

And so they turned their back on Ariadne's Stone and followed the main passage back towards the heat and sunlight.

When at last they emerged from the shadows of the cave, the sun seemed somehow abrasive on their flesh and in their eyes.

They did not speak much as they made their way down the slope towards the village, but Stephen walked the whole way as one who carried in his arms some mysterious, delicate weight.

We found Percy at the taverna, as promised, with a bottle of wine set on the table before him. "I ordered it for you," he explained, though he had already drunk much of the bottle himself, and he hadn't ordered us glasses. "I figured you'd need refreshment after your hike."

Nevertheless we sat down with him.

"How was the labyrinth?" he asked, and from his face I guessed he had known about the caves. I found myself at a loss for words, but this seemed to tell Percy more than anything I might have said. He nodded, and his eyes gleamed.

Later, as we drove on to Phaestos, Percy explained the caverns to me. The Minoans had used them as a quarry, millennia ago. Before the discovery of Knossos, many people thought that they were, in fact, the source of the Labyrinth myth. Even today they are known locally by that name. They are apparently vast, almost unending, and for the most part they remain uncharted. He told me that throughout the years of Crete's turbulent history—during the wars against the Turks in particular—the caves served as a hideout for the Cretans whose homes and villages had been destroyed by the invaders. Provisions had been stored there, and a spring of water found deep in one cavern. This is where the spirit of freedom held out, he said, whenever Crete fell under foreign rule.

I noticed a look of sadness and pride on Ianos's face as Percy described the hard history of his homeland.

Last night, after visiting the ruins of Phaestos (a Minoan palace less grand but more intact than Knossos), we stayed in the village of Agios Ioannis. We stayed up late, talking, and at one point Ianos brought out a flask and proposed a toast to his homeland. Percy told me it was raki. "This is what the men of Crete drink when they outgrow ouzo," he said.

It was bitter and strong, and coursed almost immediately to my head.

"If you like raki," Ianos said, watching me sputter, "you should come with me to my village, to Apodoulou. There they make the finest raki in all of Crete."

Percy laughed at me, and at what he called Ianos's "Cretan persistence" about his hometown. But by then it was very late. I was exhausted and only wanted sleep.

And yet Ianos would not relent until I had promised. "Good!" he said. "I will show you my village—the jewel of Crete!"

Percy was laughing at me the whole time.

And so I've agreed to trek over Mount Ida with Ianos to visit his village on the other side. Percy won't come. He says he has better things to do than break his neck on the slopes of Mount Ida, though he has offered to come up to Apodoulou when our excursion's done, to bring me back to Heraklion.

In Stephen's study, Grace furrowed her brow. Here was something she had not known. Certainly it was nothing Stephen had ever shared with her.

She thought back through the many letters he had sent her from that time. They had often described Heraklion—his friend Percy, his work on the Linear B tablets, his internship at the museum—but never had there been any mention of this mountain trek with a Cretan youth named Ianos to a village called Apodoulou. Even his visit to the cave at Gortyne, for all the space it occupied in his journal, had never come up the few times Stephen had told her the story of his time on Crete.

She pressed into the journal again. It lay before her now flat and still, like a great tablet of stone etched with some indecipherable mystery, and as she read she felt a strange and foreboding weight pressing on her heart.

CHAPTER SIXTEEN
Mount Ida

A WEEK OR MORE LATER, STEPHEN FOUND HIMSELF WAKING GRADUALLY with the dawn at the mouth of a cave on the slopes of Mount Ida, two days into his journey with Ianos across the mountains of Crete. It was the music of the birds he became aware of first. They murmured playfully somewhere in the woods beyond the cave, drinking deeply of the dawning light and offering back an orison of song with every fresh draught. The hollow of the rock magnified the sound, distorting it until it became a cacophony of notes, indistinct and echoing.

Stephen had been vaguely aware of the sound long before he realized he was, in fact, awake. He sat up and rubbed his face, rough with two day's stubble and still heavy with sleep. He didn't hurry to get up. The cavern's floor had left his body stiff, and a damp chill in the air made him reluctant to leave the warmth of his bedroll.

He saw the crumpled bundle of Ianos's own sleeping roll lying next to him, abandoned, and knew he was alone.

He rubbed his face again, collecting his thoughts. He remembered back to the start of their journey two days ago. He had taken an omnibus from Heraklion to Timbaki, the colourful market village on the southern coast of Crete, where he and Ianos had arranged to meet. After their trip to Gortyne last week, Ianos hadn't come back with Stephen and Percy to Heraklion. Stephen had needed to attend to some work at the museum for a day or two, so Ianos had gone on ahead to gather their supplies for the excursion. The village of Apodoulou was just a short day's hike from Timbaki, but they had agreed to journey to the peak of Ida first, and then come down on Apodoulou from the far side. The light that came into Ianos's eye as he described the view of the sunrise on the peak of Mount Ida had convinced Stephen it would be worth the climb.

So Stephen had taken a bus to Timbaki to join up with Ianos and begin their trek. His friend had been waiting for him by the side of the road where the bus had dropped him off, with the tether of a well-loaded pack mule in one hand and two walking sticks in the other. He'd taken Stephen's rucksack from off his shoulder and strapped it to the mule with the rest of their gear. He'd then offered him one of the walking sticks.

"You will want this before long," Ianos said with a grin.

Whether it was because Percy was not with them and he felt especially at ease, or because he was close to his village now and felt especially at home, Stephen wasn't sure, but Ianos no longer attempted to speak English. His Greek was quick and often idiomatic, and although Stephen felt he had become rather fluent in the language over the last two years, still he found it difficult at times to keep up.

Ianos had explained that their route would bring them to a village called Kamares, where they would spend their first night, and then on to the Karmares caves where they would spend the next. From there, they would embark upon a five- or six-hour journey to Mount Ida itself, and the day after that they'd undertake a full day's hike over the ridge and down into the valley, where they would come at last to Apodoulou, probably before evening.

They had shared a leisurely cup of Turkish coffee in Timbaki, as a toast to their adventure, and then set out. Ianos had led the way through orchards, past vineyards, and along narrow footpaths, winding steadily up towards the mountains.

Before long, that first day had grown hot and the path dusty. The mule rocked wearily beneath its load, the tatters of its tail scattering the black flies that clung lazily to its rough-haired hide. Stephen soon grew thankful for the walking stick Ianos had thought to provide him.

Despite the heat, Ianos had been indefatigable in his enthusiasm. His conversation was incessant, though at times his Greek tripped from phrase to phrase in a way Stephen found difficult to follow. Often he whistled the stray notes of some Greek folk song or other, sometimes humming snatches of a melody or raising his voice with the random phrases of some obscure lyric.

That first day's hike had been a casual affair, with only four hours of actual walking, though it had taken them the whole day to accomplish it. Towards the middle of the afternoon, just as the heat was reaching its apex, they had come across an ancient orchard of almond trees, gnarled and leafy and just breaking into blossom. They had lingered there through the hottest hours of the day, stretched out luxuriously in the almond-scented shadows, and swapped stories while the mule cropped casual mouthfuls of grass. Only when the heat had begun to wane in earnest did they set out again, arriving at Kamares with the setting sun.

The following day, which had brought them to this cave, had been much the same. The journey itself had been less than a five-hour hike, but between a late start from Kamares and a long lunch in the middle of the day they hadn't arrived until dusk. Ianos knew the place with all the intimacy of a good friend, however. Even in the fading light, he had found a path that led off the main road and brought them through a wooded grove until they found the cave—not the Kamares Cave, he explained, which they would visit the next day, but rather a small alcove in the rock that Ianos and his father had discovered years ago when he was a child.

"I've slept here many times on journeys between our village and the villages on the far side of Ida," he had told Stephen as they arranged their sleeping gear. "Not many know it is here."

That night had been profoundly satisfying for Stephen, sitting with Ianos in the deepening twilight, warmed by the yellow glow of their fire while the last red rays of sunset bled across the mountaintops. Their dinner had been modest—a few loaves of flatbread with some cured meat, a couple handfuls from a bag of almonds and sultanas, and three or four long drinks from a wineskin, filled with "the best wine in Crete!" which Ianos had brought from his home in Apodoulou.

However simple the fare, the glorious view and gracious company of so good a friend had made it seem to Stephen like a celestial banquet. Towards the end of their meal, Ianos produced a brown paper bag and held it out towards him.

"A gift from Apodoulou," Ianos said, uncovering a pressed cake of dried figs. "Last year's fruit, but still good."

Stephen tasted one, and the grainy sweetness seemed to touch something deep in his soul with a profound feeling of contentment.

Ianos had then begun to sing, spontaneously and unselfconsciously. "This is a rizitika," he explained. "'Tis tavias. A song of the table."

The melody was haunting, the words drifting about Stephen mysteriously, like smoke in the flickering firelight.

"'Weep not for the Eagle who must fly in the rain,'" Ianos had sung, his voice rich and low. "'Save your tears for the bird who has no wings.'"

The last light of the sun had nearly gone by the time the song was over, but Ianos started immediately into another, strange lyrics that Stephen did his best to understand.

"'You wild goats and tamed deer. Tell me where you stay in the winter? In the precipices we live; the caves in the mountains are our winter quarters.'"

Between such songs they talked at length. Sometimes Ianos explained the words, other times he let them linger enigmatically. More than once, they lapsed into a profound silence that seemed to say more than any words might.

The fire had long since died away and the night was palpably dark when at last they found their way to their sleeping rolls. Even in the darkness, though, Ianos had continued to sing faintly to himself as they lay there, staring blindly into the blackness overhead. Stephen had drifted off to sleep with the words of his song haunting his thoughts: "'Friendship is the most beautiful thing in the world. My heart is full: my heart knows how to repay.'"

His head still echoing with the stray threads of that final melody, Stephen sat up fully in the morning light of their cave and crept from his bedroll. He shivered and reached for the knitted sweater he had brought against these chilly mountain mornings. He pulled it over his head and found his shoes, lacing them and rising to his feet. He looked around again, wondering where Ianos might have gone. He rummaged through his rucksack and found a towel and tin cup; taking these, he stepped out into the morning light.

He stretched himself stiffly. By now the sun had pulled itself fully from the final peaks of the distant mountains, and he squinted at it as he tried to get his bearings. Ianos had pointed out Mount Ida the day before, when it had first come into view as they approached the Kamares caves. He had thought it very distant and inaccessible then, but in the morning light it loomed imperiously, so close now that he wondered if he might not reach out and touch it.

A path wound along the edge of the woods between the trailing patches of scrub pine on the right and a great wall of rock on the left. Ianos had pointed this out the night before, too, and told him it led to a place where there would be water for drinking and washing. Stephen followed it a short way from their camp, rounded a crumbling ridge of limestone, and found himself standing at the edge of a shallow valley, a dell hemmed in by sloping shoulders of rock. The cypress and pine were thicker here, and the grass greener, strewn with blooms of crocus and hyacinth. A snow-fed stream slipped through the valley's basin, filling the air with the murmur of clear water over cold stone.

Ianos was here. He had come to bathe, it seemed, for he was still shirtless and a linen towel had been spread out to dry on a great boulder beside him. He sat on a rough dais of piled rock at the edge of the stream, his back to Stephen. His hair clung in wet curls to the nape of his neck, and his bare shoulders warmed in the sunshine.

Stephen stopped. Ianos appeared to be so immersed in the moment that he hesitated to disturb him. One foot swung loosely from the rock, reaching almost to the stream; the other was tucked up beneath him. He held to his lips a wooden flute, which he played with great skill. The valley itself was trembling already with birdsong, but over this, or perhaps in response to it, rose the winding notes of Ianos's flute. The tune was very sad, but also somehow hopeful, and it made Stephen think of rain in dry places.

Ianos stopped playing abruptly, though the rhythms of stream and writhing birdsong continued. He turned and saw Stephen standing silently at the top of the trail. Suddenly Stephen felt that same sense of self-consciousness as when he'd first met Ianos at Knossos many months ago.

It passed quickly, however, as Ianos rose and smiled.

"Kalimera! Good morning Stephen!" Ianos reached for his linen towel and ran it roughly through his hair to dry. He stepped from his spot on the rock and pulled his shirt down from where he'd hung it on a tree limb. "You'll want to wash, I expect. You clean up and I will get the fire started for breakfast."

He came up from the stream to where Stephen was standing and clapped him on the shoulder.

"Careful!" Ianos said. "There is nothing purer in the world than the water of Mount Ida, but it is very cold."

A small fire burned at their camp when Stephen returned from his morning wash, still flinging the towel through the wet locks of his hair, more to warm his head than to dry it. Ianos was right: the water had been unexpectedly cold, and its effect on him bracing.

Ianos had boiled water and prepared coffee. It was done after the Turkish style, very sweet and black with heavy dregs of coffee and sugar lurking at the bottom of the tin cup. They took this with some more bread and cured meat— another modest meal, but Ianos assured him there would be a veritable feast waiting for them when they arrived at Apodoulou the following day.

As they ate, Ianos talked over the day's journey.

"Today we will hike to the cave of Zeus on Mount Ida," he said, "and perhaps to the summit after that. It will take us five hours to reach the cave, and maybe another three to the peak." He looked at the sun to gauge the time. "We could reach the cave by late afternoon if we leave directly. We can rest there as long as you like and then continue on to the summit by evening." He cast a thoughtful eye at the gleaming peak of Ida. "The next day we will come down by the southwest, into Apodoulou."

When breakfast was finished and their gear repacked on the mule, they set out. Now that they were walking upon the mountain heights, the air was refreshingly cool, and Stephen proceeded at times like someone waking from a dream. Every breath, it seemed, was sharp with mountain scents, with sage and cypress and wild thyme, and every ridge they crested seemed to offer fresh vistas of the Cretan countryside.

They talked and laughed and sang continuously. Ianos taught Stephen here and there the odd line of more rizitika.

"Tis stratas," he explained this time. "A song of the road."

Stephen, in return, recited scraps of the Greek poetry he had memorized during his studies. And because they were journeying to the fabled site of Zeus' cave—that secret spot where, according to all the ancient stories, the father of the gods had been reared and raised—they took turns saying what they knew of this myth, too.

"The god Chronos was the ruler of earth and sky," Stephen explained. "He had been warned that his own child would cast him down and rule in his place. And so he devoured each of his children as they were born to his wife Rhea, lest any of them should grow up to overthrow him."

And so the story was told. How Chronos had swallowed each in turn—Hestia, and Demeter, Hera, Hades, Poseidon. Five children in all. But Rhea had mourned grievously for her children, and when Zeus at last was born she hid him away on Crete.

"She bundled a stone in swaddling clothes," Ianos added when his turn came. "And offered it to Chronos instead. He swallowed it whole, thinking it to be his son."

And he told then how Rhea had taken Zeus and hidden him deep in the very heart of Crete, in a cave on the side of Mount Ida. He had been nursed there by the mountain nymphs, suckled on the milk of Amalthea, the sacred goat, and fed by bees with ambrosial honey.

"Eventually Zeus came against his father Chronos and cast him down, assuming his place as the king of all the gods," Stephen said. Walking in the very shadow of Mount Ida itself, he felt the story taking on contours he had never felt in it before. "Rhea, they say, represents the Earth Mother. Chronos is a deity of the sky, like his father Uranus. So his marriage with Rhea represents the sacred union of earth and sky. It's all symbolic, of course. And Chronos is also Time—the god of time—so the story can be seen as a metaphor for the way in which Time, eventually, steals all things."

Ianos listened patiently to this, and then finally set to laughing at Stephen's heady book-learning. He clapped him roughly but kindly on the back.

"Perhaps," he said. "But Stephen, these stories are not important for where they come from or why they were first told. These stories are important for what they put into our hearts as we hear them."

Stephen squinted up at Ida's peak, gathering silver wisps of cloud about it as the morning lapsed into the afternoon.

They did make it to the peak by evening, arriving just as the sky was turning grey with the dusk. They found a lonely chapel at the very summit—the Timios Stavros, Ianos called it—the Chapel of the Holy Cross. It was a small stone structure, more like a hermit's hut than a church, but it was always open to wayfarers, and at least it offered shelter from the wind that swept the mountaintop at this height.

Ianos found some candles in one of their bags and lit a few against the thick darkness of the chapel's windowless interior. In the soft glow of the candlelight they made out the dim shapes of frescoes painted on the walls, icons of the Virgin and Child placed reverently against the stone, and an ornately carved crucifix on a makeshift stone altar. Overhead, the light danced wraith-like on a cluster of hanging simulacra. Stephen had seen these in churches at Athens and knew what they were: small tablets of tin stamped with images of people or ailing body parts, which pilgrims to this holy place had left behind in hopes of finding healing or blessing.

They sat up late into the night talking about everything they had seen that day.

"The Curetes danced around the cave," Ianos explained, still mulling over the myth of Zeus. "The story says they sang and danced and clashed their spears against their shields, to drown out the noise of the baby wailing, and to keep Zeus hidden from his hungry father." Candlelight gleamed in Ianos's eye as he spoke. "We still remember the dance of the Curetes. Crete is full of dance, of course, but perhaps our dances are learned from them, the Curetes and their protection of the baby Zeus. There are as many dances on Crete as there are seasons of the soul!"

He rose and, as if to punctuate his point, performed a spontaneous leap into the air.

"The pantosalis!" he exclaimed. "The Dance of the Five Steps."

Entirely undeterred by the close space and dim light, Ianos stamped out the five steps of the pantosalis, as though it flowed from some deep, unheard rhythm somewhere in his heart.

Shy and laughing, Stephen allowed himself to be pulled to his feet and taught the steps, too. Ianos provided the music in the simple beat of his clapping hands, the stone walls ringing with the sound like a clash of bronze on bronze, of spear, perhaps, on shield. And as he did, he explained what it meant for a Cretan to dance: how to dance was to discover the spirit alive within the body, how to dance was to know thyself, how to dance was "to want nothing, fear nothing, and be free!"

Ianos taught him other steps, too. Drifting gracefully about the stone floor he clapped out new rhythms, one after the other: the sytros, the round dance, its rhythms undulating and pulsing, and the siganos, the slow dance, its steps easy and gentle. He showed him also the sousta, the feather-dance, although he explained, laughing, that this dance was for pairs, for men and women to dance together; but he taught Stephen the man's part anyway and explained to him the woman's, and there in the shadow of the chapel, Stephen learned it, too.

Far away, the bright horn of the moon rose silver over Mount Ida, gleaming down on the straggling spring snow. Yet it was close. Closer than Stephen had ever been to it. The chapel was windowless, of course, so he could not see it, but in his heart he somehow knew that he danced awash in moonlight. And the air rang with the clatter of Ianos's clapping, and sometimes with his shouts of delight, and often with Stephen's laughter, late into the night.

He stayed awake for a long time after they'd stopped dancing. Ianos lay sleeping in his bedroll at the other end of the chapel, and only one of the candles was left burning, casting a weak circle of light in the sanctuary. Stephen had taken it and placed it on the stone altar, where he sat a while in utter silence. He looked up at the simulacra, glittering overhead at the very edge of the candle-light. The tin shapes—a hand, an eye, a face, a foot—floated above him, turning in the shadows. He thought of the pilgrims who must have come to this place and left them here over many years, full of faith and desperate for healing.

He looked at the crucifix on the altar and thought suddenly of Grace. He hadn't thought of her in earnest for many days, and it troubled him in this moment to realize that.

Grace, of course, had always gone in for things like this: healing and redemption, crucifixions and resurrections. She'd always had a deep faith, deeper, at least, than his own. He admired her for this, of course, but whenever he had tried to pray with her, or join her at church, it left him feeling like an outsider looking in on a world he knew he was not part of.

He looked again at the simulacra and wished he had one to leave on Grace's behalf.

Not that he gave much weight to the stuff of prayer and piety, of course; he had seen how history was littered with man's failed attempts to grasp the sacred. Still, in this mysterious place, where even the oldest of myths seemed somehow real, it was easier than it ever had been for him to believe that the Divine could still be petitioned, that blessings and miracles could perhaps be besought and bestowed. If it were so, he wanted intensely in that moment both a blessing and a miracle for her.

He knelt there for a long time, and though he wouldn't say he prayed, when he rose and found his way at last to his bedroll, there were bright tears of remorse staining his cheek.

In the morning, however, they stepped out into the most glorious sunrise Stephen had ever seen, the view in every direction shimmering faintly with the allure of distant places. Apodoulou lay on the southern slopes of Mount Ida, Ianos said, about a day's hike from the summit. He was eager to begin, eager to prove to Stephen at last that all his boasting about his village had not been for nothing. So they loaded their mule after a light breakfast and prepared to depart.

But before they left, Stephen stood silently, momentarily, at the very peak of the mountain. The sky was brilliantly blue, and here, at this pinnacle of the earth, he had a growing feeling that he had at last landed, as though every road in his life had been leading to this single peak. Grey-green in the distance, other mountains stretched out around him, the vision panoramic, but to Stephen, all the world seemed far below, hazy and mute and still.

He looked to Ianos, who was already finding a path through the thinly gathered snow, leading the mule away down the southern slope. He took a deep breath of the mountain air, exhaled slowly, and turned to follow.

CHAPTER SEVENTEEN
The Lemon Grove

THE FIRST THING STEPHEN NOTICED AS HE AND IANOS ROUNDED THE final bend that led into Apodoulou was how closely they were being watched. Elderly ladies sitting on the porches of their homes nodded at them as they passed. Barefoot children stood in doorways, curious about the stranger Ianos had brought home with him. He was well known to all the village children, it seemed, for often he laughed and teased them, setting them to flee, giggling, behind their doors.

The path wound its way past modest homes, whitewashed and well-kept. There were some fenced fields, and a small church with a humble cemetery of unadorned headstones. Though their journey from the summit that morning had been tiring, Ianos's step was light now, borne up perhaps with a joyful sense of homecoming. Stephen had to quicken his pace somewhat to keep up.

"Khaireta! Ianos!" someone called out. They were passing the local kafenion, where a handful of men were enjoying an afternoon kafe, gathered in a tight knot around the open-air tables. One of them gestured them over. "Erthate kai na kathísate!" Come and sit!

Ianos stopped to talk with them, his words loud and energetic. Stephen smiled to himself as he listened. Cretans engaged in conversation with such enthusiasm, he thought, that it always seemed to teeter just on the edge of some passionate argument. The men asked about the strange guest Ianos had brought with him. Stephen could feel their eyes on him as Ianos introduced him as a friend and colleague from his work at the Heraklion museum.

"Welcome to Apodoulou!" one of the men said, speaking with tentative English in a good-natured attempt at hospitality. Someone offered him a coffee while another found them both a seat at the table.

"Efkharisto," Stephen replied, accepting their offer and sitting among them. *Thank you.*

Their interest in him seemed to intensify when they discovered he could speak Greek. They probed him cheerfully for news, as much to hear his clumsy accent as for the gossip fodder it provided. They laughed loudly to hear the roll of their language in his mouth, and often repeated back to him what he had said, exaggerating his awkward pronunciations. Even so, they seemed genuinely pleased with his efforts.

"So unlike the vacationers one generally sees in Heraklion," one of them said, "with their dictionaries and their maps." His pantomime of a bumbling tourist leafing through a phrasebook was met with laughter and agreement by the whole group, and Stephen found himself laughing along.

Their interest intensified even more when they learned he had spent time in Athens. They hedged him in with their attention now, eager, after the way of the Cretan, for gossip about the mainland. Every germ of news Stephen mentioned, however small, was batted back and forth between them at great length, and their enthusiasm left him sifting every grain of his memory for something more that might interest them.

Before the last sip of coffee was gone, the men were offering him hearty claps on the back and even heartier professions of friendship.

"Any friend of Ianos who can speak Greek and knows Athens is welcome as a friend in Apodoulou!" someone said with a laugh.

"Philoxenia," Ianos explained when at last they had risen and set off towards his house. "It is our country's sense of welcome and friendship. Philoxena is more than just hospitality on Crete. It is a way of life. A form of art. A man is bound by honour to his guest and he does not take that bond lightly." He struck Stephen on the back as they walked. "A Cretan can offer you no greater gift than his friendship, for that comes from his soul and will last until death."

They followed the path through to the far edge of the village. The buildings were scattered widely here, the way lined with spreading olive trees that cast long, mottled shadows over the road. They passed into a broad field, bright and shimmering in the afternoon sun. It was set with long even rows of green vines, ablaze with brilliant yellow blossoms in the spring sun.

"My father's vineyard," Ianos said, and his eyes shone. "The flowers came early this year. Soon the grapes will begin." He fanned his arm to indicate the view. "My father owns the largest vineyard this side of Mount Ida."

At the far end of the vineyard, just before the hills began to rise sharply again, stood a large whitewashed house. It was not so much grand as it was elegant, though it was indeed the largest building Stephen had seen in Apodoulou. It gleamed lustrously in the sunshine, confident of its simple grace. A low wall of stone enclosed a wide courtyard at the front of the house, with an ancient plane tree of epic proportions standing at the very centre, filling the space with fragrant shade.

Ianos led Stephen along the near edge of the vineyard and up towards the house. They entered through a weathered wooden gate and stepped into the courtyard's scented shadows. The yard was empty and still but for the stray breeze that occasionally stirred the branches of the plane tree.

"My father, I think, is not home. I will go in and see." Ianos tethered their mule to an iron ring set in the stone wall. "Are you thirsty? I will find us something to drink."

He entered the house and left Stephen to wait beneath the twisting branches. Stephen watched the door through which he had gone a moment, and then looked idly about him. A narrow path led to another gate at the other end of the yard, and Stephen could see the limbs of citrus trees, some still bearing the last of their winter fruit, dropping over the wall. He wandered over to look, and passing through the gate, found himself standing in a lazy grove of lemons, stretching out alongside the house. The leaves were bright and green, the scent sharp, the grass beneath dappled with shadows. From somewhere at the heart of the grove came the gentle cooing of a wood pigeon.

He thought he heard a murmur of laughter as he entered, faint but clear, and wondered if it was not simply the breeze in the trees that made the noise. The gate sighed closed behind him and he stepped forward. The light was very soft, here; again the pigeon sounded from somewhere far away; again a laughing breeze stirred the tree limbs.

There was no path, but the trees were set in even rows and well-tended. He followed a corridor of the orchard for a ways, the limbs nodding in the breeze with ripples of dark green leaves and the odd flash of bright yellow fruit around him. The scent was very rich, like wine almost, and Stephen took a deep draught of it.

He came to a clearing, at what he supposed was the heart of the lemon grove, where the shade of the trees parted and gave way to a wide space brimming with the late afternoon light. A fig tree grew in the centre of the clearing, looking very ancient and very wise. He stood before it, lost in thought, somehow mesmerized. It had already flowered, and although a few of the bright red blossoms still lingered on its limbs, every branch was crowded with close clusters of early fruit, very small and hard and green. Stephen reached out to touch one, and a memory of the honey-sweet figs he'd eaten in the cave at Karames came to him.

His hand lingered, brushing against the green leaves, fingering a bud of early fruit.

Suddenly he heard the sound of a woman's laughter, at his back. He turned quickly, as though caught at something he ought not be doing.

She stood alone at the edge of the clearing, watching him from among the spreading trees. For a moment he felt paralyzed, like one meeting a doe in a dusk-lit wood, silent and motionless lest it should startle and flee before he had seen it fully. Her gown was bright white and dappled with the shade, reaching slowly from graceful shoulders. It swayed just above her ankles, where her bare feet pressed into the grass. She held her apron up against her waist, and Stephen could see that the pocket it formed was full of newly picked lemons. Her hair was long and dark, falling in a single thick braid over one shoulder, strands of it caressing her brow and cheek whenever the breeze moved over her face. She was young, and compelling laughter shone in her dark, almond-shaped eyes. These she turned fully on Stephen.

"The figs are not ripe," she said, speaking Greek. A smile moved across her soft cheek, like a light spreading up from her throat.

Stephen found himself clumsy with his words. "I—I am waiting for Ianos." He looked past her and up towards the house.

She laughed again, a laughter that sounded more natural to her than breathing. "Yes. But the figs have only just begun. They will not be ripe until the fall."

Again that shy feeling of having been caught at something swept over Stephen, and he dropped his hand, which was still slightly raised towards the fig tree.

She pulled a lemon from her apron and held it towards him. "The season for lemons is just ending; the season for figs is not until the fall."

That radiant smile flashed across her face again, and another breeze pulled a strand of hair across her brow. She tilted her head to let the wind sweep it clear of her face, and then held out the lemon more earnestly. Stephen stepped forward and took it from her, somewhat confused.

"You know Ianos?" she asked. "Are you a friend?"

"Yes. I'm Ianos's friend." As though the words were an invitation, she stepped from the lemon trees and into the clearing, past Stephen and towards the fig tree. "Do you also know Ianos?"

She laughed softly at this. "Of course. Everyone knows Ianos. This is his village. His father is Nikos Leventi." She looked intently at the fig tree a moment. "We all know Ianos."

He felt the shyness in him very strongly and kept his eyes lowered, watching only the press of her heels divot the grass as she stepped up to the tree. He looked at the lemon she had given him, as though it was suddenly, mysteriously, a very important thing.

She touched one of the hard green buds. "You must wait for the figs. They are still just green." She pulled and plucked, breaking off a single fig and cupping it in her palm. "I have always thought that figs are a female fruit," she said vaguely, as if to herself. But then she looked at him suddenly. "Do you think? Is the fig male or female?"

The question confused Stephen, and it showed on his face. She laughed again and looked back at the newly budded fruit in her hand.

"How do you know Ianos?" she asked.

Stephen opened his mouth to answer, but at just that moment they heard Ianos's voice drifting through the trees. "Stephen? Where are you?"

The call seemed to startle the young woman. She dropped the fig and looked up towards the house. Again Ianos's voice sounded, and with a motion that might have been the spring of an ibex at the approach of the woodsman, she turned back towards the lemon grove. She gave another soft laugh and then hurried away; Stephen could not tell if it was flight or dance that had carried her off.

"Wait!" he said suddenly, unexpectedly. She did not stop nor turn, so Stephen called after her. "Who are you? What is your name?"

She stopped and turned, laughing. "I am Ariadne!" she said as though it were a very obvious thing and then turned away again.

She was gone when Ianos at last emerged from the lemon trees.

"I've been looking for you," Ianos said. "My father and sister are not at home. Perhaps they are in the village. But no matter. Come, we can wait for them in the yard."

Stephen said nothing. He looked down and realized he was still holding the lemon the young woman had given him.

"Stephen?" his friend asked. "You look like you're just waking up. Perhaps the walk from Mount Ida's finally caught up to you? Come. I've found us something to drink. I am sure they will be along shortly."

Dearest Grace, he wrote that night, sitting alone in the cool of the evening, beneath the great plane tree in the centre of the courtyard. The rest of the household had gone to bed long ago, but he had stayed up to write. He'd scratched out a thought or two in his journal about the journey to Apodoulou, and then turned to write a letter to Grace. It had taken him a long time to decide what he might say.

Dearest Grace,

As summer approaches I find myself buried deeper than ever in my work at the museum. Only two months remain in my internship, and I feel very close to decoding the Linear B tablets at last. Percy says that we are on the verge of a breakthrough. It is exciting, but something of a pity, too. There are so many sights to see on this island, and yet here I am, always buried in work.

Though it is so often tedious, still I would not trade it for anything. Just think, Grace, what value such an experience as this will have for my career when I return. Any school in North America would take me on after this, I think. And then think of the life we can begin together. Only a few months to go, and I cannot wait till then. Meanwhile, know that I love you dearly and miss you terribly.

Yours, Stephen.

CHAPTER EIGHTEEN
Philoxenia

IANOS OFFICIALLY INTRODUCED STEPHEN AND ARIADNE THAT FIRST evening in Apodoulou. She stepped through the gate of the lemon grove and into the courtyard of the villa while he and Stephen were sitting in the cool shadows of the plane tree, still recovering from their long trek down from Mount Ida. Strangely, she made out as if she were just arriving home from some errand or other, as if her chance encounter with Stephen only hours earlier had never happened.

"Stephen," said Ianos, rising as she appeared at the gate. "This is my sister, Ariadne. Ariadne, this is Stephen Walker. A friend."

There was a heartbeat of silence, and if Ariadne intended to acknowledge their previous meeting, nothing in her face suggested it. Stephen didn't know if it was Ianos's presence that made her now so shy, or if there was something more to it, but she kept her face lowered, and for an elusive moment she would not lift her eyes to his. She lingered by the gate. The apron of her white dress was smoothed down over her waist and the lemons she'd gathered were gone. Her dark braid still fell over one shoulder, and in the evening's dimming light it looked exquisitely soft and rich.

Stephen rose, too, feeling awkward and overly formal.

She kept her eyes down for a heartbeat more, then lifted them to meet his. "I am pleased to meet you, Stephen," she said, and the same smile he had seen under the fig tree flashed across her face. It left Stephen fumbling with his words.

"I am happy to meet Ianos's sister," he said at last.

She inclined her head, and the smile shone now in her eyes, but otherwise she didn't move.

A thousand thoughts flooded Stephen's mind at once. She appeared not to require any further ceremony of introduction, as though she already knew him completely, and yet he found himself wishing strongly that she might. He thought to offer her his hand but did not, uncertain if it was quite proper to do so, or if she would take it even if it were. The strange thought that she might refuse his touch left him self-conscious.

"We have been to Ida," Ianos said. There was something vaguely stern in his tone, as though he disapproved of his sister's manner with his friend. "We hiked down from the summit this morning."

The light flashed a final time in her eye and then her mien became demure once more. She lowered her gaze and spoke softly, but still the words struck Stephen as bold.

"I hope he will stay with us long?" She asked it of Ianos but clearly spoke it to Stephen.

Stephen fumbled with his words again, but before he could say anything, Ianos offered an uneasy laugh.

"I fear I must apologize for my sister," he said. "Without our mother, she has had to play the role of the hostess for this household." He looked steadily at her as he spoke. "She is young, though, and so you must pardon her forwardness."

At this, Ariadne inclined her head in a simple nod of welcome, and then moved from the gate towards the house.

"Father left for Timbaki early this morning," she said. "He should be back before dark. I will prepare something for our guest and you to eat while you wait for him."

She passed into the villa.

Stephen was quiet for a moment after she left, and then somewhat tentatively he said, "She is very lovely."

Ianos laughed, quite easily now that they were alone. "Yes, and she knows it. She is restless, though, and she often finds life at her father's vineyard tedious. I suppose it's to break the tedium that she acts so unabashed."

"And her name," Stephen said. "Like the villa in Heraklion?"

Ianos shook his head. "It was the British who named their villa 'Ariadne.' That had nothing to do with my sister's name. My mother had always loved the old stories, and she insisted on naming Ariadne after the daughter of King Minos, from the story of the minotaur. My father used to say, 'If she is an Ariadne, then that makes me a king!' But the name has belonged to Crete for thousands of years, and you'll find it all over this island."

It was some time before she came from the house again, bearing a tray of good things to eat: bread and cheese, a dish of olives, a plate of askordoulakoi, a decanter of wine. She spread a linen cloth on the table that stood beneath the plane tree and set out the food. She took a seat with them as they ate, though she herself did not partake of the meal.

They were well into the food when their father Nikos arrived home from his business in Timbaki. He greeted Stephen warmly when Ianos introduced them, taking his hand and clapping him on the back.

"I welcome you to Apodoulou," Nikos said gregariously. "And to my home!"

He went into the house to wash up from his journey and then returned, sleeves rolled up, as he dried the back of his neck with a cloth. He sat with them at the table and poured himself a generous glass from the decanter.

"And how do you like Apodoulou?" he asked, taking a large piece of bread from the tray and breaking it in half to eat.

"I like it very well," Stephen said. "It is beautiful."

Nikos looked at him closely. "There is no place more lovely on earth than Apodoulou. Ianos tells me that you and he have worked together at the museum in Heraklion? I suppose then you have unlocked all the ancient mysteries of this island?"

He thrust a piece of bread between his teeth and grinned at Stephen.

Though Nikos had clearly passed along his dark eyes to Ianos, Stephen could see little else of the father in his son. The older man had a profuse head of dark hair, which he wore oiled and combed backward. His brows were heavy and often seemed to glower, giving the set of his eyes a kind of smouldering intensity even when they were well at ease. He wore an imposing beard and thick moustache, as dark as his hair, though it was streaked in one or two places, beneath the lips and at the temples, with just enough grey as to give him a stately air. He laughed frequently and showed all his teeth when he did; often they stood out starkly against the darkness of his beard.

Ariadne sat very straight and composed in her father's presence. Gone was any hint of the playfulness Stephen had seen in the lemon grove, or even the boldness he had glimpsed when Ianos had introduced her. She was an attentive hostess, however, directing her guest not to be shy in eating his fill, refilling his wine when his cup was empty, and holding out the plate of askordoulakoi when he seemed to lag behind Ianos or Nikos.

"Please," she said, "enjoy these. They are a specialty of Crete. A delicacy."

Towards the end of the meal, she returned to the house and re-emerged with a plate arranged with pastries, sweet with honey and stuffed with almonds. She offered Stephen the first piece, as their guest, and as he reached for one he thought he saw that same smile he had seen in the orchard pass briefly across her eyes.

Throughout their meal, Nikos plied Stephen with questions—about his time on Crete, about his work at Heraklion, about his homeland in Canada—expounding pontifically whenever a stray answer or sideways comment from Stephen seemed to demand it.

"Did Ianos show you the caves?" he asked. "And what did you think? So many people make such a fuss about them—those holes in the rock! Little do they know what they were used for, when Crete was at war with the Turks." A loud report of laughter punctuated statements like these. "Did you like Athens? Everyone thinks it is the centre of the world! Pah! Just a stink hole full of people if you ask me. It's only because the west wanted Athens to be there, that it's there. *They* built up Athens, made it the capital—not the Greeks!"

A bang of his palm on the tabletop might follow so earnest a statement as this.

He was, of course, thoroughly gregarious all the while, intensely so, but something in his tone, or perhaps in the way he so clearly kept control of the conversation, left Stephen with the lingering sense that Nikos Leventi was in fact holding court. He felt it especially strongly towards the end of the evening, that he was being weighed, and how he received Nikos's various edicts and verdicts would determine whether he would be found wanting.

The moon was out and the darkness complete when at last they left the table. If he had passed the man's scrutiny Stephen could not tell for sure, but Nikos took his hand before they retired for the night and pulled him into a strong embrace.

"I am glad you are here with us," he said. "Welcome to Crete from Canada, Mr. Stephen Walker. My home is your home!"

Percy arrived the next day, towards the middle of the afternoon. Stephen and Ianos were sitting in the courtyard enjoying a late luncheon when he appeared at the gate. Ianos rose to greet him, smiling broadly, but the smile faded quickly when he saw the look on Percy's face.

Stephen saw it, too. "What is it Percy?"

"We received word at Heraklion a week ago—just after you left, Walker—that work at the museum is ended until further notice. Most of the expats and British nationals are being sent home."

"Closing?" This news caught Stephen entirely off-guard. "Sent home?"

"Things on the continent have taken a bad turn with Germany," Percy explained. "Hitler's in Czechoslovakia now, and they say he's got his sights set on Poland. The Brits are beginning to mobilize. They're making every able-bodied man twenty-one years or younger train for the service, and they're starting to talk about conscription. It's total chaos on the mainland. The administration at the museum is sending home most of their staff. They're paring down operations to only the bare essentials."

"And you? Are you leaving?"

Percy grinned thinly. "No. The powers-that-be have said I'll be more useful to the effort here on Crete than I would be back in Britain, for now. The museum is asking me to undertake the arrangements for getting everyone home in one piece. From what I can tell, travel is going to be a nightmare in the coming months."

"But Percy, our work on the Linear B?"

Percy's thin smile folded into a grimace. "It will have to wait, I suppose. It's hardly 'bare essentials.' And anyway, I'm sad to inform you, but your internship has been discontinued, effective immediately. You're not British, of course, so I can't get you home to Canada, but I can at least arrange for passage to the mainland, and maybe on to Britain from there, if you want it. I realize this is sooner than you expected to leave, but it may be your best chance to get home for a long time."

While they conversed, Ariadne came out from the house where she had been working at chores and stood beside her brother.

"Is it quite safe to travel?" Stephen asked.

"Quite," said Percy. "It'll take you a hell of a lot longer than it should to get anywhere, but it is safe. We aren't at war, Walker—though I won't say that the word hasn't been bandied about a fair bit, and I can't say how long it will be so. But for now it's safe."

Stephen still hesitated

"I should tell you formally, too, that the museum can no longer accommodate you with room and board," Percy added. "If you don't leave, it will be yours to determine where and how you'll stay."

"He can stay here, if he wishes to." This came from Ariadne, listening at Ianos's elbow. She said it in English, and it was so unexpected that all three men turned to her. She didn't waver, however, and looked back at her brother boldly. "He is our guest, Ianos, and your friend. Is it not right for us to open our home to him if he is in need?"

Ianos hesitated for a moment and then seemed to acquiesce. He turned to Stephen and nodded. "You are our guest," he said. "If you need to stay, you may."

"You needn't stay," Percy interjected. "There's a steamer set to leave Heraklion the day after tomorrow. I can still find you a berth on it if you want. It's your decision, of course, if you wish not to take it, and there may be another in the coming weeks, a month or more perhaps, but I cannot promise anything after today."

Stephen stood there silently for a moment. He thought about the work he had been doing in Heraklion, now ended so abruptly. He thought about the long journey ahead, home to Halifax. He thought about yesterday's trek down from the summit of Mount Ida. He thought about Grace. He looked again at his friend, with his sister standing slightly behind him, and at Percy.

A great weight seemed to swing in his spirit then. It happened quickly, and neither Percy nor Ianos would have noted the turmoil in him, but longing and anguish and disappointment all collided at once within. He pressed his eyes together, shutting them against the looming decision he must make.

"I will stay here," he said finally. "At least until we know what's going to happen on the continent. Perhaps this will settle down quickly, uneventfully." He added this last part as if he were saying it to convince himself, not Percy.

Percy appeared to understand, and nodded. "As you say. I am sure the hospitality of the Leventi family is greatly appreciated. I cannot stay long, Stephen, if you're not planning to join me. There's a driver waiting for me, and we have business still in Timbaki to attend to before we're back at the museum tomorrow. I will pass along your decision to the authorities in Heraklion." He shook Ianos's hand firmly, and then reached for Stephen's.

Stephen took it, but remembered suddenly the letter he had written for Grace. "Please, one minute, Percy." He went quickly into the villa to retrieve the letter, and returned, placing it into Percy's hands. "Could you post this for me? It's a letter home. I wrote it yesterday."

Percy gave him a questioning look. "You don't wish to write one that will explain these new developments?"

"It will do for now," Stephen said quickly. "Let's wait to see what the coming days bring. No need to worry anyone for nothing."

And that was how Stephen came to live in Apodoulou with the Leventi family in the spring of 1939. In the weeks that followed, other opportunities to leave Crete presented themselves, but with each passing day travel from the island seemed more and more fraught with difficulty, and he let them pass by.

The early spring eased luxuriously into bright summer, heady with sun and lavish with fruit and flower; but though the days were serene, the swirling rumour of war overshadowed all with grim uncertainty.

For his part, Stephen settled well into life with the Leventis. As it became clear that his stay might last many months and not just weeks, he took on work in the vineyard, helping with whatever chores needed doing and tending the vines alongside Ianos and his father.

There was certainly much to do. Though the threat of war was enough to grind museum work to a standstill, the sun continued to warm the southern slopes of Mount Ida as it had done for millennia, and the grapes continued to ripen in their leafy corridors, entirely indifferent to the military machinations of important men in faraway nation-states. It was new work for Stephen. In his time at the digs in Athens, of course, he had grown used to long hours in the unrelenting sun; and to be sure, there was something about his labour in the vineyard that did remind him of those days. But even so, the work had a shaping effect on him. By the time the summer had flowered in earnest, he was well burnished by the sun, his arms leaner than they had been, his hands stronger albeit rougher and more calloused.

During this time, his friendship with Ianos continued to deepen. He came to appreciate, even at times to anticipate, his good-natured laughter over unexpected things, his generous comradery, the enthusiasm with which he took hold of whatever task each day brought.

It was his sister, however, who stood at the centre of Stephen's interest. She tended to her roles at the villa with a rote sense of duty, and what she did she did well, if somewhat mechanically. Meals were always laid out just as the men came in from the field. Fresh water was set out for them to drink during the warmest part of each day. The rooms in the house were meticulously cleaned, the wash hung regularly to dry, the gardens around the villa well-tended.

Seldom did Stephen glimpse again the bold, almost brazen transparency he had seen in her that first day under the fig tree. Certainly it never showed when Nikos was around; and even in Ianos's presence her demeanour was often guarded, though the two clearly shared a close bond, and Ianos seemed genuinely concerned that Stephen should know her and like her.

In rare moments, however, and fleeting glimpses, he sometimes sensed it: a flash of light in her eyes when they happened to meet his briefly across the table, maybe, a flush of colour in her cheek that faded before he could name it.

This was how he found her at the villa late one morning as he came in from the vineyard while Nikos and Ianos were still out working. The courtyard was already filled with sunshine, so full that even the shade of the plane tree could not abate the heat. A space along the stone wall had been planted with herbs and flowers, and she was crouched there, inspecting them carefully.

A colourfully dyed scarf covered her head from the sun and her hair was pulled up beneath it. She wore a linen dress with a brightly embroidered apron around her waist, and in the crook of one arm she carried a shallow basket which she had already half-filled with various sprigs of herbs, an aromatic bouquet of green leaves and brightly scented flowers.

Her back was turned to him and her head down, so for a moment she did not realize he was there. He watched as her fingers moved nimbly among the sweet-smelling leaves, turning, plucking, and pruning so intently that he wondered if he ought not to interrupt. He didn't know much about plants, of course, but he knew that the shrub she worked at just now was rosemary; and he was quite sure that the red and violet flowers growing at her feet were pansies.

Suddenly she lifted her head and turned to look at him. She rubbed her forehead with the back of her hand—it was quite warm in the sun—and smiled faintly, still crouched by the rosemary. The same awkward confusion he'd felt in the lemon grove trembled through him.

"You've quite a garden there," he said at last, his voice dry from the heat.

She lifted out of her crouch, holding the sprig of rosemary she'd just plucked, and looked at it a moment before turning her dark eyes to his. "They are all useful plants," she said, placing it in the basket.

"Is that rosemary?"

"Yes. There's rosemary." She took a step along the wall, brushing her fingers across brilliant flowers and scented leaves as she came to them each in turn. "These are columbines. They're very pretty. And this is called fennel, in English, I think."

"You speak English very well," Stephen said.

She said nothing for a long moment, examining the bright yellow flowers of the fennel. "I was a young girl when my mother Eunice died," she said at last.

"And because I was too young for my father to care for, and because he had the vineyard here to worry him, he sent me away to Heraklion."

"How old were you then?"

"I was eleven when I left—what is it now, eight years ago? Nine? I lived with an English family there. The father owed Nikos a favour, and the mother took me under her care. I helped to clean house and care for the children. She was the one who taught me to speak English."

She did not look up as she told her story, but rather stepped slowly along the wall, examining the flowers closely.

"She also taught me to garden. She told me once that plants learn all the secrets of the earth. They are taught them by the soil, through the roots, and store them in their leaves. It is because they have drunk so deeply of the earth's wisdom that they are so useful." She was quiet a moment, and then added, "Is that not a strange thing to say?"

Stephen was at a loss for words, but she didn't seem to require an answer.

Ariadne stepped again and pointed. "There is rue. It is a very pretty plant, I think." She touched the pale yellow blossom. "Rue means sadness, doesn't it? A strange name for so pretty a plant. There are daisies. And these are violets."

She plucked a violet and placed it in her basket, then she plucked three or four daisies, holding them together in a bunch.

"Tell me of your home, Stephen Walker," she asked suddenly. "Is it quite nice? You seem to be in no hurry to return to it."

This caught Stephen off-guard. "Well, my home is not nearly so interesting as yours, I suppose, nor so lovely… as this island, I mean."

"This island is very small." A distant look came into her eyes, but she lowered them to stare intently at the daisies she clutched in her hand. "Especially when you're like I am, you come to the edges of it very quickly."

Stephen nodded. "But it is very beautiful."

She smiled again, her bold smile, but something very sad seemed to linger at the edges of it. "I suppose, but beauty can only carry a heart so far and so long. Surely one needs more than beauty?"

Stephen did not realize it at first, but he had taken a step towards her.

"You are happy, Mr. Stephen Walker, to be at liberty to come and go as you do," she said enigmatically. "My world is this vineyard, this villa, our village. My brother and my father. Even with flower gardens and lemon groves, you come to the edges of it quickly."

"It is lovely, all the same."

She laughed, and he could not tell if it was dismissive or welcoming, but she lifted the bunch of daisies she had picked and placed them against his chest, for him to take.

"There," she said. "Some daisies for you. I must get the rest of these inside or they will wilt."

She turned towards the house, her movement fluid, and when she was gone Stephen looked down at the flowers she had given him, as though he were discovering them for the first time.

———————

Many weeks became many months, and the days passed by with a dream-like quality. As summer came through the brightest and hottest of its days and the season waned into autumn, the time for the grape harvest arrived. It came early this year, and before August had started in earnest members of Ianos's extended family began to gather at the vineyard, some from Apodoulou itself and others from neighbouring villages, to help with the harvest. The pace of the work intensified, and the days started very early and did not finish until quite late, well after the heat was gone. Stephen often fell into bed at the end of the day utterly exhausted, but also pleased and well-spent.

During these days, he found himself spending far more time with Ariadne than he had until now, though they seldom spoke. There was so much for her to do to ensure the men were provided for, and she often took long turns in the vineyard herself, filling her own share of the large wicker baskets they used to harvest the grapes. Consequently, neither of them had much time to spare for pleasantries. She did take her meals with the men during the harvest, however, and often sat with them during breaks for water, saying little but clearly enjoying the company as a sharp change from the lonely monotony of the household chores. In this way, she was always present to Stephen's awareness, moving at the edges of his peripheral vision, as it were, sometimes very close for brief moments, and other times at the far end of the vineyard with Nikos or Ianos. But wherever she was, he remained deeply aware of her presence.

Once she brought water to him directly while he worked away by himself in a corner of the vineyard. This was a rare moment. The other men had moved to an entirely different part of the vineyard, but Stephen hadn't yet finished in his row of vines and had remained behind. He was so intent in his work that she was standing much closer to him than he realized when at last she spoke.

"Are you thirsty?"

He looked up from where he crouched at the vine. The sun had not yet risen to its full height and it was immediately behind her head, so that he had to squint to look at her. He saw that she cradled an earthenware pitcher in one arm.

"Parched," he answered. "This is hot work."

She held a dipper, which she filled and handed to him. "Yes, it is hot. But one gets used to the heat." She looked at his nearly full wicker basket. "It is a good harvest this year. These will make excellent sultanas when they are dried."

He drank deeply, water spilling over his chin and down his front. He handed the dipper back to her and nodded. "It is very good. I'm happy your father has allowed me to stay. This is hard work, but I enjoy it."

"You take to it well," she said, in a perfunctory tone, as though she were exercising some great restraint. "It is a very good crop and there's much to do. I am sure Father is pleased to have one more set of hands to help. You may leave this basket when it is full and join the others. I will return and bring it up to the villa for you."

She turned to go.

"Ariadne—" he said it before he realized he had spoken; she turned back. "May I—?"

He gestured at her pitcher. She said nothing but refilled the dipper and handed it him, her eyes fixed. He drank again, and though he was watching her closely as he did so, no water spilled this time.

"Thank you," he said.

"It is hot work."

"Not just for the water. I mean for opening your home to me in the way you have."

She nodded, then looked up the vineyard towards the villa, away from him. "Philoxenia," she said. "What is the word in English?"

"Hospitality."

"Yes, but it means more. Love for the stranger, does it not? Philoxenia? This is a way of life on Crete." She turned her eyes back to him and they were alight with something Stephen could not name. "And I am very glad to give you philoxenia, Mr. Stephen Walker."

She smiled and turned up towards the house. Stephen watched her leave for longer than he might have had he not been alone, and then stooped again and finished filling his wicker basket with grapes.

That evening Nikos, Ianos, and Stephen sat together around the table under the great plane tree, sharing a drink of raki before turning in. They had lit a lantern against the falling darkness, and it glowed brightly in the centre of the table. The drink was harsh, and it told on Stephen's face, but Nikos only laughed and stuck him on the back.

"Drink deep Mr. Walker!" Nikos said. "A good glass of raki will take even the worst stiffness out of those muscles, and we need you ready tomorrow for more!"

Ariadne was there, too, but she did not sit with the men. She drifted in and out of the shadows, occasionally coming to the table with a tray of food, bringing the bottle of raki and pouring more when Nikos called for her to. Stephen found himself acutely aware of her coming and going.

"It was a good day's work today, Stephen. With you to help, we may finish the harvest early this year." Nikos clapped Stephen's back again and laughed to see him stagger somewhat beneath the blow. "If your body holds out on us, that is! Not too sore, I hope?"

"Not too sore."

Nikos motioned towards the house, and then Ariadne was there, pouring more raki. Her braid was loosened tonight, and the dark tresses of her hair swept down as she leaned forward to pour.

"We make the raki strong," Nikos was saying, "because the work is so hard. Strong drink for hard work!" He drained his glass and sighed. "And you have earned your raki today, Stephen Walker!"

They were quiet then for a long moment, until finally Nikos rose from the table.

"It is late," he said. "And tomorrow comes early. We should sleep."

The older man drifted through the darkness to the house, but Ianos did not rise with him, so Stephen remained sitting a moment longer, too.

"My father likes you, Stephen," Ianos said after some time. He said it quietly and it was difficult for Stephen to read his tone.

"Does he?"

"I can tell. He's never had a foreigner to help with the harvest like this. That is more than mere hospitality. He has embraced you."

"Embraced me?"

"With philia—"

"Philia?" Stephen repeated. Then he said it in English. "Love?"

"Friendship." Ianos corrected, also speaking English. "Welcome, family, embrace. I know my father, and I can see that he has extended you his philia."

Stephen said nothing, absorbing this. Finally, he said the thing he had wanted to say to his friend for a long time. "Your sister—"

"She has gone to bed," Ianos said, looking over his shoulder toward the house. "It's not quite proper for her to sit up with the men after her father has gone to bed."

Stephen swirled the raki in his glass, still largely undrunk. "She is very lovely."

"She is like our mother. Eunice was very lovely, and it broke my father's heart deeply when she died. Ariadne was too young to remember her well, but she has grown up very much the same."

"I don't know if I've ever met anyone quite like her."

"Our mother was like her. Though perhaps not so spirited as Ariadne is. Without Eunice to give her a proper upbringing she has grown up with something"— Ianos grinned affectionately—"something not altogether tame about her."

Stephen nodded, remembering lemon groves and fig trees.

"She has embraced you, too, Stephen. You know that?"

Stephen looked closely at his friend. "She has?"

"Philia. I can see she has offered it you. She has embraced you—welcomed you. Do you welcome her?"

The words seemed to hang in the lanternlight a moment. Stephen was unsure what to say. "What do you mean?"

Ianos laughed at his confusion. "We are Greeks, Stephen, not Arabs or Turks. Protective brothers, maybe, but not overlords. Ariadne is free to love whom she loves. And I know my sister, Stephen. She has embraced you. You are a foreigner here, and this is not your home, but I know my sister, and if you can love her, she will not refuse you."

Stephen was silent at this, so silent that finally Ianos drained the last of his glass and rose to leave, but not without placing his hand on his friend's shoulder and leaning in to repeat it.

"If you can love her, Stephen, she will not refuse you, I think."

Ianos took the lantern with him when he left, but even so Stephen sat up for a long time in darkness, staring thoughtfully into the night.

CHAPTER NINETEEN

Sousta

ONE MORNING TOWARDS THE END OF THE GRAPE HARVEST, WHEN THE intensity of the work had waned somewhat and a spare hour to think and write did not seem as much of a luxury as it had in the earliest days of autumn, Stephen found a quiet place in a corner of the vineyard to sit with his journal. He had chosen a spot in the bright sunlight near where they had spread the grapes to dry, and the air here was heady with their scent. His work that morning had been to turn these grapes so they would dry evenly, and by the time he was done the sun had grown quite hot. Ianos and Nikos had left for the day, journeying down to Timbaki with their donkey, bearing great baskets full of sultanas to sell at the market there. They would not be home until late in the day, and in the meantime there was not much to do but enjoy a rare moment of solitude.

He found a rock large enough to serve as a seat and opened his journal. Until today, he'd only had time to scribble out the barest sketch of his thoughts in passing, though he had put down something of his experiences each day. There had been a great tumult growing inside him for many weeks, however, and he knew that setting it all out in the pages of his journal would help him to know clearly what he really thought and wanted.

He lifted his pen to the page and wrote out a single sentence.
It is her.

He stared hard at those words. They seemed both to beckon and accuse him, so sharply that he began writing again, more quickly.

I have been here almost a full four months now, and every day, it seems, draws me closer to her than I had been before.

Like the pull of a current to the edge of the falls, maybe, I find myself pulled towards her, almost inevitably. Ianos says that she has welcomed me, extended me philia—that most enigmatic of all loves—and I am aware of it, too, at times intensely. In the fleeting glimpse of a smile that fades almost before it appears. In a stolen glance that lingers, but never seems to alight—

He put his pen down suddenly and passed a heavy palm down over his mouth and chin. Taking a deep breath, he began a second time.

What a fool I am to write like this—to let these thoughts see the light of day! And what if Grace could read such things, to see them set down so plainly? What pain it would cause her, she who has waited so faithfully for me to find my way home. Would I really throw that back in her face, now?

And yet that world—home—seems miles away and ages ago, and shrouded from me by unshared roads and rumours of war. Would she receive me back now, even if I were to come home? Will she when I do?

And all the while there is Ariadne, continually at the edge of my thoughts. I can't, it seems, take my mind off her. Like that day I caught her dancing alone in the lemon grove, she drifts as gracefully in and out of my imagination, continually moving to some music that only she can hear.

He leaned back wearily and tilted his face up towards the sun, his eyes closed and his brow creased. The memory floated across the red flood of sunlight that burst against the blackness of his eyelids, and he let it linger a moment.

It had been some weeks ago. Ariadne had not come out the vineyard with water when she'd been expected to, and Nikos had sent him up to the villa to look for her. He hadn't found her in the house, so he had wandered through the gate that led into the lemon grove. The fruit was heavy now, with the season, and the morning somewhat breezy, so the tree limbs swayed freely, setting the ground beneath them to dancing with dappled shadows.

He had come upon her near the very centre of the grove. She was dancing beautifully, though she neither sang nor hummed, and apart from the gentle sigh of the wind in the leaves, the grove was altogether silent. It seemed to Stephen as though she had come to the grove under the pretence of gathering lemons, because a half-filled basket rested beneath a tree not far from her, but it was clear she had abandoned it for the simple delight of dancing among the shifting shadows.

Words cannot contain how pure and artless she seemed to me in that moment, he wrote, although he felt clumsy and crass to put it down like that. *She was alone, and yet every swaying tree limb, it seemed, was her partner. Her own gown, floating and drifting with every graceful movement, was her partner.*

In the sunlight where he sat writing, she danced again across the vision of his memory. He saw again her weightless feet press against the ground and spring, vaulting lightly into the air; he saw her land again, and turn and leap once more, to no other rhythm than the murmur of the breeze at play among the leaves.

It had been only a moment before she became aware of him, and she stopped dancing immediately. Her breath was somewhat short, and her cheek slightly flushed, though if this came from anything more than the mere exertion of her dance, there was no indication of it in her poise; she showed neither shame nor shyness. Rather, she looked at him directly, almost proudly, and flashed him an easy smile.

"And do you wish to dance, Mr. Stephen Walker?" she said, still catching her breath.

The invitation had caused him, in turn, to flush. "Your father asked for you. It is nearly time for a break and we—"

She waved a hand dismissively. "And you are thirsty. Very well, I will attend to it. I suppose there are better things to occupy ourselves with than dancing." She stepped to the abandoned basket and retrieved it. "My father would certainly say so."

"You dance wonderfully." He had felt foolish to say it but wished to offer her something for having interrupted her.

She had flashed him another easy smile at this, but her words belied the look on her face: "When there are so few chances for great delight," she said vaguely, "one learns to abandon one's self completely in the simplest of pleasures."

Those words had echoed strangely in his heart for many days after, and sitting on the rock now, in the sunlight of the vineyard, he set them down in his journal.

––––––––

Grace read his words with unfocused eyes, sitting alone in his silent study. She had read through the last number of pages as though each word cost her a drop of her life's blood. Never before had she heard him even utter the name Ariadne, let alone give any hint of the compelling young woman she now met in his journal. His entries through this time were often hurried and clipped, but even so they could not disguise the burgeoning attraction that had so obviously flowered between them.

Years of wasted waiting passed through her mind in an instant, sharpened to a searing point of white-hot light. Those long-pledged promises to return to her arms, his professions of great love and deep longing, empty excuses for lingering on Crete when he long since should have returned—every letter he had ever written her—echoed like taunting laughter in her mind.

The usual questions that come to those in moments of great pain rose in her heart—why? and why not? and how? and how could?—but there was no one, of course, to ask them of, and no way to answer them that would have made any difference.

She dragged a distraught hand through her hair, bringing it to rest in a great fistful at the back of her head. She shook her head and blinked her vision clear. There was nothing she could do now, of course, but to keep reading. The need to know loomed so large and suddenly in her that it crowded out even the pain.

So she reached and turned the page.

She found me once writing in my journal, standing near to me and peering over my shoulder with a kind of playful curiosity.

This was at the table in the kitchen of the villa, early in the morning before the work for the day had begun. Nikos was there, too, sharpening a pruning knife, solemnly grinding it on the stone and testing its edge occasionally against his thumb.

She teased me about the journal: "Stephen Walker, always so serious whenever he writes in his book," she said, or something like. I was self-conscious and closed the journal, but she persisted. "Please," she said, "Do not let me interrupt."

I opened it again and began flipping through the pages shyly, when she put out her hand suddenly on the page.

"I know this," she said.

It was the sketch I had made at Knossos, of the bull vaulters. I asked her about it. She explained how she'd seen the fresco at Knossos once, when Ianos had brought her there.

"It is such a wonderful picture," she told me. "I have always loved it. It is very wild, isn't it?"

I tried to explain to her about the ancient Minoans; I tried to tell her about the bull-dancing rituals. She was especially intrigued to learn that among the Minoans, the women vaulted with the bulls as well as the men, that they were honoured equally in the ritual.

This seemed to satisfy something deep and unspoken in her...

———————

"And once again Stephen Walker writes his serious thoughts in his serious book."

Ariadne's voice broke through his reveries while he sat with his journal on the rock. He hadn't noticed her approach, but she was standing over him and teasing him, much like she'd done that morning in the kitchen, in the exchange between them he had just finished writing about.

He closed his journal and looked away.

"My brother and my father are still in Timbaki," she said, "and I do not know when they will return. But it is nearly noon. Perhaps you are hungry?"

"I am. Though I still have some writing I wish to do."

"Put away your book a moment," she said, laughing freely. "If you will come with me, I have something I would show you." She turned and gestured with a nod. "Please, come."

Stephen rose from the rock and came after her. She led him up towards the villa, through the courtyard to the gate that opened into the lemon grove. She said nothing as they walked, and Stephen was unsure if he was meant to speak, so they went along in silence.

They passed through the gate and followed a path down one of the orchard's evenly spaced corridors. The grove was still richly verdant for so late in the season, and the limbs of the trees pressed close to each other. Stephen had to stoop often to avoid the branches, and when it seemed he was lagging behind Ariadne suddenly reached out and took his hand, as if to help him keep pace. The touch of her fingers against his caught Stephen off-guard. They were roughened from the work of the harvest, of course, but for all that very warm and gentle. An impulse rose in him to let go her hand, but an even stronger impulse yielded to it, allowing himself to be led.

The trees parted and they came to the clearing, the ancient fig tree standing in its very centre like some great monument, or perhaps some enigmatic shrine. She released his hand then and stepped towards the tree. He felt strongly that he ought not to enter the clearing unless invited to do so, so he remained where he was and watched her closely. Though he stood in the shade, the air was very warm here, and close.

She turned. "Stephen, what are you doing there? Come. I've something for you."

So he stepped forward and she gestured towards the tree.

"They are ripe," she said, reaching. She pulled one limb lower, to show him. Here and there from beneath the broad green leaves flashed glimpses of dark purple.

"They are ripe?"

"This is the season for figs. You cannot pick them until they are fully ripe. If you pick them too soon, they will not ripen at all. But they are ripe now. Try one." She reached and plucked. "Have you eaten ripe figs before, right from the tree? There is nothing so lovely, I think." She released the limb and it sprang gently back to its place.

Stephen took the fruit she held out to him. It was almost enigmatically purple, and slightly warm from the sunlight. He turned it in his palm. The skin was firm and a bit rough. He looked at her sceptically, and then, because she smiled at him so earnestly, raised it tentatively to his lips.

"No," she said, laughing again. "Not like that—you'll get sore lips that way!" Then she plucked another fig and held it out so he could see. "This is the proper way to eat a fig."

She turned it over and pressed both thumbs at the base of the fruit. Pinching, she split it into two halves, both bursting with soft pink flesh. She gestured to him to do the same, and so he turned his fig and pulled it apart as he had seen her do.

"And now you can eat it safely," she said.

Watching her closely, he lifted one of the halves to his mouth and bit away the flesh. It was grainy with seeds, of course, but very sweet.

"It's good," he said, still chewing.

"Some choose not to eat the skin." She put her half of the fig into her mouth in one bite. "They simply suck away the flesh. But I find it very pleasant to eat the whole fig, skin and all. Try it."

He placed the second half of the fig into his mouth. With the skin, it was more difficult to chew, but he found it somehow more substantial, more satisfying. He nodded at her.

She didn't place the second half of her fig in her mouth, but instead began to speak, very softly, and Stephen could not tell if she was speaking to him or to herself.

"It is not so bad, living here with them," she said. "They are both good to me, each in their own way. Ianos especially. Nikos loves me as a father ought to love his daughter, but he is a hard man and expresses it very rarely. Especially since my mother died. But Ianos, he loves very deeply, and it shows in everything he does. And I am happy here, most often. At least, there is little cause for unhappiness. Although," and here she looked almost piercingly at him, "although that is not quite the same thing, is it?"

There was a pause then, and though Stephen had finished chewing, he said nothing.

"No," she said at last. "I am not unhappy. But—"

"But?"

"What do you long for, Stephen Walker?" She spoke so softly now, the note in her voice so plaintive, that Stephen didn't know what to say.

But she said nothing more, so after a moment he answered. "I am not sure anymore. I wonder sometimes if I've lost everything I once longed for. Or if I discovered it maybe, already, and found it wanting."

"But you have known longing?"

It was his turn now to speak vaguely. "When I came here, I came full of longing. To see the world, to taste it and touch it, to… I don't know—to come into contact with something old and rich and true and deep, something that would—" He could not say it properly in Greek, so he finished in English.

"To find something that would help me get past the everyday stuff of life, to something beautiful that I thought lay behind it. Something transcendent."

"And did you find it, this... something... transcendent?" She also said it in English, so the words came very tentatively.

He looked at the fig rind he hadn't eaten, still held absently in his hand. "I think perhaps I have, though I do not think I can have it, or keep it." There was a perplexed note in his voice, which Ariadne heard as pain.

"It hurts to long for something you know you cannot have," she said. They were quiet together for another long moment, and then she smiled sadly. "We are not unlike each other, Stephen Walker. We are both trapped, it seems. For me it's the shores of this island, my prison. And for you? What is it that has trapped you?"

She spoke very tenderly when she asked him this. More tenderly than she had spoken to him before now. Even so, Stephen said nothing. After a moment he looked into her eyes, and because she was smiling, he smiled, too. But there were tears in his eyes.

"Come," she said, and she touched his hand lightly, though she did not take it as she had done before. "It's getting towards midday, and we've not eaten. As sweet as they are, a fig makes for a very light meal. Come, I will get us some food."

———

She led me from the lemon grove then, back the way we had come. And as I followed her out, I let be true what I have known to be true for many days now, though I have resisted it, and tried to have it otherwise.

I love her.

Though the words pain me to see them written out so simply as all that, to finally admit it, it is a great, great freedom. I have no idea what this will mean for me, of course, or for Grace—oh, God, I would do anything not to hurt her—but the human heart sometimes wanders paths along which reason and logic cannot follow.

And even if I were to find my way home—if any place that is not this place can ever be called home anymore—

even if I were to find my way back, how could anything ever be the same after this, knowing what I now know to be true about my heart, that I have given it away to her?

And so Stephen Walker came to love Ariadne Leventi, the daughter of Nikos Leventi, a Cretan grape farmer from the village of Apodoulou, with whom he had come to stay during the tumultuous days before the war.

Grace stared hard at the words, and read them a third, then a fourth time, through a burning haze. She could feel a rush in the pit of her stomach, as though the ground had suddenly given way and she was falling freely.

Strange thoughts swirled through her mind, verging on the delirious. She thought for just a minute that the bull on the photograph above the desk had leapt from the frame and lunged towards her, as though it stood alive and breathing heavily, filling the whole room with its bulk. Not that it had, of course, but if it had it could not have been more oppressive than the thought that weighed upon her in that moment, a truth that never in all the years of their life together had she ever guessed at: that he had loved another—had given away his heart on Crete—and she had never known.

There was a roar of blood in her ears, and to her swirling thoughts it sounded sharply in that moment like hideous laughter.

She sat up suddenly and looked around her, blinking stupidly.

She was alone.

Her hand trembled as she reached for the journal again, and though it took great effort to do so, as though the paper were made of stone, she turned another page.

CHAPTER TWENTY

Kismet

THE HARVEST FINISHED EARLIER THAN USUAL THAT YEAR, AND BEFORE the end of September the last of the grapes had been brought in. To celebrate, Nikos hosted a great feast at the villa. As far as Stephen could tell, the whole of Apodoulou might have been invited, besides all the extended family members from the surrounding villages who had lent a hand in the work. Guests kept arriving throughout the afternoon, and by the time dinner was served the courtyard was brimming with people and humming with talk and laughter.

Stephen had never quite experienced a joy like that which filled the Leventi home that day. Later in his journal he tried to set it down in words, but nothing seemed quite to capture it. It was heady and wild, to be sure, but also warm and hospitable, profoundly playful, yet full of great wisdom.

Britain had announced its declaration of war some weeks ago, but the grim news from the continent had only recently reached the rural ears of Apodoulou. And it may have been that the looming shadow of what was to come gave this year's harvest celebration an especially fervent edge. It was as if the people were trying by some extraordinary effort to prove that ordinary life could go on in the face of so great an uncertainty.

Whatever the reason, the feast Nikos Leventi held on the last day of September that year was as princely an affair as anything Apodoulou had ever seen. For a long afternoon and late into the evening, food and laughter and wine and song flowed liberally, as though each were trying to outdo the other in abundance.

What Stephen remembered most was the dancing that followed the meal. Long after the sun had lowered itself behind the hills, the courtyard throbbed with music and movement. Ianos brought out his flute, of course, but he did not play alone. Other men whom Stephen recognized from the village had also brought instruments. One rattled a tambourine while another hammered out a rhythm on an earthenware drum. Two men played lyres, the traditional instrument of Crete, their bows dancing gracefully over the strings with melodies that evoked hazy thoughts of distant times and ancient places. The bows of both men were adorned with finely crafted silver bells which jangled in time to the music and added to the song a hint of shimmering cacophony.

The music swelled and urged and beckoned, and whatever song the musicians chose, the crowd in the courtyard seemed instinctively to know what steps came next. They swayed and leaped, clapping hands and stamping feet. Stephen recognized some of the dances—some were steps Ianos had taught him that night on the peak of Mount Ida, others were variations on dances he had seen among the locals in Athens—but he hesitated. He was painfully self-conscious, and though he laughed and clapped along to the more urgent rhythms, he felt far too foreign to join in. Instead he watched from the edge of the courtyard, near the wall where Ariadne's garden was planted, mesmerized by the music and dizzy with the pulse of the beat.

The dance was changing, though, and now the musicians struck up a tune that the whole courtyard seemed to know before its first three notes were finished. "Sousta!" someone in the crowd called out joyously; the younger women clapped and the men cheered, and then the crowd separated into two throngs, by gender, preparing for the dance between the men and the women.

Two or three of the village men jostled over to Stephen and took him firmly, almost roughly by the arm. "Come, Stephen Walker!" they said affectionately. "Come and dance the sousta with us!"

Stephen's self-consciousness intensified, but he remembered again that evening on the summit of Mount Ida, and let himself be led into the centre of the courtyard. The music swelled and urged and beckoned yet more, and Stephen took his place alongside the rest of the village men, facing the group of women who had arranged themselves opposite them.

There was a great laughter and loud noise of applause as the dance began, and every dancer but Stephen knew their step intimately and intricately as the men and women came together. Stephen watched the man dancing next to him, and tried clumsily to mimic the step, always just a quaver behind the beat for all his effort. Someone somewhere cried out "Sousta!" a second time, a few hollers filled the air, and then in unison everyone in the courtyard but Stephen began to clap along with the beat.

They had come together now, the men and the women, and when Stephen looked up this time, Ariadne stood before him, smiling radiantly. Her throat was flushed, from the exertion of the dance, and when she laughed her breath seemed shallow, but still she clapped and called to him—"Sousta, Stephen! Sousta!"—and smiled more radiantly still. It was the smile that finally undid him, and forgetting himself at last in the insistent pulse of the song, he smiled back and began to clap along. "Sousta!" he shouted.

The men and women linked arms now and spun about one another with great abandon. Ariadne took her place at his side and put her arm through his, and Stephen remembered how Ianos had showed him this step, too. He began to spin with her then, and even though at any other time he might have felt intensely silly doing so, he threw his free arm up into the air just as he saw the other men do.

The courtyard flew about him wildly, but the whole while his eyes were fixed on her. The hem of her skirt, he noticed now, was intricately embroidered and arrayed with many tassels which floated wistfully about her ankles as they spun. At her throat, she wore a jangling necklace of gold coins—old Venetian coins, he would later learn—that she had pierced and strung together in a fashion common among Cretan girls. These rang brightly in the lanternlight, seeming to leap along the collar of her dress as she moved to the music.

The song changed subtly yet again, and on cue the men and women parted once more, clapping and kicking their feet. He tried as best he could to keep her in view as the throng shifted, but then they were pairing up with new partners, and a village girl he did not know had taken her place. They danced and moved again and he found himself among the men once more, arms linked and hands held; then again the music swept him towards a new partner, linking arms and spinning about.

The moon had appeared before the sousta was done and the musicians finally set aside their instruments for a short rest. Ever the generous host, Nikos had set out great jugs of wine on a long wooden table near the house. The crowd was hot and thirsty from the dance and many found their way over to take some refreshment. There was much boisterous laughter and more than once someone clapped Stephen's back, congratulating him on having made it through his first Cretan dance so well.

"We will make a son of Crete out of you yet!" laughed one.

The light in the courtyard was much dimmer now than when the dancing had started, of course, and between the press of bodies and the faint dizziness he felt from having danced so freely, Stephen found himself disoriented. He looked about for Ariadne but could not find her in the crowd.

He pushed through to an open space in the courtyard and looked again. This time he saw her, and before he realized he had done so he gestured to her; but he needn't have, for she was already making her way over.

"You dance well, for a foreigner," she said playfully.

"Your brother taught me."

Her laughter sounded to Stephen like a ripple of water in moonlight. "Ianos taught you to dance?"

He could not tell if the note of incredulity in her voice was also playful.

"You have had a good tutor then," she said. "Ianos sees dancing as something almost spiritual, you know. He would not teach just anybody to dance." She was quiet a moment and then: "And did Ianos teach you to dance the sousta, too?"

The question seemed so odd to Stephen, but if it was meant playfully, nothing in the tone suggested it this time.

"He told me that a day might come when I'd be glad I knew it," he said.

"And are you glad today, Mr. Stephen Walker, that you can dance the sousta with us?"

"I am."

"Well," she said. "My brother has taught you to dance like a Cretan, then, and you have learned it well."

She watched the crowd. They were refreshed now, and rested, and preparing themselves for a new dance. Ianos and the other musicians had taken their place with their instruments, and the murmur of happiness was welling up once more.

Suddenly Ariadne took his hand in hers. "Come with me, Stephen!" Though whispering, she said it intently as she squeezed his hand. "There is a place I would like you to see."

She slid her hand up to his wrist, clasping it firmly, and to Stephen she might as well have taken the opening of his heart in her palm and crushed it there. His throat felt very dry from the dancing, and his voice sounded hoarse.

"Where?"

"Come," she repeated enigmatically.

The crowd was taking its place around them, hemming them in as they took positions for a new song, but she held his wrist and led him across the courtyard. He followed her through the gate and out over the space of lawn before the villa, past a stone wall, and down among the moonlit shadows of the vineyard. Once or twice he tried to ask where they were going, but she laughed off his questions and said nothing.

She moved quickly now, almost running, and he followed her along one of the vineyard's shadowed corridors until he was deep among the vines and far from the villa. Only then did she let go his wrist. It was quite dark here among the foliage, although the moon was bright overhead, and he could barely see her moving in the dim light ahead.

"Ariadne?" he said. "What are we doing here?"

Still she said nothing.

The music of the next dance had started in the courtyard; he heard a jangle of the tambourine and the faint note of Ianos's flute, but it all sounded very far away now.

"Ariadne?"

"Stephen!" she whispered, just loudly enough to be heard in the darkness. "Come along. I am right here in front of you!"

And then she turned and ran ahead of him. In the faint light, it only took her a few steps before he couldn't see her at all.

The sound of her laughter came from somewhere further down the corridor of vines, and he stepped forward.

"Ariadne!"

He was whispering, too, though they were far enough from the villa that none would have heard him had he spoken outright.

"Ariadne, it's so dark! Where are you?"

There was no reply, but he thought he could make out the grey shape of her gown as it drifted around a corner and disappeared down another corridor. He moved as quickly as he dared in the dark, and when he reached the corner he could just glimpse her faint shape moving away from him before the shadows enveloped her once more.

"Ariadne!"

This time she replied, and her voice sounded as though it was coming from some inaccessible place. "Stephen! I'm over here."

He was completely disoriented now, and when he called out there was a note of exasperation in his voice. "Ariadne, where are you?"

"I'm only just behind you," she said, laughing.

And when he turned towards the sound, he thought he caught another glimpse of her, on the other side of a wall of vines. He pushed into the vines directly, and though their tendrils pulled at him and their leaves clung, he made it through to the other side.

She was standing in the full moonlight, by a low stone fence that marked off the southwest corner of the vineyard, no longer shrouded by shadows. She was looking out to the south with her back turned, but this time when he stepped up beside her she did not run. From this point, the land sloped quite sharply to the south, and in the moonlight the surrounding hills framed a clear view of the sea, far away and silent.

"If you look closely from this spot," she said, "you can see the moon shining on the waves out there. It's hard to see sometimes, but the moon is bright tonight. Can you see it?"

He looked in the direction she was facing, but he was still confused. "Ariadne, I—"

But she did not wish for him to speak, it seemed, because she interrupted him; and when she began, he could hear in her voice none of the playfulness with which she had led him here.

"When Ianos and I were children, some nights after the house was asleep, we would sneak out here to play in the vineyard at night—what do the English call it? Hide and seek? Ianos was not good at the game and often gave himself up after a few minutes. But I was younger and took it far more seriously. Once I hid so well, and for so long, that Ianos went and woke our parents to find me. He was worried something had happened to me. Father was furious, but Mother took up our cause and bore the worst of it for us."

She kept her gaze on the faint glimmer of moonlight on distant waves, but her tone dropped.

"That was before she died, of course. I remember very little of her now, and what I do remember is often difficult for me to make out. But I remember the day my father told me she had gone away. I wept, I remember, and Ianos with me. We fell asleep together, weeping. But that night, when it was quite dark, I came out to this spot alone. I don't really know why, but there was something comforting here, surrounded by the vineyard at night, and that faraway glimpse of the sea in the dark."

She trailed off silently and Stephen knew he ought not to speak.

"It was easier to cry here," she said at last. "After that, I often came here at night, to be alone with my sadness. Sometimes I even slept here, in the moonlight. Nikos was so lost in his own grief, of course, that he seldom noticed, and he seldom said anything even when he did. Ianos knew, in those days, but he knew enough not to intrude, I guess, because he never came out to find me, and he never asked me not to go—though often when I came back in, sometimes very late, he was sitting in the kitchen for me, awake and waiting. But we never spoke of it."

She reached out and took his hand, though she held it very loosely.

"By the time that first summer was over, everyone knew my father could not handle raising a girl of eight by himself. Someone knew of an English family in Heraklion that might take me in, and Nikos, I guess, was too lost in his pain to do otherwise, so he sent me off."

The silence that followed was long enough that Stephen at last ventured to say something, but it seemed Ariadne still wished him not to speak, for she cut in on him as soon as he began.

"Can I trust you, Stephen Walker?" Even in the faint moonlight Stephen could feel her dark gaze on him.

"Trust me?"

"Do you know the Turkish word kismet? How do you say this in English—kismet?"

"You mean destiny?"

"Yes, destiny. Kismet. The notion that some things are meant to be, that sometimes when two people come together it is as if some unseen hand has pushed them towards each other. This is what we call kismet, the fated pathways of our lives. Do you believe in kismet, Stephen?"

"I did once, but I'm afraid I'm far less fatalistic than I used to be."

"It is not fatalistic; it is destiny. I believe very much in kismet, and I have thought for some time that perhaps you are mine." Her grip on his hand became slightly less loose. "You are an answer to many things I have hoped for, for a very long time. And I can't imagine it was an accident that brought you to me. So I want to give my heart to you. Maybe I already have, I don't know, but—"

"But—"

"But can I trust you?"

"Ariadne, I—"

"I know you will say I can. But I also know there are things you have left behind to be here, things you wish not to return to, perhaps. Dark thoughts, maybe, that you write down in your book when no one is listening? You told me once that you had come here to find something that would take you beyond the everyday stuff of life. And perhaps you have found it here—I hope that you have—but when all this, too, becomes for you the everyday stuff of life, what then? Can I trust you then? Or will the same yearning that brought you to me take you away from me again?"

Stephen was very quiet, and she did not speak. Both strained their eyes for the faraway glint of the moon on the Aegean, in silence.

Finally Stephen spoke, and when he did the words came cautiously.

"Ariadne, I don't know if this is kismet or not. It is true that it was a kind of yearning that brought me to you, but I do not know if there was some deeper destiny than that. And—" He paused for a weighted moment, taking both her hands in his. "And I do know that I love you. Whatever the circumstances that brought us together, I know this much is true. And if you will trust me with your heart, I'll do my best to prove worthy of it." She said nothing, so he added, so softly that it was more said to himself than to her, "God knows you already have mine."

There was another long silence. Then, whether it was the invisible hand of kismet that moved him towards her, or something far simpler than that, he was not sure, but he leaned forward. She did not withdraw into shadow this time, but leaned towards him, too. Her eyes were closed, and in the moonlight she looked to him almost unapproachably lovely, though he did approach nonetheless.

A harsh noise interrupted them suddenly, startling them back to an awareness of their surroundings. The noise sounded again—a reverberating crack ringing out from somewhere near the villa—and again it came, and again. By the fourth time, Stephen had placed the noise; it was the report of a rifle, pealing out into the night.

"They are firing guns to celebrate the end of the harvest," Ariadne said, and there was a faint note of anxiety in her voice.

Another report of rifle fire sounded through the night, and it was answered by two or three more.

"We will be missed," she said, turning towards the house. "Come quickly!"

Stephen turned, too, and a new chase ensued through the vineyard as she fled through the shadows and back towards the house, with Stephen close behind her.

————————

They were wed before the winter, on October 29, 1939. Stephen's journal was mercilessly precise in its record of this event.

He was a foreigner, of course, living on Crete without a home or an income, but he was also a westerner, and the gossips of Apodoulou satisfied themselves with the assumption that, as a westerner, he must inherently possess the means to support a wife. And anyway, Nikos had welcomed him into his house and consented to the match, so no one in the village spoke out against it. Indeed, those villagers who had seen them leave together, hand in hand on the night of the harvest festival, smiled knowingly among themselves and agreed that the marriage was not merely acceptable now, but in fact a moral necessity.

Although the two had lived together under Nikos's roof for many months already, when they announced their intention to marry Ariadne was promptly spirited away to live with an aged great-aunt in the village. To ready them for a proper Cretan wedding, the villagers told Stephen, the bride and groom must be apart for at least the month during which the preparations were made.

The whole ordeal was so novel to Stephen that he later wrote about it in great detail. The dowry arrived at the villa the morning of the wedding, with enthusiastic shouts of good will, and a traditional firing-off of guns to greet it. A great crowd of villagers brought it up from the home where Ariadne was secluded, and Nikos set out a generous table of sweets and wine for their refreshment while the bridegroom inspected it all. Feeling like an outsider, Stephen was rather awkward in this task, but the villagers aided him immensely, picking through every item and commenting on each one. It was mostly practical stuff—linen, furniture, crockery, and whatnot—though a number of the items clearly had a symbolic value that Stephen could only vaguely guess at, things like coins, flowers, cottonseed, and sugar. The villagers warmly assured him that such gifts would bring his marriage rich blessings and much happiness. Stephen, of course, had no money to offer for the traditional bride price, but Nikos clapped him heartily on the back and assured him that he could work out his payment in the coming months at the vineyard.

When everyone there had personally approved the dowry on Stephen's behalf, they packed it all away into Nikos's home, and the preparations for the ceremony itself began. Ianos had provided Stephen with a traditional Cretan outfit, which he did his best to wear authentically. Many of the villagers sent up a cheer when he emerged from the house dressed like one of them, and with a good number of firm handshakes and pats on the back he set out down the road that led into the village. Ianos walked closely at his side, as his future brother-in-law, although a growing crowd of well-wishers thronged him the whole way.

Nearly the entire village was crowded around by the time they arrived at the house where Ariadne waited for him, and at Ianos's prompting Stephen called her out. The atmosphere was joyful, almost boisterous, but everyone grew suddenly sombre when she emerged and stood smiling brightly on the threshold. She was dressed simply but beautifully in a traditional wedding gown of rich black, her dark hair done up in an intricate braid and her dark eyes shining. They set out together for the church, and now only the wedding guests escorted them, though the whole crowd still shouted out their congratulations and milled about happily long after they were gone.

In the village church, they came before the priest who said the rite. The ceremonial communion wine was offered them, Ariadne drinking first and watching Stephen with wide, dark eyes the whole while, and then Stephen taking his turn at the cup. They were given honey and nuts—symbols of God's sweet blessing on their union, they were told—which they ate together, chewing gravely. A prayer was prayed, a blessing invoked, and the ceremony was over.

They emerged from the church as husband and wife, clasping hands and beaming. The throng of wedding guests crowded around again and swept them up together along the road to the house of Stephen's new father-in-law, where, as was the custom, the bride's father had prepared a grand wedding feast in celebration of his daughter's union.

CHAPTER TWENTY-ONE

Hymenean

THE WEDDING FEAST LASTED A FULL THREE DAYS. IT WAS CUSTOMARY FOR the bride's father to host a prolonged celebration as a sign of his lavish generosity, and Nikos Leventi, it seemed, was unwilling that any should doubt his munificence. The doors of the villa were thrown open to neighbour and kin alike, and over the course of the next three days throngs of people came and went, food and wine flowed without end, and the courtyard rang regularly with song and dance and laughter.

Very late on the first night of the celebration, Stephen and Ariadne slipped away from the feast and disappeared together into the villa. Though no one spoke of it outright, their going was noted with great approval by the wedding guests, and one or two of the elderly women passed a quiet smile between themselves, as if to acknowledge that they would not see the newlywed couple again until morning. The closest anyone came to discussing it openly was Nikos, who gave a good-natured laugh when a yellow light in the second floor of the villa, the window that looked out from Ariadne's room, blinked suddenly out and went dark. Someone said something to him about his little girl becoming a woman and he laughed happily again, and that was all.

In the corner of the courtyard where the musicians played, Ianos noted their leaving, too. He lifted his flute and started a familiar tune. His friends joined in and someone struck up the melody, singing loudly, if somewhat drunkenly, the words of a traditional Cretan wedding song:

> My bride! Tree without stars, moon without stars!
> Bride of my house, where will you go to blossom and bear fruit?

———————

That same day, on the other side of the world, a heavy rain soaked the city of Halifax, and a rather restless Grace sat impatiently in the meeting hall of the Barrington Street Mission, watching grey runnels of rainwater streak the window, as she waited for the Sunday service to be finished. It was late in the afternoon. The mission staff had finished serving and cleaning up from the day's meal and, as they did every Sunday, they gathered with the men for a Sunday afternoon prayer service.

Often ministers from the various congregations that supported the mission were invited to lead, though this particular Sunday an itinerant preacher with loose connections to the Salvation Army was visiting and they had asked him to speak. He had a spontaneous style and an urgent tone, rambling freely without notes or organization, but he had a pithy sense of humour and a rich wealth of homespun wisdom which made him very easy to listen to.

Grace was more used to the careful preaching of Reverend Elliot, however, who made his point with great economy of language and seldom strayed far from the text. As a result she found it difficult to concentrate on what the preacher was saying. Her thoughts drifted continually back to the most recent letter she'd received from Stephen, over a month ago now but still fresh in her mind, which explained how the growing tensions in Europe had made travel from Greece impossible, and he did not know when it would be safe for him to return.

Not long after it had arrived, of course, war had erupted with a great tumult around the world, and the last of her hope had been smothered in it.

With a great effort, she forced herself to focus on the preacher's words. He had chosen the Parable of the Prodigal Son as his text, and however far he rambled, he continually returned to this one central theme: that the Father never gave up waiting for his wandering boy to return.

"And so we see in our text today," he said, "that even when he was still a long way off, the Father saw him coming and rushed out to meet him. And we are left wondering: how *did* the Father see his son at such a great distance, except that he was watching for him? And waiting for him?"

The rain rushed against the windowpane, and the sound made it hard for Grace to pick out the words.

"And we know, too, that the son must have been away for some time. He had, after all, come to the end of his wealth. So if the Father saw him a long way off on the very day he came over the hill and home, then surely, *surely*, the Father had been waiting and watching *every day* that he was gone. Patiently, lovingly, longingly waiting for his wayward son to return."

The preacher then wandered into an earthy story about his dad's hunting hound on the farm back home, who waited interminably on the steps of the porch whenever his dad left for the day, whose ears would prick up whenever he started for home, even when he was a long way off, and who would rush out joyously to greet him well before he ever entered the yard.

He assured them all that he was speaking only reverently when he suggested that Our Heavenly Father was not unlike that hound, waiting interminably for us to return to him, and then he launched into something she could not follow about a mystic poet named Francis Thompson, who once called the Lord the "Hound of Heaven."

Despite his assurances, it did not seem altogether reverent to Grace to compare God to some faithful hunting hound waiting for us on the porch of heaven. Was he really as loyal as all that? she wondered absently, watching the rain beat tirelessly against the window. She had never thought before to use the word "loyal" to describe God, and it made her uneasy to hear it spoken so plainly. Reverend Elliot would speak about the faithfulness of God, certainly, his love and mercy, of course, but Grace had never heard God described quite like this before.

"But so it is with the Lord," the preacher was saying. "He is unswervingly loyal to his own. Though they may wander, he does not drift or move. And—" his tone here took on an earnest edge "—and the moment they turn their feet towards him, he will rush out with open arms to welcome them in!"

He meandered into another personal story, this one pertaining to his own prodigal past. He described a life of dissipation and wild living before he'd met the Lord, making indistinct references to his struggles with drink and gambling, which mercifully the Lord had delivered him from.

"Because the minute I turned my feet towards home—towards him, I mean to say—that *very minute* he came rushing out to meet me, to greet me, and save me!"

Many of the men listening were nodding, and more than once a furtive hand rose to wipe away a quiet tear. But Grace was still wrestling with that one word the preacher had spoken, the word she had never heard spoken of God before: loyal.

There wasn't much time to mull it over, however, because the preacher moved then into a time of prayer. And unlike the typical ministers who led the service from time to time and who always offered a carefully measured pastoral prayer from the pulpit, this preacher flung the doors wide, urging any and all who wished to encounter the loyalty of the Father—the way the prodigal son had in the story—to come forward for prayer, even in that moment.

"Give your prodigal hearts to the Lord," he said, and something almost musical danced at the edge of his voice. "Come home to the Lord and discover how truly loyal he is to his wayward children."

A number of men arose and went forward, and even though she had found it so hard to focus on his words throughout the sermon, something suddenly sprang up in her heart, spontaneously and somewhat terrifying to her, and she found herself longing to go forward, too, and discover beyond hope that what this stranger had told her about God was true.

She looked around timidly. There was a knot of people at the front now and the preacher was praying over them earnestly, often placing his solemn hands on their heads or shoulders. There was some weeping here and there, and once or twice someone cried out. The scene struck her as very tender, but she also noticed very quickly that none of the mission workers had gone forward. Only the men who used the mission, who depended on its charity, had responded to this invitation for prayer.

Though she had an overwhelming desire to join them, she told herself the invitation must not have been for her. At any rate, she stayed where she was and resisted the urge to take her place among this throng of prodigals as they stepped forward into the loyal embrace of their Heavenly Father.

Grace was drenched when she finally arrived home that evening. The weather had not let up all afternoon, and though she had brought an umbrella with her the walk had been long and the rain slanting, so that it had not protected her much. She had a chill when she came through the door and hung her sodden overcoat to dry, though she wondered if she was not trembling because of what she had heard at the mission that day. Certainly, the longing she had felt at the end of the service still lingered with her.

She changed into dry clothes and made herself a hot cup of tea. She had it in mind that when she was quite warm again she would find the great family Bible in the parlour and reread the spot in Luke the preacher had been speaking from. She wished to linger one more time over this strange story of so patient a God.

Before she could, however, there came an unexpected knock at the door.

It was Margaret. And even if she had not been without her umbrella and soaked by rain, Grace would have known from the look on her friend's face that something terribly urgent was the matter.

"It's Beth," she said unsteadily. "And Wallace. Their little Johnny has been ill all weekend and is getting worse. The doctor's been by, and… oh Grace, they're worried he won't make it through the night. Please come… Beth's asked us to."

Margaret's father was waiting with a car in the street. Grace saw the headlights glistening in the rain beyond Margaret's shoulder. She nodded and grabbed her overcoat—still dripping from her walk that afternoon—and leaving her tea untouched on the table she rushed out into the rain to help.

Wallace met them at the door. "Beth's in the nursery with him," he said softly. He was clearly trying to hide the worry in his voice, but the look in his eye betrayed his best efforts to sound reassuring. "The doctor thinks its infantile pneumonia. It's been so cold and damp, after all. But he's administered a good dose of prontosil, which should help. It's a sulfa drug, you know, and it's new, but he says it's the best treatment for pneumonia there is. We're to watch him through the night and give him another dose in the morning. If he gets worse, we're to bring him in. Though I'm sure he'll pull through."

He gave a weak smile as he said this last part, and Grace knew he was trying more to convince himself than he was them.

"May we see her?" Margaret asked.

Wallace did not say anything more, but nodded and led them down the hall.

They found Beth in the nursery, hovering over the crib with her hands clutched together and pressed against her lips. Her distress was palpable in the air, and the room was deathly silent. They could hear the faint ticking of a clock, and the baby's laboured breathing, but only if they listened for it. It was so weak and intermittent.

They stepped up to Beth's side and looked with her into the crib. They knew at once that the situation was very serious. His dark hair was plastered with fever against his head, and he lay perfectly still and pale. He was uncovered, because of the fever, and they could see the laborious rise and fall of his little chest as he struggled to breathe.

Grace placed a hand on Beth's shoulder, and she felt her friend stiffen at her touch. She was entirely at a loss for words, so she stood quietly and looked a long while at this little baby boy as he worked so hard to keep his body breathing.

"The doctor says the prontosil will help," Beth said at last, her voice trembling. "He says that if it does its job, the fever should break by morning and then his breathing should improve."

"Of course, it will," said Margaret feebly. "Beth, is there anything we can do?"

"Do you think we might pray?" Beth turned to her friend and her eyes were raw with unshed tears.

"Of course, dear," said Margaret, and she directed a look towards Grace. "We can pray for you, can't we, Grace?"

"And for him?" Beth said.

"Yes, of course." Margaret put her tender arms around Beth's shoulders. "Come, let's find a quiet place to sit. Look, Wallace is here and he can watch him while we're in the next room."

Beth allowed her friends to lead her out from the nursery into the parlour. They sat together on the chesterfield, Grace and Margaret each taking one of Beth's inert hands in theirs. She said very little, though she did repeat once more what Wallace had told them at the door, that the doctor had been by and administered a dose of prontosil, that they were to take him in if he did not improve.

"Shall we pray, dear?" asked Margaret, and she began speaking softly and squeezing Beth's hand. She called on God in his providence to protect her friend's helpless baby and asked him in his wisdom to impart peace and mercy to them all.

Grace felt as though there was something missing in the prayer, that they might do more than simply throw themselves on the faceless providence of God, but when she tried herself, she could do no better. She breathed out a broken stream of words, asking vaguely for God's will to be done on earth as it is in heaven, for God to comfort and console, but she could find nothing else to say.

It felt woefully incomplete, of course, but when they were done Beth squeezed their hands and looked at them meekly. "Thank you," she said quietly. "It helps to have you here."

They stayed with Beth through the night. She and Wallace took turns keeping vigil over their sick child, and once or twice they took a long time in the nursery together. Sometimes when Beth emerged, she would suggest in a shaky voice that she thought perhaps Johnny was looking better than he had, though most often she simply looked distraught and said nothing.

Towards three o'clock in the morning, the vigil was clearly taking its toll on these harried young parents and Grace was able to convince them to get some sleep.

"I'll take a turn watching. And if you do have to take him in tomorrow—" They started to protest against Grace's acknowledgement that this might in the end be necessary, but by now they were far too exhausted to see it through. "*If* you have to take him in tomorrow, you will want all the strength you can get. Please. Sleep. I will wake you if there are any changes at all."

In the end, they gave in and found their way to their beds for a few fitful hours of sleep. Margaret was already curled up on the chesterfield, having given in to weariness an hour or more earlier, so Grace crept quietly into the nursery by herself to stand a lonely watch.

The room was dark, but a light was on in the hallway, and with the door left slightly open there was just enough to peer dimly into the crib. There was a tomblike silence in the room, broken only by the baby boy's faint breaths, a tiny rattling sound that only exaggerated the oppressive stillness of the room. She watched him closely for a moment and became suddenly aware that she was holding her breath.

She let out the softest sigh and reached down gently to touch the baby's feverish forehead. It was very warm, and the hair was damp. She kept her fingers quite still, so as not to waken him, and closed her eyes.

"Please Lord," she prayed, and she did not realize it but she was praying out loud, in a broken whisper. "Please Lord, not him, too."

It felt as though the words were coming to her from somewhere far away. A picture rose in her mind of a young boy and young girl reading *The Odyssey* to each other on the sunlit sand of a silvery seashore; and then another, quickly after that one, of a drowned face lying serenely in a casket far too small to seem proper, in a heartbroken church somewhere, and a family of three clutching hands, dressed all in black to mark the gaping wound they now carried together. She saw a forlorn tombstone in a churchyard then, and a girl slumped in the blue-tinted shadows of a stained-glass window, alone and weeping until a boy came to her side.

"Please Lord, spare him, at least." As she whispered these words, it did not feel as though they were hers, but she said them again, almost inaudibly, and when she opened her eyes she saw that she was lightly stroking the child's hair.

She thought of Stephen then, somewhere far away, buried amid the debris of the ancient world he had unearthed. She remembered embracing him a final time, the night before he'd left. She remembered the heartbreak of this last letter she had received from him, with rumours of war, and risk, and danger, and death.

She looked sadly into little Johnny's beautiful face, hauntingly serene as it burned with fever, but she had no tears now. And an unexpected tenacity glimmered somewhere deep inside her. She stroked the child's brow once more and her hand came to rest on the top of his head.

"If," she whispered into the darkness, "if I am here and he is there, for no other reason than this—that I might be here to intercede for the life of this child—if that were the only reason we must be apart, it would be enough."

She fell silent and absently reached her free hand to the locket around her neck. She clutched it tightly, as if clinging to a final piece of flotsam from a hopeless shipwreck in a dark storm. And then she let it go.

Please Lord, she prayed a final time, without words now, but with something groaning inexplicably and inexpressibly in her heart. *Please Lord, spare this child, and it will be enough.*

Her hands did not grow warm this time, the way they had so long ago, that day she had prayed on the steps of the Barrington Street Mission for the man with the aching tooth. But even so, Grace felt suddenly sure that the child would not die. She was, in that moment, more sure of this than she had been of anything she had ever hoped for before—so sure that the word hope hardly seemed to fit, and yet it was hope, for it was the substance of something she knew but could not see. This child would live.

She lifted her palm from the boy's head, and though he stirred softly he did not wake, and she crept from the room, closing the door quietly behind her.

———————

The fever broke sometime after five that morning. By seven o'clock, he had improved enough that a hopeful tone stole into the whispered exchanges Wallace and Beth passed between themselves. His breathing became steadily more even and his body cooled, so that by eight o'clock, the time the doctor had set for his next dose of prontosil, they were even beginning to wonder if it was necessary. They did give him the medicine, though, and shortly after he began to fuss for food, the first real healthy noise he had made in two days.

Margaret called up her father to bring them home shortly after nine. Grace was due at the mission that afternoon and hoped she might still get some sleep before the morning was gone. Her parents were out when she arrived home, but she found her way into her room and collapsed on her bed without undressing.

She was exhausted, of course, but sleep would not come. She lay on her back staring blankly at the ceiling, her mind racing with everything she had been through since yesterday. She thought briefly of Beth and Wallace and their baby boy, her prayers in the thin hours of the morning, and wondered if everything would be different for her after this night.

Her mind went even further back. She thought of the preacher at the mission that evening, his rambling sermon about a prodigal son and a patient father, the urgent invitation to embrace the loyalty of God.

She thought about nothing at all for a moment, her mind falling so still that she might have drifted into sleep. But then suddenly she turned in her bed and slipped from the edge, down to the floor on her knees. She knelt beside the bed and pressed a furrowed brow against folded fists, like she had done as a child, and she prayed. She muttered something indistinct but reverent, about guilt and regret, whispering her desire against the bedspread.

But if you can use all this yearning and emptiness and ache and longing in some way, Lord, for something good, I willingly give it to you.

"If it might have been different than this," she said, mouthing the words, "I'd have given anything for it to be. But what I wish, I suppose, does not matter nearly so much as what you want, and so..." She fell into stillness again for a long time. But at last she said it: "And so if this really is the only path for me to walk, so long as you will walk it with me, I will see it through to the end."

She untangled her fingers and opened her hands, and whether the palms were cupped to receive something, or to offer something up, she did not know, but she lifted them before her and said it once more: "So long as you will walk it with me, Lord, I will see it through to the end."

A long moment of perfect stillness followed, and when she finally crept back into bed she felt as though she were, indeed, nestling into the most loyal arms in the world. For the first time in a long while, the faint light of a distant smile crept across her face.

———————

Ariadne woke that night, the last night of the wedding feast, from the depths of a deep and happy sleep. She was still bleary with slumber, and it was only as she reached out for him tenderly in the dark that she noticed he was not there on the bed beside her.

She lifted herself to her elbows.

The window was open and a scented breeze played among the curtains. The moon was bright, and the stars, too, and their grey light mingled with the shadows of the room. She could see him standing at the windowsill, silhouetted against the starlit sky, stark still and naked from the waist up. His body looked pale and slight in the moonlight.

"Stephen?" she said sleepily. When he didn't answer, she sat up fully. "Stephen? Are you well?"

The air was warm, but somehow the light on Stephen's shoulders shone very coldly, and she trembled. His head was bowed and she wondered if his shoulders weren't shaking slightly.

"Please, my love, come back to bed... I... need you to keep me warm..."

She meant it tenderly, even playfully, so she was startled to see him suddenly sink to the floor at the sound of the words. He doubled over, and even in the dim light she saw his body heave as though wracked by sobs. But there was no noise, and he said nothing.

She moved to the edge of the bed, alarmed. "Stephen! My husband? What is the matter?"

"Please Ariadne," he said, his voice trembling. "Please don't worry for me. It's nothing… I had a troubling dream, is all…"

She waited a moment. There was a tone in his voice she had heard before, and though she was now his wife, she knew there were still some gaps between them she could not yet cross, however much she wished to.

"A dream?" she repeated.

He lifted his head from where he was hunched over and looked up towards the moon, but said nothing more.

"It is late," she said at last and opened her arms towards him. "And you are cold and I am lonely. Please. Come back to bed."

And because she beckoned him, he rose. He found his way through the shadows and into her arms, and she enfolded him there, holding him closely against her side. She felt him press his face into her, and somehow she knew he was smothering tears against her body, though he still made no sound. And because she loved him very much, she stroked his head softly until he was still and they had both fallen asleep.

CHAPTER TWENTY-TWO
Grace

LOST IN THE SHADOWS OF A FITFUL DREAM, GRACE THOUGHT SHE SENSED movement, as though some monstrous weight was turning towards her in the gloom. She was vaguely aware that she was dreaming, but that knowledge only made her dread more oppressive, not less, because she wasn't sure she could waken if she tried. Somewhere far away, beneath all light and thought and consciousness, a great horned beast lifted its hoary head and awoke. Its gnarled form rose to stand in the darkness, and Grace began to run.

A snort rent the silence, and in the way one knows things one cannot see in dreams, Grace knew the misshapen body had lurched forward, searching for her. Lumbering footsteps sounded behind her, and though she could not smell it she knew that a terrible rancour, like the noisome air of some long-buried decay, came with it through the twisting shadows.

Grace's heart hammered against her breast, and the drumming of it roared in her ears. She stumbled and rose, and ran again, and always those slow, disfigured limbs moved after her. The darkness reeled now as passages and pathways opened in every direction all around, writhing tunnels winding more deeply still into the dreamscape of her subconscious. But every corridor she staggered into only opened onto new and deeper passageways, and always the turbid air throbbed with the stench and snorting of the inexorable presence that stalked her.

She could not tell where they came from, but words formed in her mind. Had she seen them written in his book somewhere? *The Bull of Minos, the Labyrinth, the tread of Ariadne, the Minotaur.* Their images swirled like mist across her vision and she felt something primal and terrifying seep in at the edges of her heart. The beast snorted again, and she wondered if that wasn't its breath she felt burning at the nape of her neck. She lunged forward again, staggered, and fell a final time.

A horned shadow loomed above her, a beast born of shame and sin hidden for ages in the blind corridors of an enigmatic labyrinth, fed for decades on the vitality of her youth, and now it reached at last for its prey in the very heart of the maze that had kept it secret so long. She could not scream; the stench was suffocating in this place, and the weight of its presence overwhelming. Nor did she know if she wanted to. Perhaps here, at last, she might make the ultimate sacrifice and finally find her rest. She lifted her throat with a terrible resignation and waited for the horrid touch of those monstrous horns.

Grace opened her eyes widely, parted them like wild lightning, and with a searing burst of perfect clarity she awoke.

At last she understood.

The room had grown dark. The sun was setting now, and as she became aware of her surroundings she discovered that she was lying unexpectedly on the floor of the study. She could not say how she got there, or how long she had been lying like this, but as she sat up she saw that the floor beneath her was stained darkly, as though she had been sick and then collapsed into a delirious sleep.

She looked around the room. The desk still stood where it had always been, and from where she sat on the floor it loomed over her at an ominous angle. She stood and saw that the awful book was still there, lying open to the last page she had read. She moved very slowly to it and lowered herself numbly into the chair. She sat perfectly still for what seemed hours, eyes blank, mouth still, head inclined over the pages.

But she was not reading now.

She understood.

There was rage inside her, bubbling up with questions she had long since given up asking. Though before she might have turned with these to prayer, she could not, or would not, now.

Because she understood.

She quaked as words like *betrayal* and *deceit* formed in her mind, and with them a profound weight of shame.

She pressed her palm against the travel-worn pages and held them there a long time.

She clenched her fists.

And then the understanding erupted from her, bursting from her body with a trembling heave. The journal smote the wall violently and flew open, pages fluttering apart along the spine. It tumbled to the floor and lay there haphazardly. The force of the blow jarred a framed picture from the wall and it slid to the floor. The glass shattered. She saw, ironically, that it was a wedding photograph.

She placed her arm parallel to the surface of the desk. There was the briefest moment of indecision, and then, with a heave, she flung her arms wildly across it. Papers, letters, stacks of books, and shards of broken pottery together spewed from the edge, scattering like some startled flock of carrion birds. They fanned, broken across the floor, some clattering against the wall. A bottle of ink shattered, staining the floor with a spreading pool of ink and glass.

Desperate now, she heaved open the desk's top drawer. The carefully arranged contents looked somehow contemptuous to her—a pen, a pencil, a magnifying glass, a letter opener—so orderly and precise amid so much chaos. She began to empty these things, flinging them to the floor, methodically at first but with growing determination. She clutched and flung and clutched again and then opened and disembowelled other drawers, and when these all were empty she rent each one from its sliders and hurled it violently to the floor.

When she rose at last and stepped away from the desk, she did not feel the shards of broken glass that cut the soles of her feet. She ignored the sting of the ink at the wounds as she stepped up to the bookcase, trailing a greasy smudge behind her. She stood there, cradling her barren bosom in empty arms, looking over the titles through blurred vision. They seemed so smug to her, suddenly, and she trembled almost violently with understanding. She pulled one from the shelf and weighed it in her palm: *Homer. The Odyssey. With English Translation.*

It burst open with a chaotic flutter of pages when she flung it to the floor. She moved frantically now, flinging volume after volume from the shelves. Pausanias' *Description of Greece, The Complete Poetical Works of Shelley, The Palace of Minos* by Arthur Evans. One by one they clattered down.

She had grown almost frenzied in her purging, until at last she came to rest on a single book, *The World Atlas*, left alone in the corner of one shelf. Its fall, when she threw it down, actually broke the covers open, and the many newspaper clippings folded between the pages splayed wildly across the study floor.

She staggered over to the next bookcase, which held the broken pieces of pottery he had so painstakingly assembled. She hesitated, of course, because she knew they were precious, but then, nearly unaware she had done so, she pulled one down and let it fall. Almost as if she hadn't heard the clatter of breaking earthenware, she reached and dropped another, and then another, and soon she was clearing the shelves in clumsy armfuls until the floor beneath her was treacherous with broken clay.

When the shelf was empty, she held it firmly, bracing her weight and heaving weakly against it. She wanted it to topple, to descend in a great crash of dust and debris and smother her, to bury her finally beneath all the lies and secrets it had hidden for so long.

But it would not budge. She heaved again, but she realized it must be anchored to the wall and she did not have the strength to wrench it free. The thought stuck her like a blow. Fifteen years ago—ten, even—when she was younger, she might have, but not now. She'd been stronger then, and in her weakness now regret rose up unbidden despite her every effort to choke it down. If only she had tried then, when she'd had the strength.

Why had she not tried?

As if in answer, her blind gaze happened to fall on the framed photo hung above the desk, the enigmatic fresco, the fabled *Bull of Minos*. Suddenly this image of three youth vaulting a wild dancing bull seemed almost obscene to her, and she grabbed it frantically.

At last she formed the words.

"Why!" She was looking at the photo when she said it, but she was not of course speaking to it. "Why did you put me through this?"

And because there came no answer, she threw the picture down as hard as she could, with all her remaining strength. It exploded in a burst of glass and wood. She gave a deep groan and collapsed to the floor, her body wracked with violent sobs, though no tears came. She was very thirsty, and very tired, and at last she was aware of a pain in the soles of her feet, but still she sat among the broken debris of the study and groaned, until her thirst and weariness and pain became overwhelming, and she could groan no more.

———

The night was waning, dim with a promise of grey morning, when Grace finally left the study. The house was still dark and shrouded with silence, but she stepped blindly down the hallway, dragging her wounded feet behind her and reopening the cuts that had clotted. She walked tentatively, looking pale and faint when the last of the seeping moonlight happened to slip across her bare arm or throat as she passed a window.

She found her way to the kitchen. Scattering a box of salt and some baking soda, she rummaged through a cupboard until she found a tin of tea, knocking a can of coffee to the floor in a great mess as she pulled it out. She didn't especially want tea, but she hoped that by going through the motions of brewing some she might steady her nerves, so she dragged a kettle to the sink and filled it.

At the window by the sink, she looked out over the lawn, misty and indistinct. Across the yard, far below the window, she saw the ocean trembling against the beach. She closed her eyes and listened for the familiar sound of waves on sand, but the window was closed, so she heard nothing. She opened it to listen and a damp breeze filled the room. She breathed deeply and wondered if she had ever smelled the sea the way it smelled in this moment, in these dull hours before dawn. A vague thought washed over her that the waves were calling to her, but it faded quickly, before she could grasp it for what it was.

The kettle clattered over the burner. A blue flame skipped once and then coughed to life beneath it. She pulled a mug from another cupboard, placed a teabag into it, and set it next to the stove to wait for the water to boil. She then leaned against the counter at the window and breathed deeply once more of the salt sea air.

The murmur of the waves reached her again, and in the confusion of her shame she was sure it was beckoning to her, whether inviting her or summoning her, she did not know. She listened closely and heard it more urgently than before, and before the thought could fade this time she answered it, and walked over to the patio door.

The twilight seemed to welcome her, softly and gently as she stepped out into it. She stood on the porch for a long time, staring down to the beach and the endless stretch of grey sea. The lawn was littered with daisies, and even in the faint light she could just make them out. It occurred to her that she had once thought them very lovely, though in this light they seemed so pallid that she wished, irrationally, that they were not there, at least not this night.

She stepped down the porch, towards the sea. The grass was wet with dew and cold to her feet, though it eased the pain of her wounded soles. It was not clear in her mind where she was going yet, but she moved deliberately, crushing the daisies beneath her, the hem of her dress growing wet and laden as it brushed against the taller grass.

When she finally reached the beach, her wounds made it hard to walk on the rough sand. A sharp rock bit against her heel, causing her to stumble, but she rose and stepped forward without stopping, moving to the very edge of the water as it churned back and forth along the strand. The waves seemed to shimmer in the final throes of the moonlight, and the sound of it became haunting to her, plaintive even. Far away, in that secret place where Helios rises, where Zeus was born—as Stephen might have said long ago—the sun was easing itself at last from the shivering water. She could see the first real glimmer of its cold light on the farthest edge of the horizon, but still the night was not through.

A thought came to her unexpectedly, of Willie and the day he had drowned. Why had she not rushed in after him? It occurred to her to imagine how life might have been different if she had, or if she had kept him from going in the first place. Would everything be other than it was now? Certainly, there would have been nothing binding her to Stephen the way Willie's death had.

She stepped forward into the sea, thinking these thoughts and wishing irrationally that she might have dared the waves to save him that day. Or kept him from going. Or followed him in. The skirt of her dress grew heavy with water as she stepped again, yet deeper, but she did not notice it much.

She must have gone deeper than she thought, and when the next wave came against her it was startlingly cold, tearing a gasp from her lungs. She braved it, however, and stood there as solidly as she could while the undertow sucked the sand away from around her feet. She dared to take one step further, a sense of defiance growing in her, as if she were confronting the surge of the water with these impossible what-ifs.

But the next wave, when it came, exploded against her body with great force, and the pull of it as it drew away swept her off-balance. When she regained her footing, she was deeper than she had been, and the weight of the water in her dress seemed to draw her downwards. Another wave came quickly on the last, and an icy sting clenched about her chest, sucking the breath from her lungs.

It came into her mind that she had gone too far, but the sand beneath her feet was dissolving again with the retreat of the last wave, and she could not steady herself to go back. She wasn't even sure she wanted to. Was this what it had been like for Willie, she wondered, the day they'd lost him? Or for Stephen?

This thought was not fully formed in her mind when the next wave overwhelmed her, pulling her from her feet and lifting her further into the water, drawing her out with irresistible force. She put her feet down but could not find the sand beneath her, and the next wave swept over her with dreadful urgency.

A horrible panic surged in her then, but also, alarmingly, a kind of desperate resignation. She gasped for air when her head came up, but the next wave tumbled over her, and with it came a kind of soft, grey light. She thrashed as frantically as she could, of course, but there was something there, somewhere, urging her to let go. She fought it back, but when the next wave came that grey light seemed to flood her every sense. The cold was everywhere, and when the water swept back out to sea she did not resurface.

———————

In the kitchen, a neglected kettle hissed with boiling fury over a dancing blue flame, its forlorn whistle piercing the silence of the night like a terrible cry of pain. The forgotten cup of tea was ready.

PART IV
War Effort

CHAPTER TWENTY-THREE
An Eastern Canadian Port

GRACE STRUGGLED AGAINST THE SWIRLING SURGE OF THE SEA AS IT DREW her down, the grey light churning all around her until she was blind with it, or lost in it, or both. Vague images passed across her mind, and it occurred to her indistinctly that this must be what was meant when people spoke of having their lives flash before their eyes. Times and places long since passed seemed to swirl around her, each memory bleeding into the next until they came to rest suddenly and in startling focus on a single time and place.

She was standing outside her home in Halifax and she knew the date: September 7, 1939. The trees that shaded her lane were gilded with the early gold of autumn, grey skies lowered overhead, and in an instant the awful memory of those terrible times rushed over her, even as she sank against her struggling, into deep water.

Only one anxious week ago, on September 1, Germany had invaded Poland. This grim news had sparked through Halifax like a match to dry tinder, igniting fires of uneasy activity throughout the city as it prepared itself for the inevitable war that was surely now only days away. Armed guards were stationed at all the vital points of the city's gas and electric systems, Citadel Hill bristled with militant life, and the dockyard bustled with workmen long after the first day of the news had faded into night.

Then, two ominous days later, on the third of September, the rising tension had reached its boiling point, and the measured voice of British Prime Minister Neville Chamberlain sounded from every eagerly tuned radio in the nation, declaring the state of war that regrettably now existed between Britain and Germany; and later the King's voice, appealing to all loyal peoples of the Commonwealth—and surely the people of Halifax counted themselves among this number—to stand by them in their hour of need. Within days, every radio announcement, every cinema newsreel, and every newspaper headline in the city indicated Canada's enthusiastic response to that appeal.

The uncertainty of this time worked strangely on Grace's heart. She struggled often with great fear, thinking of Stephen on the far side of the world, separated from her now not only by mere distance but by the opaque and swirling clouds of war, and yet a great sense of purpose seeped into her as she watched her city burst to life with readiness to play its part. And so it was with a mingled sense of both these things, fear and purpose together, that she stood on the steps of her home that mild autumn day, September 7, 1939, and opened another envelope from Stephen, the first she had received since the dreadful announcement last week.

She had been returning from a morning at the mission and saw it stuffed into the mailbox with a bundle of other papers as she came up the steps. She recognized his thin and wandering handwriting, and though she dreaded to read the sad news it might contain, the very fact of it—that he had sent it, and the awful announcements of these last many days could not keep it from her—gave her some solace. She held the envelope briefly to her lips, breathing against it tremulously, and then pulled a free a folded sheet of paper, packed tightly with his words.

She read it over far too quickly to absorb its news, in a single glance at the page, and then, holding it separately from the rest of the mail, she came into the house. She flung her coat over a chair in the parlour and found her way to the kitchen table, where she smoothed the page before her and read it again more carefully.

August 21, 1939

Dearest Grace,

It's heartbreaking to write this, because I know how much it will hurt you to hear it, and all I can do is to apologize and wish with all my heart that things had been different. But they are not, and we must carry on with a brave face on what is.

She looked out the kitchen window thoughtfully. Something in the tone of these words struck her as strange, uncharacteristically polished perhaps, or overly restrained. She noted it but did not dwell on it for long.

Please forgive me. If I had left Crete sooner and not kept up with my work here at the museum, I know I could have spared you this heartbreak. Had I known what was coming, I never would have asked you to wait. Because what can I do now? I know I cannot ask you to wait any longer, but I know, too, that to ask you to throw away everything you've been waiting for would be far too cruel a thing to do.

Again his odd way of putting things struck her, and she paused. She looked a second time at the date—only one week before the clouds had finally burst over Europe—and wondered if it had simply been the chaos of that coming storm working on his heart as he wrote, that made his words sound so cool and distant.

I saw Professor Percy this morning and we discussed my options. He says that the whole continent is in a state of readiness now, that war is inevitable. He warned me against trying to leave Crete at this time, especially as I must travel through Italy. The trip would be dangerous enough, but more so for me, since my visa expired this spring. I would surely be under close scrutiny, as a foreigner leaving Greece and travelling through Italy without any papers. On Percy's advice then, I've decided to stay exiled on Crete for the time being.

Exile—the word filled her with a heavy weight to see it so starkly written, and she thought of a line he had sent her in another letter months ago, something about a song he'd heard in Athens, how the man in exile must put on black for his clothes to match the colour of his heart. Here at last was something that sounded distinctly Stephen.

I cannot say how long all this will last. Perhaps Percy is wrong and the turmoil on the continent will be resolved without conflict. Perhaps very soon it will be safe to travel again. I cannot say. None can. But no matter what has happened, and no matter what will happen, I need you to know that I do love you and always will.

I am so sorry that my choice has caused you such pain, but if you are able to, please find strength for these dark times, at least, in my love. I only wish I had done more, or perhaps left some things undone.

Yours always, Stephen.

She read the letter a third time, going painstakingly slow. It still struck her as somehow unlike Stephen in many places, and one or two of the lines would have felt vaguely ominous were she to have dwelt on them. *But no matter what has happened* (so odd a turn of phrase)… *or perhaps left some things undone* (such a strange way to end).

But she did not dwell on it, because of course only a week after writing these words the worst of his fears had been realized and the war had come at last. Now, more than ever, she needed the strength he offered her in his love. And so she let her uneasiness pass and clung instead to the one thing she was sure of, that he loved her.

She heard her mother calling softly from the landing of the stairs, and the sound brought her back to herself. So soft Mother's voice had become these days, Grace thought absently. Father's work in the Marine Service had grown grim since Britain's declaration of war, of course. He had only been home once in the last week, and then they had stayed up far into the night, talking over softly and sadly what it might mean for him, should Canada follow Britain into the conflict. Mother's voice had never really lost the sad tone they had used that night.

"Grace, is that you home, dear? I was beginning to worry."

She felt suddenly a profound need to be strong for her mother's sake, if nothing else. She folded the letter carefully back into the envelope and rose from the table.

"Yes," she said with a note of determination in her voice that she did not expect, "I am home."

Grace sat breathlessly by the radio only four days later and heard the terrible pronouncement that everyone expected and dreaded still more. It sounded thin and static-muted from the speakers, for all its ominous portent.

> Canada has taken up arms against the German Reich… on behalf of Great Britain and all her peoples… on behalf of France and Poland… to help the persecuted of the world and to fight for freedom as this country knows it.

Her parents were both with her that grey Monday morning, September 11, 1939. The news had been rumoured for many days, of course, but to hear the announcer at last reciting this formal declaration of war, so calmly and determinedly through the popping airwaves, gave it a kind of hypnotic surrealism. The three of them listened stoically as the proclamation was read.

> Now therefore we do hereby declare and proclaim that a state of war with the German Reich exists and has existed in our Dominion of Canada from the tenth day of September 1939. Of which our loving subjects and all others whom these presents concern are hereby required to take notice and govern themselves accordingly.

"So we have entered at last," said her mother in a hushed voice. She gave her husband a weighted look. "Oh, Edward, what is going to happen to…"
But the sentence hung unfinished in the air.
The radio carried on with the report.

> The King received the Canadian High Commissioner, the honourable Vincent Massey, in audience Sunday, and has issued a proclamation that "On the advice of His Majesty's Privy Council in Canada, the Dominion is at war."

Mother began weeping quietly. They all knew that Father's division in the RCMP had been preparing for war for many months now, and Mother was acutely afraid that Father would find himself fighting on the Atlantic.

For his part, Father sat pensively in the great armchair by the radio, listening with a furrowed brow and a stone-still look on his face.

Grace thought she ought to weep, but strangely she found she could not. She reached out and squeezed her mother's hand, and she felt something very strong flicker in her heart as she did so.

At last her father spoke. "We'll do what we can," he said, and Grace thought she heard something almost satirical in the strained note of heroism in his voice.

She was on the floor, kneeling near the radio, her forehead bent in studious concentration. Though her mother and father were too numb to look at her closely, if they had done they might have seen a strange light come into her eyes, of quiet hope, perhaps, or daring determination. At least now—she knew it clearly in her heart even if she could not bring herself to admit it—there was at last a concrete reason she and Stephen must be apart, something beyond any decision she or he might make to change it.

She dared not face the fact that she might, in fact, be grateful for this awful announcement, but neither could she bring herself to weep.

Her mother came down from where she had been sitting on the sofa and knelt next to her, her face streaked by slow tears; she held Grace close, cradling her head gently against her shoulder, though it was not clear to Grace if she did so to comfort her or to soothe herself.

Her father rose stiffly from the armchair and walked over to where the two women knelt. He put his hand lightly on Grace's shoulder, squeezed it determinedly—and Grace wondered if there wasn't something desperate in his touch—and then he wandered wordlessly from the room.

Grace continued to sit by the radio long after her mother had finally let her go and followed after her husband, but still the light in her eyes was hopeful, and it did not dim even when she reached to turn off the radio and the room fell at last into a deathly silence.

In the tumultuous months that followed, Grace moved through her responsibilities with a great resolve to do her part. The gears of the city's war machinery shuddered, groaned, and ground slowly forward into dutiful motion all around her. Within a month, a brood of antiaircraft guns had appeared, perched on the rooftops of downtown buildings and scattered among the hills that surrounded

Halifax Harbour. The skies overhead throbbed with the constant drone of aircraft. Ominous drills were practiced periodically throughout the city, with urgent announcements blaring out their enigmatic signals: "Attention all light-keepers in the East Coast area! Instructions A—A for apples—will be carried out!" Alarms like this would sound unexpectedly from the radio, so that no citizen could forget for long how terrible a thing lay on the horizon.

And then came the young men. The city streets became regularly choked with throngs of them, some clad in the blue uniforms of the Air Force but the majority by far wearing the darker blue of a Royal Canadian Navy recruit. This might have been hard for Grace, to pass these heroic bands of adventurous young men on her way to and from the mission, and to realize Stephen was not among them, but she refused to dwell on it and only plunged herself deeper into the work she was doing to help with the war effort.

Throughout October and November, as a dismal winter advanced on the east coast, swirling with dreadful reports of torpedoed ships and sunken vessels in the frigid waters of the North Atlantic, the furnaces of Halifax's military industry were stoked and fanned, and Grace felt strangely warmed in its awful glow.

One morning in mid-December, she found herself standing at the waterfront and watching a transport fleet creep slowly from the harbour and fade, ship by ship, into the dense fog that enveloped the city.

The day was leaden with sleet and she had been wandering along the waterfront, thinking deeply about Stephen, of course, but also her father and mother. Father had been deployed to escort merchant vessels across the Atlantic, and this had taken a hard toll on Mother.

Grace was hunched into her collar against the cold, so lost in thought about all this, that it startled her greatly when a ship's foghorn suddenly bellowed out over the water. She looked up and saw that she had wandered much further down the waterfront than she had intended. The sight of many dark ships being loaded with endless lines of khaki-clad youth brought her up short, and she realized in a moment what she was seeing. There were a handful of others who had been passing at just that moment and had stopped to watch. Grace stepped up to join them.

This was the second convoy of the First Division of Canada's war effort, heading out over the Atlantic to join the struggle in Europe. The rumour was that the first convoy of this division had already left some two weeks earlier under the strictest of secrecy, and this second one was leaving in much the same way. No crowds had gathered to wish it a celebratory farewell, no ceremony or shore bands marked the moment of its departure. Indeed, it was only by accident that Grace happened to be at the waterfront the hour it left, to see it off.

It did not take long for the morning's sleet to gather on her still frame, and soon her hair had become crusted with it, her face rubbed raw with the cold. But she did not shiver, though she was in fact dressed rather lightly for the weather, and she could not look away. There was something mesmerizing, if not a little absurd, in these long lines of bright-eyed young men, their youthfulness and vitality obscured by the formless greatcoats they wore, the weight of their duty belied by the easy swing of the rifles swaying at their shoulders, almost playfully, as they stepped forward by the thousands.

There was a hum of adventure among the men, a daring kind of enthusiasm, but beneath it she sensed a dark note of uncertainty no one wished to acknowledge. She wondered about whoever and whatever these men must have left behind—sweethearts and close kin, friends and family—to answer the inexorable summons of war.

A wind picked up and the sleet swirled, but still she did not shiver—and though she wrapped her arms about herself, it was not against the cold. As she watched the men boarding the furthest vessel from her, a soldier on the gangplank stopped momentarily in his file and turned his bravely beaming face back across the waterfront. It seemed he was searching for the familiar face of a loved one, or perhaps he just felt overwhelmed in that moment with the newfound pride of being a soldier. She could not tell from her distance. But she saw him suddenly lift a gloved hand and hold it high. Even from so far away, she recognized the gesture. His two fingers were raised in an eager V, the hopeful pledge of victory. He waved the hand briefly to no one in particular and, turning back to the file, vanished into the ship.

Without realizing it, Grace nervously lifted her own hand and opened her palm tenderly towards him. The motion was almost imperceptible, but she waved, and then raised her tremulous fingertips against the numb flesh of her cheek. An unspoken petition welled up suddenly in her heart and she found herself unexpectedly praying, against whatever might come, that God would cherish the sacrifice these naïve young men were making, and honour it somehow in the great mystery of his providence.

The sleet became more substantial and determined now, but still she remained watching, praying silently however it struck her to do so, until the last of the ships had been filled and one by one they slid out across the greasy sheet of Halifax Harbour, vanishing like phantoms into the clinging mists of December.

Only after the last vessel was finally lost from sight did Grace finally pull up the collar of her coat and turn pensively but confidently through the snow and away from the docks.

––––––––––

The first wartime Christmas came and went and the new year dawned coldly on an ever-intensifying struggle. Soon every vessel that pulled into Halifax did so with thrilling stories and fearsome adventures to report. The German invasions in Europe had displaced the navies of many European nations, and many of these in desperation had established bases of operation in Halifax, setting up temporary headquarters in the previously unused buildings that lined the waterfront. The streets were regularly thronged with sailors from all around the world, and often, as Grace moved among them on her way to and from her work at the mission, she felt as though she was wandering a city that was no longer hers.

Yet throughout that brooding first year of war, even as the battle of the Atlantic grew feverous in pitch, she did not lose the determination she had brought with her from the docks that dismal December morning. Letters still arrived from Stephen describing the war effort on Crete, how it had disrupted his work at the museum and yet made travel from the island so impossible, but these came far less frequently than they had before, and sometimes months passed without even a whisper of his name. But even so, the simple fact that he was hers, and knowing it was so, gave her a sense of purpose that carried her through the darkest times of that first bleak year.

When the next wartime Christmas arrived, the men and women of Halifax were determined it should still be glowing with merriment and good cheer, however portentously the clouds of war had gathered over the city.

A few months after Christmas, the government would require a careful rationing of goods as part of the war effort, but these measures had not come yet, and if anything the industry of war had brought a kind of heady prosperity to the city's economy. Food, drink, and clothing were to be had cheaply and abundantly, a welcome change to a city still tender with the wounds of the Great Depression. Halifax had issued a precautionary ban on the traditional coloured Christmas lights that year, but that did not seem to dull the city's festive spirit. Every frozen plane of ice, it seemed, jostled with skaters, theatres and cinemas distended with crowds, and homes glowed with abundance and cheer throughout the season.

Many of the families in Halifax had young servicemen over for Christmas dinner that year, determined to do their part by opening their homes to the newly minted soldiers who found themselves gathered in the city from across the country, waiting their turn to cross the Atlantic and join the fray. The Stewarts themselves billeted a farm boy from Saskatchewan, of all places, turned prospective sailor in the RCN. Robert Holden was his name, and he had only been in Halifax a short while. He was scheduled to leave in the new year. Her parents spoke about hosting him as their Christian duty, but for Grace there was something more to it; his presence at their table seemed to point the way to an inaccessible place she desperately wished to be.

"Good evening, Mr. and Mrs. Stewart," Robert said politely when he appeared at their doorway on Christmas day. "Miss Stewart."

He was in uniform, of course, and this combined strangely with his youthfulness to give him a kind of radiant glow.

"Welcome to our home, Mr. Holden," Mother greeted him. Though sincerely hospitable, her tone struck Grace as unnecessarily formal.

"Thank you, ma'am." Robert doffed his white cap, still smiling, and looked all the more aglow. "Please, call me Robert."

Father extended his palm and he gripped it tightly.

They led him to the dining room. There was something very compelling about him, and Grace caught herself watching him closely as he took his place at the table. She guessed his age at eighteen, possibly nineteen. He was brilliantly blonde and carried himself with the confident poise of a boy newly stepped into the vigour of his manhood. His eyes were startlingly blue, like a baby's almost, she thought, though surely there was something hard in them, too, like ice perhaps, or steel. They seemed to her remarkably like the eyes of an untried warrior.

Father said grace.

"A toast?" Mother suggested, lifting her glass.

"Yes, a toast!" It was Grace who spoke. She raised her glass, too. "To all the brave young men overseas," she said, and she let her eyes meet Robert's briefly. "May God go with them."

Robert lifted his, too. "To a speedy victory," he added, but his eyes looked away from Graces as he did.

The glasses touched and Mother echoed the sentiment. "To a speedy victory. May God go with them!"

As dinner was served, Grace found herself wanting very much to say something that would both nurture whatever remained of the boy in this young man, and also strengthen whatever it was of the warrior she saw in him. She remembered the young man who had flashed the V of victory at the docks last year, and of younger boys before that. She thought of Richard who was even now somewhere overseas doing his part in the Royal Navy, and even briefly of Stephen stranded on Crete because of the war, and she suddenly desired intensely to impart some strength of her own to this untested farm boy from Saskatchewan, as though every boy she had ever known or lost had come together in him.

"Peas?" Mother lifted the lid from a dish of their finest china, steaming dully with green peas. It seemed such a mundane thing to do in that moment that Grace cast her a look.

"Thank you, ma'am." Robert smiled affably as Mother spooned the vegetables onto his plate.

"And mashed potatoes?"

"Please."

Mother and Father were too polite to mention the war at the table, Grace knew, but in the presence of this uninitiated warrior she found it all so pointless and superficial.

"Ham?"

"Yes, please."

"Thank you."

"Here's some gravy."

Something in her bubbled over at last, and without thinking she said, "Are you at all afraid... of fighting in the war?" She had meant it empathetically, but it came out entirely wrong.

The gravy ladle clattered awkwardly and her mother fixed her with an incredulous look. "Grace—?"

Robert looked suddenly uncomfortable, and very childlike in his discomfort.

There was a long silence. Grace shot a furtive glance in her father's direction and saw that he was scowling.

As though trying to mop up a clumsy spill, she sought to repair what she had done with a flood of words. "I only mean that I can imagine it must be frightful, going out into... well, who knows what... and not knowing what to expect. Certainly, I would find it frightening, and I would hardly hold it against you—or any man, for that matter—if you did..."

She trailed off, seeing that she was only making things worse.

Robert looked profoundly uncomfortable now, and what she had thought was the gleam of a warrior in his eyes had faded. In its place was a transparent and innocent shyness.

"Well, I... I suppose it is," he said. "Frightful, I mean. But we all do what we can. And it's better than working a losing farm back home. When it comes to that, I don't even know if I really had much choice. My brother went over, too, with the first division, you know? I guess I'm only a bit behind him."

He lapsed into a silence, but no one said anything, so he said more.

"My mother didn't like us going off, though. That's for certain." He looked towards Grace, though he would not meet her gaze. Perhaps it was just the flicker of the candles Mother that had lit at the dinner table, but she thought she saw a glimmer in his eyes. "Boy, she cried. She warned me not to get hurt, which I guess is a pretty funny threat. 'Don't get hurt or else!'" He laughed ironically, but the glimmer was unmistakable now. "My father, though, he said it was for the best. There's no way the farm could've kept us all going anyway. Don't get me wrong. He didn't say so, but he didn't like us going off neither. But all he said to me was, he said, 'Go and make me proud, Bobby.' So I don't know, but maybe if I focus on doing that I won't have to worry about being afraid. I don't know."

His voice remained steady, but the sadness in it was unmistakable. He let her eyes hold his at last, despite the glimmer in them.

"But if you mean about dying, I can't say," Robert added. "I hope I'll be able to be brave, but really, in the end, who isn't afraid of dying?"

Grace flushed with shame, wishing deeply that she had not made their guest so vulnerable in this way. "I am sorry. I didn't mean to… I—I'm sorry."

Now it was her turn to look away, and she trailed of feebly.

"Well, we mustn't worry about that tonight." This came from Mother, making a valiant effort to salvage the situation. "This is Christmas, after all, and of all the days of the year we needn't dwell on such dreary thoughts as that today! Here, Robert, let me refill your glass." She flashed a look at her daughter and then smiled warmly at their guest. "Don't mind Grace. You know, we do see so much of the war here. I mean, ships are being hauled in all the time. And the refugees and such. It's all so overwhelming that sometimes it's hard to be sure what to say about it, or how to speak of it."

"No, it's all right, ma'am." Robert looked again towards Grace and now the glimmer was gone from his eyes. "It's just that, you know, I've never been to sea before—I mean, I've never even *seen* the sea before. A prairie boy like me, well hell…" He caught himself and looked at Mrs. Stewart. "Beg your pardon, ma'am. But you know, I'd be nervous just going out to sea on a pleasure voyage, to say nothing of sailing in the navy! I guess it's only natural to be a little nervous." He smiled, and Grace dared to think she caught the glint of the warrior shine briefly in his eyes once more. "But I'm ready, you know? I'm ready and willing to take it to those Krauts, and that's no lie."

Her father laughed gruffly. His face had never recovered from the brooding look that had overshadowed it when Grace had first broached the subject of the war. "I've seen a lot of young men going out with the same enthusiasm, Robert," he said. "It's a kind of courage, I suppose. Keep it. You will need it."

"Thank you, sir." He seemed unsure how to take the remark. "I hear you're in command of a corvette for the navy?"

"I used to work for the Mounties, in the Marine Division. With the war, the navy's commissioned me to run escort for the convoys."

"Well, you must have your share of—" Robert stumbled for the right words.

"Adventures?" Mother suggested politely, but with a slight note of nervousness in her voice.

Father laughed again, almost unkindly, and repeated it. "Adventures?"

"Well, I suppose it must be exciting sometimes."

"Well, maybe they're adventures for me, because I survived them. And they're definitely adventures for you because you have no idea what it's really like. But for a lot of young men—and these are boys I'm talking about, no older than you and some far younger—for a lot of them its no adventure out there. It's horror. Absolute bloody horror."

"Dear!"

"I'm sorry. But I just don't want him to buy any of that nonsense about adventures at sea. Because it's all rubbish. There are no words to describe what it's like—the constant fear, wondering if you're the next one to get torpedoed. Those bloody U-boats are like demons, damn them! Ships will just suddenly burst into flames like that! And you'll be sunk before you even know where the strike came from. The worst is watching another ship get it. First because there's nothing you can do to help—I mean, this time of year the sea kills almost as quickly as the fire does—but more because you know the bloody submarine is still down there, and all you can do is just wait around hoping you're not the next one to get a torpedo up the—"

"Dear!" There was a reproving tone in Mother's voice now, and she placed a gentle hand on her husband's forearm.

But he shrugged it off and struck the table abruptly. "Well, they sunk the bloody *Athenia*, for the love of God! A bloody civilian ship, I mean! A passenger vessel. If they wouldn't stop at that, where will they stop! So keep your enthusiasm, Robert, because you'll need all you can spare, but make no mistake what you're stepping into when you step onto that boat come the new year."

"Edward, please." Mother was weeping, very softly though quite obviously, and her voice had grown plaintive. "Not tonight. It's Christmas."

The table fell silent.

Robert swallowed.

"Have some more ham, Robert. Please." Mother's eyes pleaded as she held out the platter.

"Well… thank you, ma'am." He inhaled deeply. "This dinner sure is swell. Almost makes me forget I was away from home. And that's saying a lot, too." He smiled nervously.

"Please…" Grace had trouble finding the words, but both her mother and father had lapsed into a heavy silence, so at last she spoke. "Please, Robert, don't let my father's roughness intimidate you. He's seen a lot this last year and it's made him speak sometimes a bit more directly than he might otherwise do. But I know he means it kindly." She looked sadly but gently at her father. He still did not speak, but the look on his face did soften. "He has lost some… boys… like you… you know, that he cared for very much… and that makes it hard sometimes to stand on pleasantries, I guess. But he wants you to be encouraged tonight, don't you, Father?"

He nodded quietly, looking down and studying the mashed potatoes on his plate intently. "And I want that for you, too, Robert. I wish I could say something to encourage you, because I can only imagine how hard it is, and how hard it will be. So for what it's worth, please do know that I will keep you in prayers. It's not much, perhaps, but it's what I can do."

"Please, Miss Stewart," Robert began, and the affable light returned to his smile when he said it. "Please don't think of it. I understand what Mr. Stewart means. And about the prayer? To me it's worth a great deal."

———————

Edward Stewart sat at the table long after Robert had left and Mother and Grace had cleared the dishes away. He kept the bottle of wine and his glass with him, and even after the bottle was drained he continued to sit, staring blankly over the table.

Like his outburst with Robert that evening, episodes like this—of sitting silently with a bottle late into the night—had grown far more frequent for him. Not so frequent as to be truly alarming, perhaps, but they clearly troubled Grace's mother, who would stand in the doorway of the dining room and watch him silently sometimes for hours.

Tonight he was still sitting there when she finally went off to bed, alone, leaving him to nurse the last of his wine at the table by himself.

Grace lay in her bed and heard her mother pass as she retired to her room. She knew Father was still sitting up in the dining room, and after a deep breath she rose and crept quietly out to see him.

She could not tell if he noticed her standing there—he had drunk a good deal of wine that night—but she stepped very softly to stand next to this strong, stoic man who was her father. She placed a hand on his shoulder. He didn't acknowledge the gesture, so she sat next to him and let her hand come to rest on his forearm. Still he stared blankly at the empty table before him, but neither did he shrug off her touch as he had done with her mother at dinner, so she leaned in towards him, whispering a quiet prayer.

"Please, Lord, do not let me lose him," she said very softly. "Not like this, at least. And if by being strong I might somehow keep him from drifting away, then please: make me strong enough for that."

It was so quietly spoken that she did not think he could have heard, but as she slowly pulled the wineglass from his grasp, suddenly he leaned his head against hers weakly and began to cry openly.

She cradled her father's head against her own and stroked his hair soothingly, as he often had done for her when she was a child and hurt. As she did, she felt a faint light glimmer to life within, and a great strength flowing out from her.

CHAPTER TWENTY-FOUR
Rumours of War

THE INNER STRENGTH GRACE HAD DISCOVERED THAT NIGHT AT HER father's side continued to grow through the coming year as she threw herself into the war effort with great resolve. She did not see her courage for what it was, of course. She simply saw how great the need was—her father's long days at sea, her mother's sleepless nights, her work at the Barrington Street Mission. It exhausted her to be continually moving towards the hurt of others like this, especially as the mission evolved into a hostel for servicemen on shore leave. Yet with her weariness came a profound sense of purpose, and even, occasionally, an overwhelming sense of peace.

This was probably the only reason she found it somehow bearable the day she came across that headline announcing the German invasion of Crete and she was forced to accept the fact that she might never see Stephen again.

It was a mild morning in the early summer of 1941. She had been scouring the daily paper for anything to do with the war in the eastern Mediterranean, as she did every morning. There was far too much to report on, and places like Greece were rather distant corners of the globe, so she seldom found what she was looking for. But every now and then she would come across a passing update on the battle in the Balkan, perhaps, or some frustratingly brief word on the conflict in Greece, and she would know darkly that the war had taken a step closer to him. Today, however, the headline glared at her, its import unmistakable: CRETE FALLS TO NAZI ONSLAUGHT. The article provided few details, but the headline was enough. His island had been captured.

Even then she refused to despair. She brought the paper up to her room and sat on her bed with it. She carefully clipped the article, and then reached for the world atlas she kept on her nightstand. This was Stephen's atlas, and the day he'd left for Greece in the summer of 1937 he had given it to her, wrapped up neatly with coloured paper and tied with a length of ribbon, while they'd stood together for a final moment on the pier. She had thought it an unusual gift at the time, but he explained that it'd been his grandfather's and was very precious to him. He had even told her a story from years ago, from when they'd first met on Prince Edward Island, how he had wished to give it to her then but had been too shy.

"You can see things in it, if you look hard enough," he had said enigmatically. "Or at least, it will remind you of things—faraway and forgotten places." And here he'd given her a warm smile and the brush of a kiss on her cheek. "Perhaps it will help you to follow me as I go… or at least to keep track of me while I'm there."

Of course, that had been almost four years ago now, and for a long time the atlas had sat unopened on a shelf in her room. But when the war had erupted and reports began to swirl chaotically around her, about battles fought and nations falling, she'd turned to the atlas to help keep it all straight.

This had started a couple of years back, when a story about Italy's invasion of Albania had left her wondering how close the conflict had come to Crete. She had pulled the atlas from off the shelf to look up the locations, and discovered that Albania was still some ways from Stephen yet. And anyway, the article had explained that Albania had been a puppet state of the Italians already for years, so it did not trouble her too greatly. Still, she'd clipped the headline carefully and taped it to the page. On a whim she'd found a pen and written a brief line on the map, next to the clipping: *Lord, I place him today into your hands, please keep the war away. April 10, 1939.*

Over the following years, the atlas had become a strange combination of scrapbook and prayer diary for her. Whenever she came across a news article reporting on the advance of the war in the eastern Mediterranean, she would clip it out carefully and fix it to the relevant map in the atlas, often scratching out a brief word of prayer on the page next to it. These reports were few and far between—the focus of the news in Halifax was really on Northern Europe and the battle raging on the Atlantic—but enough news came by that she was able to track the slow creep of the conflict southward.

As she flipped through the pages on the bed, she came across a handful of articles she had collected last year that had followed the Italian invasion of Greece. The first of these was taped to the map of Italy, dated October 29, 1941. She lingered to read it again.

GREECE SAYS "NO!"
Italians Mobilize for Invasion

Athens, October 28—Greece is preparing for invasion today after firmly refusing an ultimatum to allow Italian troops into the country.

Greek General Metaxas was woken early yesterday morning by Emanuele Grazzi, the Italian Minister in Athens, who delivered the ultimatum. The details are unknown, but sources report that the Greek leader's "No!" was unmistakable.

Patriotic demonstrations in the city today suggest that the nation has united itself now under the unpopular Metaxas, against the Italian enemy. Sir Michael Palairet, the British Minister in Athens, was cheered this morning from the balcony of the British Legation, where he promised Britain's support in this struggle "against the Enemy of all the Free World."

Many consider the Italian ultimatum to be nothing more than a pollical charade. Italians have already been massing in Albania and it is rumoured that they have been preparing for this invasion for many months. This made the ultimatum all the more infuriating for the Greeks. The mobilization of Greek troops was furious today, as soldiers piled onto trains, firing hundreds of rounds into the air in their enthusiasm.

She remembered first reading this report last year. It had seemed to her that the inevitable was finally underway, that the war was turning towards Stephen in earnest. Next to the report she had written: *Lord, keep him safe and bring him back.*

On the facing page of this map there was an article dated just a few days later:

ITALIAN INVASION STALLED
Germany Claims Ignorance of Italy's Plans

Athens, November 4—After almost a week of fierce fighting, the Italian advance into Greece has ground to a halt. In the Pindus Mountains of Northern Greece, where civilians and children helped in the fighting, the badly outmatched Greek army was able to stall the Italian advance.

Many suggest that Italy had severely underestimated the Greek opposition, and had expected a triumphant march into the country.

Sources say that the Italian army was not even provided with proper engineer units as a result of their miscalculation.

This defeat will undoubtedly prove an embarrassment to Mussolini, who undertook the Greek invasion to distinguish himself in the eyes of the German Reich. In a statement issued today, Hitler expressed exasperation at the failure of the Greek campaign and denied any prior knowledge of the invasion.

This report had seemed so promising, and such a clear answer to the prayer she had penned only days previously, that next to it she had simply written: *Amen and thank you, Lord!*

From this point onward in the atlas, the maps of the Eastern Mediterranean were now scattered with headlines. As she flipped past them on her way to the map of Crete, the story they told of the Italian campaign filled her again with all the tremulous hope she had carried through the last year as it looked more and more likely with every passing day that Italy would be repelled from Greece altogether.

The headline, ITALIANS PUSHED BACK TO ALBANIAN BORDER, had been dated December 10, 1940. Then came GREEK ARMY ESTABLISHES RIGHT FLANK AT PROGRADETS, ALBANIA, from December 30. Then RAF DOWNS 27 ITALIAN AIRCRAFT OVER ALBANIAN FRONT, from February 29. And ROYAL NAVY WINS VICTORY OVER ITALY IN AEGEAN, from March 30.

She had followed the campaign as closely as these infrequent reports allowed, watching it all unfold from her distant vantage point on the opposite side of the world. The prayers scrawled next to the headlines were a strange mixture of desperate petition and brazen hope, and she found herself beseeching God earnestly on behalf of the people of Greece, as though Stephen's fate was intimately bound up with theirs.

For a time, it looked as though God would answer her prayers and Greece would stand.

It would not last, however. Turning the page, she came upon a map of the Balkan peninsula, to which she had fixed the article that had nearly shattered her hope altogether. It was dated April 7, 1941. She had clipped it out only a few months ago and taped it into this place, scratching a bit from the Psalms next to it— *"Yea, though I walk through the valley of the shadow of death, I will fear no evil."* She read it over again before moving on.

GERMANS LAUNCH DOUBLE INVASION IN BALKANS
Belgrade, Greek Port, Both Bombed

Athens, April 7—Shortly before dawn yesterday morning, the war in the Balkans intensified as Germany launched what has proved to be the simultaneous invasion of Yugoslavia and Greece together.

Relentless bombing throughout the day has reduced the city of Belgrade to rubble. Though exact numbers are unknown, estimates place the casualties in the thousands. This attack comes only weeks after defiant Belgradians deposed the Regent of Yugoslavia for signing the Tripartite Pact with Hitler, allowing him access to the Yugoslavian railway systems.

Later the same day, the harbour of Piraeus, just south of Athens, was bombed by German raiders. The Clan Fraser, a ship loaded with munitions, was hit in the attack, and the resulting explosion destroyed most of the harbour. Eleven other vessels were sunk.

Elsewhere in the Balkan peninsula, fighting intensified as Germany made its long-expected entrance into the war in the Balkans known.

She thought back to the day she had first seen this headline, tucked away in a corner of the paper as though it were a detail hardly worth mentioning in a war that had engulfed the entire world with such terror and tragedy.

And yet for Grace there could be no news more difficult than this simple announcement that Germany had entered the battle on the Balkan peninsula. She didn't have an especially firm understanding of how this development might affect the direction of the war more generally, but she knew well what it meant for her personally.

Germany had turned the brutal engine of its war machine towards the Eastern Mediterranean, and however valiantly the Greeks had stood against the Italians, it was little likely, save by the grace of God, that they would resist the advance of the German Reich. She had seen too many headlines announcing the fall of too many nations to think it might be otherwise.

Her hands had trembled the morning she clipped the article and set it in place in the atlas, knowing that the chances of seeing Stephen again faded with every day. Even so, she had felt somehow vindicated, as though her long wait through deep ache and great sacrifice was her own private act of resistance against the foe.

The next article she'd uncovered had confirmed her worst fears, and if her longsuffering were an act of resistance, it was put profoundly to the test as the shadow of war took another step toward Stephen.

SALONIKA, MACEDONIA FALLS
Greek Homeland Open to German Advance

Athens, April 10—After three short days of fighting, German Panzer divisions took the Macedonian port of Salonika yesterday. This defeat led to the surrender of all the Greek forces east of the River Vardar. Greek and Dominion forces alike have been pushed back to undisclosed locations along the northern line.

With Salonika now fallen into German hands and Yugoslavia likely to fall too, many fear it will leave Greece vulnerable to attack from both the eastern and western fronts. Should Greece fall, it will leave the Allies with no access to the continent.

The events moved swiftly forward from that point. The next map she came to showed the Attica peninsula, and Athens, and the Aegean Sea. The news article fixed to the page was dated a mere ten days after the previous story, and it bore the grim news that the battle had at last reached Athens.

AIR BATTLE RAGES OVER ATHENS
Evacuation of City Imminent

Athens, April 20—The skies over Athens today were the stage of one of the most terrific battles yet of the Balkan campaign. Perhaps not since the Battle of Britain has such valour been on display.

Against terrible odds, 15 fighters—all that remained of three Hurricane squadrons—took on over 120 German aircraft. In a show of great courage and skill, the RAF pilots reportedly downed 22 enemy aircraft for a loss of only eight of their own. Long after the air raid sirens in Athens had gone still, word of this great victory buzzed about the city.

Despite valiant efforts such as these, the retreat of Allied forces continues. Reports indicate that all along the northern line, Greek and Dominion forces have been pulling back. Though some remain optimistic, many expect the order for the evacuation of Athens to come any day now. Just last week, a crowd of British civilians stormed the

British Legation in Athens, demanding to know the plans for their evacuation.

Next to this was taped another clipping from the week following, that bore even grimmer news.

ATHENS EVACUATED TO GERMAN INVADERS
Swastika Raised over Acropolis

Alexandria, April 26—German troops marched into Athens in the early part of the morning today, after paratroop units took Corinth to the west. The German army was swift to crush all opposition, and the swastika was flying in the centre of the city before the sun set.

The fall of Athens comes only two days after the British army received its official evacuation orders. Since then, sapper divisions have been busy destroying munitions dumps and fuel depots to prevent their falling into enemy hands.

With British and Dominion forces pulled out and new headquarters established on an undisclosed island in the Aegean, Athenians could do little but watch as German forces occupied their city.

Alongside this article, she had penned another line from the Psalms. Reverend Elliot's preaching text that Sunday had been Psalm 2, and he had spoken more passionately than she had ever heard him speak before, about the Lord's sovereignty in the midst of the unspeakable turmoil that had engulfed the world and how, although nations may rise and fall and take up arms against nation, even so the Lord's purposes will be realized in the end. He spoke also of how even now the Lord stands untroubled amid it all, a shelter for any and all who will take refuge in him.

It had struck Grace so profoundly and she had continued to mull it over many days later. So when she read this article announcing the fall of Athens, she had written next to it in the atlas: *Why do the heathen rage and the peoples of the earth conspire in vain? He who sitteth in heaven shall have them in derision.*

But even as she wrote it, she knew that, barring some great miracle, the fighting was sure to come to Crete at last and, barring some greater miracle still, Crete was as likely to fall as had the rest of the Balkans. So under the verses from the Psalm she had added, *But please Lord, bring him through and home at last to me.*

And now, here she was, a long month after the fall of Athens with one more news article to put into place, a single brief paragraph announcing that the worst had finally come to pass. She flipped forward a few more pages until she found a map of Crete. Smoothing the atlas flat on the bed, she reached for tape and secured the headline to the page.

CRETE FALLS TO NAZI ONSLAUGHT
Greek Island Abandoned by Allied Forces

Alexandria, June 2—Arriving exhausted and worn, the last of the Dominion evacuees from Crete arrived in Alexandria today. After days of ferocious fighting, British forces finally received the order to evacuate the island on May 31. On arrival in Alexandria, many battalions fell in and marched off proudly, refusing to look like a defeated army. Though reports vary, it is guessed that some 1,500 troops were unable to be evacuated from Crete and were taken as prisoners of war.

She stared at the map with a stoic determination not to cry. There was a time, years ago, when she would have wept bitterly, and yet there was so much hurt all around her that she hardly felt she could afford the tears now. So many, it seemed, needed her strength—at the mission, among her friends, and here at home with Mother and Father—and deeper still there lurked a thought that she dared not face but knew to be true without acknowledging it: that at least now she had proof that he remained on Crete only because he had no choice, not because he wished to stay away.

At any rate, no tears came, however deeply her heart was breaking.

She reached for the pen, but stalled. She could think of nothing suitable to pray next to this dreadful news. She poised herself pensively over the page for a long time and still no prayer came.

At last she thought of his locket. She had not worn it since her prayer the morning after the vigil with Beth and Wallace, but she knew exactly where she had left it. She rummaged through the drawer of her nightstand and brought it out. Opening it carefully on the atlas, she unfolded the slip of paper she had placed within. She reread it three times, then a fourth, and finally a faint smile of quiet resolve flickered dimly to life on her face. She leaned forward and with a very steady hand wrote the words into the atlas.

Set me as a seal upon thine heart, as a seal upon thine arm, for love is strong as death; jealousy is cruel as the grave.

CHAPTER TWENTY-FIVE

Barrington Street Mission

THE MONTHS THAT FOLLOWED THAT FATEFUL MORNING CAME AND WENT for Grace at a frantic pace, each day coming fast and full on the heels of the last. She had recently received a new assignment at the mission, becoming the Director of Recreational Activities for the servicemen, and that spring Reverend Elliot had asked if she would oversee the War Effort Salvage Drive at St. Christopher's. All this, coupled with her regular role as the principal organist at the church, kept her so busy that she seldom had time to pause. But she welcomed the responsibilities and found herself regularly saying yes to more. Somehow they kept her mind off the dark speculations she was prone to whenever she sat still with her thoughts for any length of time.

She especially liked serving the servicemen who came and went at the Barrington Street Mission. It was touching to see the uneasy combination of the soldier's brazenness and the schoolboy's shyness, mingled in different degrees on the faces of the young men she met there. In some small way, ministering to their individual and often unspoken war wounds helped to ease her own.

It was like that the morning she came across two young men with sea-weathered faces and thick foreign accents, sitting at a table laid out with a variety of board games—a chess set, a deck or two of playing cards, and a backgammon board.

One of them touched her elbow as she bustled past on her way to or from some duty or another. He gestured at the backgammon board and in very clumsy English said, "You… like… playing?"

Grace stopped and smiled warmly. "Oh, I'm sure I'd love to, but I don't really know how to play, and anyway, I'm needed in the next room."

The young man shrugged—he looked surprisingly young, Grace thought, and she wondered if he hadn't perhaps lied his way into the service—but his companion was slightly older and not so easily put off. He gestured as well. "But we can... teaching you... no?"

Grace smiled just as warmly at him but shook her head gently. "I'm afraid I really don't have the time to spare just now. But if you like, I could ask one of the other women to..."

She looked around the room, but all the volunteers were already occupied—there were so many men all the time, and their need for connection always so great that no one, it seemed, ever had the time to spare. She lingered a moment, then sat at the table.

The older of the two clapped his hands together and smiled broadly, while the other opened the backgammon board enthusiastically.

"You... are... much kind," said the younger man in his halting English.

Grace watched him lay out the pieces. "You speak English well," she offered. "Where are you from?"

The older man raised one eyebrow in confusion. "Eh?"

She tried a different tack. "Your home? Where is your home?"

He smiled widely again. "Ah! Home!" He placed a battered sailor's hand on his chest. "Me, Greek. Me, Georgios... He, Alexis... We... have home... in Greece."

The sentence took great effort, but as he said it a new light shone in Grace's eyes. She thought of Stephen, far away, and the recent news about the fall of Crete. She tilted her head with curiosity and instinctively placed a hand on the young man's forearm, where it rested on the table.

"Greek?" She repeated. "Are you from Greece?"

He smiled again and laughed. "Yes," he said, touching his chest once more with his palm. "Yes, Greek. Come here..." He waved his hand here as if miming the motion of a boat. "...come over sea... from Greece."

"How has it been in Greece since the invasion?" she asked quickly. The man furrowed his brow, struggling to understand, so she tried again. "The war? In Greece? War? How does it... go?"

"Ah..." The man gave a long, plaintive sigh. "Yes... war... in Greece. Very bad. Very bad."

The smile on Grace's face faded, but she kept her hand on the man's arm and even gave him an encouraging squeeze.

"I'm so sorry," she said. "And I understand. The war is very bad everywhere. I can only imagine how hard it must be for you to be..." Her words faltered, so she swallowed thinly and started again, speaking more to herself now than to him. "I only ask because there is someone whom I love—very much—in Greece, and it's been a long time since I had any word from him. And I thought perhaps you might—" She looked at him closely and trailed off until she was merely whispering to nobody at all. "But of course you wouldn't. How could you?"

The Greek man looked intently at her. He clearly did not understand, but he recognized the look on her face, and with a nod he placed his free hand on hers with a reassuring grip.

"Georgios and Alexis... we come by..." He looked at Alexis and said something fluidly in Greek that she did not understand. Alexis said something in return, at which Georgios nodded. "We come by *Kalypsos*," he finished.

Now it was Grace's turn with a furrowed brow. "I'm sorry. I don't understand what you mean. What is *Kalypsos*?"

He nodded with a wide grin. "Yes! *Kalypsos*!"

Alexis smiled, too. He mimed with his hand again, like the movement of a wave on water.

"I'm sorry. I really don't know *Kalypsos*. I don't know what you mean."

The grin faded slightly. "No?" he said, and he shrugged subtly. That spark of contact she had been profoundly aware of a moment ago seemed to be fading, and she longed for it not to be lost.

"Maybe I shouldn't have even asked," she said quickly. "It's just that my husband is in Greece. Well, he's not really my husband. Not yet, anyway, but he will be... and anyway, he's in Greece, trapped there because of the war. Though he's not really fighting in the war, only he went there as a... as a..."

She couldn't finish. The story seemed all so convoluted to her, and she knew it was impossible Georgios would ever understand. She barely understood it herself. She smiled at him weakly.

Alexis motioned to them both that the board was now ready, and Georgios set about, in the most limping English imaginable, to explain the game to her. But Grace's mind was stuck, it seemed, in a tangle of thoughts she had not dared to wander for a long time.

"I really am sorry," she said softly as he continued to explain the game. "It's just that I am desperate for news of him. Anything. I haven't seen him for more than four years and now he's trapped there and I don't know what's become of him, and I guess it just occurred to me that you might have some news. Any news." She hesitated and then took one more chance. "Are you, by any chance... are you from Crete?"

He stopped and smiled, recognizing the word in what she said. "Kreta?" he said. "Crete?"

She nodded, the spark of connection flaring again briefly. "Yes, Kreta. Yes! Are you from Kreta?"

He laughed lightly and shook his head. "No. Me no Kreta. Me... Thessalonikou."

She repeated it slowly. "Thessalonikou?" The spark was fading again and with a great disappointment, she looked away.

From the corner of the crowded common room, a piano clanged merrily to life. The three of them turned toward the sound. The woman playing wore the same hospitality crest as Grace wore. The mission had a rather small selection of sheet music which was played in a relatively steady rotation, so before the first measure was quite finished Grace already knew the tune. It was a lilting wartime melody called *The Sailor's Betrothal Ring Song*.

The woman started to sing: *"A sailor and his sweetheart stood on a creaking pier..."* Grace had heard it often enough by now that she knew the words well, though they struck her with a kind of bitterness to hear at just this moment, with her mind on Stephen the way it was.

A crowd was gathering at the piano, a handful of servicemen in khaki and navy and air-force blue, sauntering up to listen. The tune repeated and crescendoed towards the finale, one or two of the men picking up the melody and joining in at the end.

A round of applause went up when it was over, and one or two voices called out their favourites next. The woman at the piano smiled amiably and almost without pause launched into a series of popular tunes, one quickly after the other: *The White Cliffs of Dover*, *You Are My Sunshine*, and *A Nightingale Sang in Berkeley Square*. For some of the tunes, the men joined in; for others, they stared off distantly while the music washed over them.

Her two Greek sailors were drawn in by the music well enough that they had abandoned the idea of a backgammon game, so Grace took her leave of them with another warm smile, but not before a very disappointed shadow crossed her face.

Of all the days in the many years of Stephen's exile, that chaotic summer of 1941 was probably the hardest for her. By 1941 the battle in the North Atlantic had become terrifically intense, and the city of Halifax was faced daily with new and dreadful reminders of it: rumours of U-boats lurking the dark waters just beyond the submarine defence net that spanned the entrance to the harbour, constant blackout orders and air raid drills, regular government statements urging every responsible citizen to purchase gas masks and know how to use them. These realities made it impossible for the city to forget for long that Canada was indeed at war, and that Halifax was, in fact, the country's only "frontline city."

Grace took all these worrisome inconveniences in stride, however. It was the overcrowding of the city with men that really troubled her. As an assembly point for the convoys of soldiers venturing out into the dangerous waters of the Atlantic, and as a key hub in the tenuous connection between war-harried Britain and her allies, Halifax was swarmed with men from all over the world. One local newspaper report summed it up in this way:

A crossroads of the United Nations, where men of man lands and races pass day after day in the course of work or leisure—that is the corner of Barrington and Sackville Streets as World War II has made it.

And it was true. The waterfront was crammed with ships from all over the world, navies left homeless by German invasion. The docks were choked almost daily with refugees, the streets swollen with crowds of them. Throngs of international sailors competed with the already overcrowded Canadian servicemen for what little lodging there was to be had, all of them waiting for their turn to cross the ocean and play their part in the war.

Grace felt profoundly for them all, knowing none were there, really, of their own choosing.

But not everyone in the city took so charitable a view of the situation. Every now and then, a grumbling editorial would appear in a local paper, wondering when Halifax would be given back to the Haligonians to whom it rightfully belonged. The city's population had, after all, nearly doubled in size since the start of the war. And truth be told, none of the displaced men and women who found themselves dependent on the city's strained hospitality liked the situation any better than anyone else. Tensions hung palpably in the air, and Grace was often acutely aware of it.

What made it worse, of course, was the interminable waiting, not just her own for Stephen, though that was hard, but everyone's, for anything. No one in Halifax had anything to do, it seemed, other than to wait. Restless soldiers on leave waited out their precious few days of respite from battle, fresh servicemen waited to embark into who-knows-what, sea-hardened sailors waited for their ships to be repaired and resupplied, and native Haligonians waited for their lives to go back to normal. It might have made the wait for Stephen easier to bear, to know she was hardly alone in her waiting, but the chaos of so many people flooding the city with so little to do and nowhere else to go was itself troubling.

Scarred deeply by what they had been through in the war, and turned loose on a city that seemed not to want them, bored servicemen wandered the streets, looking for some way to vent their pent-up energy. Alcohol was under strict wartime rations, of course, but bootleg drink was easy enough to come by if you knew where to look for it. Prostitution and other illegal trades had begun to fester, it was said, in the city's dark underbelly. Occasionally the newspapers blazed with letters to the editor complaining of sordid drunkenness in the streets, of brawling and assaults on a too-regular basis. Many young women had taken to brandishing large hairpins when they walked downtown, to defend themselves from the unwanted attentions of raucous, often drunken soldiers.

It was Grace's suggestion that the mission do something practical in response to the growing tension and creeping chaos. Other such organizations—the YMCA, for instance, and the Knights of Columbus—had already opened hostels along the waterfront for men in uniform with nowhere else to go, and it was Grace's idea that the mission might do something similar. They organized recreation and scheduled activities for the servicemen as an alternative to drinking and brawling, and recruited volunteers, mostly women like herself, who wanted to do their part in the war effort. They sat with the men in shifts, looking almost defiantly cheerful, laughing too loudly at poorly told jokes, engaging almost zealously in gracious games of checkers or crib, listening intently to sad stories as they served coffee and sandwiches to the throngs of lonely men who so outnumbered them.

This was their service. It was certainly Grace's, and she threw herself earnestly into it, showing hospitality to the war-wounded of the world.

And so it was that she had found herself sitting around an unplayed game of backgammon with Georgios and Alexis that afternoon, these two unexpected strangers from Greece, of all places, asking for even a wisp of a rumour about Crete. She had met men from all sorts of distant places in her work at the mission, of course, but this was the first time she had ever encountered anyone from so close to where Stephen was, and it had awoken some deeply buried thoughts in her. If they could have come from Greece, mightn't Stephen himself find his way back eventually? There was a glimmer of hope in the thought, but also something unsettling.

The encounter with Georgios and Alexis sat uneasily with her the rest of the day. Even after her work was through that night, she continued to turn it over restlessly in her mind as she walked home. The streets were dark—they were under strict blackout orders for fear of air raids—and the darkness seemed to close in threateningly around her. Whether she was running from something or running towards it, she couldn't have said, but she walked at a very steady pace, her thoughts lost in a troubling maze of uncertainty.

"Hey, doll! Where y'goin' in such a hurry?" A catcall from the street ahead made her suddenly aware again of her surroundings.

She looked up and saw that she was approaching the Orpheus Theatre. The sidewalk was overflowing with men in sailor's uniforms, waiting for the show to open. It was so crowded that she would either have to force her way through or step out onto the road to pass. There was a rowdy murmur among the sailors as they milled about, though one or two military police stood sentinel nearby, keeping them all in check.

"Wanna see a movie picture with the boys tonight?" It was a different voice that called out this time, and a ripple of raucous laughter spread across the crowd. Someone whistled.

There rose in her a strong impulse to cower as she passed, to sink into her collar and cross to the far side of the street. But unexpectedly something flared in her—it was not anger, but rather a great resolve and with it an even greater strength. She forced herself to slow her pace and square her shoulders. She looked as calmly as she could into the crowd, and as she did all the uncertainty she had been carrying that day seemed to dissipate.

"I'm afraid I can't, boys," she said. "I'm needed elsewhere. And after all, I am spoken for. Now, if you'll just let me by, I'll be on my way."

She was aware of a note in her voice she'd never heard in it before. It was not quite playful, but far more confident than she felt. She was determined not to be cowed by a crowd of lonely sailors.

"Ah, c'mon, doll!" The catcall was less threatening in its tone this time, though more spirited. "C'mon and have some fun with us. I ain't been to shore for months!"

Grace had stopped fully now, deeply aware of a resolve forming in her that she would pass by on the sidewalk. This crowd of leering men would make way and let her through, and they would do it civilly, too.

"And if this is your first shore leave in months," she said, "it would be a shame to waste it all on wishing for a thing that will most certainly never happen. Now be a gentleman and let a lady on her way."

Her heart pounded thunderously as she said it, but her face remained almost miraculously calm.

Another round of laughter rose up at this retort, and one or two of the catcaller's friends gave him a teasing shove.

The din was just dying down when a familiar voice rose up from the crowd. "Grace? Is that you?"

The crowd of men murmured raucously again, but among them one sailor pushed his way forward till he was facing her.

"Grace?"

It was Richard. She had not seen him in over a year, though she knew through Margaret that he was still serving in the British navy. She smiled, and despite the rowdiness of the circumstances there came an almost maternal tenderness into her eye.

"Fancy meeting you here!" he said with a wide grin.

"Fancy indeed. And are these friends of yours?"

"I suppose they are," he said, casting a laugh at the others. "Though I guess when you're in the navy you can't really judge a man by the company he keeps."

Another lively murmur rippled among the men and one or two of them jostled with Richard, pushing him playfully. He stood his ground, though, and when the din had died down again he offered her the crook of his arm.

"Can I help you on your way?" he said.

Grace smiled, still very tender towards him, but shook her head. "No. I'm sure I wouldn't want you to miss the picture."

Once again there came a ripple of laughter and one or two teasing words were flung in Richard's direction, but he was undeterred.

"At least let me clear a path for you through this band of ruffians," he said. He turned to his friends and made a sweep with his arm. "Make way, boys, there's a lady coming through."

They parted for her now, and though her heartbeat still roared in her ears, she walked calmly by. And though he needn't have, Richard walked beside her for a short way.

When they were through the crowd and the sidewalk was clear again, Richard stopped her with a brief hand on her elbow.

"So you see, Grace," he said suddenly. "Your prayers have been answered."

She turned towards him and raised an eyebrow. "My prayers?"

"You said you would pray for me, didn't you? Or did you think I was too drunk that night to remember?"

She laughed in spite of herself, remembering that cold walk from Margaret's house on New Year's Eve before the war.

"I couldn't tell," she said honestly. "Though you were quite drunk."

"But you did pray for me?" He was still speaking playfully, but she sensed an earnest note of expectation in his voice.

"Yes I did, Richard," she said softly, and truthfully. She touched his hand where it rested on her elbow and then leaned in briefly and gave him a gentle kiss on the cheek. "And I will keep doing, so long as you need me to."

The crowd of men must have still been watching them, because the cheer that erupted at the sight of her kiss made her blush, though the street was too dark for Richard really to notice.

He let go her elbow. "Well, Grace, it seems to be working. I won't say there haven't been some close calls, but here I am still. So keep it up."

And he started moving back towards his friends, though he walked backwards, so as to keep his face turned towards her, watching her with a wide grin.

―――――――

The house was impenetrably dark when Grace finally arrived home that night—more precautions against the threat of air raids, though it seemed darker than it needed to be. Father was away again, somewhere in the Atlantic.

Grace found her way up the porch, blindly, and fumbled at the door with the key. Once inside she called out softly to her mother, though there was no answer and the darkness of the house seemed to exaggerate the silence.

She called again, and stepped down the hall. She saw a faint glow coming from the kitchen and moved towards it. When she came through the door, she saw her mother with her back turned, working at the counter in the light of a single flickering candle.

"Mother?"

The woman was intent on her work and gave no response. As Grace came around to her side, she saw that her mother was pouring a greasy mass of chicken fat into a great mason jar, working carefully not to spill anything in the dim light. Recently the call had gone out for housewives to help in the war effort by preserving all their cooking fat. Apparently the glycerine in the fat was needed to make explosives. Some stores had even offered special incentives: *"Now you can pour that burning oil down der Fuhrer's back!"* read the adverts. *"Bring in your fat jars for a 10% discount on all groceries!"* It seemed like a bit of a cynical ploy to Grace, but her mother, determined to do her part, had already filled a great collection of jars with chicken fat and bacon grease, hoarding them in a congealed mass in the kitchen.

"Reverend Elliot stopped by this afternoon," Mother said at last, though she did not look up from her work. "He had the report for you on the salvage drive at the church."

"Oh?"

There was a teapot on the counter and Grace reached for it as they talked. It was still hot—Mother must have made it not long ago—and she poured herself a cup. Tea was under strict rations and the teabags Mother had used, Grace knew, were already on their third tour of duty. It had to be taken black, too, and unsweetened, what with sugar under similar rations. It was not especially bracing to drink, but as if to make up for it Mother had made it scalding. Grace blew gently on the cup a long while before taking her first sip.

"He says that we've collected all the used tin cans they need," Mother explained, "and that what's needed now are old rags. You know, for cleaning guns and equipment and what have you. I've taken down one or two dresses—I don't really wear them anymore anyway—and made them into rags." She paused. "Even the wedding dress."

Grace watched her mother closely in the candlelight. She saw that her hands trembled slightly when at last she set down the pot of grease she had been pouring out.

"And do you suppose rags are needed as desperately as all that?" Grace asked softly.

"Who knows what's needed?" Mother said with only the faintest hint of despair in her voice. "Today it's old rags that are going to win this war, tomorrow the only thing standing between us and victory is a jar of grease." She looked weakly at her daughter through the candlelight. "But we do what we can, Grace, don't we?"

This was the twelfth day her father had been out at sea, and he was already two days overdue returning. This had happened once or twice before, but each time was harder than the last for her mother. The spark that had glimmered to life in Grace when she'd stood before the crowd of sailors at the Orpheus still burned like a faint ember within her, and she stepped towards her mother as if to warm her with it.

"We do indeed do what we can." She reached through the candlelight and put her arms around her. "Oh Mother," she whispered, and she felt the tension tremble through her mother's body as she leaned heavily against her daughter. "We do what we can. And perhaps, so long as we do, we may get through this in one piece yet."

Mother let her daughter embrace her for a moment and then slowly pulled away and walked quietly from the kitchen, leaving Grace with her weak tea, scalding hot, and an unspoken prayer burning silently in her heart.

––––––––––

The next morning, on her way to the mission, Grace decided to follow Water Street, along the docks. Ships of many nations and every description lined the wharves, and as she approached Salter Street she stopped and looked out for a moment over the crowded harbour. There was a ship docked near to her that caught her attention. It looked like a merchant ship, and it bore its name in bold letters which she recognized from the Greek alphabet. Years ago when she and Stephen had been courting, he had tried to teacher some of the rudiments of the Greek language—for fun, he'd said, though they hadn't gotten very far. Even so, she knew enough that she could sound out the name emblazoned on the side of the ship: *Kalypsos.*

She remembered Georgios and Alexis from the day before. "We come by *Kalypsos!*" the young man had said. Though she had not understood then, it suddenly became clear to her. This was their ship.

She stared at it for a long time. It caught her off-guard to think that this boat was here in Halifax from Greece, that it might have, for all she knew, been docked at some time or another in Crete itself, or at least sailed by its shores.

Uneasiness darkened the horizon of her thought. If it was here, she wondered very briefly, mightn't he have come also?

It was too dark a thought to follow, and she had no idea where it might lead her, so she let it fade as quickly as it had occurred to her.

But still she stood there, staring at this ship called *Kalypsos.* She thought of her father fighting fiercely somewhere in the Atlantic, and of her mother gathering great jars of grease to help him home safely, of Richard in his navy blue uniform waiting restlessly for a show to open at the Orpheus, of Georgios and Alexis sitting sadly in the mission, desperate for human touch. And like a bright light flooding a shadowy place, a great, wordless prayer groaned suddenly within her, and with a petition on her lips that she could not put into words—like the stopper in a gap between great peace and deep turmoil—she found herself yearning but without any ache on behalf of them all, trembling with a deep need she knew instinctively would be met.

And when at last she turned and walked away from the dock, her feet were steadier, and her heart lighter than she had ever felt them to be before.

CHAPTER TWENTY-SIX
Before the Dawn

THE WATER PULLED HER DOWN INEXORABLY, AND HER WHOLE BODY clenched against the clutch of it, the last strength of her final breath nearly spent. A creeping blackness grew in her mind, edging out all but the most vivid of thoughts. Those that did come came quickly, shining with intense precision against the otherwise impenetrable darkness. They faded just as quickly, blurring one into the other until all sense of time and place was jumbled together into a pinpoint of white-hot light which etched out these final images with searing clarity.

Grace saw that miserably grey morning in 1941, when an awkward junior officer had pressed his letter—what she would come to know as Stephen's final letter from Crete—into her hand with rote words of sympathy. The officer had recounted the harrowing history: how three soldiers, one British and two New Zealanders, had escaped by raft towards Egypt after the surrender of Crete; how one of the New Zealanders had committed suicide along the way, and the British soldier had died of heat exhaustion before they landed at last at Sidi Barrani; how the third was barely conscious when they found him, washed ashore with his derelict raft. And somewhere amid this man's incoherent ramblings, he had said this, and said it clearly: a man named Percy had made him promise that this letter would find its way to her; the Brits had then passed the letter along to the Canadian War Office, who had seen to it that it arrived in Halifax.

She had grown used to heart-wrenching stories—indeed, she had heard any number of them from the men she met at the mission—but the ill-fated journey of this tattered letter seemed so impossibly tragic that even if it had not been Stephen's letter, it would have moved her deeply.

With a slight groan, she sank to the steps of the porch while the rain streamed down around her. She opened it carefully and extracted a single folded page as though it were a priceless artefact.

"Miss Stewart?" The junior officer ventured this question clumsily. The rain came down steadily, but not so strong that it hid the tears blinking hotly in her eyes, and he was uncertain how to respond to this sudden display of such deep feeling. "If there is any loss, Miss Stewart, the Department of National Defence would like to…"

He trailed off, as if hearing for the first time the stilted tone in his own voice as he extended these formalities of condolence.

"Thank you," she said without looking up from the page still folded in her lap. "Thank you, but I don't think you quite understand the nature of my loss."

The officer cleared his throat. "No, perhaps not," he said, and though his body stiffened his tone was reflective. "I suppose everyone's loss in this war is its own kind of grief." He trailed off again, watching her closely. "At any rate, Miss Stewart, you do have our sympathies."

She looked up from the letter to thank him, but the words choked in her throat.

"Thank you," she said at last, very faintly.

The officer straightened himself again and turned to leave.

She sat there for a long time on the porch, alone, with the chill of the rainwater soaking her, until she could not tell if the tremble in her was from her sadness or from the cold. At last she unfolded the page and smoothed it over her lap to read.

The words returned to her now, even as the ocean pulled her down into its final depths.

If this letter, by some miracle of fate, does actually reach you, please do not cling to some false, empty hope…It would hurt me deeply to know that you held on for nothing.

She had once thought this enigmatic statement to be so selfless—that despite his great love for her, Stephen would offer to release her from the pain of holding on to him like this.

Now at last she understood it for what it really was.

I have decided to stay on Crete, to fight against these horrors... I am sorry if I have failed you, if my staying to fight alongside these people causes you pain. Please do not double that pain by hoping vainly for my return.

This was no heroic sacrifice, as she had chosen to see it then, as if Stephen were simply flinging himself into the same struggle against the war that she herself was fighting daily on the home front of Halifax. This was a betrayal, and a cowardly one at that.

Had Stephen simply offered her the truth, she might have chosen differently. She might have let go at last. But he hadn't. And she never had. A lifetime of sacrifices offered blindly on the altar of this lie rose up starkly to accuse her.

Randomly she remembered passing the great, theatrical windowpane of the T. Eaton Company one vibrant spring morning in May 1943. Earlier that week, the Halifax papers had triumphantly advertised the long-awaited arrival of infant-sized gas masks. After existing almost four years under the vague threat of a German gas attack, Halifax could finally rest assured in the fact that gas masks designed specifically to fit children were now available. The advertisement that had announced this fact had struck Grace as far too congratulatory, given the grim reality that made it necessary: *"Gas masks for infants of 1½–5 years of age have just arrived and can be secured at the T. Eaton Company."*

She remembered a dull pain of great emptiness aching inside her the day she had stood there at the shop window, transfixed by these miniature rubber masks on display. Without realizing it, she had stepped up very close to the glass, drawn by an intense longing. They had seemed so grotesque to her, yet somehow comical, like finely detailed playthings in a child's chest of toys, with those bulbous glass goggles and the protuberant face covering, that long serrated hose winding clumsily from the nosepiece. It had made her think unexpectedly of Beth's little Johnny, who was still just young enough to be fitted for such a mask, but old enough now to be tempted greatly to play soldier with it. Certainly Willie, at that age, would have wanted to.

She was not aware that she had done so, but she lifted a hand somewhat plaintively to touch the glass. The emptiness gaped inside her and she pressed her eyes closed against it, resting her forehead against the windowpane—she had come close enough to the window that she might have pressed her whole body against it had she not been standing in public. A vision had formed in her mind of a beautiful, nameless infant face sealed fearfully but safely behind those lolling plastic goggles, this ghastly child's plaything breathing into it the breath of life. And as it came to her like that, the emptiness inside widened into a great chasm.

A powerful impulse to have one had come over her then, and with it a trembling determination, like some primitive instinct wakening within. She had entered the store furtively, and without finding the courage to look the clerk in the eyes, she'd purchased one. The staff placed it for her in a paper bag, and she'd carried it hidden among some other items she had bought that morning downtown.

Arriving home, she had gone directly to her room and set the gas mask on her bed. She'd stared at it blankly for a long time, as though she were standing at the utter edge of the emptiness it had opened inside her and peering down into a dark void. She'd tried to laugh at herself for such melodramatic thoughts as she had been having lately, and shoved the gas mask surreptitiously under the bed. Before she left the room, however, she had taken a furtive look in the mirror to make sure her eyes were quite dry.

These pictures of the past flashed across her memory almost too quickly now to place them.

She saw herself standing on the corner of Granville Street, trembling with fantastic wonder as she surveyed the aftermath of the revelry that had erupted through the city earlier that week. It was the ninth of May 1945, and the world had thrilled with victory only two days ago, when German Radio at Flensburg had announced the final surrender of the remaining Nazi forces.

For a city like Halifax, where the military population nearly outnumbered the civilian, this one word had fallen like a haphazard match tossed carelessly onto a pool of spilled gasoline. Victory celebrations had ignited throughout the city, and before long the more unruly of these had erupted into victory riots. Led primarily by a throng of sailors on shore leave, a mob of servicemen and civilians alike had stormed through the city, and for two chaotic days Halifax had reeled in a frenzy of drunken vandalism and senseless looting. Shop windows had been smashed, victory flags pulled down, debris and goods flung out into the streets. Two buildings had even been lit ablaze in the anarchy.

She had seen the photos in the paper on the morning after the riots. They showed streets lolling with unabashed revelry, Citadel Hill littered with men and women alike, carousing with a near hysterical sensuality.

A long time ago, when was studying at university, Stephen had told her in passing about the ancient Maenads, who had worshipped the god of wine, Dionysus, with terrifying rituals of drunkenness. The bacchanalia, he had called it, and he'd described the satyrs and nymphs who joined in the frenzy. Staring at those stark photographs of the Halifax riots, it had occurred to her to wonder if they were not somehow akin to those ancient rituals.

Haligonians had been outraged at it all, of course. Military and civilian police, along with a great force of troops brought in by rail to help secure the peace, had patrolled the streets in strength. Arrests were made until police cells and city prisons were bursting with prisoners. Investigative commissions were appointed, inquiries made, restitution paid. Eventually life in Halifax would find a normal pattern again.

But in the first days of calm after the worst of the riots, Grace had wandered downtown to see for herself. Standing there and surveying the destruction, she had trembled with a strange mixture of fear and wonder. It had shocked her to see such great joy expressed with such terrible abandon, and yet she had marvelled darkly to think that all this chaos might in fact be the real cost of the many years of sacrifice the city of Halifax had endured to do its part in the war.

She had wanted badly to pray, but the sight of so violent a catharsis confused her deeply, and she hadn't been able to find the words. Though she'd dared not admit it, a faint desire had glimmered in her, that her own sacrifices might be vented in this way. But the idea terrified her and she smothered it before it could grow into a real thought. Instead she had tried to feel sympathy for the revellers themselves. They had suffered through so much uncertainty for so long, it seemed, that when the final victory arrived they'd had nothing left inside but this ravenous desire for self-forgetting.

It was not a recriminating prayer, but still the words had formed with her breath on her lips: *May it not be, Lord. May it never be this way for me.*

That unspoken prayer came back to her in the sinking darkness of the water, and with it a single, final image. And she knew this would be the last.

It was the winter of 1947. Two awful years still after the end of the war, a full ten years since Stephen had left on a research scholarship to study archaeology in Athens, and twenty since the day they'd first met, he returned to her at last. This final memory was painfully vivid, all the more so because it was cast now in the light of the plain truth, and in that light she saw every detail with new clarity.

His family had accompanied her to the wharves that dismal morning, light snow tumbling through damp air and an unkind wind breathing over her from the water. She stood apart from them, though, with her arms wrapped around herself against the chill, her cheeks and nose bright with it. A gull or two came to rest near the end of the pier and screamed angrily at her. Further down the wharf, a group of longshoremen loitered noisily, talking crudely to one another.

She stepped closer to the edge of the pier, squinting out across the water like one peering across a great chasm, or one teetering at the edge of a high precipice and gazing down.

"And what did he say the name of the ship would be?" Jane asked, finally breaking the silence between them.

"He said it was called the *Aegeus*. But the lettering will be Greek."

"And when is it expected to arrive?" This from Stephen's mother.

"He said it would be after nine, but really, it could be any time." Grace did not turn towards them. Rather she continued to stare out over the water, watching earnestly and hopefully.

It was, in fact, a full three hours before the ship arrived. At one point, Stephen's mother produced a thermos filled with hot chocolate and passed around cups to ward off the cold, and towards noon Sarah and Jane wandered away to find some food, which they brought back to the wharves and shared with the others as a light lunch.

But eventually the *Aegeus* arrived, crawling almost unbearably slow across the harbour and into view. The name was emblazoned on the side of the vessel, and though the letters were indeed Greek, still she knew enough of them to recognize it as his ship.

Time seemed to collapse almost to a standstill. It was hours before the ship docked and Stephen was dully processed by customs. Grace was trembling almost uncontrollably by the time the ordeal was through, though this of course might have been the cold. She kept trying to picture him, or to form in her mind her first words when she saw him. After ten years, it took great effort to imagine what he would be like, or what she might say when at last they met.

After what felt like a purgatory of waiting, he finally emerged from the customs office near to where the *Aegeus* had docked, dragging a tattered rucksack behind him, and stood at last in view. Grace raised an involuntary hand to her mouth at the sight of him, and her eyes widened sadly. She knew him instantly, of course, but strangely she did not recognize him. His hair was long, for one thing, and oiled back. There was his beard, too, a dark shadow unexpectedly lining his cheeks. And though he smiled when he saw her, there was a woundedness in his eyes, like a scar that had healed badly and left a disfiguring limp.

And he was dressed so strangely. He wore loose-fitting pants pinched at the knee by glossy black boots. His shirt hung at the sleeves, and around his waist was a broad sash. The ensemble was entirely black, too. This struck her the most; the shirt, the pants, and even the sash that held it in place were entirely black, billowing about his body like the sail from a ship's mast. His limping eyes could not hold her gaze, and he looked down, the smile fading on his face.

But she knew him, however changed the last ten years had left him, and she breathed his name at last.

"Oh, Stephen," she said, and stepped towards him like one stepping from the lip of a high cliff and plunging over the dark precipice of his return.

He looked up again, and there were tears burning in his eyes.

"Grace," he said at last, and the voice was Stephen's, however many years had passed since she last had heard it. This, at least, had not changed. "Grace, I am so sorry to have…"

But she wouldn't let him finish. It hurt her to see him looking so dark and frail, and she could not bear the burden of his apology. She shook her head weakly and the faintest sob escaped her.

"No, Stephen, please don't. I am sorry. I waited for you. You told me not to, because you did not want me to hurt, but I did, and I have and…"

Here she swallowed hard, against the next sob that was rising in her, and she closed her eyes tightly until she knew the tears would not come. When she opened them, he was looking finally into her face and his eyes glimmered with an unspoken pain.

"And here I am at last," she finished.

She opened her arms to him then, like a hen spreading her wings over scattered chicks, gathering them into her side for healing and help. The thought did not occur to her at the time, that this was what she was doing, but that was how she saw it now. However much it hurt to do, she loved him in that moment, more sincerely than she ever had.

He stepped forward and opened his arms to her, too, and they held one another closely. She was still very cold from her long wait on the wharves, but she could feel the warmth of his body passing into her, and she no longer trembled.

Stephen quaked suddenly with an unvoiced cry of pain and squeezed her, burying his face against her neck, into the hair that fell softly over her shoulder. She lifted her hand and stroked the thickly grown hair at the nape of his neck and then lifted his face until they were looking into each other's eyes.

"I did not want you to hurt," he whispered. Tears streamed down his cheeks now, wetting his strange beard.

"Nor did I, you."

She cupped his cheek tenderly with her palm and stroked a tear away with a gentle thumb. It did not seem so then, but in this final moment of her life it occurred to her that the words that came to her next were coming from somewhere far above of her, blowing through her like a soft breeze on her breath.

"But we have. We all have. And we would have anyway. And we do. But perhaps if we hold tight to each other now, then maybe the hurt won't get the last word in the end."

She pressed her forehead against his, and felt his breath mingle warmly with her own, and then, with a deep sigh of pent-up yearning, they pressed together and kissed one another, not childishly or passionately, like they had a decade ago, but warmly and earnestly, drawing from each other strength and breathing into each other new life.

Yet there was the salt taste of tears, lingering faintly on his lips.

And at last she understood the sting of them.

He had loved another—had married another—and had left his heart behind him when he came away from Crete. The darkness of the water condensed around her, whispering a promise of numb release from that final, bitter truth. She fought it, but her strength was mostly gone. She had no more *whys* left to ask, and could not ask them if even if she had.

A final urge to pray rose in her, but she could no longer find the words, and she no longer thought she knew the one to whom she might have prayed.

The sea seemed to stop its pounding. The waves ceased to surge, and she felt herself suspended in a weightless calm of complete and utter silence. There was something soothing here, a lightness and stillness she had not known for a long time, and she opened herself to it.

The darkness enveloped her fully then, and for a final frozen moment she stopped her struggling at last.

But he had returned.

Even against the darkness, this thought flickered suddenly in her heart like a faint grey light. Whatever may have happened on Crete so many years ago, still he had returned to her, and chosen to. Despite his love for another—perhaps even because of it, she did not know—he *had* returned.

A new *why* welled up from deep within her, as if coming to her from somewhere far away. Why had he left Ariadne? Why had he come home? Had he really chosen her, and if he had, then why?

As each of these questions took shape in her thoughts, the grey light continued to grow, until she couldn't tell the difference between her longing to know and her longing to forget it all. And still the light grew, and even began to undulate, a slow, rocking caress that she recognized at last as the motion of the tide.

Consciousness washed over her suddenly like a cold wave, and she knew that she would not, *must not*, go like this. The foam of the sea surged against her sinking body, and she knew it again, as if feeling it for the first time. The water felt suddenly painful and perhaps it was the pain that gave her the resolve to struggle again.

Or perhaps the resolve came to her from somewhere still outside herself.

But however it came to her, it did, and she fought violently against the sea with the last of her fading breath. The light swirled around her confusedly. It was above her, but when she urged her body towards it, she was sinking; it drifted far below, yet when she moved towards it she was rising. She was aware of the soaked fabric of her dress pulling her down, and weakly she clutched at the cloth, tearing the buttons and pulling it open, struggling her shoulders free.

She struggled again, and the grey light foamed brilliantly all round. She was stripped now of the awful weight of the dress and felt her body floating upwards. The foam seemed to part then, or to dilate, and she felt herself lunge towards it blindly, laboriously.

Something convulsed inside, pushing her forward, and with an urgent cry of great pain she emerged at last, water breaking over her and streaming down her face, gulping terrified gasps of air as if taking a new breath for the very first time.

She coughed, and spat, and gasped again, expelling the sea from her lungs. The twilight was very dim, but through the thrashing beat of the sea she could see the shore. Her limbs were still lifeless, and yet somewhere the strength came to her to push towards it. She felt herself lifted and carried, though this might have been simply the motion of the sea, until unexpectedly she felt the grinding rasp of pebbles beneath her struggling knees, and her weight sank against the solid ground of the beach.

She crawled weakly until she thought she was fully free of the water and then collapsed, shivering numbly and breathing in ragged gasps. The grit of the shore pressed harshly against her naked flesh, and for a moment she faded from consciousness, as if dead.

But she was not dead. And eventually she found in herself the strength to lift her battered body and stumble up the long slope back to the house. Along the horizon of the sea, the grey twilight had grown red as the morning began to dawn.

Freezing from the salty chill, she stumbled deliriously through the house until she staggered before a closet in their bedroom. With hands she could barely control for shivering, she rummaged about until she found a rough woollen blanket and draped herself with it. The room reeled blackly, and she almost faded again into her pain, but instead she sank against a wall and lowered herself carefully to the floor, huddled in the blanket and focused intently on getting warm. She could not. She was trembling uncontrollably in the very core of her body and her head hummed, teetering on the edge of consciousness.

Gradually the humming grew clear and she became aware of a shrill hiss penetrating her delirium and drawing her back to from the edge. She wondered where she had heard a sound like that before, and realized vaguely that it had been screaming at her ever since she'd entered the house. With this realization came a sudden understanding; she knew the sound but was still too confused to feel alarm. It was the violent hiss of an abandoned tea kettle, whistling urgently at her from the kitchen.

She crawled weakly towards the noise, still draped with her blanket. She found the stove and pulled herself to her feet, bracing herself against the counter and reaching slowly to extinguish the flame. The kettle had nearly boiled dry, but there was still some water left.

Her shivering remained uncontrollable, but she found the teacup she had pre-pared—who knew how long ago that was now?—and poured a rolling cascade of boiled water into it, watching it blush translucently as the tea released its fragrance. She held the cup in her hands and, for the first time in what felt like eternity, felt warmth. She took a slow drink, and was somehow grateful to feel the hot water burn her tongue, if only it might somehow warm the chill from her.

When the shivering had subsided enough that she could trust her legs again, she staggered towards their bathroom and drew a warm bath. It stung her skin sharply to step into it—she was still that cold—but she fought the instinctive recoil of her body and lowered herself in. It took time, but eventually the heat stilled the trembling in her and she closed her eyes gently and let it spread through her.

It took a long time, but when she felt the strength to do so she reached for the sponge and began to rub it slowly over her body. It had been gritty with the sand of the beach and rough with a film of salt, but the impulse to clean herself ran deeper than that; she scrubbed her legs and chest and abdomen, not roughly but with great determination, squeezing her face into a grimace whenever she found a place that hurt greatly.

When she was warm and clean at last, she pulled herself from the water and draped herself again in the woollen blanket. She found her way to their bedroom and collapsed wearily on the bed, burrowing beneath the quilt and falling deeply into a dreamless, swoon-like sleep.

It was light in the room when she finally woke, but she had no idea of the time. Her body stirred beneath the quilt, aching dully with the memory of the previous night's awful violence. She felt a sickness in her still, but her sleep had been profound. She pulled herself to the edge of the bed and sat there for a long while before she found the courage to rise.

When she stood at last, she was startled by a stinging in the soles of her feet.

She stepped gingerly down the hall and into the kitchen. The floor was littered with a great mess—a spilled coffee tin, a scattered box of baking soda, an upturned canister of sugar. She returned these to their places in the cupboard and, finding a broom, she swept.

When she was done, she turned towards the hall that led to the study. She felt her courage fade slightly and had to lean against the wall until it was steady again.

The creak of the study door came at her like an accusation when she finally opened it. She was shocked to see the room so wrecked. She saw the scattered books and shattered glass, the strewn papers and broken potshards, and wondered if it was really her who had done it.

It was difficult to do, but she picked her way through the rubble, sifting it slowly. She lifted the broken frame of the desk's drawer, pushed aside a pile of trampled paper, and rummaged among the spilled books until at last she found it: *Journal and Field Notes. Stephen David Walker (1937)*. It was splayed open where it had fallen, but though some of the pages were bent, the book was unharmed. She closed it and held it in her hand, staring at the leather cover for the slightest moment of indecision.

Then she reached for the upturned chair and set it in place at the bludgeoned desk. She found the place in the book where she had left off, pressing it open and smoothing down the pages. It hurt to do so, because her body was still quite stiff, but she lowered herself into the chair, and with a kind of determined uncertainty began to read.

CHAPTER TWENTY-SEVEN
The Leventis

NIKOS LEVENTI LEANED BACK IN HIS CHAIR, WATCHING STEPHEN WITH a sharp eye. It was a late evening in the trailing days of spring, 1941, and a warm breeze flitted through the courtyard of the Leventi villa, belying the palpable tension that hung in the air. He moved the edge of a scythe again and again against a sharpening stone, with a grating rhythm that left Stephen visibly unsettled.

Ariadne appeared at the table and reached to fill her father's glass. Both men turned their attention to her briefly, and Stephen felt himself mercifully released from his father-in-law's gaze. Ariadne moved with great composure, but she cast a quick glance in her husband's direction, an anxious look that warned him silently to take care.

"Father," she said softly. "Stephen has been through much, and he is exhausted. I believe you ought at least to hear what he has to say."

Nikos fixed his eyes on his wine glass and would not look at his son-in-law. "And so I will. No one is keeping him from having his say. I only wonder what a foreigner could possibly know about the matter—the battle for Greece or the defence of Crete?" There was a note of steel in his voice, and he dragged the blade of the scythe across the stone again, distractedly. "But go ahead. Speak, if you have anything to say."

Stephen opened his mouth, but no words came out. He sank back wearily into his chair and lifted his gaze to the silhouetted network of limbs and leaves overhead, etched blackly against the deepening shadows of the evening sky. He and Ianos had just arrived from Heraklion that afternoon, thirsty and aching from a two-day trek over the White Mountains. They had completed the long march in a single push, both anxious to see their village again, and both burdened with the dreadful news they carried. Throughout the trek, their way had been haunted by the incessant drone of the German Luftwaffe, as squadron after squadron crawled back and forth across the sky, raking the clouds with their spreading black wings. After a long night of endless walking, and a longer day to follow, they had finally arrived in Apodolou towards dinnertime on the second day, ragged and harried from their fearful flight.

Nikos clapped the sharpening stone loudly on the table. The sudden sound of it startled Stephen, and his mind flashed involuntarily back to Heraklion, the day before. He saw the ground heave again, in his memory, great eruptions of debris spewing up and pelting over him while German bombers rained down hell on the city.

The attack came so suddenly that not even the distant murmur of the planes had registered a warning before the first bombs struck. A second before it all began, the street was as serene as any Stephen had ever seen in Heraklion. He and Ianos had been to see Percy at the Villa Ariadne the day before, and they had been sitting down to coffee at an open-air kafenion, readying themselves for the journey home. Ianos had just made some droll comment or other, and the two were batting it back and forth between them with light-hearted laughter without the slightest sense of danger.

A second later, a thundering force had flung them brutally to the ground.

The roar of it was so loud that it passed and left Stephen levelled well before he could determine where it had come from. And even as he collected his scattered wits and began to piece it together, the ground pitched vehemently, flinging concrete and brick down around him, roiling like a frenzied tide beneath his feet. He felt his body lifted and thrown through the air, felt it shudder convulsively as it struck something hard, and again a blinding rage of sound broke over his senses.

After what seemed an eternity, the earth finally stilled. The hail of burning rock had stopped and the dust settled. His head rang painfully, but he fought the delirium of it, clinging as tenaciously as he could to consciousness.

Time passed fitfully, but gradually he realized he was lying against a wall, half-hidden in the debris. He lifted his head as best he could from where it lay in the dirt, but his body would not move. The thought stuck him acutely that he had been paralyzed by his fall, and he felt panic closing about his lungs like a fist.

He heard a stifled moaning from somewhere far away and clung to the sound, pulling himself to full consciousness by its tenuous lifeline. More sounds became distinct to him through the humming in his head then, and he knew he heard a woman wailing hysterically somewhere nearby.

They had been bombed.

The thought took shape in his mind at last, and as it did it intensified his fear that he had, in fact, been paralyzed. He struggled earnestly now to move but could not. The panic in his chest squeezed tightly, but he forced himself to remain calm. He focused his senses as well as he could, testing for feeling in his arms and legs, until he became aware of a throbbing pain in his shoulder. It hurt, but it was a great relief to know he still felt anything, and as he focused on the pain he realized that his arm was pinned down beneath his own weight. He tensed his muscles, heard a shifting of plaster and stone slide from his back, and felt his arms move.

At last he was able to lift himself to his hands and knees, bowing his head between his shoulders. The moaning was less muffled now, and the woman's scream had reached a feverish pitch. He felt he might vomit.

But he did not, and after another long moment he found the strength to stagger to his feet. He looked around at the destruction and again the urge to vomit swept over him, a second shockwave. The street that only moments ago had been alive with light and laughter now smouldered sulphrously. Near him a man writhed, impaled through the belly on a great timber flung free in the first explosion. Another moaned softly, still breathing but crushed beneath the tumbled remains of a wall. Others lay in haphazard positions, pinned beneath heavier, more gruesome detritus.

But he had survived. He felt his bruised body incredulously. The effort extracted acute pain from deep inside him, but the pain assured him it was true: he was alive; he had survived.

He began picking his way through the grisly scene. A dreadful thought arose in his mind, and it started him on a frantic search. His mouth was very dry, so when he tried to call out, no sound would come, but at last his voice rasped free from his lungs.

"Ianos?" He staggered through heaps of broken stone which he could not recognize but must have been the remains of the kafenion where they had been sitting. "Ianos!"

It was so silent for so long that Stephen feared the worst, but then, distantly, he heard his friend's voice, smothered beneath the rubble.

"Stephen?" he called faintly. "I'm here."

"Where, Ianos? I can't see you!" He moved clumsily and fell to his knees, scrabbling up again and searching more feverishly than before.

"Stephen?" The sound was clearer now and terribly, almost ominously calm. "My legs are trapped, but I'm here."

He scrambled over another heap of stone and slid down to his hands and knees as it tripped him up, but even as he did he saw his friend's face, still smiling, it seemed to Stephen, unless it was an awful grimace of pain. Ianos was trapped beneath a fallen heap of brick and plaster.

Stephen pulled frantically at the debris, and even after his hands had become raw and bleeding he continued. When the last of it was cleared, he helped his friend slowly to his feet.

"Are you all right?" Stephen asked. "Can you walk?"

"I am. I think I can. I will try."

Stephen draped his arm across Ianos's shoulder and carried the better part of the man's weight as he gingerly tested his legs. He had suffered worse than Stephen, but only slightly so, and they found he could stand after all. His ankle was badly turned, and Stephen knew now that what he had taken for a smile was indeed a wince of excruciating pain.

Together they looked over the ruined street. Other survivors had begun to emerge from the wreckage, staggering deliriously through the drifting smoke, searching and calling out names desperately. Some had pulled broken corpses from the rubble, wailing over them with a dreadful cacophony of heartbreak.

"I'm thirsty, Stephen," Ianos said. His voice was feverish.

Stephen realized then that he, too, was profoundly parched, and this sudden awareness of thirst momentarily distracted him from his other agonies. They staggered forward together, each clinging to the other to keep from falling, in search of water.

They found none, and as the hours dragged on their thirst began almost to choke them. They joined up with a ragged group of survivors sorting through the dead to look for the living. It was gruesome enough labour, but as the day grew hot, an unbearable stench of death rose in the air, mingling inextricably with the other horrors of the scene—the smoke, the cries of agony, the broken bodies—so overwhelmingly that he might have retched with it had he not been so terribly thirsty. Great swarms of flies appeared, bloated and hideous, come to feast on the carnage. And still the piles of the dead grew, until they lined the street and he was numb to the sight of them, delirious with the reek and aware of nothing now but the unquenched thirst in his parched lungs.

The horror of that day welled up in Stephen's eyes again when he finally brought them level with Nikos's gaze and found the words to answer his challenge.

"But you don't understand, Nikos. You weren't there. And I don't think you realize how serious the situation is. Athens was surrendered. *Surrendered.* The Germans have occupied the whole of the mainland. They will come for Crete."

"So let them come!" Nikos said defiantly. "And we will show them what kind of fight it is that burns in the spirit of this island."

"Fight?" Stephen was not sure if it was exasperation or fear that welled up in him, but he felt an urgent need to make Nikos feel the weight of the threat that loomed over them. "Do you really think that Crete can resist a force like the one that's coming, Nikos? Greece is *fallen*! Fallen. And if all the strength of the Greek army couldn't turn back the Nazis, what makes you think we will? A handful of grape farmers and shepherds, armed with pitchforks and scythes?"

Nikos scoffed dismissively, but there was something ominous in the bravado of his laugh. "We are more than shepherds and farmers, Stephen. We are Cretans! And we will fight like Cretans when the time comes to do. This is not the first time we've had to defend our homeland. Before the Huns it was the Turks, and before them it was the Venetians. We have a long history of defending what is ours, Stephen, and if the Huns come—" Stephen opened his mouth to interject, but Nikos roared him silent. "*If* the Huns come, they will find that we've learned the lessons of that history well!"

Stephen was about to answer when he felt a warm hand alight on his shoulder. It was Ariadne, warning him with a touch to stay silent.

But Ianos spoke up in Stephen's place. "But you *weren't* there, Father," he said. "And you *didn't* see. They bombed Heraklion without warning. And they have been doing the same across the island, bombing civilian and military targets alike. Women and children, soldier or civilian, it makes no difference to them. Mr. Percy says they're trying to force the British to move the last of their planes down to Egypt, so that the island will be utterly defenceless. And he says they will do, too."

"Mr. Percy?" The bluster in Nikos's voice took on an aggressive edge. "What does that drunkard know about this island, and the spirit that burns here? I'll be damned if I'll trust the fate of my homeland to the likes of Percy!" He slapped the scythe on the tabletop, as a kind of exclamation point to his words.

Stephen closed his eyes tightly, forcing down his frustration. They had talked with Percy the day before the bombing, and in his mind's eye he could see him again, sitting across from him at a table, on the veranda of the Villa Ariadne.

He was Lieutenant James Percy now, of course, no longer the affable archaeologist but looking just as crisply clad in his military uniform as he ever had when dressed for his work at the museum. Because of his military background, and more importantly because of his intimate knowledge of the island and its people, the British army had recruited him to help in the fortification of Crete. The work had been slow and often disheartening. A furious fight was raging for Greece on the mainland, and little could be spared to arm this island, either in ordinance or in soldiers. They had set up a weak battery of anti-aircraft guns in the hills around Heraklion, however, and established a makeshift aerodrome for the RAF south of the city. And when Athens had finally fallen and the Allies were forced to flee south across the Aegean, Percy had helped to coordinate their evacuation to Crete.

"We've had another troop of wounded arrive from the mainland," Percy was saying.

The grounds of the Villa Ariadne had been hastily converted into a makeshift hospital, and its once serene gardens were crowded with evacuees, the wounded and war-weary, men harried and haunted by the horrors they'd seen.

Percy indicated them with a nod from the veranda. "And look at them, Walker. Have you ever seen a sorrier looking lot? Exhausted. Half-starving. It's a wonder the evacuation didn't kill more of them than the Germans did themselves. And the bloody Luftwaffe was at their heels the whole way over." The long days working at an impossible task had clearly taken a toll on him, and his voice was uncharacteristically terse. "But then, the whole operation has been a botched job, beginning to end. We lack the most meagre semblance of order, and the discipline among the soldiers is a disgrace. There've been scuffles with the locals, men stealing food and such. They're even saying two soldiers killed an islander at Canea."

He passed a heavy palm over his weary face.

"God only knows where all this is leading us to, Walker, or where the end of it will be," said Percy. "But I can promise you this: the fight will come to Crete before it's all said and done."

Stephen nodded. For months now, the skies had been dark with the shadow of the Luftwaffe as planes passed overhead on their errands of destruction; and for longer still, the waters around the island had been thronged with fleets from the German, Italian, Greek, and British navies, vying with each other for victory.

The prevalent opinion among the locals, of course, was that the Aegean Sea would serve as ample enough shield against any German invasion. Even when the Cretan army division had set out to fight the enemy on the mainland, and Cretan families were forced to bid their sons and husbands a fearful farewell, most had clung blindly to the belief that the war would never cross the sea to trouble them directly.

But for Stephen, all the signs were there, that Crete was to be the next stage for this dreadful drama that had engulfed the globe. The day was closer than any dared believe.

"You should get out while you still can, Walker," Percy was saying. "Things are grim now, but they're going to get bloody well brutal before long. You should hear the stories the troops are bringing with them from the mainland. We'll get no quarter from the Germans, I can tell you that."

"Is it even possible now? To get out, I mean? It feels a little late for that."

"And maybe it is, but I just don't want you to say I didn't warn you. We're standing in the eye of a dreadful storm, Stephen, and it's about to break over Crete in a deluge of blood."

"Nikos thinks the Germans won't come for Crete, that they've moved as far south as they'll go. He says—"

"And let Nikos say that." Percy's voice was dull with the effort to supress his exasperation. "And let him go on saying that until the swastika is flying from every flagpole on the island, if it makes him feel better. Typical Cretan bluster. But anyone who knows anything knows that this island is the next target, whether Nikos wants to admit it or not. And what have we done about it, really? A few batteries of artillery, a half-built aerodrome with a dozen planes, and those held together with chicken wire? There's not half the men here, nor a quarter of the equipment we'd need to hold this island. And we're not about to get more."

Stephen rose from the table and stepped towards the edge of the veranda to where he could see the grounds, bustling with wounded men while orderlies hurried about, making space for more evacuees as they found their way in.

A vague line from *The Odyssey* came to him then, from the scene of Odysseus's journey to Hades, and he whispered it under his breath: "I saw Minos, the illustrious son of Zeus, sitting on a throne giving judgement to the dead."

Percy heard him and understood. "Odysseus had only to go to hell and back, Walker, to get home from Troy. I'm afraid we may have further to go even than that, before this battle's done."

The sound of stone on steel rasped intrusively against Stephen's memory, and brought him back to the moment. Nikos had taken up the sharpening stone and scythe again. He worked at the blade very deliberately now, but fixed his eyes firmly on Stephen the whole while.

Despite the unspoken warning in Ariadne's eye, Stephen tried a final time: "Nikos, please listen to me. Percy says that when Crete is attacked—and he is sure it will be—when it is attacked, it will fall. I'm just saying that we must be prepared for that."

The blade stopped suddenly in the middle of a long pull across the stone. Something smouldered in Nikos's eyes, but when he spoke at last his voice was measured and restrained.

"We *are* prepared," he said. "And *if* Crete is attacked, we will fight!"

"So you say. But do you really think that we'll do what the collective strength of the Allies could not do, Nikos? With what? And how?"

"What else can we do, Stephen?" The restraint was fading in Nikos's voice, and the smouldering look flared brightly. "What else can we do? Run away? To where? Or hide? Where then?"

Stephen had no answer. Ariadne's hand was still on his shoulder, but it no longer felt warm to him.

"We could take shelter in the mountains," Ianos spoke up. "Father, you know there are places there, in the hills, where we would be safe."

Nikos scoffed, but there was a note of warning in his voice. "My son," he said, refusing to look at Ianos but fixing Stephen with a look of disgust. "My son would have us put our tails between our legs like a pack of mongrel dogs!" No one dared speak back to him then, the look in his eye was so hard, so Nikos pressed his advantage. "Do you know, Stephen, our name—my *family name*—do you know what it means?"

Stephen was unsure what to say. He looked towards Ianos, but his friend was staring determinedly at the ground and would not meet his eyes. He looked at Ariadne. There was a sad glint in her eye that he could not place, and she gave her head the slightest shake, an imperceptible warning.

"Leventi," Stephen said at last. "It's Greek for... in English, we'd say 'handsome,' maybe. Or 'gallant?' Isn't it? Leventis? A handsome man?"

Nikos laughed with something vaguely like a growl. "But do you know what it is, a leventis? For us on Crete, I mean? Stephen, leventis means man of valour! To be a Leventi is to be filled with philotimo—you know this term? Philotimo, the love of honour? A leventis is a man who will do anything, and everything, for the sake of his honour. And in this sense, every true Cretan is a leventis, because the heart of every true Cretan beats, in the end, with philotimo!"

He had risen to his feet and the growl in his voice was unmistakable now.

"So I say, let the Germans come! And so long as Crete is free they will be met with an island full of leventes—men and women fighting for their honour, and for the honour of their homeland."

Nikos reached into his sash then and pulled out something bulky, banging it down on the tabletop. The light had grown dim in the courtyard, but even so Stephen made out the cold black metal and polished wood of an antique-looking flintlock. He looked up quizzically at Nikos, who had folded his arms across his chest and was staring down at him defiantly.

"It is a relic from our fight against the Turks," Nikos said. "From another time when the levantae of this island rose up against the enemy, with philotimo pounding in their hearts. We have met the enemy before, Stephen, and we will meet him again. And so long as we do it with honour, I say, Crete will never fall!"

An ominous note rang in his voice as he said it, as if he dared any of them to suggest otherwise.

None did.

Each stared blankly at the firearm on the table, until the silence grew palpable. At last Nikos gave a little scoffing breath and, picking up the flintlock again, turned slowly towards the house, walking away and leaving the three of them wordless in the wake of his passing.

CHAPTER TWENTY-EIGHT
Ariadne

THE DAYS THAT FOLLOWED THAT INTENSE EXCHANGE WITH NIKOS HAD A surreal texture to them. The looming threat of German invasion continued to overshadow them, though Nikos made it eminently clear that he had no wish to discuss it further. Stephen and Ianos journeyed one more time to see Percy in Heraklion, to learn what else they could about the work being done to ready the island against attack. But Nikos refused to come and asked them nothing about the trip when they returned. He sat smouldering over dinner that evening and maintained a stoic, almost heroic silence for the next two days.

Work at the vineyard did not stop, of course. If anything, it carried on with a kind of valiant attempt at normalcy. It was high spring, and the fields were in full bloom, swathing the hills around the villa with verdant green and brilliant yellow. The weather, too, was splendid, glorious almost to the point of irony given the ominous threat hanging over the island. Mornings shimmered with slow-fading mist, and afternoons lingered with brilliant sunlight and soft breezes. For his part, Nikos filled each day to overflowing with chores, apparently determined that whatever fate lay on the horizon for Crete, it would not disturb the regular rhythms of life at the Villa Leventi.

And so it was that one morning when Stephen woke from a luxurious sleep, just as the sun was rising on a Tuesday in May, it took him some time to recall the truth—that Crete lay under the looming shadow of war. Even when he did, he was unwilling, at just that moment, to let it darken his groggy peace. The wood-slatted shutter of their window was open and the gentle light of a brand-new sun was seeping slowly into the room. He moved languidly in the bed and became aware that the space beside him was empty. Ariadne had already risen.

He lifted himself to his elbows, inhaled deeply, and looked about the room, rubbing his face fully awake. He saw her standing at the window, softly silhouetted against the morning light. She wore a linen nightgown, her hair done up in a kerchief so that the nape of her neck was exposed and the curve of her jawline stood out sharply when she turned and he saw her in profile. She seemed inaccessibly lovely in that moment, so he said nothing and watched silently.

She had spread a linen cloth over the table that stood beneath the window and set out a ceramic basin, pristine white. She lifted a pitcher and poured out some water. The sound of it made Stephen think of windchimes maybe, or church bells, and the spill of it caught the light with flashes of white and yellow. She set down the pitcher carefully and leaned over the basin, cupping water in her hands and splashing it over her face. The light seemed almost to fill the room then and it danced over her shoulders like dove wings, lingering like a halo about her head.

Or so it seemed to Stephen.

And he watched silently a second more while she dried her face with a rough towel and washed her hands with great care, shaking the water gently from her fingers when she was done.

His mind was racing, no longer at rest. She was almost unbearably lovely, and he felt himself suddenly, intensely unworthy of her. The light played over her so naturally that it hurt him almost to see it. But the ache was not a longing, rather a tremulous surge of guilt.

She loosed the kerchief and shook free her hair with a single motion so graceful that it reminded him of that evening they had danced the sousta together; and sitting in a chair by the window, she took up a brush and began working it into a long single braid.

The ache trembled in him again and at last he spoke, in spite of himself.

"And why did you ever choose me, I wonder?" he said softly.

She turned, and though she was surprised to discover he was awake, she tilted her head and smiled at him fondly.

"It certainly wasn't for your looks in the morning," she said with a playful laugh. After a thoughtful look, she added, "Then again, perhaps I didn't have a choice in the matter. Kismet moves in ways sometimes the heart cannot understand."

"So you say. I'm still not sure I believe in kismet, but however it happened, I am glad we found each other. These last few months would have been pretty bleak without you."

She rose, leaving her braid unfinished, and crossed the room to crawl into bed beside him. "Without me? Stephen, without me you would probably be back at your home in Canada by now, miles away from this war, and this island just a happy memory."

He moved his arm so as to open his side to her, and she nestled into him, pressing her head against his chest.

"Not so happy as this is right now," he said, inhaling deeply the scent of her hair as it came to rest beneath his chin. "Whatever may come, Ariadne, I don't think I've ever been happier than I am with you here, right now."

They lapsed into silence, Stephen stroking her hair idly.

When finally she spoke, however, her voice was noticeably pensive. "Stephen?"

"What is it?"

"Will you take me there?"

"Take you?"

"To Canada. When this war is done, and whatever's to come has come. Will you take me home with you to Canada?"

He shifted his weight and took a breath to speak, but Ariadne lifted a hand to his cheek, to silence him. "I know what you'll say, that Halifax is nothing compared to here, that it's dull and dismal and Crete is lovelier by far. But not for me it's not. For me, this island is a doorless cage, a prison without walls. And yes, I know, too, that there are things in Canada you've tried to leave behind, things you wish maybe not to return to, or to face. I've listened closely enough to have gathered that. But Stephen, this island is like that for me, at times, and if I could just get away I think I would never look back."

"Ariadne, you don't understand. Canada's no longer home to me. Not anymore. You are my home now. Halifax, Crete, it makes no difference— wherever you are, that's where my home is."

"And if it makes no difference, then it might just as easily be Halifax as Crete, mightn't it?"

"But it's not nearly so simple as that." Stephen's voice had dropped to little more than a breath, and he stared blankly at the ceiling for a long time.

But Ariadne, it seemed, had something of her father's tenacity in her, and she pressed the point.

"Promise me." She sat up and leaned towards him, taking his face in both hands and pressing her forehead against his. "Take me with you to Canada. When the war is done, take me home. Promise."

He stared intently into her eyes, and she into his, until in the end he could do nothing else but nod. "Very well. When whatever it is that's coming has come," he said softly, "and this awful war is done. I'll take you wherever you wish to go."

Ariadne could see he meant it sincerely, and she was satisfied. She smiled at him and nestled down again.

"But until then," he said after another long moment, "this island will have to serve as our home, however much you wish it weren't. And there is work to do today. We can't lay about in bed forever."

But she pressed even tighter against him. "Oh, but let's do!" she said, playful once more. "Let's not have any talk of work or worry today. Let's just laze about in bed, you and I, until this horrid war has passed over us like a hazy dream."

"And leave Ianos alone for the day with your father? That hardly seems fair." He shifted his weight to the edge of the bed and made to rise, but she clung to him.

"At the very least," she said at last, "please don't go to Rethymnon today with my father."

"But he's taking the last of last year's sultanas to market, and he may need my help with the load."

"And you'd leave your wife lonely and unattended for no better reason than that? Stephen, Nikos travelled to Rethymnon well enough on his own for decades before you came into the family. He'll manage." She held tightly to him still, and a strange earnestness came into her voice, passing almost before Stephen noticed it. "Please… please don't leave me alone today."

"Fine," he said, affecting a note of mock exasperation, though he felt very tenderly towards her in that moment. "Fine. If it will please my clinging wife, I'll work with Ianos in the vineyard today. I believe he's attending to the southern side of the vineyard today. He could use my help, too, I suppose. And will that make you happy?"

"Happier than I'd be to have you gone all day."

He swung his legs over the edge of the bed and sat there a moment. She came up behind him to hold him tightly one last time, pressing her cheek against his back.

"Oh, must you?" she asked.

"You know as well as I do that I must. He'll be up and started by now, and the fields will be too hot for working in by noon."

He put his hand on hers, and though she continued to cling to him playfully, he pulled her arms free and rose from the bed. Pulling on his trousers, he stepped to the window, and after a luxurious stretch he took his turn at the basin to wash.

When he turned back to Ariadne, she was sitting up in bed, working again at the braid in her hair and watching him intently. She looked just as lovely as before, but somehow less inaccessible than she had been, more concrete and tangible.

"You know that I love you, Ariadne?" he said, speaking to her in English for the first time in a long while.

Her fingers stopped with the braid for a moment and she looked at him closely.

"Do you?" She said it in Greek, and though her tone was still teasing, something almost imperceptible flashed across her face.

Stephen caught it before it faded, and it brought to mind for him a dozen things at once. He thought of Grace, and that tremor of guilt quaked in him again. He thought of that first afternoon in the lemon grove, after his exhilarating trek to the summit of Mount Ida. He thought of the ache for faraway things and the wonder over ancient mysteries that had driven him from his home to here, like an unquenchable thirst he had been carrying all his life. He thought of the day he'd met Percy at Knossos. He thought even of the atlas, of all things, and a windswept morning on the shores of Prince Edward Island.

And with a ungraspable flash of clarity, it occurred to him to that somehow Ariadne embodied for him all these things—as though touching her brought all of it into being. An intense sadness swept through him then, but when it passed so, too, did all these thoughts.

"Do you?" He hadn't spoken, so she repeated her question. The playful smile was alight in her face but her teasing tone of voice had taken on a somewhat more earnest tenor.

He smiled, too. "I do," he said, and he meant it deeply. He moved forward to kiss her lightly and then passed through the door.

The morning was nearly at its apex when Stephen saw the glider. The sight surprised him, because he had heard nothing. Like some great, tranquil kite suspended effortlessly in the air, drifting on a silent wind, it slid across the sky. He had been kneeling in the vineyard, sunk among the brilliant perfume of the martolouloudia, inspecting the grape blossom and pruning the vines, when its ominous shadow passed over him. He rose slowly, gaping, his pruning scythe hanging forgotten in his inert hand.

He turned and looked further down the slope. Behind him, Ianos had also risen to watch its mysterious, awful flight.

Again his gaze lifted upwards. The splayed wings and long, tapered body floated almost majestically across the brilliant blue, yet it seemed to be falling, its trajectory dropping at a perilous angle. Thick, oily plumes of black smoke sputtered behind it.

But it was so silent. Its silence seemed to fill the vineyard, so ominously that it became a dread in him.

"A glider—" Stephen called loudly to Ianos, still gaping at the shape.

The word thundered unexpectedly in his own ears even as it passed his lips. And then it seemed as if time collapsed in on itself, suspended somehow in the silence of the glider's descent. He was suddenly aware of its trajectory, and at the same moment its darkening shadow passed over the villa at the far end of the vineyard.

"They're coming!" Ianos called out.

A small, dark shape dropped then from the underbelly of the glider.

Ianos called out again, more urgently than before: "They're coming!"

Stephen thought of Ariadne alone in the house as another dark shape fell, silently. The first shape billowed open, unfurling in a mute, distant flutter of pink. A third shape dropped, then a fourth. The second shape unfurled; it was black. The third shape bloomed blackly, too, then the fourth. They sky drifted with round silken shapes like fluttering flower petals floating earthward.

It was all so surreal that it took a moment to register. They were parachutes.

He traced their drifting trajectory and saw that they would land near to the villa. He thought again of his wife, and a strange dread fluttered up from the darkest places of his mind.

He began running the narrow corridor of the vineyard up towards the house, slowly at first, but with growing speed and urgency. His legs beat rhythmically, throbbing, pummelling the earth as his run became a sprint. Never had that vineyard seemed so long to him as it did in that moment.

"Ariadne!" He heard his voice spark gutturally from his lungs. His veins swelled with fear. "Ariadne!"

He was near the gate now. His lungs hammered. He saw the latch move. She appeared in the gateway, her eyes dark with confusion. He saw her point into the sky. She had seen them, too. She reached out for him, moving towards him uncertainly. Her mouth opened to speak. He was almost upon her, but he could no longer see the fluttering shadows above him. Another lunge of his legs and he would enfold her in the safety of his arms.

Then he heard it.

Almost before he did, he recognized the sudden look on her face. The thundering report of a single pistol—echoing awfully across the hills—rent the air. Her eyes widened. And before he could even place the sound, he recognized the startled burst of blackness eclipsing the light in her eyes.

She fell forward. A shuddering heap of cloth, a stumbling cloud of dust, and she crumpled forward as if struck from behind. He had reached the gate and was upon her, but he knew—darkly, violently, he knew. Kneeling, almost falling before her with the momentum of his run, he grabbed at her, as though to pull her back from a sheer abyss. He turned her prone body, gathering her up as best he could. Clutching at the tempestuous hair splayed across her forehead, stroking her gaping face, he heard himself scream her name. She coughed then, a great clot of red erupting on her lips.

Something burst into a fine cloud of dust against the stone wall of the courtyard, near to where he crouched. In the same instant that it registered on his senses, he heard another report of pistol fire. A burst of dust exploded on the wall near him, and he found he had risen, but slowly, as though he were moving through a heavy narcotic of rage and terror.

A few yards away he saw the bulky, bundled form of the paratrooper, enveloped in a fluttering veil of pink parachute silk, struggling simultaneously with the harness of his parachute and with his pistol.

He had dropped the pruning scythe when he'd knelt to hold her against himself, but now, almost without realizing he'd done so, he reached for it again.

A blind, crimson haze engulfed him then and he surged with adrenaline. Before the paratrooper could free himself from the clumsy burden of his parachute and properly aim his weapon, Stephen rushed forward.

He struck out furiously, but as he did the fluttering parachute entangled him. The pink film suddenly exploded into a burst of red, as something hard was brought violently against his head, and he felt himself flung sideways, sprawling through the silk.

A heavy weight pressed against him then. He struggled through a red-pink, pink-red mist. The weight overbore him and he felt another blow, then another.

His grip tightened on the scythe.

Clutching at the weight above him, Stephen heaved his body forward, upward, and felt a heavy mass thud beneath him as he landed. Grappling, the two men rolled, and suddenly he was beneath that pressing, battering force again. The soldier's arm, entangled in parachute silk, struggled above him to free itself. Stephen twisted his weight, lunged again, and tried to contain the arm, throwing his whole body against it. The two bodies, invisible to each other through the parachute silk that flapped about them, strove against each other for a dreadful moment of suspended eternity.

And then, with a wild rush of inertia, Stephen's arm swung suddenly free. He felt his fist tighten around the handle of the scythe, and with all the momentum of his rage he brought it down across the great mass that grappled with him.

Again he lifted the scythe, blindly, and again plunged downwards, and again. Even after the weight beneath him had ceased to struggle and lay limp, still Stephen's arm lashed at it.

At last he shuddered still and rolled heavily to his back. He felt a hot wetness at his temple. His lungs burned as he breathed, the motion of them aching against his ribs. He tasted heat and sweat at his lips. He opened his eyes at last, and a dull, rose-coloured light flooded his vision: parachute silk—and blood.

He struggled up, disentangling himself and stepping free of the flapping silk. Looking down, he saw the body, its contours sickeningly broken, obscured between the formless pink of the parachute that shrouded it. But the pink was darkening so very slowly that for a horrible moment he caught himself mesmerized in the slow reddening of the silk.

He turned away. His fist was still locked around the scythe, but the dreadful knowledge of the awful stain on the blade kept his eyes averted from it.

As the mist of rage swirled clear, he looked up and saw another paratrooper, this time dangling from a great black parachute that had caught in the limbs of the plane tree in the villa's courtyard. The man was suspended from the ground, rocking against the tree trunk as he struggled frantically to free himself from his harness. Stephen wasn't sure if it was terror or fury in him, but he rushed forward. The soldier saw him, and his struggling changed as he began to clutch at the holster of his pistol, trying to wrench it free.

Stephen lunged with the scythe, felt the sickening shudder of the blade against flesh, was vaguely aware of a guttural scream. He heard whistling in his ears, and something burst against the trunk of the plane tree; he turned and saw a third soldier, standing free of his parachute, levelling a pistol at him. Stephen tensed in horrible anticipation.

Suddenly a great flash erupted behind him.

Turning to the sound, he saw Ianos standing amid a drifting cloud of white smoke. His arm was extended and he gripped something Stephen did not immediately recognize. He looked back to the soldier, now writhing in his death throes. Back to Ianos, he saw his friend throw away what he had been holding and pull something dark from the sash at his waist, lifting it like he had done before. Again a great sound rent the air; again Ianos vanished in a cloud of white smoke. A fourth soldier fell backwards, swallowed by the gaping black maw of his parachute.

A heavy silence fell over the courtyard then. A breeze rippled through the languid tendrils of parachute silk, but otherwise the silence was complete.

Something rasped painfully in Stephen's lungs. He stood watching Ianos through the sweat and blood stinging his eyes as the narcotic of his rage began to dissipate. In its place, a sickening awareness of what had just happened swept over him. He dropped his scythe. He felt his body ache. Ianos still held the dark thing in his hand and, stooping, picked up the one he had dropped. Stephen saw that they were, in fact, two antique-looking flintlock pistols.

"There were only four," said Ianos. His voice seemed to tear a gaping wound in the silence. "I saw four drop."

Stephen nodded blindly but said nothing, till at last the words came out in spite of himself. "She's dead, Ianos."

"I know."

"She's... dead—she..."

He turned his face away from Ianos and looked towards the motionless heap lying at the threshold of the gate. Staggering, he moved towards Ariadne. Her gaping face still stared upwards, unseeing, and a great streak of crimson, bright and still hot, smeared the front of his shirt as he pulled her weight against him and pressed it there, clutching at it desperately.

Then, cradling her lolling body in numb arms, he struggled to his feet. His mind throbbed with inexpressible thoughts as he turned to face Ianos, who looked on silently, his face streaming with raw tears.

"They... they've killed her, Ianos."

"Stephen," Ianos said, "there may be more to come. It's not safe. We must go. We must find Nikos and—"

"No!" Stephen shouted, but it was not necessarily directed at Ianos. "No, Ianos, they've killed her. We need at least to see to her body."

"Bring her into the house. We will see to it and then we must find Nikos."

Stephen stumbled forward with his broken burden, and together he and Ianos entered the suffocating silence of the villa. He did not know what to do, so he carried the body to their room, and laid it gently on the linen of their bedsheets. His shirt was gory now with blood and clinging to him everywhere with sweat.

Gathering her motionless hand into his, he clutched it between quivering fingers. A soft sob shuddered from somewhere deep within him and he lifted the hand to his forehead, pressing it to his brow. He turned it outward, opened the inert fingers, and pressed his mouth weakly against the cooling palm, buying his face into it.

He did not know how much time had passed, but finally he dared to look again at his wife's face. It gaped hollowly at the ceiling, the dark eyes empty with her final terror, lips rough with brown-clotted blood. He tried to close his eyes against the sight of it, but the image was burned with searing clarity into the fabric of his mind.

He was aware of Ianos kneeling beside him and looked towards him. He had brought a basin of water and set it on the bed. With a cloth, Ianos began to wipe Ariadne's face and clean the blood from the mouth.

"Oh Ariadne," Ianos said faintly. "Oh my sister—"

He arranged the hair about the face as best he could and very gently closed her wide eyes. His face was streaming freely with tears, but he swallowed them back and leaned forward, kissing her forehead once very lightly.

He placed one of her hands over her chest and reached to take the hand Stephen still held, to set it in place as well, but Stephen shook his head and tightened his grip.

"Please," Stephen said. "Not yet."

Ianos nodded. "I will give you the time need. I will see if I can find Nikos." He stepped from the room and closed the door quietly behind him.

The room had grown cold and dim when Stephen finally felt a hand on his shoulder. He lifted his face. It was stiff with his dried tears and streaked with brown. Her body was quite cold now.

"We must go, Stephen." It was Nikos's voice, sounding heavy and restrained from somewhere in the shadows.

Stephen turned. "Nikos, she's dead. Your daughter. They've killed her."

Nikos was unable to acknowledge Stephen's words, or else he refused to. "We must go," he repeated. "They are coming."

"But Ariadne—"

"We must go!" The older man's hand gripped Stephen firmly from the shadows. "We couldn't save her, Stephen, but we can avenge her."

Stephen looked up at Nikos's shape, indistinct in the evening light. The wideset man was burdened with a long, bulky shape slung over his shoulder—a rifle—and Stephen could make out the black shape of another gun, a German tommy gun, dangling from a strap under his arm.

It took a moment for Stephen's mind fully to absorb these details. "Where have you been?" he breathed.

Nikos did not meet his gaze, but when he spoke, the words were menacing, like the rasp of a blade on a whetstone. "Repaying the Germans for what they've done."

Another shadow appeared in the doorway.

"I've found a canister south of the lemon grove," said Ianos. "The glider must have dropped it. It was attached to a parachute. Full of supplies and gear."

His friend was just a silhouette in the doorway behind Nikos, but still Stephen could see that he was carrying weapons like his father did.

"I also saw the wreckage of the glider," Ianos added. "It crashed some miles south of here. I don't think there are more."

"There were hundreds over the skies in the north." This from Nikos, his voice still menacing. "Maybe this glider was hit as it crossed the north coast. Perhaps that's why it dropped so far to the south, and why only four troopers jumped. The gliders we saw this morning dropped dozens each. The hills were swarming with them. The fighting is focused in the north for now. I barely got through. But they will come."

"But we must bury her." Stephen was still clinging to his wife's lifeless hand as he said it.

"There is no time," said Nikos. "Stephen, the invasion has begun. The men you killed this morning were only four among thousands. There is no time."

"But Nikos." Ianos placed a hand on his father's shoulder. "We must bury her."

A deadly tension flashed between the three of them, but it passed quickly and Stephen saw his father-in-law shudder, palpably, like a rubber band pulled far too tight suddenly snapping.

Nikos stepped towards the bed and knelt next to Stephen. "Oh, Ariadne!" he said as a great sob erupted from him, and he placed his forehead on the bedclothes, against the cold body of his daughter. "Oh child, my child. Why wasn't I here for you?" He wept freely and Stephen let him take her hand from his and fold it tightly into his own.

"Come," Nikos said at last, rising and turning to his son. "Come, we will bury her."

CHAPTER TWENTY-NINE
Nikos

STEPHEN PASSED THE NEXT FORTY-EIGHT HOURS IN A KIND OF DELIRIUM, drifting blindly through an incoherent montage of forced marches and desperate skirmishes. The battle for Crete was raging bitterly across the island, and Nikos was fiercely determined to do his part, that the invader would not take his homeland without a fierce fight. Ianos fought bravely alongside Nikos, though Stephen could not tell if it was genuine Cretan philotimo that drove him or something deeper, a fear of failing his father perhaps, or his anguish over Ariadne. Stephen was swept up with them in the struggle. He often quailed at the things they did and saw, but whenever he hesitated Nikos would say something passionate about death and honour and it was enough to push him forward in the fight.

In this way, he found himself, on the morning of the third day after burying his wife, lying on his belly in the sultry shadows of a bamboo thicket with a stolen tommy gun in his hands, blinking through sweat and staring down the slope of a hill, waiting for Germans to kill. The morning was late and the heat oppressive, the hillside smouldering with dust and sunlight. Nikos had stuffed his pack with supplies stolen from the war-dead, and the weight of it seemed to intensify the heat, crushing him down.

He looked over his shoulder. Ianos was crouched behind him, loading his own tommy gun carefully, his face looking strangely sinister in the mottled shadows of the thicket. The dark shock of hair showing at the edge of his tasselled cap was plastered to his brow with sweat and his face was streaked with grime. Stephen barely recognized his friend, but when their eyes met the man gave him an unexpected smile, a look so familiar that for the briefest moment Stephen forgot the horror of what they were about to do. But then a look of steel came into Ianos's eye, and he drew back the blot of his weapon with slow, determined significance. He lowered himself to his belly and inched his way forward on his elbows.

Stephen looked out from the foliage again. The air beyond was perfectly still, untouched by any breeze. Again the weight of his pack bit against his shoulder, but he dared not move to adjust it. His clothes clung to him and his face itched with sweat, but even so he sat perfectly still, straining to hear against the ominous silence, squinting out into the dazzling sunlight.

Ianos appeared at this side. "Nothing?" he whispered, his voice little more than a soft breath of noise.

Stephen shook his head. "Where is Nikos?" he whispered.

Ianos nodded. "Down there." He pointed. "We must wait."

Stephen swallowed painfully. Trudging across the parched hills all morning, and then wallowing this last hour in a stifling bamboo thicket, had left him aching with thirst and feverishly hungry. He still had some of the rations they had looted from one of the dead paratroopers, stuffed into the front pocket of his shirt. He felt he couldn't bear his hunger any longer, so he took the risk and very slowly he pulled it out. It was a hard brick of chocolate, or it had been. The heat had turned it into a soft mess that smeared his fingers as he pulled it open. He tried licking it from the foil, but it stuck like paste in his throat. He discarded it hopelessly and reached carefully for his canteen. It was nearly empty. The few mouthfuls that passed his lips when he lifted it were warm and only exaggerated his thirst.

A sudden, distant rattling of machine gun fire startled him into new alertness. He let go the canteen and looked anxiously over the hillside. Nothing moved.

Again the report of a machine gun rent the silence. He heard men shouting then, muffled by an ambiguous distance. He sensed Ianos's crouched form tense beside him. He looked down and realized he was gripping the handle of his gun so tightly that his hand was trembling. He tried to relax his fingers, but the next burst of gunfire sounded nearer than before. The shouting was louder, too, but he could not recognize the language. German? English? Greek?

He was so intent on the noise of the skirmish that the sudden clattering of the bamboo behind him caused him to start. His fist tensed around his weapon and he turned his head.

It was Nikos, appearing through the foliage and crouching beside them. He was breathing heavily, as though he had just bolted up the hill. "They are coming!"

Ianos nodded at the signal and crawled through the shadows, further down the thicket to a new vantage point.

Nikos moved until he was crouched right next to Stephen, looking down the hillside with a hungry eye.

"A New Zealand force is driving back what's left of a German platoon," Nikos said, hissing vehemently. "They are losing ground... being driven up this hill. We must be ready."

Even as he spoke, his words were punctuated by another torrent of gunfire, not far now from where they waited.

Nikos did not look at him, but his steely grip closed like a vice around Stephen's shoulder.

"We must be ready," the man repeated. "Do not fail, Stephen. Do not hesitate, and do not fail."

And then he was scrambling through the bamboo to his own position, leaving Stephen alone in the shadows.

The noise of the battle was almost upon him now, though as yet he could not see any soldiers. But the air was agitated violently with the sound of it. Stephen swallowed again, choking his fear down past his swollen throat.

A frantic scrambling came into view down at the edge of the slope, and a dozen or so men, all dressed in black and helmeted, broke suddenly from the cover and began sprinting up the hill, pursued by an unseen onslaught of New Zealanders.

Stephen felt the pit of his stomach convulse, and a sight flashed sickeningly through his mind, of a dying German paratrooper swaying in his parachute harness from the limbs of a plane tree, writhing with Stephen's scythe in his belly. He squeezed his eyes shut against the memory, and his finger stiffened, paralyzed against the trigger of his gun.

To his left, he heard the staccato eruption of Nikos's tommy gun. A cloud of dust billowed up into the heat as one of the retreating Germans sprawled forward and collapsed.

His finger was still frozen, but another sight flashed through his mind, this time a crumpled heap of cloth, a linen dress, bleeding out by the gate to the courtyard of the Villa Leventi. His heartbeat surged in his ears, his veins trembling with adrenaline, but still his finger did not move.

Nikos's gun erupted again, echoed now by Ianos, to his right, and a searing hail burst from the stippled shadows of the bamboo. He saw two more soldiers crumple and fall, but still they advanced. The Germans were aware of the enemy fire ahead of them now, as well as behind, and they had begun firing blindly in their direction. The bamboo rattled around him as bullets bit through it, clattering harmlessly overhead.

They were nearly upon him now. The air was swollen with the chaos of machine gun fire and the entire thicket seemed to shudder with it.

He saw Ariadne flash a second time across the scrim of his memory, and something seemed to shatter within him then. His weapon jerked violently in his hand. He saw one of the Germans fall, tumbling a few feet and then lying still. Another fell, hewn down by the thundering force of his squeezing finger. He did not realize it, but an awful scream had burst from his lungs, drowned out by the noise of guns in every direction.

He was only vaguely aware that the thundering had echoed still when Nikos appeared again at his side. The hillside was littered with corpses, but the New Zealand contingent had not yet broken cover. Ianos was down among the bodies, stripping them of supplies as quickly as he could.

Nikos was breathing heavily and if he saw Stephen's distress he did not acknowledge it. "Good, Stephen. That was good." He gripped Stephen's shoulder tightly. "Now we must go. Quickly."

Nikos turned, and the dense growth of the bamboo closed around him as he moved away into the depths of the thicket.

Stephen turned his face away from the horrid scene of the hillside below. Scrambling to his feet, he followed his father-in-law into the shadows.

That night, the three of them sat huddled together in a shifting circle of candlelight, around a rough wooden table in a stone hovel somewhere on the northern slope of Mount Ida. They had stumbled across this shepherd's hut as they fled the scene of the morning's skirmish. It was inhabited by a lonely widow. Her only son, she explained, had gone off to war when the Cretan division had left to fight for Greece on the mainland, and for all she knew he had been killed in the siege of Athens. She was quiet in their presence, perhaps cowed by these three battle-bloodied men bearing weapons and besmeared with the grime of a long campaign, but she ushered them in and offered them the typical Cretan hospitality nonetheless.

"We will march to Heraklion tomorrow," Nikos was saying, inspecting his gun the whole time. "They are hard-pressed there, and we will be able to help them."

There was an edge to his voice, like cold steel, warning off any dissent from the other two men. Stephen felt an inarticulate anger bead his veins, but he said nothing and stared hard at the tabletop.

Ianos sat to Stephen's left. He placed his gun on the wooden table and leaned forward. "Father," he said. "What use will three inexperienced grape farmers be in the fighting there? What good will we do?"

A sharp look flashed in Nikos's eye, but he calmly reached for a rag and began meticulously to wipe his gun. "We will fight," he said with a measured tone. "That is the good we will do. Today these three inexperienced men killed a dozen Germans. That is our use. We will fight the Hun until every drop of blood in our veins is spent trying."

Frustration and grief burned hotly together in Stephen's heart, but he bit his lip and sat trembling with silence.

Nikos and Ianos fell quiet as the old woman entered. She did not speak and averted her eyes from the ugly weapons lying on her tabletop, but she set out a tray of goat cheese and bread. Without a word, she then retreated behind a curtain into the only other room of the hovel.

After she was gone, Nikos set to work with his rag and gun again, but the silence remained and no one spoke for a long time. They had been rehearsing the same futile arguments for the better part of an hour now, and there seemed to be nothing left to say.

Stephen leaned back and looked wearily out the window. The air outside was cool, and the night brilliantly clear, shimmering serenely with starlight. It struck him as a far more beautiful a night than it had any right to be, given the horror that had swept over the island these last three days. He looked back towards Nikos, but was much too exhausted to argue with him anymore.

Ianos, however, tried one final time to press his point. "How do we even know if the way to Heraklion will be passable?" he asked. "And once we get there, what then? If the full force of the British army couldn't resist them, what will we—"

There was the vague hint of a snarl in Nikos's voice. "And what would you have us do then, Ianos? What?"

"We could make our way to the highlands. Find shelter in the mountains. Wait to see—"

Nikos brought his palm down loudly on the tabletop. "I'd rather die than run!"

"It's not running," Ianos persisted, urgently. "It's escaping. To a place where we could regroup, maybe. Join up with others. Then we could fight safely from the mountains. Wage a real war, not these futile bursts of fighting and running and fighting and running that are accomplishing nothing."

"You'd make a coward of your father!" Nikos was shouting now.

"You'd make a fool of him?"

Nikos was on his feet then, his chair clattering backward and turning on end, but Ianos raised his voice determinedly before he could speak. "How long do you think we can carry on like this, Nikos? We hardly have any food left, and even less ammunition. If we must fight then I will fight, but at least let us fight wisely. You know as well as I do that there are places in the hills where the Germans would never find us, however hard they looked."

"I am a Leventi, Ianos! You, my son, *you* are a Leventi!" Nikos seethed at them both.

"But Nikos—"

He roared him down. "No! We are Cretans, and we will fight like Cretans! And if it means our death, then so be it. I'd rather die fighting than live as a coward!"

Stephen could not contain himself any longer. He rose suddenly, throwing back his own chair as he did, knocking it to the ground. He cast a trembling look at Nikos.

"Nikos!" Stephen shouted. "Is it not enough that we lost her? Would you lose Ianos, too, and everything? If you had listened to us weeks ago and taken shelter in the mountains when we had the chance, like Ianos wanted you to do, and I, and Percy, if we had, *she might still be alive!*"

Things happened quickly then. Nikos groaned, or perhaps he roared—it was not clear to Stephen—but the man lunged at him across the table, catching him on the side of the head with his open palm and sending him sprawling to the stone floor. Ianos lunged forward, too, coming between them and holding Nikos back as he moved towards where Stephen had fallen. Stephen scuttled away until his back was pressed against the stone wall of the hovel, and then he slowly brought himself to his feet, watching the face of his father-in-law with mingled fear and rage.

"Nikos, please!" Ianos strove against his father's weight.

Nikos let his son restrain him, but still he cast a murderous look at Stephen, breathing furiously between his teeth. "Say that again to me, Stephen," he growled. "Say it again and whether you are my son-in-law or not, I will kill you."

Stephen had collected his wits and stood staring at Nikos a moment more, his own chest heaving. Then he pushed past them both and stumbled blindly from the house.

He staggered a few paces past the door and sank heavily to his knees. The moon gleamed overhead and the light of it seemed to lay him bare. He stooped over on his hands and knees, his rage and terror distending in him until he felt he must retch.

And he did, coughing and spitting, his chest shuddering within him and an acrid taste in his mouth. Again he vomited, sobbing terribly. When he was done, he lowered himself until he was curled in a ball on the ground. He lay there in the damp earth for a long time, weeping openly, and grinding his cheek against the dirt as he did so until everything in him was spent and empty.

Gradually he became aware of a soft hand pressed against the back of his head. He started and turned to see who it was, feeling acutely ashamed of the dreadful mess he had made.

It was Ianos. His shape was silhouetted in the moonlight, and he stooped cautiously over him.

"Stephen," he said gently. "You must not let him trouble you, Stephen."

His voice was a whisper, and though it didn't register with Stephen at first, he became gradually aware that Ianos was speaking English.

Ianos looked furtively over his shoulder towards the hovel, and then spoke again. "You must not let him trouble you, Stephen. He does not mean to be so hard."

Stephen said nothing, and again Ianos reached out tentatively to touch his head.

"I loved her, Ianos."

"I know, Stephen. And I loved her also."

"Did—" Stephen hesitated to say it, but he felt he had no choice. "Did he?"

Ianos nodded and there were tears in his eyes, either that or it was the glimmer of the moonlight on his face; Stephen could not tell.

"He did," Ianos said. "But she was very much like our mother. And it hurt him so deeply when Eunice died, that I think his love for his daughter has always been mingled with that pain."

Stephen tried to sit up. His face still stung from the blow he'd received, and it was streaked now with dirt and bile. He wiped his mouth with a shaking hand.

"He terrifies me, Ianos."

Ianos shook his head sadly. "It's not him. It's this war."

"But he's so—" Stephen thought back over the last three days, and words failed him. "Brutal," he said at last.

A distant look came into Ianos's eyes. "You don't understand. He was not there when our mother died. He was in Athens when she took ill, though she had asked him not to go. And he delayed returning, too, so he didn't make it home in time and she died without him. My father loved our mother very much and he has always blamed himself for her death. The shame of it still haunts him. And now Ariadne is dead, and again he was away when she was…" Ianos trailed off for a moment and then said simply, "It's a great shame to him."

"Is that why we're fighting like a pack of cornered dogs then? Because of Nikos's shame?"

"We are fighting for our homeland, Stephen, for our honour. You are not a Cretan, so you can't know what that means. But there are some fates worse than death. For a man like Nikos, to lose your honour is to lose everything, and disgrace is almost too great a thing to bear."

"But how long will we carry on like this? How long can we?"

Ianos looked back towards the hovel one last time. "Until he has won back his honour or can no longer fight," he said vaguely. "One way or another, the end will come."

A silence fell between them then, and they both became aware of how gently the night had fallen, however awful the events of the day had been. Somewhere nearby a goat bleated, otherwise the mountain air hung perfectly still all around them.

Finally Ianos spoke. "It is late and we'll be leaving before the dawn." He stood and extended his hand to Stephen, raising him to his feet after him. "Come, we should go in."

But they stood motionless for a moment, facing each other in the moonlight. Suddenly Ianos moved and clasped his arms firmly around his friend. Stephen lifted his arms and tentatively closed the embrace.

"Whatever is to come," Ianos whispered, "I swear this oath tonight: that I will love you, Stephen, as I love myself." The words seemed so strange to Stephen, but then he added, more strangely still: "May God call the enemies of Stephen Walker to account."

Stephen didn't know what to say in response, but he felt a mysterious strength come into him with the words, such strength that at last he held his friend firmly in return and said, "I too swear to you my friendship, Ianos, come what may."

And so I swore this oath of friendship to Ianos, though the words struck me so strangely: "May God call the enemies of Stephen Walker to account."

But I suppose it won't be long until the oath is put to the test, because we've decided we will march to Heraklion tomorrow after all. Nikos's will, it seems, cannot be opposed. There is something emerging in him that horrifies me, though I've seen so much horror these last three days that it's all begun to blur into one endless waking nightmare— Nikos, the Germans, Ariadne, Ianos.

Yesterday we stumbled across a massacre of German soldiers. Some twenty or more men lay slaughtered in a tranquil olive grove. The work of Cretan locals, it seemed, from the crude violence of the killings. Some were still tangled with their parachutes in the trees, some were hewn down with axes or scythes—all stripped of their weapons and ammunition.

And their boots had been stolen. This struck me the most: in the midst of so ghastly a scene as this, those bare, pink feet seemed almost farcical. I don't know if I expected the feet of the invaders to be scaled or clawed or what, but they were just so human, their feet. Soft soles, five toes. It was the humanness of their feet, I think, that repulsed me most.

So tomorrow we march to Heraklion and God knows what we will find there. We may be marching to our deaths, but after so many days of living hell, death may not be so unwelcome as all that. Nothing can bring her back, of course, but a valiant death, at least, might atone for my failure to protect her. And if I play some small part in defending this place from the enemy, then maybe her death won't have been for nothing.

God how I loved her.

Grace looked at the date of this journal entry—May 23, 1941—three days after the initial attack. The entries that followed were disjointed and somewhat incoherent, as though Stephen were only jotting down events as best he could, in the haphazard moments between fighting and running and fighting again. Even so, she began to piece together a vivid picture of the battle as it raged across Crete, and as Stephen played his role in it, the atrocities of war he had both witnessed and participated in.

She read about the skirmishes they pitched against the Germans in the hills around Heraklion, about the devastating carpet-bombing attack on the city the Germans launched in the days that followed, about the gruesome day he and Ianos had stumbled across a slit trench, filled with the machine-gunned corpses of New Zealand soldiers, their hands all tied securely behind their backs. She came across the feverish record of a long, dry trek across the White Mountains, escaping from Heraklion to God knows where, as well as his account of a surprise attack on a marching patrol of Germans in which twelve soldiers had fallen beneath the invisible hail of his gun while he fired down from the hills above them.

It was heartbreaking to read, but it also explained the brooding silence that had so often filled their days together after Stephen had returned; some of the horrors were, indeed, unspeakable.

She became aware an inarticulate pity growing gradually in her hurt. She fought it at first, but it spread through her warmly—despite his betrayal, perhaps even because of it—and as she turned towards the final pages of the journal, she could not tell if it was a sense of recrimination or compassion that drove her to discover, at last, the truth.

PART V
Minotaur

CHAPTER THIRTY

Sfakia, 1941

"BASTARDS!" THE NOISE OF THE SURF ALMOST DROWNED OUT PERCY'S voice, but he cupped his hands to his mouth and shouted again, bellowing the insult across the water. "Bloody, whoreson bastards!"

This loss of composure was so unlike him that Stephen felt profoundly unsettled to see it, and he stood there awkwardly, unsure of what to say.

Percy shouted indistinctly a third time, then let his hands collapse to his side in exasperation. After taking a breath, he said it once more for good measure, muttering to himself in a distraught tone: "Those bloody, bloody bastards."

They were standing at the edge of a cliff, looking out over the Libyan Sea. The night was very dark, littered chaotically with a tattered scrim of clouds that drifted slowly southward on a sauntering breeze. The moon was hidden, and the few stars that broke through gave little light. Stephen strained his eyes against the gloom, but although he could hear the sea rolling restlessly off into the distance before them, he could not see it. Even so, he knew that somewhere out there on the invisible horizon, trailing a stench of smoke behind it like a blood streak, a British destroyer limped southward with the clouds. It was the fourth and final vessel of the fleet come to Sfakia to evacuate the Allies from Crete, and though it bore hundreds of men to safety, still it left thousands behind to face their fate at the hands of the Germans.

"How could they?" Percy asked into the darkness. "There must be five or six thousand of us still waiting to be evacuated. How could they just abandon us like that?"

The question was obviously rhetorical, but even so Stephen ventured an answer. "They said they would return," he offered weakly, "that they'd come back for the rest—"

A dismissive scoff from Percy brushed the suggestion aside. "Did they indeed? They only said that because they knew there'd have been riots among the men had they said anything else. God! There was almost a mutiny as it was. The entire battle for Crete has been botched. We shouldn't have expected the evacuation to be any different."

"Then you don't think they'll—"

"Come back for more? I know they won't. Didn't you notice how the senior officers were given the priority, and the enlisted men left to fend for themselves? And no one would give anyone a straight answer on the evacuation plans? I wouldn't be surprised if this was the plan from the start—to save their own sorry skins and leave the rest—leave us—to fend for ourselves."

Stephen persisted naively. "But they couldn't have! Shouldn't the officers have stayed with their men? They couldn't really have abandoned them, could they?"

Percy turned to him, and in the dark Stephen could feel the cynicism dripping in his voice. "Trust me, Walker. There's nothing so ennobling about the rank of officer that you wouldn't give up every shred of your dignity, if it meant you got to save your own skin in return." He fell into a brooding silence, but not before whispering the epithet a final time. "Those goddamned bastards."

Stephen felt something in him deflate. In the ten days since the first German parachute had cleft the skies of Crete with violence, he had seen for himself the indomitable spirit of the British army over and over again: doomed charges of exhausted bayonets against an unrelenting hail of machine gun fire, undaunted courage against impossible odds, valiant last stands. He had seen New Zealanders, Australians, and Brits fight fiercely together for a land not their own, in a struggle made theirs only by their shared hatred of the enemy. And he had fought alongside them, too, beaten back and losing ground until there was no ground left to lose. They had retreated at last to Sfakia, a tiny fishing village on the southern coast where the British command had promised they would all be evacuated to Alexandria. It turned out to have been an empty promise for most of them. After so brave a struggle as these men had been through, this final betrayal was too bitter, almost, for Stephen to accept.

"But will they really leave all these men behind?" He knew the answer but still could not face it.

"Make no mistake. The lucky few who got off today will be in Alexandria by morning, and the officers will be at tea by midday, justifying their cowardice behind some smokescreen of rank and necessity. They'll keep the press from reporting the true number of the soldiers left behind, and none but us will be the wiser."

"Then what will we do?"

"Surrender."

Percy's tone was matter-of-fact, but still the word fell between them like a death knell. For a fleeting moment, the moon broke through the clouds and in the sudden light Stephen made out a look of grim resignation on his friend's face. The man gripped Stephen's shoulder, a gesture clearly meant to be encouraging, but there was something terribly ominous in the weight of his hand, the palm heavy, the fingers inert. A look of great sadness flooded his eyes then, so palpably that Stephen was almost relived when the clouds shifted and the darkness fell over them once more.

"We should rejoin the others," Percy said at last, dropping his hand from Stephen's shoulder. He turned and began to pick a slow, blind path down from the edge on which they stood.

Stephen looked out over the water a moment more, but there was nothing to see, so at last he turned, too, and followed.

After a short scrabble through the dark they came to a thicket of scraggly trees, shifting dimly with shadow and firelight. They pushed through the branches and entered a makeshift bivouac where three men sat around a frugal campfire, reclining with what seemed to Stephen an almost satirical luxuriousness, given the horrors they had been through these last ten days. They had spitted a great haunch of meat over the fire and looked for all the world as though they were princes sitting down to a sumptuous feast. The meat was somewhat burned, but Stephen was hungry enough after days of campaigning that it seemed to fill the whole clearing with a maddening smell.

At the far side of the camp, at the very edge of the firelight, he could make out the hunched shapes of Nikos and Ianos, sitting apart.

"Do you think it's a wise idea to light a fire, Marlowe?" Percy said by way of greeting.

"Go to hell, Percy!" came the New Zealander's response. "The fight's over. And anyway, we might as well enjoy one last feast before the surrender, mightn't we?"

Marlowe lifted a large piece of meat, skewered on the end of his bayonet. He tore off a bite and kept speaking with his mouth full.

"Don't suppose you'll be offered such a meal in a German prison camp," he added.

"You said it, Marlowe," agreed one of the others, a New Zealander named Duncan. "But then, I don't plan on finding myself in any prison camp."

Marlowe held out his skewer of meat. "Here, Percy, help yourself. There's plenty to go around."

Duncan agreed. "Don't stand on ceremony. It lacks some flavour maybe, but still, meat's meat."

"What is it?"

The third soldier, a man named Peters, laughed at him: "What difference does it make? You wouldn't turn down real meat, would you? After the jaunt we've had across this island? Here, Walker, there's some for you, too."

Duncan held out some of the meat on his own bayonet. "Call it Cretan mutton, if you will. Anyway, it beats the hell out of the bully-beef and biscuits we've been choking down for God knows how long."

Stephen took the bayonet and bit ravenously into the meat. Like the other men routed here by the Germans, he'd been fighting far too hard on far too little, with precious few rations and even less time to eat them in. He swallowed before he had finished chewing. It was very tough, and if it was better than bully-beef and biscuit, it was only barely so.

"Cretan mutton?" he asked sceptically after he had forced it down.

A look passed between the three New Zealanders, and then Marlowe explained: "It's donkey, Walker. Ass. Compliments of the New Zealand Fifth Division. Duncan here caught it ambling unattended outside Sfakia. He and Peters dressed it up themselves."

Stephen's mouth fell open. He had been just about to take a second bite, and the meat hung frozen before his face.

Marlowe laughed again. "Well, it's meat, isn't it? It won't kill you."

"Think of it as a delicacy," Duncan suggested. "Even your two Greek friends there ate some."

Stephen looked uncertainly towards Percy, who was already chewing heartily, far too hungry to put on squeamish airs. Duncan, Marlowe, and Peters laughed loudly when at last Stephen grimaced and took his second bite. They cut themselves each another portion and together they all fell to.

Ianos had ventured closer to the fire and joined the men in their food and talk, but Nikos remained at the edge of the clearing, silent and erect, watching intently.

This unlikely band of seven derelicts—a Brit, a Canadian, two Cretans, and three New Zealanders—had formed during the trek across the White Mountains as the Allied forces made their final retreat to Sfakia.

The last ten days had run one into the other in a kind of surreal haze, and even now it was difficult for Stephen to put all the details together coherently. After the awful dispute in the shepherd's hovel on the slopes of Mount Ida, Nikos's will had intensified, and neither Stephen nor Ianos had any heart left to resist it. So they had followed him to Heraklion where they'd been plunged into a waking nightmare, holed up in the very bowels of the city. The combat was almost inhumanly fierce there, but after five gruelling days of blood and fire they were, in the end, overcome. The main force at Heraklion had been evacuated by sea, but the remaining battalions had fled south towards the makeshift hospital the British had established at Knossos, and Stephen, Nikos, and Ianos had been able to intermingle with these retreating soldiers and so escape capture.

At Knossos they'd met up with Percy, who was still doing his part to help the British command at the Villa Ariadne to maintain some semblance of order. He had been working with little food and even less sleep for days, and the shadows under his eyes were blue with exhaustion; but still he wore a brave face and continued to work unflaggingly, as the dead and dying poured in from the city. Even after the order came to abandon Knossos, he remained behind, determined to do what he could to help the wounded who could not be evacuated.

When it had finally become obvious that nothing more could be done to salvage the situation, he'd joined up with Stephen, Ianos, and Nikos to slip away to the southeast, even as German troops rolled onto the grounds of the Villa Ariadne. There were German mountain divisions patrolling the hills now, and the four of them had been driven east into the White Mountains—indeed, they'd been forced to travel well east of Rethymnon before they could safely bear south towards Sfakia and the coast.

They'd met Marlowe and the other New Zealanders among the soldiers fleeing Canea. Marlowe was severely lame from a festering bullet wound in his upper thigh, and the soles of Peters' feet had been worn raw from marching bootless. Despite being uninjured, Duncan hadn't been willing to abandon his friends, so the three men had been straggling badly when their battalion began the breakneck descent down the final path towards the coast. Percy and Stephen had stopped to help them, and a vague comradery had arisen. Their battalion had actually been one of the few to be evacuated when they arrived at Sfakia, but Marlowe's wound had caused the group to lag and miss the boarding. Peters and Duncan were determined to stay with their friend, and so they'd all been left behind together.

"And what do you think will happen tomorrow?" Marlowe asked suddenly.

They had finished gorging themselves on donkey meat and were each lost in thought, watching the flames of the fire with blank expressions. The sound of his voice brought Stephen sharply back to the present.

"We'll capitulate. The Germans will take us captive, and we'll probably be marched back to Canea to become official prisoners of war." Percy laughed ironically. "You lads might just as well have spared yourselves the trip across the White Mountains and stayed at Canea—"

"I'll be damned if I'm going to be taken prisoner." The tinge of steel in Duncan's voice left no doubt that he meant it. "I'd rather be killed fighting, and take as many of those bloody Krauts with me as I can before I go."

"We could try to escape," Peters said. 'The highlands would keep us well hidden. And with Walker's connections among the locals—" He nodded here in Nikos's direction, who still sat at a distance. "—we could probably avoid capture."

"You could, Peters," said Marlowe. "But I'd be buggered, with this lame leg."

No one wanted to acknowledge how badly Marlowe's injury was hindering them all, so instead they fell into a grim silence.

Suddenly Peters erupted with exasperation. "Damn Brits!" He flung his bayonet down in disgust, and then followed it with his empty canteen. "God damn them!"

No one said anything else, and the silence fell again, more ominously than before.

"Well," said Percy at last. "Let's at least wait to see how the situation looks in daylight. Anyway, there's nothing to more to be done about it tonight."

Each man knew this was so, and eventually one by one they found a spot to lie down by the fire and watch as the last of its light danced itself into embers. Soon everyone but Nikos was asleep, but he sat in rapt attention throughout the night, keeping his stoic vigil, with his machine gun resting idly across his lap.

The next morning, the seven of them agreed that Marlowe's injury really did make escape impossible, but they decided at least to break camp and find a better spot to hide from the German patrols. Marlowe was in no shape to attempt the mountains again, so instead they crept along the shoreline, hiding in the undergrowth and among the rocks, taking turns supporting their friend's weight as they went.

Towards mid-afternoon, they discovered a hollow in the face of a cliff that came down directly to the water, and though the climb up to it took an excruciating toll on Marlowe, it was cool with shade when they reached it and large enough to hide them all. They collapsed inside, completely spent, and dreading any discussion of what they might do next.

Nikos did not wait long, but said something in Greek about scouting for Germans, and then left. Ianos lingered reluctantly a moment after his father had gone, but eventually he left, too, though not before flashing an apologetic look at Stephen.

After a restless moment, Peters said he would see if he might not find them something worth eating, and left as well.

Duncan and Percy did their best to tend to Marlowe's wound, now inflamed and oozing after the morning's strain, and Stephen perched himself at the mouth of the cave, watching the shoreline nervously.

The day was nearly gone and the shadows of evening were lengthening when Ianos came scrabbling over the rock and up to the cave, speaking excitedly in broken English.

"I've found a boat!" he said. "Stephen! Mr. Percy! I have found a boat."

His news was met with a tentative enthusiasm, more anxious than it was hopeful. No one wanted to say it aloud, of course, but the possibility of escape had flared up suddenly in each man's thoughts. Stephen and Duncan followed Ianos back to the boat, to make sure, while Percy stayed behind with Marlowe.

True to Ianos's word, some hundred yards or more from the cave he brought them to a shallow inlet where they found a derelict boat lying overturned in the water, slapped gently by the waves. It was a small aluminum affair, possibly the abandoned life raft of some navy ship or other that had been lost at sea. It had a huge dent in the bow, but the hull was whole, and after righting it and testing it, none of them doubted it was seaworthy. There was even the better half of a broken oar, which they could use to launch and steer it.

They dragged it further up onto the gravel of the beach, and then gathered together a clumsy tangle of bamboo stalks and cypress limbs to hide it.

Percy and Marlowe were waiting eagerly for their report when they got back to the cave.

"It would carry the lot of us," Duncan said eagerly. "No doubt of that. And I don't expect it would have much trouble on the open water."

Percy knew the waters south of Crete well enough to give the idea a serious weighing; he scowled at the ground, lost in thought.

"We might make it across to Egypt; at least it's not impossible," Percy said. "What do you think, Ianos?"

"If there are no storms... or bad winds..." The Cretan answered with a nod.

"I'm not saying it would be easy," said Percy, more to himself than the others. "Indeed not. We'd need to be well supplied—water being the primary concern, of course. And I don't suppose it'd be a Sunday afternoon in the park lying out under that sun during the day."

"Egypt would have to be—what?—four hundred miles?" Duncan said, weighing the plan for himself. "How long would it take?"

"Who can say? For a destroyer it's more than an eight-hour voyage. But then, we'd be drifting entirely at the mercy of the sea, and who knows what to expect of that? I'd guess three days, maybe four, but that's nothing more than speculation."

"Three or four days?" repeated Duncan.

"Five at worst," said Percy.

"We could make that." This from Marlowe, who leaned forward enthusiastically. "I know we could."

Stephen had been listening silently, but at last he spoke up. "Five days on the open sea? Do you hear yourselves? The exposure would be like the desert at the hottest point of the day, and no way to hide from it. It doesn't seem like much now, but it's a long time to be drifting aimlessly. You'll die of thirst, if you don't get bombed by a Stuka or something first."

"You'd rather get taken by the Germans, and sweat it out in some prison camp?" Marlowe asked.

"No. I'm just trying to be practical. No point escaping the Germans only to die of thirst on the open sea."

Duncan was already working out the problems. "We could bring a stock of water, rig up some sort of canopy maybe."

"And how would you avoid detection from the air?" Stephen asked.

"We'd have to take our chances on that."

"But really, Duncan, where would you find enough water to—"

"Damn it, Walker! What would you have us do?" The New Zealander's frustration got the better of him. "Spend the rest of the war like an animal behind barbed wire? Have you heard how they treat their POWs? For the love of God, I'd rather die bobbing about in the middle of the ocean than face that!"

Percy spoke up. "Look. We've each a canteen. If we scavenged, we could probably produce three, maybe four more. That's nine or ten, let's say. If we could fill those, and we rationed carefully, we'd have enough to last a good five days. I'm not sure about any canopy. We've nothing really to fashion one out of, but we'd just have to do our best with the heat."

"We've got to try." Duncan was clearly resolved, and Marlowe nodded with him.

"We've no choice," Percy said firmly. He gave Stephen a close look. "You see that, don't you, Walker? We really have no choice."

"Where the devil is Peters?" This from Marlowe. In their enthusiasm, they had not realized how long he had been away till now.

"He should have been back hours ago," said Stephen. "And Nikos, too."

They looked at each other with drawn faces. No one wanted to consider the possibility that either of them had been captured, or worse, but the implications of their absence, as it slowly dawned on them, left them acutely aware of how urgent it was, now, that they escape.

Peters had not returned by nightfall, and the group's fears grew ominous. For his part, Nikos came into the cave just as the last light of the evening was fading. He said nothing about what he had been doing, though when they pressed him he said that, no, he hadn't seen Peters. He mentioned some German patrols he had seen in the hills nearby and warned them that they ought not to light a fire tonight.

But even after it had grown fully dark, Peters did not return, and a terrible dread hung over them when they finally lay down with empty bellies, trying fitfully to fall asleep.

It took a long time for anyone to drop off. Stephen had been lying stiff and wide-eyed, staring up into the blackness of the cave for what seemed like hours, when finally he heard Percy speak to him in hushed tones from the darkness.

"You don't intend to come, do you, Stephen?"

Stephen did not speak at first, but Percy waited silently for his answer, so long that finally he said, "I can't, Percy."

"Is it because of them, Ianos and his father?" It was not a judgment, nor an accusation, but in the utter blackness of the night Stephen felt it as both.

"It is… it's because of her, Percy."

"She is dead, Stephen." Percy's reply was far more tender than Stephen had ever heard his friend speak to him before, but even so the words were piercing. "And your own death won't change that."

"Is it more likely I'll die here? Or out there on the open sea?"

"Fair enough. But understand that you are not a soldier. You've been fighting this war as an irregular, and if you are caught by the Germans you will be taken for a criminal, not a prisoner of war."

Stephen blinked blindly in the darkness. "You don't understand. I gave up everything to be here with her... and now that she's gone, I don't know if I could go anywhere else, even if I wanted to." He fell so quiet that they could hear the lapping of the tide on the rocks outside the cave. Percy waited patiently and said nothing, so at last Stephen added, "But... but if by doing something honourable—heroic, maybe, I don't know—in this fight... if by that I might somehow redeem something I've lost, then I don't know, but maybe her death might mean something in the end."

He felt foolish saying it, but it felt true to him as he did. He shifted his weight and turned towards the place where Percy's voice was coming from, and though he could not possibly see his friend, he knew that he was looking at him.

"Does that make any sense to you?" Stephen asked.

"It sounds ridiculous."

But even in the dark, Stephen knew he was smiling at him gently, and that he meant it kindly.

"But I guess love itself is ridiculous, when it comes down to it, and war is no better," Percy said. "So if by staying you can make sense of it all, then I won't press you to go. Only..."

"Only...?"

"Only, what about Grace?"

"Grace?" Stephen pressed his eyes closed tightly.

"You told me once that loved you her, too."

"And I do. I do. But after what I've done—what I've become—it wouldn't be right. I couldn't ask her to take me back. The shame it would bring on her would be too horrid. And she would, if I did—take me back, I mean. I know she would. But it wouldn't be right."

Percy sighed softly. "No. I suppose not. At least, I suppose you would know better than I. Only, I wonder if it would be worse to return to her than to leave her alone for good? You know, don't you, how unlikely it is you'll ever leave Crete now, if you don't leave with us?"

"Percy," Stephen said quietly, "you told me you wouldn't press."

"And I'm not pressing. But at least I want to be sure you are sure before we leave you behind. This is probably your only chance to escape."

Stephen did not speak again, but stared savagely into the dark. Percy waited for a moment, and when no answer came he finally said a resigned, "Good night, Walker," and after a while Stephen could hear the uneven breathing of his sleep.

Marlowe muttered once or twice from the depths of some terrifying dream he was having, and Duncan was snoring more gently than he had any right to, given the circumstances. But other than that, the cave was filled with the soft noise of the surf down below, and little else.

Even after he was quite sure everyone was sleeping as best they could, Stephen lay wide awake, turning Percy's words over and over in his mind.

When the weight of them finally became unbearable, he sat up and groped through the darkness until he found Ianos's pack. He knew Ianos carried an electric torch in it, and after rummaging about blindly for a moment he fished it out. He crept back to his own bag then and found his journal and a pen. He crawled to the far corner of the cave, where he knew the light would not wake the others. Turning on the torch, he tore a single blank page from the journal and began to write.

Dear Grace,

It is awful for me to write this after so many years of lying to you. Not just because of the terrible shame it is for me to tell you at last, but more importantly because of the hurt that it will cause you. For it will hurt you, Grace. I know it will.

I wish I had the strength to have told you the truth a long time ago, when everything was simpler and it might only have set you free from loving me, instead of shattering you in the way it is bound to do now. But I couldn't, at least I didn't, and now, after waiting through years of uncertainty, I can't imagine the agony it will cause you to discover it at last.

That I have loved another.

I have fallen in love with someone else. I did not want to hurt you, much less to betray you, or disgrace you, which is why I kept it secret from you. Nothing is more loathsome to me now than this lie, and though I can't bring myself to ask for your forgiveness, I will at least give you the permission to hate me for it.

Hate me, the way I hate myself, for the agony I've caused you. Or if you can't do that—and knowing you, Grace, it's not likely you could—if you can't do that then at the very least leave me. Let go of me and follow whatever path your fate will lead you down without me.

Because I love another. And because I can't leave that love behind, I will stay on Crete. I must stay here, and fight, or die fighting. There really is no other way.

I am sorry that I have hurt you. I am sorry I ever lied to you. Know that I have always cherished you, but know, too, that I love another, and be released from ever having loved me.

Stephen.

When he had finished writing, he stared at the page in the light of the electric torch. He reread it several times, and each time he tried to imagine Grace somehow receiving this letter, and reading it herself, and knowing the truth at last. He shuddered, not for himself, but for her.

And then he closed his fist over the page tightly, crushing it into a crumpled ball. He was about to toss it aside, but at the last moment he opened it again, smoothing it as best he could against his thigh. Then he folded it carefully and tucked it into the pages of his journal.

He tore out a new page, and after a deep breath, began a second time.

Dear, dear Grace,

If this letter, by some miracle of fate, does actually reach you, please do not cling to some false, empty hope. Know that I am alive, and that I love you desperately, but it seems so unlikely I will ever be home again. It would hurt me deeply to know that you held on for nothing.

The words came quickly, and he scratched them down without looking back at what he had written. When he was finished, he folded the page furtively, tucking it into the breast pocket of his shirt. Then he crawled back through the darkness and lay down again, though he did not sleep, and when the morning light finally crept into the cave, his eyes were raw and his face stiff with dry tears.

———

Peters had not returned by morning. They all agreed that if he was not back by evening, they would have to give him up him for lost and escape without him. There was a dispirited argument between Percy and Duncan about this, but it didn't last long. They all knew that the risk of being found by the Germans grew by the hour, and if they didn't make it away soon, they never would.

They spent the earliest hours of dawn hunting in the hills above them for fresh water and anything they might carry it in. The search was less fruitful than Percy had hoped. They did find two canteens on the bodies of some unburied soldiers, but even with those, in the end, they only had five canteens of water between them. Even Duncan had to admit that it seemed foolhardy, if not suicidal, to brave the blazing sun of the open sea for who knows how long with such little water as that. But the group was resolved. And anyway, they had long since passed a point of no return, so they all agreed that they would have to make do.

Stephen had wanted to give them his own canteen, but Percy insisted that in the coming days he would need it just as much as they.

They waited through the day without speaking much. Each man was far too consumed with worry to talk, and even if they had wanted to, they were too hot and hungry to have found the energy for it. Marlowe's wound had flared dangerously, and he spent most of the day drifting in and out of a feverish delirium. At one point he burst into a fit of frenzied, unconscious screams which they did their best to smoother, terrified that it would give away their position to the Germans.

Evening came at last, and with it a merciful break in the heat. Peters had still not returned, and though Duncan and Percy exchanged some words about waiting just a bit longer for him, they all knew they had already waited too long, and they would have to leave him behind. It took some time for Marlowe to navigate the path down from their cave, and it was fully night when they finally came to the place where the life raft was waiting for them. The sky was clear, however, and laced with moonlight, the water glimmering as it swept forwards and backwards in the inlet. Only Percy, Marlowe, and Duncan were going, but

Stephen, Ianos, and Nikos had come with them, to see them well launched and wish them godspeed.

At the last minute, Percy pressed Stephen one more time to come with them.

"You know I can't, Percy. I really must stay and fight now."

"And what about your home? Your family?"

Stephen thought fleetingly of Halifax. He remembered the awful fight he'd had with his father right before he left, and wondered if his father was worried for him now. His mother would be, he knew, and so would his sisters Jane and Sarah. He thought of Grace, and the pain he'd caused her.

But his grief for Ariadne burned so brightly in his heart that it eclipsed everything else.

He looked back at Ianos, standing stoically at his elbow, and even at Nikos who stood a few yards off, watching them.

"This is my home, Percy, and this my family," Stephen said. "I couldn't live with myself if I turned my back on them now."

"Then it's decided, I suppose." Percy looked long and hard at his friend, measuring him carefully in the moonlight. "You're a fool, Stephen. I probably should have told you that long ago."

And then something came into his voice that Stephen had never really heard from him before, something almost paternal. He placed his hands on Stephen's shoulders and held him at arm's length.

"But then, I've never admired a fool more."

Stephen laughed in spite of himself. "If I'm a fool, you're a sot… though I don't think I've ever admired any man more. I wish you luck."

Percy laughed, too. "A sot, he says? Well. I've been called worse. But don't forget everything this sot has taught you. Not that it will be of much use to you as you face what's to come. But maybe someday it will."

"Maybe someday you and I will sit down over a good glass of malmsey and find the wits to crack the Linear B at last."

"One can hope, Walker. Until then…"

And Percy enfolded him in a quick embrace, clapping him on the shoulder roughly but kindly, and released him just as quickly.

"It's time we were off," Percy said, turning to Duncan and Marlowe.

They pushed the aluminum life raft into the shallow water. Stephen and Ianos held the boat steady while the three men climbed in and arranged themselves carefully. Marlowe was in agony as he pulled himself over the gunwale, and it took him a long time to find a sitting position that he could bear. Stephen watched him nervously, but the New Zealander put a brave face on it and eventually the three of them were as settled as they were likely to get.

Ianos and Stephen pushed the boat further into the water, until they were sure Percy could handle it with the broken oar. The water was at their waists now, and Ianos had let go. But Stephen held on a moment, and just before releasing the raft he spoke to his friend a final time.

"Percy?"

"Walker?" Percy shifted his weight until his head was close to Stephen's at the gunwale.

"Percy, can you—will you promise me—?" As he spoke, he reached into his shirt pocket and pulled out a folded piece of paper. "This letter must reach Grace, Percy. Promise me you'll get it to her."

Percy looked carefully into his friend's face, and then he took the letter form his hand. "I'll do what I can."

"Promise me."

"I promise."

Stephen was satisfied. He braced his shoulder against the boat and gave it a final heave, sending it off to its fate. But still he stood for a long time in the waist-deep water, watching it drift away until the darkness had engulfed it.

———————

The next morning, Nikos was adamant that they leave as quickly as possible. He was already afraid they had stayed too long at Sfakia, and every second they remained intensified his fear that they would be captured. So long as Percy and the New Zealanders were with them, Nikos had lingered in the background, brooding pensively but saying little. Now that it was just the three of them again, the indomitable will returned with full force. At his order, Ianos and Stephen prepared for a trek into the highlands, where they might "fight the Hun on our terms, not his."

They were well on their way into the White Mountains when they saw a sight Stephen would never forget: the captive soldiers of the abandoned British force, being marched by the Germans from Sfakia to the prison camp at Canea. It was Nikos who saw them first. Motioning to Stephen and Ianos, he crouched under the cover of the foliage to watch their passing in silent respect. The line was two, sometimes three wide, and it stretched interminably in both directions along the mountain path. Thousands of men—four thousand, if there were a dozen—marched along numbly, mere spectres of the soldiers they had been.

As far as Stephen could tell, only a handful of well-armed Germans kept this great, broken mass of beaten men in line. He felt something sink in the pit of his stomach, an overwhelming sense of defeat, mingled with a strange feeling of awe.

He was startled suddenly by the rattling burst of a machine gun close beside him. He tensed and turned towards the sound. The noise erupted again, and then he saw Nikos, standing proudly, out in the open, firing his gun into the air in a reverent salute to these, their captured allies. There was a poignant look in his eye, and Stephen wondered if this was what he had meant when he'd spoken of philotimo.

Stephen rose, too, and Ianos with him, and together the three paid homage to these thousands of men who had given everything in their struggle for freedom, firing round after round into the air.

The Germans were quick to reply with their own volley of gunfire, and as a hail of bullets fell burning among them, Ianos grabbed Stephen by the shoulder and pulled him down. Nikos was already moving up the slope and over the ridge, beyond the reach of German gunfire, and without looking back a final time they turned and followed him, fleeing deep into the cover of the hills.

CHAPTER THIRTY-ONE

Chryssoscalitisa, 1942

THE DAYS THAT FOLLOWED BLED INTO WEEKS, AND THE WEEKS INTO months. Nikos drove the three of them ferociously, a little band of andartes, as Ianos called it, though whenever he did Nikos glowered at him threateningly.

"We are not guerrillas, Ianos," he insisted. "We are apeleutherotes—freedom fighters for Crete!"

But whatever they called themselves, still Stephen found himself doing things that horrified him to think about, whenever he ever found time to scratch down a record of it in his journal. This he still kept with him, though it seemed so unlikely now that anyone would ever read it. Many of the pages had been soiled with the dirt of their haphazard campaign, and one or two stained badly with blood, from when he sat down to write in it without remembering to clean his hands first.

It was true that the mountains allowed Nikos to fight the Germans on his own terms, and though theirs was not the only band of freedom fighters on Crete, the man showed little interest in joining with a more organized resistance effort. He preferred to fight in intense bursts, attacking viciously and unexpectedly from the cover of the hills, and then retreating again into the mountains where they would lurk until their next opportunity to lash out at the enemy. They looted what supplies they could from the Germans they killed, and though they never raided any of the locals, those that provided them with food did so at great risk to themselves, and sometimes out of an obvious but unspoken fear of Nikos.

"They've taken to calling him O Tauros," Ianos told Stephen once as they followed Nikos into a shepherd's hovel where he had arranged for them to spend the night. "They love him. But then, few have the heart to do otherwise. O Tauro tes Kretes—the bull of Crete!"

This nightmare succession of pitched skirmishes and aimless mountain marches began to eat away at them, though, and Nikos seemed to fight more and more savagely as the months wound on with no end to the German occupation in sight. He took to collecting trophies from those he killed, usually insignias cut from the uniforms of fallen soldiers, though once Ianos had to prevent him forcibly from cutting off a dead man's finger to get hold of a steel ring he wore. A bitter argument had erupted between the two of them over this, but in the end Nikos had acquiesced and taken the man's dog tags instead. Stephen had looked away.

It may have been this particular skirmish that brought their little band of andartes to the special attention of the German command—it was far more violent than any other they had fought till then—but whatever the reason, German patrols hunted them unrelentingly over the next three days. Even their usual mountain haunts could not hide them, and more than once they came very close to being captured at last.

They were driven south and west, out of the hills towards the coast. Even though Nikos knew paths the Germans did not, they were running out of places to flee to and eventually found themselves banging urgently, just as the sun was setting, on the wooden doors of a white-washed monastery on the western coast. It was built high on a cliff overlooking the Libyan Sea, a place Ianos called Chryssoscalitisa, the House of the Golden Steps.

It took some time for the door to open, and when it did two monks stood timidly in the doorway, with a third man standing behind them. From the deference the other two gave him, they took him to be the abbot. He spoke first, and though he did not know them, he clearly recognized why they were there—armed as they were and streaked with the grime of battle and flight.

"Come, my sons," he whispered furtively as he ushered them in. He said very little but seemed to know exactly what was needed. "If you have come to seek refuge with Our Lady of the Golden Steps, you may take what help we have to offer, only come quickly."

He spirited them through the softly lit sanctuary of the church, into his own cell at the back of the building. The room was a modest space with a bed and a writing desk, a few book-lined shelves, and a rough wooden floor. A single oil lamp burned atop the desk, and in its light the abbot cast a knowing look over the gaunt shadows lining each man's face. He lingered especially over Nikos's, reading it carefully, as though he knew more deeply than he could say the hurt that drove him.

Stooping, he pulled open an expertly hidden panel in the floorboards, revealing a low cellar, carved into the rock beneath the room. He had them lower themselves in—there was no step—and when the they were all pressed into the small space, crammed in with their packs and gear, he returned the floorboards to their place. Only the faintest light fell down to them through the slats between the floorboards, drifting with dust and casting thin lines across their faces.

"Please wait here," came the voice of the abbot. "Say nothing and keep as still as you can. I will return when it is safe to do so."

Stephen could not tell how long they hid there. Time seemed not to move in that tomb-like space. The air was very close, heavy with a damp smell of must and the stench of their own bodies. He was exhausted from days on the run, but there was no room to sit, and the cellar's ceiling was low, so neither was there room to stand up straight. He leaned as best he could against the stone wall, and in the press of the room he could feel Ianos, leaning against him wearily.

Hours passed, though Stephen could not say how many. He was beginning to wonder if the abbot hadn't abandoned them, and was even about to say so, when Nikos raised a warning finger and scowled at him to be still. He stood rigid, listening with piercing intensity. Stephen listened, too, but heard nothing, until, faintly and far away, he detected the sound of a scuffle.

Voices could be heard coming from the far side of the abbot's door, and muffled by the floorboards. Even so, Stephen could tell there was tension in the voices, determination in one and a great apprehension in the other. He sensed Ianos go taut beside him and heard a metallic grinding as Nikos slowly drew back the bolt of his machine gun. The air of the cellar felt suddenly stifling to him, and he realized he was sweating profusely.

"This is a house of God!" the abbot shouted, his voice growing louder as the door opened and he came into the room. He was speaking very rapidly in Greek and anxiety tinged his voice. "We are monks, not soldiers!"

The reply sounded harsh and guttural. It took a moment for it to register with Stephen that the speaker was German, but his heart surged and his vision narrowed with adrenaline as it occurred to him what was happening. Nikos lifted his gun slowly and brought the very muzzle of it to rest against the cellar's ceiling.

The abbot clearly did not understand what had been said to him, so he spoke again in Greek, louder than before. "On your honour! Do not commit violence in a house of God! We are men of God!"

The shadow of a booted figure passed over the floor then, and again a German voice spoke, rough and incompressible. The tramping of more feet sounded, and though Stephen could not tell how many, the room was filled with men now. His fingers tensed almost instinctively over the trigger of his rifle.

Now another voice was speaking. It was German, too, but it spoke Greek—at least, a broken parody of the language—and Stephen listened intently.

"Father Abbot," it said, and to Stephen it was almost sickeningly composed, considering the circumstances they were in. "We mean no violence to you… the German Reich has never… wanted… harm to the people of Crete."

The abbot did not reply, so the voice continued.

"Father. You and I should be… friends. Certainly the Reich is your… " The foreign words came to him only with great labour. "…friend. You say you are men of God. Who am I to think otherwise? But if you are… then why would a man of God wish to harbour killers? And traitors?"

There was a long silence, and Stephen cast a terrified look in Ianos's direction. He had also lifted his gun against the floorboards and pinned it there rigidly, his breath held in one great apprehensive inhale.

"We are harbouring no such men at Chryssoscalitia!" came the abbot's reply at last. "This monastery is a place of worship! We are men of prayer, not war!"

The German speaker was clearly straining at the edge of his composure. "Are you so? And would a man of prayer really lie to an officer of the German Reich? These men have committed crimes of war against the German people. Now, show us where they are." The voice barely suppressed a shout. "Show us where they are hiding or share their guilt with them!"

"Again, please, we are men of—"

But the German officer shouted him down violently, the façade of composure discarded at last. "It is not a wise thing to try my patience, Father! Would you dare to hide your crimes—the crimes of your people—behind this empty show of faith?"

Stephen heard boots shift overhead, and the noise of a machine gun bolt being drawn back sharply.

The abbot spoke again, and there was an eerie calm in his voice. "There's nothing you could do to me that I would fear to suffer. I am a man of God."

The crunch of a rifle butt brought hard against bone shuddered through the air, and the German's voice exploded. "So you say! And say, and say! Man of God or of the devil, it makes no difference to me!"

Another blow fell and the floorboards rattled with the noise of a falling body. The booted weight of the German moved, seeming to tower over the fallen man.

"We will find these savages, and when we do, you can join them in hell for having harboured them!"

He gave a stern command in German, and the men with him moved into action. The floorboards trembled fiercely as the soldiers began systematically to dismember the room, upending the bed, dragging the desk away from the wall, and pulling shelves to the floor.

Stephen winced. Ianos tensed. Nikos did not move, his eyes glittering. Together they poised their weapons and waited against hope for the search to turn them up.

But it did not. After an unbearable space of time, the soldiers seemed satisfied that they had thoroughly ransacked the little room. And whether it was the prayers of the abbot or blind luck—Stephen refused to decide—their hiding place remained secret. Stephen heard the heavy tread of boots overhead as the soldiers trooped out, shouting to one another in German. He then heard the voice of the officer as he hovered momentarily over the huddled mass of the fallen abbot, still crumpled on the floor.

"The German Reich thanks you for your cooperation." He still spoke Greek, though the tone in his voice suggested that he found it a distasteful thing to do. "We will find these criminals, Father, and if we discover you have had anything to do with their escape, we will be back."

A loud tread of feet sounded one last time, and the room was cast into a deathly silence.

For a long time, Stephen could sense no movement above, nor did he relax his grip on the handle of his gun. The room was so still for so long that he began to wonder if the soldiers had, in fact, killed the monk.

But then, after what seemed an eternity, a quick, urgent whisper sank down to them. "Do not move," it said. "They are gone. But do not move."

The planks creaked as the abbot lifted himself, stood, and moved in the direction of the door.

Stephen turned towards Ianos in the darkness. His friend's face was lifted close to a slat in the floor, straining to see.

After a long time another whisper descended to them. "I will go and see. Wait. I will return."

His footsteps passed from the room and everything fell into silence again.

Many more hours passed. Stephen was painful hungry by now and unbearably cramped, parched, and beginning to feel feverish. He sweated heavily, too; it ran down into his eyes, but they were far to cramped for him to lift a sleeve and wipe them clear. And anyway, the abbot had warned them not to move.

He was teetering deliriously on the edge of a feverish sleep when a scuffling of feet overhead caused him to jump with another surge of fear; though these feet sounded as though they were sandaled, not booted as the Germans had been.

The floorboards shifted and the panel was removed. A whiff of fresh air spilled down over them, and though the light was dim it was enough to make Stephen blink as he peered up. Two monks looked down on him. One held an oil lamp. The abbot stood behind them.

"They are gone," the abbot whispered. He nodded at the two monks, who reached down and helped them up from the cellar.

They were painfully stiff from having been buried so long, so it took some effort before all three stood upright again, besmeared with sweat and blinking blindly in the abbot's cell.

"Come," said the abbot curtly. "We must go. You cannot stay."

He gestured to the door and led them anxiously from the room and into the sanctuary. It was quite dark, and except for the candles burning near the iconostasis at the front of the church, the place was suffused with shadow.

The abbot shuffled through quickly, with his head lowered. Ianos and Nikos followed close behind, but something brought Stephen up short.

At the centre of the iconostasis, glowing with the golden light of a dozen or more candles, lit in reverence at its feet, there stood a vivid image of Jesus. It was an icon he had seen before, though never quite like this. Two piercing eyes looked out from a serene face—so serene as to appear almost, but not quite, stern. Jesus's long hair was bound back, and he lifted two fingers, in blessing perhaps, or for some more arcane reason. Stephen could not tell. But it felt as though the saviour were in that moment reaching out to him.

The icon was gilt with gold, and it caught the flickering candlelight from a thousand different directions, dancing in the halo about Jesus's head.

But the eyes were what caught Stephen, and stopped him, and drew him to linger. One eye—and he couldn't help but believe this was so—looked slightly upward, scanning a distant horizon for signs of heaven, perhaps. The other eye—and the effect was so subtle that he wondered at first if it wasn't a trick of the light—gazed forward, directly forward, as though he were looking straight through Stephen, into the utter depths of his soul.

Something warm swept over him, but the feeling was not altogether pleasant, and he shuddered.

"The Pantokrator." The voice of the abbot came softly from behind. He had noticed Stephen linger at the icon and had come back to retrieve him. "Christ the Almighty."

Stephen stumbled with his words, and he was surprised to discover he was whispering, almost inaudibly. "I have seen this before, Father."

"And so may Christ watch over all your paths, my son. But come, they may be back, and we are at great risk so long as you are here."

Stephen allowed himself to be led away, though not without one last plaintive look at this image of Jesus, Omnipotent. They passed through the sanctuary and out into the courtyard. It was not yet morning, and far away Stephen could hear the familiar sound of the tide in the moonlight, yards and yards below them.

Nikos gripped the abbot firmly by the hand. "I thank you, Father. You have saved—"

"I have saved no one. 'For all who take up the sword will perish by the sword.' This is the teaching of our Lord." He looked deeply into Nikos's face, and when he spoke next it was not clear if he was addressing the soldier, or the bereaved father, or the vineyard-keeper standing before him. "I have staved off death, maybe, but no: I have saved no one. But you must go now. You have put us all at risk so long as you're here."

Even as he said it, he pushed a sack into Nikos's hand.

"Here," the abbot said tersely. "There is medicine and water and some food— what little we can spare. Take it freely, but please: go."

Nikos nodded and shouldered the bag. He turned towards the path that led down from the monastery. Ianos fell in behind him. Stephen did, too, but at the last minute he turned back to the abbot.

"Thank you, Father," Stephen said.

The abbot nodded. "Go in peace, my son. And may Christ the Almighty go with you."

The monastery doors closed softly at his back, not unkindly but urgently and irrevocably. Ianos and Nikos were already picking their way down the path. Without lingering over the thoughts that welled up suddenly in his heart, Stephen adjusted his pack on his shoulders and set out after them.

IN THE DAYS THAT FOLLOWED THEIR BRUSH WITH DEATH AT Chryssoscalitisa, their activities fell into a more consistent pattern, marked by fewer but more strategic incursions against the Germans, and longer intervals of hiding in the deepest cervices of the mountains, at the very heart of the island. They had established a makeshift base in a cave near Gortyne, stocked with whatever munitions they could steal from the enemy, and any provisions they could glean from the locals.

Nothing seemed normal anymore—indeed, Stephen wondered if he would ever use that word to describe anything in life again—yet the rhythm they found, of planning a foray, sometimes for months at a time, executing it as well as they could manage, and then disappearing again into the hills, at least had something predictable about it. They weren't trained for this work, of course, and often woefully ill-equipped, but the hard edge of Nikos's will pressed them on if they wavered, and somehow it was enough to carry them unscathed through even the closest of calls.

And so an uneasy year passed. Nikos's collection of war trophies slowly grew, with the badges and dog tags of fallen men mostly, though there were some more gruesome mementoes among them, trophies which even Ianos could not dissuade him from taking. The name which the locals had given him, O Tauros, stuck with him and even began to gather the aura of legend. Many of the villagers whispered in hushed tones about the exploits of O Tauros, though these were usually grossly exaggerated, and even the Germans had begun to speak of him. Der Stier, they called him, the despised Bull of Crete.

Stephen knew for certain that the Germans had been tracking a resistance fighter known as O Tauros and were determined to capture him, the day he learned about their plan for Apodoulou. Ianos had caught word of it from a young shepherd who often served as a contact for them, watching the movements of the German patrols and then reporting back to Ianos through an elaborate system of signals they had established between them.

"They say that if the Bull is not turned in by tomorrow morning, they will execute seven villagers in Apodoulou, as accomplices to his war crimes," Ianos explained to Nikos with a look of horror on his face. "Nikos, we can't let them die! We must do something."

"And what would you have us do?" There was a familiar edge in Nikos's voice.

"We could turn ourselves in?" Ianos himself sounded unconvinced as he said it.

Nikos narrowed his eyes. "Has this year of fighting meant so little to you that you'd throw it all away so quickly as that?"

He did not lash out, but Stephen and Ianos had no doubt from his voice that he would if they mentioned the idea of surrender again.

Even so, they did set out for Apodoulou that evening. The trek took the better part of the night, but they were at least moving under cover of dark, and they reached the village just as the sun was breaking over the eastern slopes of the terraced hills around the village. Stephen had not been to Apodoulou since the day they had buried Ariadne, almost two years ago.

They knew the countryside intimately, of course, and positioned themselves in the cranny of a hill overlooking the central square. From this vantage point, they could see most of the village at a glance, but they knew it would be impossible for anyone looking up from the street to see them.

The morning was warming quickly, and the wait seemed interminable, but eventually a commotion started up in the square and a troop of uniformed men filed in, moving with great precision.

The village gathered, and even at a distance Stephen could tell from their huddled shapes that they were abjectly terrified.

And then, pushing roughly through the crowd, two soldiers appeared, shoving seven bound bodies towards the south side of the square. They often fell, and were pulled roughly to their feet until they were all standing in a trembling line, in sight of the whole village.

An officer stepped forward and bellowed something harsh in German. There was a timid-looking Cretan standing near to him, wringing his cap in his hands. The officer looked sternly at him and shouted the words again. The Cretan cleared his throat and translated, tentatively, as though every word pained him to say it. His voice was not strong, but he spoke so that the whole village might hear, and Stephen was just close enough to make out what he was saying.

"You have been charged and found guilty," the man began, "of acts of resistance against the German Reich… of giving aid to the enemy… and of associating with those who have murdered German soldiers." The translator looked hesitantly at the officer again, who shouted out something else. "For these crimes of war… and for the guilt of your people, you are hereby sentenced by this tribunal to be executed."

A whimpering moan rippled among the villagers, but the German officer shouted a command to his soldiers, who raised their weapons in a single motion. A dreadful pause followed, so long that Stephen wondered if the officer was waiting for something to happen, for someone to step forward perhaps, or for someone to plead their case a final time.

But nothing came. In fact, an awful stillness seemed suddenly to fall over the square.

From their distance, Stephen could not know if it was in fact the case, but it seemed to him that the trembling line of bound men stood defiantly straight in that moment, and cast an unflinching look in the direction of their executioners. Certainly they made no noise. And though some of the villagers looked away, and one or two had collapsed to the ground in grief, no one moved.

But there was a terrible cry of anguish screaming in Stephen's heart. He shifted his weight forward and opened his mouth to speak.

Instantly, the steely vice of Nikos's hand gripped him by the forearm. "Stay," he whispered coldly. "Make no noise."

"But Nikos—"

But the grip tightened, holding back his words. Suddenly a dreadful rattle— the staccato report of many guns firing at once—filled the air, and as it did Stephen pulled against Nikos's grip, ripping his arm free. But he did stay, and he made no noise.

A thin cloud of smoke drifted slowly across the square, mingled with a faint wisp of dust that had been kicked up as the first three bodies fell. Someone was crying pitifully, but otherwise the square was ominously still.

But only three had been killed. Four of them still stood together. At first Stephen wondered if the soldiers could have missed at such close range as that, but gradually he understood that this was part of the macabre play the officer was staging, for he started barking something again in German.

"This does not need to be," the translator said in Greek, his voice trembling. "This is only what comes of harbouring the one they call the Bull. But if he were taken into custody… or handed over to us… then no more blood would need to be spilled."

There was a terrible silence then. No one said anything, and though Stephen turned to look at Nikos, it was impossible to read his face.

At last the officer grew tired of waiting. He spoke out the charges again, and the man beside him translated sadly, wringing the very life out of the cap in his hand.

"You are charged and found guilty of giving aid to the enemies of the German Reich, and of war crimes against the German people."

"Nikos!" The scream almost broke out of Stephen's heart, though he kept his voice restrained, for fear of discovery. "We must do something! We can't let them die for us!"

Everything happened quickly then. Nikos's hands writhed and flashed like lightning. He gripped Stephen powerfully by the hair and pulled until his head bent back in pain. Almost as quickly, his other hand smote against Stephen's face, clapping over his mouth and smothering his words.

At the very same time, the air was ripped apart once more with the sound of gunfire, over and over, while four more bodies fell.

Stephen screamed against Nikos's palm, but the sound of the rifles in the square drowned out even the muffled noise he made. Nikos then pressed his full weight against him, pushing him down until their heads were very close together, his mouth right by his ear. He tightened the grip on his mouth mercilessly.

"Shut up!" Nikos whispered. "Do not speak, or by all that's holy you will never speak again! They are not dying for us. They are dying because they are Cretans, and they know the meaning of honour!"

"Father!" Ianos put his hands on Nikos's shoulders, trying to pull him free, but Nikos pushed back, shoving his son away. In doing so he had to release his grip on Stephen's hair, and Stephen was able to wrestle free of the hand clapped over his mouth.

The square was still moving with people down below, so none of them dared to speak openly, but Stephen stood seething in rage. He looked hatefully at Nikos, who towered before him, breathing heavily.

"Don't tell me that we must do something." Nikos's voice had dropped murderously still, but quiet as it was, it seemed to echo in Stephen's head. "I *am* doing something. Do you really think by surrendering we might have spared their lives? Rather we would have simply joined them in dying, and then who would avenge them? No, Stephen! You cannot place this guilt on me. I will not bear it. But—" and he flashed Stephen a rapacious look when he said this "—but I will avenge it."

Down in the square, the translator was speaking on behalf of the German officer a final time. "Let this… justice… be an example to all loyal… friends of Germany. Do not resist the rule of the Reich, and do not assist any who do. Any man, woman, or child who shelters… or in any way helps these fugitives will share in their guilt. And they will share, too, in their punishment."

The German's voice rose loudly then, and he looked up into the hills to the north and to the east as he shouted this next part.

"And to the cowards who resist the German army through guerrilla tactics," came the translation, "ambushing and murdering German soldiers in cold blood… let this be a warning to you. Your people share your guilt… and one way or another justice will be served!"

The soldiers left the square after this, though the villagers rushed forward and gathered up the bodies of their fallen loved ones. Even from this distance, Stephen could hear them wailing in grief, a single plaintive note that pierced the air.

Hot tears streamed down Ianos's face, and Stephen blinked back his own. His mouth bled slightly from where Nikos had struck him, and the taste of blood on his lips infuriated him. But Nikos had already turned away and was preparing his pack for the trek back to their hiding place at Gortyne.

This journey took far longer than it had for them to come. They were forced to wander far up into the highlands to avoid the patrols in the lower hills, and the day had become excruciatingly hot, so that they had to stop a number of times for shade and rest.

No one said a word the whole way. Once or twice, Ianos opened his mouth to speak, but the gloom hanging over them was so grim that he seemed to think better of it and fell quiet.

Even when they reached their cavern base at Gortyne, still no one spoke. Stephen retreated to a recess of the main antechamber and flung his pack down in disgust, collapsing to the floor after it.

Ianos busied himself with the pretence of preparing a fire, though it never got lit, and Nikos took an electric torch and disappeared for a long time down one of the cave's side tunnels. This was the same cavern Ianos had shown Stephen on his first journey to Gotyne so many years ago, and there was no end of pathways to wander if one wanted to lose one's self in anger or grief.

It was late when Nikos reappeared. No one had yet spoken, but he found a spot in the centre of the antechamber and, lighting a kerosene lamp, began to hunt for something in his pack. The kerosene was scarce, and normally Nikos kept it under the strictest of rations, so the soft yellow glow surprised Stephen when it suddenly sprang to light.

In spite of his anger, he sat up and looked towards his father-in-law. To his surprise, the look on Nikos's face was disarmingly serene—though that might have simply been the dimness of the light. He met Stephen's eyes for the briefest of moments, and then looked down at something he had pulled from the pack.

"Come here, Stephen. I have something I would like you to see."

However serene his face looked, the tone in Nikos's voice was quite severe and not to be refused.

The memory of the dead at Apodoulou still burned in Stephen's heart, but almost against his will he rose and moved towards him. He sat down in the circle of lamplight, though not facing Nikos. Rather, he glared blankly into the darkness that led towards the heart of the cavern.

"These belonged to my brother," Nikos said at last, and he spoke as though he was choosing every word with great labour.

Stephen looked at Nikos's hand and saw that he was holding a loop of amber-coloured beads, the traditional komboloi—the worry beads—that so many Cretan men carried with them. He had seen them once or twice among Nikos's effects, though he'd never thought much of them before.

"I've never heard you mention a brother," said Stephen.

"Demetrios was his name. And these belonged to him." He moved the beads deftly through his fingers, so that they glinted in the dim light, one after another as they passed his thumb and index finger. "He gave them to me just before he left for the war."

"The war?"

"Against the Turks, for Greek independence. That was more than twenty years ago now. Every red-blooded Cretan with a drop of philotimo in his veins wanted to join the fight, of course. And the Leventis were no different—only… well, I was just married to Eunice at the time. Ianos was still nursing, and she— his sister—she was on the way. So I didn't have the heart to leave them. And anyway, Eunice begged me to stay."

When he reached the last bead in the loop, he flicked the strand with a practiced hand and started again from the top.

"Demetrios, too, he said it wouldn't be right. He told me to stay behind and look after her, that he would go for us both. He promised he would kill twice as many Turks, to make up for me staying behind. And he gave me these komboloi the day he left. He said I should use them if ever I was tempted to worry for him."

Nikos looked up from the beads and fixed his son-in-law with a look. There were no tears in his eyes, but still Stephen thought he saw an immense sadness in them.

"Well, Demetrios died at Smyrna. They say it was a Turkish cavalry charge that took him. We never saw his body, though, so we can't know for sure. And twenty-one years later, all I have left of him is a silly string of useless beads."

Stephen took a breath to speak, but Nikos started in again.

"Of course, Eunice died barely a decade later. Consumption took her, after a bad winter. So maybe it was for nothing I stayed behind, since I lost her all the same. And she left me with two children I couldn't raise. Though of course I still had my worry beads."

The motion of the komboloi suddenly stopped and he closed them in a tight fist. When he looked up, the familiar glint in his eye had returned.

"Stephen, there was nothing we could have done today. And they say the Germans are rounding up villagers for slaughter at random, all across this island. So I can't say if those who died today died for us or not. But I will say this: I have lost people I love to war, and I have lost in peacetime, too. And as far as I can tell, there's not much that separates the two. Fate, it seems, takes whomever fate will. But if I can do something to resist what is happening to my homeland, whatever it may be, so that when fate takes me I can go honourably, then I will do that. I would rather loose those who are dear to me by fighting for them, than by doing nothing."

Stephen turned the words over in his mind for a moment. The edge of his anger had dulled, but bitterness still burned hotly at the back of his throat.

"That may be, Nikos. But still all the honour in the world won't bring them back."

Nikos looked down at the worry beads. "No, I suppose it won't." Then, after a pensive moment, he added, "Well, the kerosene is precious. We mustn't waste it."

Then he reached and extinguished the lantern, plunging them both into sudden darkness.

CHAPTER THIRTY-THREE
Mount Ida, 1944

THAT WINTER WAS ESPECIALLY HARD ON THEM. THE WEATHER WAS unusually cold, particularly in the highlands where they now spent the majority of their time, hiding from the Germans and waging their desperate campaign. Food was scarce and often Stephen went days without a solid meal. The locals still supported them as well as they could, but German reprisals on the civilian population grew increasingly brutal, and they knew that whatever help they accepted put those who gave it in terrible danger.

That fall, they'd received word of a massacre in the villages around Viannos, in the west—some twenty villages razed to the ground and more than five hundred people slaughtered. The news had devastated Nikos. He had retreated into the darkest corner of their cave for a full day or more, and when he finally emerged there was an air hanging about him that Stephen found profoundly unsettling but impossible to read.

After Viannos, Nikos started reaching out to other freedom fighters on the island, especially the notorious leader of a guerrilla band from the region around Anogia, a self-styled warlord named Bourdzalis. Through the winter and into the spring, he had a number of meetings with Bourdzalis's men, who came to visit him in his hideout near Gortyne. These visits increased in frequency as March passed into April. The details were shrouded in the most ominous of secrecy, but Stephen gathered that an important incursion was in the offing, one that, Nikos assured him, would be a great victory in their struggle against the Hun.

Stephen and Ianos pressed him to know more, but Nikos refused to say anything, scowling them into silence if ever they brought it up. Many uneasy days passed, and more guerrillas from Anogia came and went, until one day, towards the end of April, Nikos unexpectedly summoned them both to join him in a far corner of their hideout, where he had lit a lantern and spread out the tattered map of Crete that they used for plotting their incursions. All three of them crouched together in the conspiratorial lamplight.

Nikos leaned in until they were sitting very close together. "There is a mission underway," he said quietly, "to capture the German they call Kreipe."

Ianos's mouth gaped open. "Capture General Kreipe?"

Even in the furthest recesses of the mountains, they knew the name—a decorated soldier and the commander of the German forces stationed on Crete.

"How—?" Stephen began, but Nikos lifted his hand.

"The less you know, the better. Just know that the British are leading it. There are agents in Crete already, and have been for months now, in hiding. They have recruited Bourdzalis to provide cover for the mission. He's organizing a band of freedom fighters to help." He looked at Stephen and Ianos firmly, his eye glinting in the dim light. "And we are to join him."

It was clear that for Nikos there was no room for discussion of this point, but Stephen tried nonetheless. "What use could we possibly be in a mission of that sort, Nikos?" he asked incredulously. "We're hardly trained for espionage, or equipped for it."

"Our part in this operation is small, Stephen, but if we play it well we may help to bring a great enemy of our people to justice. The British intend to take Kreipe at Heraklion. They will bring him by foot across the mountains, to the coast. I can't say where, because I've not been told, but a boat will meet them there and bring him south, to Egypt. What's needed are men to take up positions around the Villa Ariadne on the day of the abduction, to provide cover, and, if the mission should fail, create a diversion to allow the British to escape." Nikos was gesturing at the map the whole time he explained this. "Ianos, you and I will take up a position here. And if it comes to it, we must draw the German patrols away to the west as best we can."

There was something inexorable in Nikos's voice as he reviewed the plan. Stephen had heard the tone often enough to know that it could not be refused, so he took a resigned breath and spoke.

"You and Ianos?" Stephen asked. "You said you and Ianos would take positions there. What's my part in all this madness then?"

Nikos nodded at him grimly. "Of course, the Germans will be hunting all over the island once the cry goes up that Kreipe's been taken. And the search will be fierce. You must take up a position here, on Mount Ida, along the route that the

British will be taking over the mountain. From there you must scout for German patrols and report to the andartes who will be escorting them to the summit. I'm sending you, Stephen, because you will be able to translate, if need be."

Stephen looked at the spot Nikos pointed to on the map. He wore an incredulous look on his face, but a thought formed in his mind that perhaps here was a chance to do something more than simply shoot haphazardly at random Germans from the hills. Certainly if Kreipe were taken, it might make some real difference in their endless struggle for this island, and for all he knew it would give real purpose to the chaotic months he had endured following Nikos in his personal war against the enemy.

He exhaled heavily. "When do we leave?"

So it was that Stephen found himself trekking alone in the last days of April 1944 on the eastern shoulders of Mount Ida, on his way to rendezvous with the guerrillas who would be escorting the British agents over the mountain. It was midspring and the weather was warm in the lowlands, but a miserable mist had fallen over the upper slopes of Ida, drizzling with rain and bitterly cold. He could not see further than a few yards ahead of him, but he knew the path he followed well enough that he did not fear getting lost. He was moving just below the snowline and the way was treacherous with straggling patches of ice.

Nearly soaked from the mist and trembling with cold, he had seen no Germans, but the fog was so thick that he doubted he would, even if they were only a few yards away. He crouched as low as he could get and stopped, listening intently. The press of the mist seemed to amplify the sounds. He thought he heard a wood pigeon coo somewhere nearby, or the trickle of a stream somewhere not far from that, though it might have been a trick of his ears.

He shifted his weight to rise, but suddenly a scuffling noise froze him in place. He held his breath and did not move for a long time. He was just beginning to wonder if he hadn't imagined the sound when it came again, closer to him, the sound of something moving with light steps among the rocks.

He lowered himself slowly, until he was lying on his belly against the ground, and looked as hard as he could into the impenetrable fog. There was an outcropping of rock on the slope just above him where he might get better cover, but he dared not move even an inch. His ears roared now with the sound of his own heartbeat, and when he let out his breath slowly it sounded alarmingly loud to him.

The noise came a third time, only yards ahead of him, invisible in the mist.

And then it stepped into view: the shaggy flank and striped coat of a wild goat, picking its way delicately among the rocks. And whether it was because the mist kept him hidden from it, or for some other reason Stephen did not know, the animal didn't seem to have noticed him lying there, holding himself perfectly still on the path ahead of it.

Despite the surge of panic which had not yet faded, still Stephen noted how lucky he was to have encountered such an animal in a moment like this. Because this was not some stray goat wandered off from some shepherd's hovel somewhere; he could tell by its distinct markings and the delicate curve of its horns that this was a kri-kri, the rare Cretan ibex. Once or twice, Ianos, who was admittedly the best shot among them, had brought one back to the cave at Gortyne after the longest of hunting trips into the furthest reaches of the mountains. He called it the agrimi, the "wild one." They were certainly worth eating, and food was scarce, but also extremely rare and only the most skilled of hunters ever came across them.

Stephen was hardly the most skilled of hunters, and it struck him as so unlikely that he would come face to face with an agrimi, of all things, there on the slopes of Mount Ida, that he could not help but watch, spellbound, as it nosed its way gracefully among the mountain grass and loose rocks.

As though he were glimpsing something spectral, or sacred even, he lay motionless and prostrate, awash in a deep awareness of his great, great fortune. The ibex took another step in his direction and then it suddenly lifted its head and fixed him with a piercing eye, tensing its haunches to run. It did not bolt immediately, but rather stood frozen, and for the most ephemeral of moments these two creatures—this lonely man and this wild goat—stared at each other.

Stephen couldn't say why, but thoughts long buried suddenly sprang to his mind unbidden. He remembered Ariadne—dancing with her to celebrate the harvest, receiving her philoxenia in the lemon grove, holding her as she coughed out a great clot of blood and slipped away forever in his arms.

He remembered further back than that. He thought of Grace—how long had it been since he had thought of her? Of holding her, confused but determined, the day they'd buried her brother. Of meeting her that night on Chocolate Lake. Of a dying seagull set free together.

Had the letter arrived, he wondered? He thought of Percy then—the day he had happened upon him while sketching the ruins at Knossos, his first invitation to the Villa Ariadne, an unmailed postcard. Stephen himself had been meant to return the next day, to Halifax, and home, and Grace, and yet of course he never had.

Once again it washed over him how unlikely it was that he should cross paths so closely with an agrimi on the slopes of Mount Ida in the middle of this horrific war. It was as if—and the thought was powerful in him, however foolish it made him feel to acknowledge it—some unseen hand had brought it to him, or he to it, in this moment, for this reason. If such a hand did such things, he thought, then surely it had done this.

An overwhelming desire to touch it came over him then. The animal had not eased the tension in its haunches, but neither had it fled away. So very slowly Stephen shifted his weight forward, hoping to reach out to it with a cautious finger. The movement was almost imperceptible, but it was enough for the startled animal at last to take flight. It sprang lightly up the slope, and before a handful of yards separated them, the mist had swallowed it and it was gone.

Stephen was still frozen, mid-reach. There were strange tears in his eyes that he could not explain, and then—to hell with whatever German patrols may be lurking nearby—he let out a great groan, burying his hands in his face and weeping for a long, long time.

That same day in Halifax, on April 30, 1944, Grace received an unexpected and somewhat unlikely call on the telephone from Margaret. There had been an accident on the pier, she explained. A fire had broken out on a ship that was moored there. The seamen had fought it as well as they could, but three men had been killed and one very seriously hurt before it was brought under control.

The news was sad, Grace admitted, but stories like these had become somewhat common fare in the years since the war had come to Halifax. Even when Margaret explained that it had been a British ship, Grace still didn't grasp what she was saying.

"It was Richard's ship," Margaret said at last. "He was the one injured so badly in the fire."

"Oh dear." The words hardly felt adequate to the news, but they dropped from her lips with great, ominous weight.

"Well, his father's at sea, and he's British navy, of course, so the rest of his family is at home in England," Margaret went on. "But he's far too badly hurt to travel. And... and he's asked to see you, Grace."

"Me?" She sounded surprised, but somewhere deep within her she knew it was so almost before Margaret told her.

"Well, he's alone here, and he's got no one else. I suppose it makes sense."

"Yes," Grace said faintly. "Yes, I suppose it does."

"Though I should tell you, Grace, he's very badly burned. It's not my place to say, of course, but I don't know how long he has."

Grace agreed to see him and thanked her for the call, but she stared at the phone pensively for a long time after she hung up. She tried to imagine him lying there, alone and dying in a strange hospital room, and a flood of what-ifs washed over her. Almost as if she were trying to keep the flood from overwhelming her, she reached for her coat and stepped out into a dismal Halifax afternoon.

She found him in a quiet ward of the Halifax Infirmary on Morris Street, lying in a pristine white hospital bed in the gentle care of the Sisters of Charity. A white-clad orderly led her to his bedside, and even as she approached she could tell he was as Margaret had said—badly burned and holding on to this world with only the weakest of grips. The room was full of wounded men, but it was serenely, almost ominously quiet. It had four large windows at one end, facing west, and golden light flooded in through the gossamer curtains.

"Are you in great pain?" she asked when she was standing at last at his bedside.

Both his arms were misshapen beneath many layers of gauze, and aside from his left eye and his mouth, most of his face was heavily wound in bandages. The question seemed stupid to her as she asked it, but so great a flood of compassion had overwhelmed her at the sight of him that she could think of nothing better to say.

"Oh," he said. His voice was almost inaudibly raspy, but she could tell he was trying to sound gallant, for her sake. "Only when the morphine wears off, otherwise it's all just a hazy dream."

His left eye was watering profusely when he turned it to her and tried to smile feebly.

"And is the morphine worn off now?"

"Mostly," he said, and he squeezed the mist from his eye, blinking it clear. "But it's okay. My next dose is within the hour, and this way I'll remember this visit well after you're gone."

"Margaret told me about the fire."

"And so the Germans didn't get me after all."

"No. I suppose they didn't. Oh, Richard."

Words escaped her then, so at last Richard said, "I wanted to tell you I'm sorry, Grace."

"Sorry?"

"Well, you told me not to carry a flame for you, but you know that I couldn't help it."

She reached out and placed her palm on the bandaged mass that had been his hand, but very lightly, hardly touching him at all for fear of causing him pain.

She closed her eyes gently. "Please, Richard, you needn't apologize."

He laboured through a great distressing cough, and when he could finally speak again he said, "Please, Grace. Let me be sorry. Because even though you told me not to—and God knows I wasn't true to you—even so, I carried a flame. Somehow, thinking that you were here like this helped. When it was very dark, you know?"

She nodded compassionately, and though she did not know it the gilded light of the setting sun was falling into her hair, setting it ablaze, so that for Richard, through his burning vision, it seemed she bore a delicate halo about her.

"Did I use you for that?" he asked after another pause. "Was the thought of being with you one day just a selfish way of getting through the horror? And if it was, was that unfair to you? I'm only asking because... well... I think I may die. And if I do, I will be carrying a lot of things with me into whatever it is on the other side. War is hell, like they say, but at least if I could be absolved for this one small thing, then maybe it will absolve me of it all." He blinked again, and then, with a faint vestige of his old familiar grin flitting at the corners of his mouth, he said, "Listen to me talk! Maybe the morphine hasn't worn off after all."

The barest laugh escaped her, but she swallowed it back. "Oh, Richard. It's not you who needs forgiveness."

A merciful silence fell over them for a moment, and then Richard spoke again, and his voice seemed somehow clearer. "Is God..." he began tentatively. "Is God really like Jesus?"

"Like Jesus?"

"The stories you hear in Sunday school, you know, about the man who loved those who didn't deserve it, who never turned away the sick unhealed, the Good Shepherd seeking the one lost sheep, or what have you. Is that really what God is like? I don't suppose I would be afraid to die, if when I do meet God, he's just like Jesus."

"Is God like Jesus?" She repeated the question quietly. "Well, I've always lived as though he were. Certainly, anything I've come to know of him, he's like that."

It was difficult for him to nod, but she could tell he had.

"Yes, Richard, he is," she said more convincingly. "I believe so anyway. I don't know I could have made it through... all this if he were otherwise."

He sighed raggedly. "Well then, I guess it won't be so bad as all that."

They were quiet again for a moment, and from a nearby bed came a half-stifled groan of immense pain.

"Will you pray for me, Grace?"

She nodded, and to Richard it was like the sacred light in her hair was scattering in every direction. She lifted her hand and placed it on his bandaged forehead, whispering softly that the love and mercy of God might carry him through whatever was to come. Her eyes burned hotly, and as she spoke she became aware of a great warmth spreading from her.

But she actually said very little by way of prayer, and as her hand lingered there in silence she was sure she heard a voice speaking softly in her heart. She had never heard God speak to her in prayer before, at least never so clearly as this, but the silence was perfectly unbroken in that moment, in that hospital ward, and she had no doubt of what she was being told.

It will not be wasted, said the Voice. *It has not been for nothing and it will not be wasted. Every sacrifice, every tear, every yes to every opportunity to live true—they were my sacrifices, and my tears, too. I lived them in you, and through you, and they are working together for you an unbearable weight of glory that will be a marvel to all when it is revealed at last. Believe me when I tell you that not a second of it will go to waste.*

Richard had closed his one good eye and was breathing peacefully, more peacefully than she had yet heard him breathe, so she leaned down and kissed him gently on the forehead, above the eye in a spot where his face was not covered with gauze. The smell of ointments and antiseptic was strong, but she inhaled anyway and then touched her forehead to his, thinking he was asleep.

But when she began to straighten herself, his wounded hands shifted, as though he were reaching for her, and he turned his head very slightly in her direction.

Though something in her told her strongly she ought not to, something still deeper said, *It would not be wrong if you did, and it may help immensely.* So she leaned a bit further towards him and kissed him lightly but tenderly on his mouth. His lips tasted repulsively of salt and blood, but it was not that kind of a kiss. And anyway, he did not have the strength really to kiss her back.

"It will be okay, Richard," she whispered, standing up straight again, and something in her assured her that it really would be.

———————

She did not visit Richard again, and she learned from Margaret that he died a few days later. The Sisters of Charity had done all they could, of course, but he had been badly burned, and it had really only been a matter of time.

"But they said he died peacefully," said Margaret when she told Grace the news. "They made particular note of that, that he died, almost, they said, almost serenely."

And though she cried softly to hear it said, deep in her heart Grace knew that it was so.

CHAPTER THIRTY-FOUR
Gortyne, 1945

AFTER HIS FATEFUL ENCOUNTER WITH THE KRI-KRI ON THE SLOPES OF Mount Ida, the months seemed to pass for Stephen in a nightmarish blur. Word reached them through the underground that the mission to abduct Kreipe had been successful. Their part in it had been smaller even than Nikos had expected, however. He and Ianos had joined with Bourdzalis's men, as arranged, but on the eve of the abduction the British agents had changed their plans and dismissed them all, determined to undertake the operation without their help. Apparently, there'd been reason to believe the Germans had spotted some of them while they were hiding in a ramshackle grape press outside Heraklion, and the British had been afraid that their presence endangered the mission.

Nikos was bitterly disappointed to have missed this chance to win some glory for his people, and though the British gave each of them a gold coin for their trouble, he tossed his aside in disgust on their way back to Gortyne.

For his part, Stephen had seen nothing worth reporting in his scouting mission on Mount Ida, and said as much when he'd rendezvoused with the andartes who were preparing to escort the British over the crest of the mountain with their prisoner. His trip back to Gortyne had been dogged by German patrols, however, who were out in force by then and hunting for the kidnapped general. But he had wandered the goat tracks and shepherd trails often enough that he was able to find a route that kept him out of their reach.

And so life fell into another unbearable stretch of delirious months holed up in their cavern fortress.

The slow deterioration Stephen had noted in Nikos began to accelerate sharply. Often he lost himself for days at a time, wandering the recesses of the cave as if he were hiding from something, or searching for it. He slept very little, and his face grew to be lined with ugly shadows. Sometimes he sat perfectly still, glowering into the unseen distance, and saying nothing for hours at a time. Other times he'd start into an incoherent diatribe about the war, or the Germans, or the Italians, or the British. He never shouted when he did, but the low timbre of his voice, flecked with foam and heavy with pent-up feeling, was worse.

Once Ianos had tried to speak into one of these ramblings, to calm him with a quiet word, but when he did his father lunged at him so viciously that if Stephen hadn't intervened he was sure blood would have been spilled.

They had very few engagements with the Germans anymore. They did join with Bourdzalis once or twice in the fall for a series of major offensives near Canea, and in the early days of winter Nikos led them in one of the most viscous incursions Stephen had yet participated in. Nikos hadn't taken any war trophies home from this skirmish, but to Ianos and Stephen's great dismay, he strung up the bodies from the limbs of an ancient olive tree, grotesquely mutilated, and left them there as a defiant message to whomever might find them first.

Stephen didn't have much heart to write in his journal anymore, though he felt that someone ought to record what was happening to them—as a witness, maybe, or a confession. Of course, the thought of anyone actually reading what he'd written dismayed him.

Once he and Ianos had a long, whispered debate about giving up the fight, but it ended in frustration. After all they had seen and done, they knew the Germans would show them no quarter if they surrendered, and it was likely that Stephen himself would be taken for a foreign spy, if he himself were ever caught.

And so, in the end, they agreed that there was nothing for it but to continue to follow Nikos in his feverish war of resistance.

On a clear autumn day in October 1944, Ianos returned to their hideout at Gortyne after a clandestine trip to Heraklion, where he had travelled to gather news.

"It is over," is all he said as he entered the cave.

Both Stephen and Nikos looked at him sharply.

"Over?" said Nikos, and there was a glint in his eye. He had been sharpening a bayonet; he held it poised over the whetstone.

"They say the Germans have given up Crete. They've withdrawn from Heraklion already, and they say they'll be leaving Canea in a matter of days. And the word is they've given up Athens on the mainland, too. Nikos, the struggle for Crete is over… and won."

"Lies." Nikos's reply was sudden and terse. There was something vaguely threatening in his tone, but he went back to sharpening the bayonet as though Ianos had not spoken.

"But Father—"

"Lies!" He looked up from his work with the blade, the threat in his voice unmistakable now. "This is some ploy to draw us all out of hiding. You watch. We'll lay down our arms and come down from the hills, and the Germans will be waiting for us."

"But Nikos," Stephen said, "the rumour's been going around for weeks that the Germans are getting ready of pull out of Crete. You know this as well as I do. Surely this can't be—"

"Lies! I will not listen to them, and I will not be taken in by them!"

Stephen bit his lower lip. He had certainly seen Nikos like this before, many times in recent months, in fact. But there was an edge to the man's obstinance this time that deeply troubled him. He turned towards Ianos, and to his alarm there was a look of real fear on his friend's face. The young Cretan would not meet Stephen's eyes, but he swallowed hard and tried to speak calmly to his father.

"Nikos, please listen to me," he said carefully. "I saw the ships pulling out of Heraklion harbour for myself. And I've spoken with some of Bourdzalis's men, who confirmed that Canea is all but abandoned. This is great news. This is a day of great victory—"

"Bourdzalis's men?" Nikos cut in sharply. "Bourdzalis's bandits, you mean! If it's not a lie of the Germans, then it's his lie. He's wanted for months to bring our work for the resistance under his control. I know that he's planning to set himself up as some kind of a chieftain over Crete when the war is through. For all we know, he is in league with the Germans himself!"

"Father, listen to what you're saying! It makes no sense! How could Bourdzalis—"

But Nikos roared him down. "I am telling you: you have swallowed the bold-faced lies of the enemy! So be a fool if you want to be, but I won't be taken in! And I swear, Ianos, I'm not going to let my own son lie to my face. So if you try to again—by all that's holy, I swear it—I will kill you!"

Stephen shuddered to hear this exchange, and he couldn't contain himself for long.

"Nikos!" he yelled, leaping to his feet. "What is wrong with you? It's over! Can't you see? We've won. The Germans are giving up the island, and it's over. Good God! Have you gone utterly mad?"

"Mad!" Nikos bellowed. "Will some foreign whelp stand there and lecture me about madness! I'll show you the meaning of madness!"

The older man rushed forward. He still held the bayonet, and except that Ianos stepped between them Stephen was sure he would have buried it in his chest.

"It's not enough that you've become a fool?" Nikos roared at his son. "You'll turn traitor on me, too?"

He shoved him to the ground with tremendous force, looming over him and breathing violently. The bayonet shook in his hand, and there was blood on the blade.

Ianos pulled himself up. His arm was bleeding, and he clung to it with his good hand. "Father, I know the toll this fight has taken on you. You know I've always fought it with you. But please believe me: there is no need for it to continue. It's over."

Nikos snorted, and when he spoke his voice was murderously calm. "And if I hear either of you suggest as much again, you will both die as the cowards you've become."

He swept past them, still brandishing his bayonet, and stormed out the entrance of the cave.

Stephen watched him silently as he passed, and when he was gone he came quickly to Ianos's side.

"Are you hurt badly?" he asked, inspecting his friend's wounded arm.

Ianos looked stunned as he pulled his hand away and discovered it wet with blood, as though he had not realized till now that he had been cut.

"Yes, I am hurt very badly." Ianos stared hard at the blood on his palm, and then looked into his Stephen's face. "What will we do, Stephen?"

Stephen had pulled off his shirt and was using it to staunch the wound. It was bleeding freely, though it might have been much worse, and it would probably heal well enough if he kept it bound.

"What can we do? There's no reasoning with him when he gets like this— and I've never seen it so bad as this before." He wound the arm tightly with the shirt. "We could go without him."

Ianos had tears in his eyes, though these may have been from the pain of his wound. "No," he said weakly. "Stephen, we can't. Not in the state he's in. God knows what he may come to—or do—if we left."

Stephen looked towards the entrance of the cave. "I'm not sure he wouldn't have killed me if you hadn't stepped in." He turned again towards Ianos. "I've seen murder in his eyes before, Ianos, and it was there just now."

Ianos's injured arm lifted only with great difficulty, but he raised both his hands and placed them on either side of Stephen's head, bringing his forehead to rest against his friend's. The tears were unmistakeable now.

"Promise me," Ianos said, "that you will see this through with me, whatever it may be that needs to be done. Just as we've been through everything together, promise me you'll go through this with me, too."

"May God call the enemies of Ianos Leventi to account," said Stephen vaguely, remembering that night outside the shepherd's hovel on Mount Ida.

"Promise me," Ianos insisted.

Stephen lifted his hands now to his friend's head. "I promise, Ianos. I will."

Nikos did not return that night, but he was sitting at the entrance of the cave when they awoke the next morning. He was watching them silently and sharpening his bayonet again. He didn't acknowledge Ianos's injury, or even the words they had exchanged the day before. All he said was that he had been to see for himself, and he knew now that this rumour about the Germans surrendering was sheer nonsense. He forbade either of them from mentioning it again.

Stephen tried to protest but was cowed into silence. Not only that, Nikos went on to say, but he also forbade them any more excursions from the cave, except with his express permission.

"It's too dangerous out there," he explained ominously, inspecting the edge of his bayonet as he spoke. "It's liable to get you killed."

Later Stephen and Ianos took stock of their supplies. They had food enough to last some six weeks, maybe seven if they rationed severely. Ianos knew of a spring of water trickling down between the rocks at the heart of the cave, and though it tasted awful they could drink it easily enough if it came to that.

The worst thing they discovered, however, was that their weapons were all missing—guns and ammunition, blades and bayonets alike. Nikos must have hidden them away while they were sleeping.

Only once did they risk trying to reason with him again, revisiting the same arguments about the Germans having left Heraklion.

"Father," Ianos pleaded. "I saw it with my own eyes."

But Nikos's response was so violent that they despaired of ever persuading him and gave up trying. Stephen insisted that they should leave him and escape to Heraklion themselves if they could, but Ianos refused.

"He is still my father, Stephen," he said in tears one night, "however lost he may seem."

And so the most horrific months of any Stephen had been through since the start of the war ensued. They never found their own weapons, and Nikos stalked about the cave with his machine gun continually loaded and his bayonet strapped at his side. Sometimes days would pass where he said nothing at all; other times, when he did speak, he was terrifyingly incoherent. And still he refused to let either of them wander far from the cave, except for one or two trips into Gortyne for supplies, which he always accompanied them on—as an armed escort against the enemy, he explained—never letting them out of his sight. Even these stopped after the villagers began speaking openly to them about the German capitulation.

Many times Stephen woke in the middle of the night with his heart racing and wondered if it might be better if he just ran off. But whenever he did, it seemed, Nikos was sitting in the entrance of the cave, his silhouette hunched in the pale moonlight that fell through the opening, working away with his bayonet on the whetstone. Once Stephen was even startled awake in the middle of the night, with Nikos holding the lantern close to his face, looking spectral in the oily light and peering at him with lunatic eyes.

Except that he kept track of it in his journal, Stephen could not have said how long this went on. Their foodstuffs were dwindling and they had resorted to drinking the cave water, but Nikos showed no signs of improving. If anything, he spiralled deeper and deeper into whatever it was that had taken hold of him. Often they heard him muttering to himself vaguely as he went about whatever busy work he found to fill his days. And though he must have slept sometimes, when he awoke in the night Nikos was always there, watching him.

Ianos and Stephen both knew this could not continue much longer, though neither of them knew what to do. Stephen was beginning to feel his own grip on sanity weaken, though writing in his journal did help with that, and Ianos was sinking into despair from watching his father's spirit slip so helplessly away. Something had to give.

And then, one moonlit winter night in the early days of 1945, it finally did.

———————

Stephen awoke in the middle of the night, wild-eyed and wide awake from the depths of a frantic dream. These occurred almost nightly now, but this one was so vivid that he was drenched with sweat and burning with clarity. Pale moonlight fell into the mouth of the cave, and it must have been a brilliantly clear night, because the light reached further than he had ever seen it do before.

Nikos's silhouette lay near the opening, but when Stephen's racing heart had calmed enough that he could listen, he heard his father-in-law breathing so steadily that he knew he must be asleep.

He pulled himself gingerly from his sleeping roll and groped through the shadows until he found Ianos, lying nearby.

"Ianos," he whispered as loudly as he dared. "Ianos, wake up!"

It took some time to wake him, and the noise his friend made as he started from sleep so alarmed Stephen that he clapped his hand over Ianos's mouth and brought his own mouth close to the other's ear.

"Ianos, stay quiet. Your father is asleep."

Ianos nodded slightly and Stephen pulled his hand away.

He listened until he was sure Nikos was still asleep, and then he said, "This can't go on, Ianos. We're losing him by the hour, and if he doesn't get help soon, he may be lost for good. I think we need to go—"

Stephen's cheek was pressed close enough to Ianos's own cheek that he felt his friend shake his head feebly in the darkness.

"We need to go to get him help," Stephen insisted. "In Gortyne, if we can find it, or if not then in Heraklion, or Canea."

"He would take it as a great betrayal." Ianos's voice sounded weak, as though it were struggling under some unseen weight. "It might break him if we did. I'm sure it would."

"I'm not sure he hasn't broken already, Ianos. Certainly us staying here—with him, in this madness—it's not doing him any good. And there's no way he'd come with us."

There was a long pause then, and because he was crouched so close to his friend's body, Stephen could feel a great tension shudder through it.

"I know you are right," Ianos said at last, "and we may be able to help him yet. Only, Stephen, it will break him terribly if we leave." But even though he said this, Ianos shifted his weight and made to rise. "Come, he sleeps so fitfully now that this might be our only chance."

It took some time for them to blunder through the darkness and collect what they needed for the journey. They dared not make even the slightest of sounds, and of course they couldn't risk a light. In the end they only had a single pack, stuffed with a canteen of water and rations enough to last a day, but it had already taken a long time to gather even this much, so they decided it would have to do.

As it was, they had taken too long. They were moving as silently as they could, creeping past his softly breathing form and standing almost frozen in a white beam of moonlight, when Nikos suddenly opened his eyes and stared at them. Stephen could see them glitter dully in the pale light.

"Where are you two slinking off too then?" he asked menacingly.

"Father, we—"

"And are the traitors creeping off to hand me over at last?" Nikos cut him off, pulling himself to standing. He had been sleeping with his tommy gun in his hands, and he waved it at them haphazardly as he got to his feet.

"Nikos, you aren't well," Stephen said. "We want to get you help."

"Stop it!" The antechamber of their cave echoed with the roar of his voice. "For all I know, this foreigner has been in league with the enemy all along. And has he pulled you in, too, Ianos? Has my own son turned traitor on me?"

"No, Father, but we must get help. This can't go on—"

"I said stop! I won't listen to these treasonous lies, and I will silence them myself if I have to!"

Something slipped in Stephen at that moment, and it came rushing out of him like water from a broken dam. "God damn it, Nikos! Would you listen to yourself? You're raving like a lunatic! Look at him! That's your son there; he's no traitor! And look at me. It's Stephen, your friend, your daughter's—"

This was too much for Nikos. "Don't speak to me about my daughter!"

He exploded towards Stephen, catching him on the jaw with the butt of his gun and dropping him heavily to the ground. He stood over him viciously and pointed the weapon downwards. Stephen's breath froze in his chest.

Ianos lunged forward and jerked the barrel of the gun sideways, even as Nikos squeezed the trigger. The cave fluttered with a staccato flash of light, trembling with the noise of it as the bullets rattled harmlessly off into the dark.

"Father, please!" Ianos cried.

Nikos struck him on the side of the head and he fell, too, tumbling away from the moonlight and down into the shadows of the cave.

Stephen was already on his feet and had pressed back against a stone wall, where he hoped the darkness would hide him.

"Nikos! Listen to the sound of my voice!" Stephen shouted. "It's me! We don't want to harm you, but only to help."

But Nikos was no longer present to them. He roared and fired his gun blindly into the cave. Nothing hit Stephen, but he could hear round after round ricochet off the stone near him. The noise was deafening.

When it subsided, Stephen leaped forward and pelted down the cave's main tunnel into an even deeper darkness. He stumbled against an unseen stone and fell—a lucky fall, as it turned out, because just at that moment Nikos fired again, this time towards the sound of his movement, and the shots rang loudly over his head as he went down.

When the gunfire stopped a second time, Stephen lay in pitch blackness, breathing hoarsely and wondering what he ought to do. He could hear Nikos shouting blind murder at him from the entrance of the cave, but no more shots came, and he guessed he must be reloading.

"Ianos?" he shouted desperately. "Ianos!"

There was no answer.

He tried a third time. "Ianos, please!"

Except for the sinister sound of Nikos readying his gun, somewhere up towards the moonlight, there was no noise.

At last Stephen lunged to his feet again with a great scuffling of stone and shale. Nikos's gun was ready by now, and he fired at the sound. It was far to dark to have hit him, of course, but even so, the rocks around Stephen rattled with a terrifying ricochet of bullets as he pressed forward, finding one of the cave's many winding passageways and losing himself completely down a lightless corridor.

CHAPTER THIRTY-FIVE

Ariadne's Stone, 1945

IT WAS IMPOSSIBLE FOR STEPHEN TO SAY HOW LONG HE LAY THERE IN utter blindness. It might have been hours—certainly the fluid oozing from the place where Nikos had struck him with the gun had congealed, and his shirt collar was stiff with dried blood. But his pulse still pounded furiously in his head, so it could not have been that long. In either case, he was thirsty, almost sickeningly so. He could see absolutely nothing, but even if he could have it probably would not have helped much. He was hopelessly lost.

Strange sounds whispered at him from every direction: the noise of vapours exhaling from one of the cave's many winding tunnels, a slow drip of moisture from somewhere far away, the faint scuffle of tiny feet overhead, which he thought might be bats, disturbed by his being there. The darkness magnified these sounds so that they echoed in the air, swirling past him and all around like wraiths in the shadows. He thought for a second that he heard the sound of sinister laughter somewhere nearby, though it was so hard to tell in such perfect darkness as this.

Then a great shifting of earth sounded—and this was unmistakeable now, like the noise of a heavy weight moving over loose stone. He sat up rigidly, frozen still and listening in desperation. His breath was alarmingly loud in his ears, but however hard he tried to still it, it only sounded louder to him. The noise did not come a second time, so very slowly he shuffled forward, moving on his hands and knees in an unseen direction.

He groped along the ground until he came to the solid fabric of the cave wall. He used this to lift himself slowly. His knee throbbed from where he had fallen on it in his flight from Nikos, but it could still bear weight.

Again his imagination spiralled manically in all directions as he stood in the pitch black and it washed over him how inescapably lost he really was. He thought he heard the monstrous shuffling of something lumbering towards him, and he was sure he felt savage fingers reaching for him through the gloom. He swallowed feverishly and tried to calm the trembling in him. It took all the heart he had in him to do it, but he began moving forward, blindly, with his hand against the cave wall to guide him.

And then he saw a flash of pale light, the feeble beam of an electric torch unmistakable in the darkness. It danced in a swinging arc, searching the tunnel from side to side, and he could see the silhouettes of stalagmites and stalactites emerge from the shadows like jagged teeth as the light swept over them. Stephen crouched down till he was almost prone on the ground, though he kept his weight poised to fight or fly.

The light paused, then shifted, and began to creep along the stone wall in Stephen's direction. His heart roared thunderously in his chest. There was nowhere for him to run to in this dark, and if he stayed where he was, he was sure to be found. He held his breath as the light swung in another arc and fell at last on his hunched form. He squinted into it, but all he could see was a single dazzling star of light, pointing him out.

Without thinking he leaped towards it, and though he wasn't armed, still he grappled with the shadow behind the light as fiercely as he could, tumbling to the ground on top of it and pummelling with his bare hands. The figure roared something frantically, but Stephen knew he could not give him even a second to find his bayonet or level his gun.

The invisible mass beneath him grappled back, taking hold of Stephen's forearm and pinning it against his own chest. He reached his other arm around Stephen's torso and hugged him tightly against himself. Stephen struggled, but the other held tighter still.

"Stephen," it said. "Stephen, it's me! Ianos."

Somehow the familiar voice registered against Stephen's terror and he recognized his friend. He stopped.

"Oh God, Ianos. Ianos… I am so sorry—"

"It is all right. I'm not hurt, and it was dark."

"No," said Stephen. "About it all. Your father is lost, I think, Ianos, or at least he's very nearly so. And I'm the one who brought him to the final step over the edge."

Ianos had dropped the light in their tussle, and he groped to retrieve it. When he had it again, he brought it up between them so Stephen could see him. The angle of the beam cast ghastly shadows over his face, like a death mask, but even so Stephen could see the terrible sadness in him. His eyes were hot with tears, and in the torchlight they glinted tragically.

"No, Stephen. It's not your fault. He's been slipping away for months now, and maybe longer than either of us knew. I knew it would come out eventually, though I hadn't thought it would be so awful as this."

Ianos looked around him with his light.

"Do you have any idea where we are?" Stephen asked after a long time.

His friend did not answer right away, but he pointed the light pensively down the mouth of one of the many tunnels gaping open before them.

"Come," Ianos said at last. "I think it's this way."

He reached out and took Stephen's hand in his own, and they began picking a slow way forward. The light was so dim and the path so uncertain that this was the only way to be sure they would not stumble. Stephen was sweating terribly, but Ianos's palm felt unexpectedly cool against his own.

They moved on like this for what might have been hours, though time was impossible to gauge in the heart of that cave. Periodically Ianos stopped and flashed his light around him, thinking, but he said very little. The eerie sounds still whispered at them from the shadows, and once or twice Ianos brought them down suddenly into a crouch, extinguishing the light, because he was sure he had heard someone moving nearby.

Eventually they came to a place where the air did not press so close, and Stephen guessed that they were in a large chamber of some sort. When Ianos cast the light in a wide sweep, it revealed heaps of stone piled in many places. Here and there were the openings of other tunnels, leading into and away from the chamber. The light did not reach the far side of the cavern, though, and the ceiling was lost in blackness overhead.

Ianos stepped forward. "I think," he said tentatively, "that I know this place."

He swept his light in another arc, and a huge finger of stone came into sight, a great, single pillar of rock standing erect in the centre of the cave. It was as if—and the thought seemed to come to Stephen from a distant memory—as if it held up the darkness looming all around it.

"This is Ariadne's Stone," said Ianos. He was whispering, but a note of great relief sounded in his voice. "We've been here before. And if we can only find the pile of stones that marks the right tunnel—our tunnel—we will be able to find our way out."

Ianos moved the light over the stone and Stephen recognized it, too: Ariadne's Stone, the primeval marker set up by ancient hands to point the way through the labyrinth and out again. Ianos had shown it to him on their first visit to the cave at Gortyne, many years ago.

"And so maybe we're not as lost as we thought," Ianos said, risking a faint laugh in the silence.

At that moment a guttural cry erupted from the shadows and a huge mass, almost inhumanly savage, lunged at Ianos, sending the light sprawling and bringing him down heavily. Stephen could hear a furious struggle as the two men grappled with each other in the dark, but he could not make anything out.

"Ianos," he screamed. "Nikos! Stop it! You'll kill him!"

The electric torch was lying many feet from them, and Stephen could see its weak light shining at some skewed angle against the rocks. He stumbled towards it, bringing his shin painfully up against a heap of stone, falling hard, and scuffling forward on his hands and knees. When he reached it, he turned it towards the noise of the fight, and saw the shape of Nikos, hunched wildly over his son and throttling him brutally with both hands at his throat.

"Nikos!" he screamed again.

Stephen threw himself forward, knocking Nikos aside. He heard Ianos struggling away from his father's reach. Stephen held the torch in his right hand, and even as he pointed it towards Nikos he saw the man hurl his weight towards him. The beam of light caught a flash of steel, and Stephen barely got his left arm up in time to deflect the blow of a knife. He felt a stinging pain in his forearm and went down again.

He heard Nikos breathing hard in the darkness and he tuned his light towards the sound. As the beam fell on him, Stephen saw that he was bearing down again with the knife, and this time he would not miss.

He cowered back, but even as he did so another black shape flung itself towards Nikos, slamming into him and pulling him down.

"Stephen!" shrieked Ianos's unseen voice. "Stephen, run!"

Stephen was still holding the torch, but his fear throbbed fiercely in his head, so he was completely blind as he scrambled to his feet.

"Run!"

And he did run. He staggered forward towards Ariadne's Stone, falling hard against it, and then, turning towards his best guess, he pelted as quick as he dared into the gloom. He reached the opening of a tunnel, marked with one of the piles of stones, and turned back towards the chamber.

"Ianos!"

"Stephen! Don't turn back! Run!"

He moved in a sightless terror then, up the tunnel. Just as he was about to turn back a second time, a shrill scream split the dark, and it came again, almost inhumanly shrill. Stephen could not tell whose scream it was, but it was followed by a deep groan—the cave seemed to shudder with the sound—and when he heard it, he fled blindly up the passageway.

He had the light, and the way was marked here with piles of stone, so he did his best to follow them. Adrenaline still coursed in him and his whole body trembled with it, but he kept his feet moving and he didn't look back until, eventually, he came to a place where cool grey light spilled into an antechamber of the cave, and he recognized at last that he had reached the entrance.

He was too frantic with terror to wonder at his luck. He rushed towards the light and came to the mouth of the cave, pushing through and bursting, it seemed, like the great exhale of a long-held breath, out into the fresh air.

It was twilight. A slow sun was just promising to break over the eastern edge of dawn, and the sky was pale with the earliest hours of the morning.

He staggered a few steps away from the entrance, slipping on loose stone and falling into the dust. He pulled himself up again and moved a bit further until his strength finally escaped him completely and he collapsed to the ground as though he would never move again. A feverish oblivion overcame him then, and though he could not say he slept, he slipped into a black fog of unconsciousness.

The sun was risen, though not yet very far into the sky, when Stephen heard a voice calling his name. It sounded weak as it reached through his unconscious stupor, but as he gradually came to it became stronger. It was calling from the entrance of the cave and sounded irreparably broken.

He rose in great pain and moved towards the sound. He would have dreaded to approach the cave again, except that the voice called so plaintively.

When he reached the entrance, he saw Ianos sitting in the dust with his head in his hands. He must have been holding great fistfuls of earth, because his hands were soiled and when he lifted his face to Stephen it was filthy, his tears tracing awful runnels through the dirt. Nikos's electric torch lay idly on the ground beside him.

"Ianos," Stephen said weakly. "Are you—"

He stopped. Ianos's shirt was sopping with blood and his palms and forearms were stained darkly.

"Ianos! You're hurt!"

Ianos shook his head faintly. He would not meet Stephen's eyes. "It's not my blood," he said.

"Oh, God."

Ianos finally lifted his eyes to Stephen and they were flooded with tears. "Stephen, it's not my blood," he repeated.

He pulled himself to standing, and staggered. Stephen rushed forward to steady him and he fell into his friend's arms, clinging tightly.

"It's not my blood, Stephen," he said a third time.

Stephen nodded wordlessly.

"He is dead, Stephen."

"Ianos, you had no choice. We had no choice. He would have killed you."

"But—he's dead... and I—"

Stephen pressed his friend's head against his shoulder, to smother the confession. "You had no choice," he repeated.

And they stood there as the sun pulled itself up into the morning sky. And whether Stephen was clinging to Ianos, or Ianos to him, he couldn't say, but they kept one another standing.

"Ianos, I am sorry. I'm sorry that I couldn't have saved you from... that... that I couldn't have saved him. I promised you I would see it through with you, whatever had to be done—and yet, I ran off and left you."

Ianos lifted his hand and placed it on the back of Stephen's head, and then brought their foreheads together. He was still weeping.

"No, Stephen. It wasn't yours to save him. And anyway, there was nothing you could have done. And—" Ianos's voice broke, but when he finally could speak again he said, "And I swore an oath to you, that I would love you as I love myself."

A deep sob escaped Stephen then, but both of them were crying openly together now, and he felt no need to stifle it.

His voice was unsteady, but suddenly Ianos started to sing, very faintly.

"'Friendship is the most beautiful thing in the world,'" he sang. Stephen recognized it as one of the rizitika he had taught him on the way to Ida so many years ago. "'My heart is full: my heart knows how to repay.'"

He sang it again, but couldn't finish, and trailed off into voiceless tears.

When they were able to speak again, after a long time Ianos said, "I think, Stephen... I think you must go now. From Crete, I mean. You must leave."

"Go? But Ianos, I—"

"No. There is nothing for you here anymore. Ariadne is gone, and now Nikos. I don't know what will happen to me. And the war for Crete is over. I'm not sure what that will mean for a handful of pitiful andartes who have been waging their own personal campaign up in the hills like this. And you, you're not a Cretan national, so who can say what will happen when the British, or the Greeks, or whoever it is that will take charge of this island, when they start looking into all we've done?"

"Ianos, I can't leave you. Not after all we've been through."

"You must. I am better off alone. There are places I can go on the island, people who will probably take me in. But not you." Tears pressed earnestly again at the edge of his voice. "This is not your home. You are not Cretan-born. So long as my father was willing to take you in, you could make it your home, but he's gone now, Stephen, and we—we—" He couldn't bring himself to say what they had done, so he simply said, "So this can't be home to you anymore. Please. You must go."

A heavy silence fell over them. Stephen knew that it was true, what Ianos was saying. His mind swirled with questions and heartache, but beneath it all he knew it was true, or at least why Ianos was saying it.

He stared hard at the ground for a long time. He couldn't find the words to express what was burning in him, but when his voice finally came to him, he offered Ianos's rizitika back to him as best he could.

"'Friendship is the most beautiful thing in the world,'" he sang, weakly. "'My heart is full. My heart knows how to repay.'"

Grace stared at the journal in stunned silence. She had no tears left to cry, but the story she had uncovered was so pitiable that even if she could have wept, it would not have been for herself. She thought of Stephen, struggling through those dreadful years of violence and horror, of Nikos slowly sinking into madness, of the blood on Ianos's hands—Stephen's journal was very clear on this detail—and her heart was crushed beneath the terrible weight of a profound, overwhelming pity.

She pushed a slow palm through her hair and took a deep breath, still staring numbly at the last pages spread open before her.

The journal trailed off towards the end, but it didn't matter. She knew roughly—at least in broad strokes—how Stephen had found his way home to her from Crete; he had at least told her this much. She knew that he had arranged for passage from Crete to the mainland in the spring of 1945, on one of the British Merchant Navy ships regularly pulling in and out of Heraklion after the liberation.

She knew that he had gone to Athens, where he'd drawn on old connections from his time there before the war, and stayed there almost a full year. Greece had been in total chaos at this time, with the Germans pulled out and the Allies taking hold, but somehow, between taking on whatever odd jobs he could find and some generous help from some old colleagues, he'd been able to scrape together the fare for travel to England.

She knew this for certain because this was where he had finally contacted his parents. They'd received a wire from him just before Christmas 1946, explaining simply that he was still alive and that he had made it from Greece to England, that he was well and more news would follow.

It had struck her as odd that he would have contacted them first, but she had been so relieved to have heard anything from him after so long that she hadn't dwelt on it.

Two more messages had come after that, one in the new year, explaining that he was working on plans to come home, and then one more towards the end of February, telling his parents that he was sorry, but he needed their help with the fare.

At the time, it hadn't occurred to Grace to wonder why he had taken so long after the liberation of Crete to finally return, from the spring of 1945 till the day he arrived home in the winter of 1947. But as she mulled over what she had just read, she wondered if it hadn't taken him that long simply to work up the final resolve, to fight through the guilt, and turn at last and face them all—his family, and her—waiting for him at home.

Of course, the whole world had been reeling in those hard days after the war, and it may have simply been that it was difficult for him to travel. Certainly it had been a great challenge for Mr. and Mrs. Walker to arrange for his passage home from England. But they had, and he'd come, and she had been there, waiting to meet him on a wet winter morning in 1947 on a pier in Halifax Harbour.

She thought over the years that had followed, in light of what she now knew. She had known that he had seen and done some terrible things during the war. He had told her next to nothing about it, but from the brooding shadow that descended over them whenever she mentioned it, she knew it must have been awful for him. She had never guessed how awful, of course, but the trauma was always there, lurking in the background of their life together.

So she had loved him. Their marriage was never like she had imagined it would be, or hoped for when she had prayed all those years for him to return, but she had tried to love him well. All the care and compassion she had discovered within her through her efforts in the war, she channelled into loving him. With the war over and won, it seemed the most natural place to direct it.

He had eventually found work teaching Classics at King's College. His time in Athens and on Crete had positioned him well for this. She had continued to serve at the Barrington Street Mission, and continued also to attend St. Christopher's. He did come with her most Sundays, though he showed little real interest in it, and she could not say if anything that happened there meant anything to him.

But it was not always grim, and there had been days when he'd laugh like he used to, a long time ago, before the war, before his fieldwork, before Willie even. There had been times, too, when he'd reach for her from the depths of some unsettling nightmare, in the quietest hours of the night, and press his body against hers for warmth and peace; and she would hold him tightly in return, for a peace and warmth of her own.

And so she had loved him as well as she could, never understanding till now how deep his wounds truly ran. But even so, she had offered him whatever grace was hers to give, to help him heal.

She reached to close the journal. As she did, she noticed a folded bit of wrinkled paper, wedged in between the final page and the back cover. She pulled it out and smoothed it open.

It had been torn from the journal—she could tell that the paper was of the same size and weight—and it had been crumpled tightly at some point.

Dear Grace,

It is awful for me to write this after so many years of lying to you. Not just because of the terrible shame it is for me to tell you at last, but more importantly because of the hurt that it will cause you. For it will hurt you, Grace. I know it will.

It slowly dawned on her what she was reading. This was a letter he had written but never sent. There had been a passing reference to such a letter in the journal, from the day he had chosen to remain on Crete and join the resistance.

She read it through slowly a number of times. *Though I can't bring myself to ask for your forgiveness,* it said, *I will at least give you the permission to hate me for it.*

"Oh Stephen," she whispered, closing her eyes gently.

Of course she couldn't hate him for what had been. He was right; it would have hurt her brutally to have discovered it in that way. As it was, it had hurt her anyway, and probably just as brutally. But she could not hate him for it. She could not love him any more—at least not in the way she had once wanted to—but even as she accepted that, she understood, too, that there was a truer kind of love growing in her, for him as he had really been, betrayals and failures and all. It was not hers, this love, but she felt it was the same love that had been at work in her, and loving her, for many, many years. And it would not pretend that she was not hurt; rather, it embraced her hurt as much as it embraced his, and it refused to hate him for it.

Whether or not she could forgive him—he'd never brought himself to ask for it, and she could not offer it now—still she could release him to that love.

It hurt profoundly, but she closed the journal at last, and as she did she felt that she was releasing a great burden in her heart.

Grace rose from the desk.

She had no idea how long she had been there, but she was stiff with sitting, and exhausted from her ordeal. She picked a careful way through the debris on the floor and stepped to the window. The Venetian blind was still drawn, but through the cracks she could see sunshine. She reached for it and very deliberately pulled it open, flooding the room, at last, with light.

CHAPTER THIRTY-SIX
Villa Leventi. 1968

THE SUN WAS WARM BUT NOT UNBEARABLY SO THE DAY GRACE STOOD quietly at the foot of a gravesite, near to what had once been the Villa Leventi, in a space of grass that had once been a lemon orchard. Some of the trees were still there, but they had not been tended for many years and had grown wild.

The villa was no longer called Leventi, of course. A wealthy landowner from Canea had bought the vineyard years ago and was renting out the house to a family from Timbaki. She'd gathered all this from the tenants themselves, who had greeted her warmly when she knocked on their door. They spoke only the least amount of English, and she knew no Greek, but she was able to communicate that she simply wanted to look around the grounds awhile. She did not have the heart to ask if she could come in, and anyway, she did not think she would have wanted to have seen their room, if she could have.

There was nothing to show that the grave was Ariadne's, only a simple stone marker with no inscription. But she had Stephen's journal with her, and from the entry he had scrawled out the day after they'd buried her Grace was quite sure it was the place, at the far end of the orchard, looking out over the hills and down towards the sea.

A wind played softly over the cloth of her dress, brushing aside the strands of her hair, and the wild lemon trees fluttered their leaves behind her. She hadn't expected it to be so serene as this, to stand at the grave of her husband's wife.

She wasn't even sure she should have come. It had taken her many months to decide, at last, to travel to Crete for herself. But there had been some small amount of money left after they'd settled his estate and she had been profoundly restless after reading his journal. She hadn't wished to share the story with anyone—not Jane or Sarah, and certainly not his aging parents—but neither could she do nothing with it. So eventually, with no clear plan for what she would do when she got there, she had booked the flight. It was the first time she had flown; indeed, it was her first journey outside Nova Scotia since her trip to Prince Edward Island ages ago.

She had used Stephen's journal to guide her to Apodoulou, and from there she'd asked around in the village until she found the Villa Leventi.

"Leventi?" said one of the few villagers who spoke any English, when she'd asked at an open air kafenion in the village square. "Leventi? No Leventis here for... many much years."

The villager had been a wizened old man, toying with a string of beads the whole while they spoke. He'd turned and exchanged a word, in Greek, with one of the others sitting at the table.

"But I only want to see the Leventi Villa," Grace had explained. "Their home—house?—where the Leventis lived."

"Ah," the man said. "House of Leventis... yes... no Leventis, but house, still here." He gestured across the village square. "Go... that road. You find house."

One of the other men had put a hand on his forearm and said something softly she hadn't understood. The older man had nodded and then looked at Grace.

"It very... sad. The... doings..." He had been at a loss for the right word in English. "The things... done... to Leventis. With? With the Leventis. Nikos Leventi die in war. His daughter, too. And his son..." He then asked his tablemates a question and they'd discussed something briefly in Greek. "He... exoristos."

She furrowed her brow, so he tried again.

"Exoria?" he said, hoping she understood the word. "Exoristos?"

But she still had not understood, so he used the best English he could manage. "His son gone after war. No one knows where."

Grace nodded and thanked him.

She'd followed his directions to the villa and, after a similar exchange with the family that had greeted her at the door, she'd found herself standing in silence before a stone marker she felt sure indicated the spot where they had buried Ariadne.

"I don't know why I'm here," she said at last, feeling very foolish to be speaking aloud, but also feeling like the moment called for it. "You and I both loved the same man, I guess. Though in different ways, I think, and for different reasons. I did not know the Stephen you knew, though I have come to. And I wonder, did you know him? The way I did?"

Of course there was no answer, and the foolish feeling grew stronger in her. Quickly she reached into her handbag and pulled out something small and dark and smooth. It was one half of a mussel shell, the kind you might find on any beach in Halifax.

"Here," she said, setting it down on the grass by the stone. "I think I want you to have this. I've come to realize that I don't need it anymore, and in a way, it was never really mine."

The wind sighed, the lemon trees shifted their limbs, but otherwise, of course, there was no answer. It was, in fact, a beautifully serene moment.

She reached into her handbag a second time and produced an envelope.

"And also this," Grace said. "Though it's not really for you. But I wanted to leave it here."

She set down the envelope. It was a letter she had written for Stephen. And though no one would ever see it, if someone could have, this is what they would have read.

Dear Stephen,

I prayed for you all the time during the war, that God would protect you, and save you, and guide you back to me. You may have no idea how earnestly I prayed. And I had no idea how earnestly he was answering those prayers. Or how much it would cost for him to do.

When it was especially hard to pray, I would wonder why things like this happen—suffering and tragedy and such—as if all that was needed to make the hurting stop was simply an explanation for it. I've come to believe that there is no answer so complete as to make it so that it doesn't hurt, only that if you are willing to live into it, something very good may come of it in the end.

Reverend Elliot, at St Chris's, told me once that in doing so we discover ourselves nearer to God than we could ever be otherwise. Something like that, anyway. And I've found that to be true.

So in a way, I guess, I should thank you, or at least let you go in peace. I always thought that what I needed was your love—that if we could have been together through the war, maybe it would have been different, or when you returned, if you could have loved me without the trauma of war overshadowing you.

But when I think through all the hard years without you—and even with you, after the war—I wonder if that wasn't at all what I needed. Rather it was just to be faithful to the circumstances I was in, and in being so, discover God's love alive in me.

I hope to leave this letter for you at her grave. I suppose it would be right if I left it at the spot where you are buried, in St. Christopher's cemetery here in Halifax. But I don't think your heart is there. It may not be on Crete anymore, either, but so long as we've been together, it was—though I never realized how fully it was until now—and so maybe that's where this final note really belongs.

At any rate, I will leave it there, and in doing so I commend you to the mystery of God's mercy.

With my sincere love, your wife,
Grace Walker

On the way back from the villa, Grace passed again through the village square. There was a modest church building at one end of it, brilliantly whitewashed, with a single bell tower and a bright blue roof. She paused in front of it, guessing that this was the place where Stephen and Ariadne had in fact been married.

The door was open and her bus back to Heraklion was not due for more than an hour, so she decided to step inside for a brief look. She felt strangely furtive at first, but the church was cool and the light gentle compared to the dazzling sunlight outside, so that it put her at ease and seemed to welcome her in.

The sanctuary was empty, and solemnly silent, but not sternly so, and the air smelled richly of incense. She stepped to the front, her feet echoing faintly on the stone flagging. As far as she could guess, she came to stand directly on the spot where they had stood, some twenty years ago. She might have expected some overwhelming flood of emotion, to be here like this, but instead she was filled with a strange feeling of profound tranquillity.

She looked up and saw at the very front of the church, on a wooden stand and venerated with a dozen candles flickering gently at its feet, an icon of Jesus.

She recognized the image vaguely, though she was not at all familiar with icons. But this one was so arresting, its gaze so perfectly serene, that she could not look away. In the dancing light it looked as though one eye was angled slightly upwards, toward heaven, but the other looked gently—so overwhelmingly so— at her directly, and she felt herself laid bare before it. The hand was lifted in blessing, and she looked closely, because it seemed to her that the palm was pierced with an open wound, though that might have been only a trick of the light.

There was no audible voice, but she felt as if she was told everything, all at once, in that moment. She saw a sick child prayed for and saved, a burned sailor loved tenderly on his deathbed, her own heartbroken father covered by her prayers as he plied the Atlantic, and her mother welcoming him home for good after the war was finally won. She saw a long line of men—sailors and soldiers, the jobless, the homeless—loved and served and helped and healed through her mission on Barrington Street. And she saw Stephen, too, fighting desperately in a battle that was not his, with her love watching over him faithfully. Every compassion, every sympathy, every mercy, every grace she had ever showed, it seemed, was laid out before her in a flash, and inexplicably she understood how, in it all, God had been loving the world through her.

I loved them all, the voiceless Word of God said to her, *with you and through you; and you could only have loved them the way you did, because all the while I was loving you more immensely than you could imagine.*

Her eyes stung as she heard this, but they were not tears of sadness, rather of an unspeakable joy. She did not recognize it, but she opened her heart to this joy as fully as she dared, though it threatened to undo her completely.

Her thoughts went to Stephen again, and she accepted it as true, that although he had never loved her the way she'd needed him to, she had been loved—and was loved now—more fully and more faithfully than she could ever know, by the One whose face she had glimpsed in this moment. And a future was shown her, in which this love continued to love the world through her in ways she could not now foresee, but she knew would be tremulously, inexpressibly good.

She was a long time in silence before the icon of Christ. And when at last she left the building—for anyone who had eyes to see it—her face was shining with a beatific light.